NOTHING
LIKE
THE NIGHT

DETECTIVE STELLA MOONEY NOVELS
BY DAVID LAWRENCE

Nothing Like the Night

The Dead Sit Round in a Ring

David
Lawrence

NOTHING
LIKE
THE NIGHT

THOMAS DUNNE BOOKS
ST. MARTIN'S MINOTAUR ≈ NEW YORK

THOMAS DUNNE BOOKS.
An imprint of St. Martin's Press.

www.minotaurbooks.com

Book design by Irene Vallye

Library of Congress Cataloging-in-Publication Data

Lawrence, David.
   Nothing like the night : a Detective Stella Mooney novel / David
Lawrence.
      p. cm.
   ISBN 0-312-32880-X
   EAN 978-0-312-32880-1
   1. Police—England—London—Fiction.   2. Triangles (Interpersonal
relations)—Fiction.   3. London (England)—Fiction.   4. Policewomen—
Fiction.   I. Title.

PR6112.A988N67 2005
823'.92—dc22
                                                            2005040703

First Edition: June 2005

10   9   8   7   6   5   4   3   2   1

To Sheelagh
and Sandy

NOTHING
LIKE
THE NIGHT

1

Although it was broad day, every light in the house was burning and Stella Mooney knew something dreadful had happened. The place cast a hard, pale glare like a lamp in sunshine. Her first move—any police officer's first move—was to call for back-up, but either she was in a black transmission spot or her mobile's battery was down. She walked up the path to the front door and the journey seemed to take an hour. The sound of the doorbell, when she rang it, was shocking: it struck through the dead silence in the house like a sudden shout. The front door had a frosted-glass panel. There were shadows on the glass. Stella wanted to turn and leave. She wanted to hurry away and be somewhere else; be someone else; but her hand went to the letterbox and she pushed it up and stooped and peered in.

They were hanging from the upstairs banister, three children in their nightclothes. She could see their legs in cartoon-character pajamas, she could see their feet, motionless and white. She was still carrying her phone and, somehow, she was able to dial without taking her eyes from that terrible sight, but as she pressed the buttons they flew off into the air like tiny birds, fluorescent blue and emitting little beeping cries.

Stella woke sitting upright. She was speaking on an indrawn breath, but had no idea of what she'd just said. She drew her knees up against the sharp pain in her abdomen and wrapped her arms round, hugging herself, stifling the sounds of her own weeping. The man beside her was fast asleep and she didn't want to wake him; didn't want to tell him about the dream that snagged in the shadows round the room.

If she closed her eyes the images loomed up: pale feet as still as stone. Stella shuddered then caught her knees more tightly. A two-tone ARV siren started thinly somewhere down the North End Road, swelled as the police driver pushed things just past the limit, then tapered off into silence. A 747 rumbled down the Heathrow corridor. *Three babies. Dead babies. One of them mine.*

Stella stretched her legs to the floor and lifted her weight off the bed as slowly as she could. A couple of floorboards creaked and the bedroom door closed with a click because there was a wind outside and the basement flat had windows that had warped and doors that showed a gap above the floor. Stella had to tug the door against the draft to close it. She went into the kitchen and poured herself a drink: it was vodka and she felt the need of it. In the basement area outside the window, sheets of newspaper and burger cartons were floating and flapping, caught by a tiny twister. As she watched, sipping her drink, a dustbin lid lifted off and smacked against the basement wall. She looked up and saw the dark shape of the street's only roadside tree seeming to furl and unfurl as the wind battered it. Clouds were traveling fast and when Stella lifted her gaze to beyond the treetop, she saw, in a cloud-break, that rarest of all London sights: a star.

The house blazing with lights was something new, otherwise it had been the usual dream. A dead-baby dream.

She ate the ice from her first drink, and went to the fridge for more, her glass in one hand, the uncapped vodka bottle in the other. She was loading and pouring when the door opened behind her and he came into the room carrying her mobile phone.

"It went off. Sorry."

"It woke you up." She dialed "last call" and checked the number.

"Well, yes. It doesn't matter." Stella Mooney and George Paterson had lived together for going on six years; it wasn't the first time police business had broken his sleep. He swapped the phone for her drink, took a swallow, then handed it back. "Are you going to call, or do you want me—" *To lie for you,* was the unspoken part of the sentence. He'd done it before.

"No. I'll call in."

She lifted the kitchen phone and dialed DI Sorley's mobile. He must have been waiting for the call, because the ringing tone lasted only a moment. She said, "It's DS Mooney, boss." Sorley gave her brief details and an address in Notting Hill Gate. "I'll be twenty minutes," she said. "Scene-of-crime people?"

"I've got some regulars," Sorley told her, "officers we like to work with. We'll have a full team by the morning. Anyone you fancy?"

Stella asked for DC Pete Harriman and DC Andy Greegan. She wanted Sue Chapman, if possible, as coordinating officer.

Sorley said, "Greegan's already there."

She took a fast shower to wake herself up: maybe in the hope of washing away the ragged remnants of the dream, though she knew that wasn't really possible. Then she walked into the bedroom and tried to find her clothes in the dark. He said, "You didn't think I was asleep . . . ?" and put the bedside light on—for her benefit, or for his own, perhaps, as she went naked from one side of the room to the other gathering what she needed. His eyes went with her. She had dark hair just long enough to tie back and was a little above average height, which meant that if she carried an extra pound or two it didn't show. She was attractive in a way that didn't strike people immediately, but the slow-burn factor, once they'd registered it, meant they kept looking. She pulled on a T-shirt and gave a little hop to help her jeans up over her backside; a sweater, then, and a sleeveless down vest, because it was early spring and the night wind could be cold.

"What time is it?"

He picked his watch up from the bedside table. "Almost three. What have you got?"

"A body in Notting Hill Gate."

"What were you dreaming about?"

"Dreaming . . . ?" She had her back to him, pulling her hair into a stubby ponytail.

"No, okay." He tried to sound amused, but there was a rough edge of anger in his tone.

She said, "Go to sleep, George. I'll call you later."

Stella slammed the door and walked a couple of streets to find her car. Street parking was a day-in, day-out battle; if you got to within half a mile of your door you were ahead of the game. The London wind wasn't cold, it was wet and thick and carried a smell of rot; when she turned a corner and came face to face with it, she had to lean forward to make headway. Two sleepers, hunched against the weather, were dug down in street-stained bags in the doorway of the local Eight-til-Late, dead to the world, trash silting up at their backs. Stella wondered what their dreams were like.

A couple of miles away, the same damp wind was blowing across the headstones and broken pillars of Kensal Green cemetery, putting up a howl when it hit the granite edges, flattening the posies of silk flowers. A dog was going through, a brindle half-hound, lean and low-backed, padding along in the pre-dawn dark, and seeming to look for something. It caught a scent and turned down between one of the aisles of stones until it came to the blocky shape of a mausoleum. The lock on the barred gate was broken and the gate stood open. The dog went in and immediately shapes stirred in the blackness; a low growling started up, coming from half a dozen throats. The pack rose and circled.

At the center of this movement was a boy of about ten. He woke, briefly, as the cool air reached him and the growling of the pack quickened his senses; then, as the incomer was accepted and the dogs settled once more, he fell back into sleep.

Stella found some wallpaper music on the radio and drove too fast through the West Kensington backstreets. There were lights shining in the Harefield Estate tower blocks: shebeens in operation, crack parties, all-night fuckfests. The wind hammered the great, gray slabs like the sea at a cliff face. She wondered whether the people who slept in the topmost flats of the tower blocks were feeling the sway. She wondered when the whores ever slept.

She thought she would never get rid of the dreams. The dead-baby dreams.

2

You could smell her before you could see her: Jane Doe several days dead, flat on her back, one arm folded across her abdomen, the other flung out so that it overhung the edge of the bed. You could see she was a woman, but that was about all because her body had gone through a number of changes: the warp and weft of death, the addition and subtraction. It was still possible to tell that someone had used a knife on her: the multiple cuts were easily visible even though the body had begun to weep; but the one that had killed her was obvious: a dark gape across her throat, like a slice taken out of a watermelon.

DC Andy Greegan had already done his work: organizing an uncorrupted path from the street to the body, putting the stills photographer and the video man to work. Everyone knew what to do. A forensics team was fine-combing the room, looking for any hint, any murmur of a clue: forensic tittle-tattle. Like them, like everyone there, Stella was dressed in a white disposable coverall. Forensic officers went silently from room to room like ghost-dancers shepherding the souls of the dead.

With the hood pulled over and tightened, DI Mike Sorley was a tubby snowman with a five o'clock shadow. Like others at the scene, he had smeared a gobbet of cream astringent under his nose and was making a conscious effort to breathe through his mouth. Jane Doe was in the bloat stage of decay and she smelled powerful. Sorley showed

Stella a photograph in a decorated leather frame: a head-and-shoulders studio shot of a young woman. She was beautiful enough to turn heads; maybe to stop hearts; certainly to break them: almost perfectly even features, apart from the mouth which was too full to be perfect, though who would have complained? A long sweep of throat; a plunge neckline that showed the rise of her breasts.

"Is this her?" Stella asked.

"Must be."

Death had changed Jane Doe: changed her dress size and her complexion; changed the shape of her face and the light in her eye. You'd have to know her to be sure. You'd have to be a loved one.

"There are two bedrooms," Sorley went on. "Both have got girls' stuff in them. In this room, the clothes fit someone her size. The other girl must be going on six feet tall."

"Where is she?"

"The other girl? We don't know yet."

"Names?"

"If we're right, the dead one's called Janis Parker. Her flatmate is Stephanie James. We've got bills, letters, credit cards, and so forth. Her passport was in her handbag."

"For both of them?"

"A couple of bills for Stephanie James. Otherwise, nothing. Wherever she is, her personal stuff's with her. Why not?"

"So, credit cards for Janis Parker," Stella said. Then: "Money? Jewelry?"

"Jewelry, yes. Not sure about money. No folding stuff in her wallet, but maybe she just hadn't been to the cashpoint recently."

"Not robbery, then . . ."

"Doesn't look that way," Sorley said, then shrugged. "But I wouldn't want to second-guess it. This is only what forensics have found: top-of-the-pile stuff. You'll need to turn the place over when they've finished."

Stella and Sorley stepped apart as a forensic officer went between them with a fine-mesh net mounted on a telescopic aluminum pole. He was netting flies. In a fresh body, there's a rough rule of thumb for calculating the time of death: 98.6 degrees minus the rectal temperature divided by 1.5 equals the approximate number of hours since death oc-curred. Jane Doe was a long way from being fresh and the pathologist would have to rely on other evidence: the time maggots take to hatch and pupate would provide more figures in the raw arithmetic of death.

Stella noticed something about the photo and about the corpse. She went closer, trying to think of Jane Doe as nothing more than a puzzle to be solved. The flesh was marbled, red and black, and swollen with gases; two maggot masses were feeding on her, one around the wound in her throat, the other in her groin. And more in-side, Stella knew, feeding and growing and getting ready to break out. She crouched down beside the body to take a closer look at the wristwatch on the outflung arm, then got back to her feet and turned to look at Sorley, but he had gone. She found him in the living room, standing close to the wall in order to keep out of the way of the forensic team that was working floors and surfaces.

"I already looked," he said. "Yes, it's the same watch as in the photo. Rolex. Very nice. Just like everything else." He looked round the room at the minimalist furniture, the wide-screen TV, the Bang & Olufsen sound system, the Damien Hurst spot painting. He didn't mean very nice, he meant very expensive. The TV was on: *España Viva.* "Close-relative ID will let us know for sure," Sorley said, "but it's her. Janis Parker."

"Who found her?"

"There's a uniform with a sour look on his face parked outside in a marked vehicle. They took the call."

Stella nodded. "Okay, boss, I'll talk to him."

"You saw the cuts on her . . ."

"I did, yes. A frenzied attack," she added, putting the phrase in quote marks.

"Let's hope so."

Stella looked at him. "Hope so?"

"Because if it wasn't that, then someone was playing with her."

The sour look belonged to PC Stuart Barley. Stella sat in the car with him and the vehicle rocked slightly with each new gust that barreled down the street. He was smoking hard, like a man who's looking forward to the next cigarette. Stella had stopped smoking, but she cadged a cigarette off him to show solidarity.

"You took the call," she said, "but who found the body?"

"I did."

"What happened?"

"Triple nine from the downstairs neighbor. A guy called Mathers. She woke him up."

"Who did?"

"The dead girl."

"She's been dead a while," Stella observed.

"She woke him up by dripping on his face. The bedroom floor is just boards, stripped and varnished; these are old houses—there'd be a bit of lath and plaster underneath. She . . . you know . . . leaked through his ceiling. He was sleeping on his back. She got him full on."

"You're kidding me." Barley looked at her and shook his head.

"So where is he?" Stella asked.

"Rinsing his mouth out with bleach would be my guess."

"You took a statement?"

"As far as I could. After the . . . whatever . . . gunk . . . came through on him he went upstairs to her flat. Thought he was getting a leak from their bathroom. Jesus," Barley laughed without smiling, "the smell of it, the *taste* . . ."

"But there was no reply."

"He lifted up the letterbox. And got the same smell, but turbo."

Lifted up the letterbox. Stella experienced a sudden flashback to her dream: a technicolor freeze-frame, brightly lit and brutal.

"You didn't take the call solo," she said.

"My partner stayed in the car. Basically, we were waiting for back-up."

"Where is he now?"

"All-night McDonald's."

"And you're having the full McBreakfast, are you?" Stella shook her head in wonder.

"We were night shift. Last time I ate anything was half-six yesterday." Barley sounded defensive.

"If you were waiting for back-up, why did you—?"

"Go in." Barley finished the sentence for her. "The downstairs neighbor woke the next-door neighbor, who had a key. Used to go in to water the plants if the girls were away."

"You should have waited for scene-of-crime."

"I know. The neighbors were getting agitated, I thought they might just go in themselves. They wanted me to go and take a look."

"Fuck the neighbors," Stella told him. "You're the police, didn't you know that? You tell *them* what to do." The atmosphere in the car had changed. Solidarity was no longer an issue. "By going in before the scene-of-crime officer has set up a pathway, you run the risk of compromising forensic evidence."

"I know, boss, I'm sorry, it was just—"

"Defense briefs love a copper like you. We've got someone in the frame and suddenly your DNA crops up all over the place and some bastard's leaving the dock with a big, shit-eating grin on his face."

There was silence in the car for a while. Barley sighed. He said, "I couldn't be sure it was a body. Could have been a leaky soil pipe."

Stella said, "Switch on the ignition." Barley did it, and she pressed the button for the electric window and lobbed her cigarette out into the street. "So you went in."

"I went in. As soon as I found her, I got the neighbors out and called my inspector. No one went in after that. I stayed by the door until your guv'nor arrived with the SOC team."

The temperature in the car suddenly dropped several degrees. "You got the neighbors out . . ." Barley switched the ignition off and a silence fell. "Are you telling me the *neighbors* went into that flat— on to the scene of crime?"

"They followed me in. I hadn't noticed. They didn't go far."

"Far enough," Stella said. She was staring at Barley; Barley was staring straight ahead through the windscreen. "Let me tell you, they went far enough."

The nearside door opened. A uniform stood there with two McBreakfasts and fries. He saw Stella and backed off a couple of paces.

Stella got out of the car, then ducked down and looked back.

Barley was still facing front, his jaw working. She said, "Eat a hearty breakfast."

Mike Sorley was coming downstairs as Stella was going back up. He said, "I'm going to get a couple of hours' sleep. You ought to do the same."

"I will. I'll go and check with DC Greegan; find out how long they expect to be. Don't suppose we've got an incident room yet."

"I'll call your mobile."

"Okay, boss."

During the previous summer, Sorley had lost a marriage and found a girlfriend all in the space of a month. The new life had brought some changes. He was still overweight, but these days you could see his belt buckle. His hair was still thinning and going gray from the temples up, but someone had told him about dandruff shampoo. Stella wondered what "get a couple of hours' sleep" might really mean.

"If I manage to get DC Harriman released to the team, I'll give him your number," Sorley told her. "You might as well get stuck in here later on when the white suits are out of the way. Give the place a seeing-to. Make up a profile on the dead girl. A profile on her flat-mate. Someone else could make a start on house-to-house."

He went down a couple more steps, then paused. "What do you reckon?" he asked. "Sex crime or domestic?"

"What makes you think," Stella asked him, "that it has to be one or the other?"

Forensics were taking temperatures: of the room, of the body, of the maggot masses. They were bottling flies and tweezering up beetles. They were taking swabs and shaking out the curtains and removing dust samples. Someone had found a couple of wasps among the pile of clothes on a chair in the dead girl's bedroom. They were drowsy, easy enough to brush off into a specimen jar. People think wasps like jam. No, they like flesh; little sharky carnivores. They feed on the body and they feed on the other bugs. Jane Doe was a table, over-flowing with good things.

The doctor had made his educated guesses and gone to write his report. Measurements had been taken: body in relation to bed, bed in relation to room. Further measurements had concerned blood spatter on the walls and floor. Items from the bathroom and from a dirty-laundry basket had been lifted and bagged for blood type and DNA comparison with the corpse; other items had been taken from her wardrobe, from her handbag, from her bedside table. Dirty dishes and glasses had been removed from the kitchen. Fingerprints had been lifted from surfaces and objects. The flat had been recorded on video and stills camera. Jane Doe herself—Janis Parker, if that was right—had been videoed and photographed from all angles.

And not for the first time, Stella thought. There was a small port-folio on a coffee table in the living room. Stella tapped the shoulder of a white figure who was getting into the crevices of furniture with a hoover, and pointed at the folder. The figure nodded to let her know it was okay to touch, then went back to the business of collecting jots and scraps that might, one day, be evidence. Stella opened the portfo-lio and saw a ten-by-eight black-and-white of Jane Doe that was more recent than the framed photograph Sorley had shown her.

The girl was smiling. She had every reason to smile. She was young, beautiful, rich. She had the rest of her life to live.

3

Patches of aquamarine sky were appearing in the cloudbreaks; they were streaked through with dawn pink, but still carried traces of the city's sul-furous orange night-time glow: a livid mix. The wind was battering trees in the park and the streets were full of waist-high, wind-borne garbage. Stella drove the half-mile to John Delaney's flat and was about to pull over to the curb when she saw the patrol car outside. She drove past, turned the corner, parked, and dialed his number.

"Delaney . . ."

"There's a red-stripe outside your building. It's not you, is it?"

"It was. They're leaving."

"Still with you and about to leave, or—"

"Have left."

"Are you okay?"

"Sure."

"Was it—"

"You're down there, are you?"

"Round the corner."

"They'll be gone in a moment. Tell you then."

Stella walked back to the corner in time to see two uniforms getting into their car and driving down the road and past her. She didn't know them, and she hadn't expected to, but there was always a possibility that one of them might be seconded to Stella's team if they needed some help with door-to-door or a bit of local knowledge. That's when she might regret being recognized as "the DS who was going into the complainant's flat as we were coming out," because only one other person knew about Stella and John Delaney apart from Stella and John Delaney. Most of all, George Paterson didn't know. George had lost count of the number of times he'd asked Stella to marry him. "You don't have to say 'Yes,' " he'd told her once, "just say 'Okay.' " Stella's secret note to herself about George was that she loved him all right, but it was a low-key thing: companionable, comfortable, non-adversarial. Her note to herself about John Delaney was, as yet, unopened.

They had met while Stella was on a case and Delaney had been drawn into her life. They had started seeing each other, and that described it pretty well—seeing each other—because they hadn't been to bed together and that made everything more dangerous. The sex was there all right, but their relationship could never be just a fling. What lay between them was unspoken, but it was strong; maybe stronger for not being talked out. Sex was the unlit fuse. Neither said as much, but they both knew Delaney was waiting for her: it was her

NOTHING LIKE THE NIGHT   13

move. He was free, Stella was not. The other person who knew all this was called Anne Beaumont, and she was bound by client confidentiality because Anne was a psychoanalyst and no one, absolutely no one, knew about her.

Stella had a key to Delaney's street door and another to his second-floor apartment. She kept them in the glove compartment of her car with a police tag attached. George had never mentioned them. Delaney was standing in the hallway when she arrived. He held out a hand, but not toward Stella: he was gesturing at the door. The graffito was direct and unadorned: YORE DEAD.

Stella said, "As a working journalist, you must know any number of people who go to remedial English classes."

Delaney smiled. "The two young policemen who called just now were a great help. I gather that one of them is taking a D.Phil. in semiology."

Stella ran her hands over the upper part of the door, above the red paint. The woodwork had been scored and hacked with something like a knife or a screwdriver. Delaney went inside and, when she joined him, was making coffee and opening a packet of croissants. His brown hair had a curl to it: uncombed; his face was narrow with flat planes to the cheeks: unshaven.

Stella said, "Were you the only one to get the graffiti treatment?"

"The only one. I didn't know it was there. A neighbor on his way to work rang my bell. I was in bed."

"It's a great life, being freelance."

"Apart from the lack of money."

"First time?" she asked.

"No, I've been broke before."

"I meant—"

"I know. Yes, first time for this: for graffiti. There were some crank phone calls."

"Just phone calls . . . ?"

"I think so."

"Think so?"

"I wondered whether I might have been followed back here a few days ago. I'd gone through a set of lights on amber and the car behind me shot through as well, so the lights must have been red: almost hit a courier bike that was jumping off early from the other junction. Lots of horn blowing and tire noise and threats. The guy was driving a red BMW. The same car drove past me when I got home. I'd had to tour round for about fifteen minutes to find a parking space, so it was odd to see him there: still behind me, in effect."

"The driver?"

"Who knows? A shape."

"He didn't stop, get out, whatever?"

"Well, I don't know. I suppose he could have driven on, parked, and walked back. I wouldn't have known who he was."

"And you noticed all this because—"

"Yeah, you're right. Wouldn't have occurred to me if not for the phone calls." He pressed the plunger on the cafetière and poured coffee into two mugs. His and hers. As he got closer to Stella, handing her the mug, he said, "You smell of something."

"What did the phone calls say?"

"Nothing. Silence on the line."

"Try one four seven one?"

"What do you think?"

"I think the caller withheld their number."

"Good guess."

"You didn't tell me about it."

"I haven't seen you for a week." In fact, it was nine days, but he didn't want her to think he'd been counting.

"All this happened in the last week?" Stella asked. Delaney nodded. She added, "Journos have enemies, don't they? You write an article someone finds uncomfortable, and you're taking a risk. I suppose you've looked at that."

"Recent articles? Sure."

"And the possibles are . . . ?"

"Yardies, oil companies, construction outfits, car dealerships, the WTO, fang-toothed fundamentalists of several persuasions, multinationals, George W. Bush, and grass-roots corruption in the police force."

"And you've made enemies? It's a mystery." She sipped her coffee, then pulled her head back sharply because it was hot. "What did they say—the uniforms?"

"They took notes. Apparently, a crime-prevention officer is going to call to tell me how to make myself less vulnerable. A lesson we could all learn." She let the remark go. Delaney sniffed the air between them and wrinkled his nose. He said, "What is it? The smell."

"Death," Stella said.

She took her second shower of the morning while Delaney booted up his computer, made some phone calls, got his day going. George would sometimes shave while she showered; it wasn't like that with Delaney: too much at stake for that kind of casual intimacy. Stella stood under the jets and massaged shampoo into her scalp, trying to wash Jane Doe right out of her hair. When she'd finished, the bathroom was full of steam; getting out of the shower was like stepping into a cloud. She looked at the foggy reflection of her naked self in the mirror, then glanced at the door, half-hoping Delaney would come in. More than half-hoping.

I'm in love with him, she thought, and he's never seen me naked. She drew a face with a turned-down mouth in the moisture on the mirror, then wiped it away. I must be in love with him because I don't know what else it could be.

She was drying her hair when her mobile rang. She had put it on a shelf next to Delaney's razor and toothbrush. The LCD display showed a number she didn't recognize. When she answered, it was a voice she knew.

"So we've got a stinker, is that right?"

"Where are you, Pete?"

"On my way. DI Sorley thought we could make a start at the scene."

"I'll be fifteen minutes."

DC Harriman's voice drifted in and out of static. "Okay, boss," he said. "I won't begin without you."

She got dressed in the clothes she'd been wearing. They felt slightly sticky, as if she'd had them on for days. Delaney was at his keyboard. He looked up as she came into the room and asked, "What have you got?" The same words that George had used.

"A body. Body of a woman."

"Near here?"

"Up by Notting Hill Gate."

"So we might be seeing more of each other." He was looking at the screen, now, as if her answer didn't matter all that much.

She said, "I stayed away—" then stopped because she didn't know what she was going to say next.

"Because it's easier to stay away."

"In some ways, yes. But it's not what I want."

He got up and crossed the room and kissed her as if it had been on his mind all the time. He was tall and had to stoop. She said, "How long can this go on?" She might have been talking to herself.

She tensed slightly, as if to pull away, but he held her close and, after a moment, she leaned in to him and closed her eyes. She was tired and her mind went briefly out of focus; she could hear all the tiny sounds in the room: the fan in his laptop, a radiator clicking, the wind outside like someone shaking a tin sheet.

Delaney said, "It's still there. That smell. It's still on you."

4

The body had gone, forensics had gone and—with the windows open wide—the flies had gone. Stella and DC Harriman made a preliminary tour of the flat, but most of what they would need had already been taken and was being catalogued.

Harriman said, "It's not a smell like any other, is it?"

The bed had been stripped to its slat base, mattress and bedclothes bagged and sent directly to the forensic lab. You could see the stain, plum-dark on the wood. Stella sat in the living room and flipped through a pile of fashion magazines as if she were at the dentist's. She opened cupboards and drawers and found what you would expect to find. She went into the bedroom, where Harriman was sifting through layers of underwear in a tallboy. Like her, he was wearing latex gloves; even so, he let the soft silks drizzle through his fingers.

She said, "I hope you're not enjoying that."

"Hating it." He opened a second drawer, then a third, digging down into each like someone searching for a gift in the lucky dip. He showed Stella a self-sealing glassine envelope that held enough cocaine for a week of happy nights.

Stella said, "Naturally."

Delving into the bottom drawer, Harriman came up with a vibrator, fleshy and lifelike, and lobbed it to Stella, who was too startled to avoid catching it. Harriman grinned. "Looks like we've got a second victim, boss. I wonder what the killer did with the rest of the body."

Stella handed the vibrator back. She said, "Put that in a place where you'll be able to find it later."

They looked behind pictures, behind mirrors, at the backs of drawers, in the pockets of clothes hanging in the fitted wardrobe, because you can never be sure where people are going to keep their little secrets. Some might even be in full view, and not be noticed for that very reason. A set of keys in a glove compartment, for instance.

They weren't sure that there were any secrets, of course, or whether they might say anything about why Jane Doe had been killed, but since most people are killed by someone they know, secrets are often a factor.

Stella glanced round the room again before leaving. She said, "What's in there?" A small suitcase was tucked neatly into the space between the tallboy and the wall.

Harriman shrugged. "I assumed it was empty, boss. Didn't forensics take a look?"

"Open it," Stella said.

Harriman tipped it onto its side and it went down with a thump.

"Not empty," he said. It had a combination lock, but the clasps hadn't been engaged. He unzipped the lid and threw it back. Stella saw neatly folded clothes, shoes arranged heel to toe. In the net compartment under the lid were a slim, silver notebook computer and a hairdryer. She unfastened the straps holding the clothes in place and leafed through. Enough for a long weekend.

"She was going on a trip," Stella said.

Harriman nodded. "I wonder where."

"I wonder who with."

They drove in separate cars back to Notting Hill nick. Stella's Area Major Investigation Pool—AMIP-5—had been allocated a large open-plan space on the first floor, and as Stella and Harriman came out onto the upper corridor they met a small procession of deeply pissed-off police officers who had been given an hour to clear the office. Harriman was carrying Jane Doe's suitcase. He grinned broadly at one of the women and got a smile back, despite the fact that he'd just helped to make her homeless. Harriman had thick, dark hair with a curl in it and a narrow gypsy face; he was twenty-six, a gym regular, and none of the girls in his life expected exclusivity.

The incident room was still being set up: whiteboards, pin-boards, VDUs, filing systems for hard copy. Sue Chapman was running the office systems. She would log everything relevant to the case: the neighbor's call, witness statements, forensic reports, the post-mortem, all the way through to any court proceedings. Her close colleague in this was Stuart Proctor, a DC, who was the exhibitions officer. He kept tabs on the hardware: any item that might be considered evidence.

Sue's desk was the AMIP-5 larder: chocolate bars, crisps, soft drinks. The chocolate bars and the soft drinks varied, but it was always salt and vinegar crisps: no variants, no substitutes. She was eating a Lion Bar and typing up the initial medical report on Jane Doe, though the name was bracketed throughout with "Janis Parker."

"Used to be a model," Sue observed. "She put on a couple of years and a couple of ounces too many and made a sideways move: editing

a fashion magazine, *Imago*. Tall girls with no tits and a bad atti-
tude." Sue was tall herself, with a wild perm; she definitely had tits,
as Pete Harriman had been known to observe.

"That's a tabloid view of models," Stella told her.

"You're right. I'm sure they're all homebodies once they come
down off the catwalk."

Stella glanced at the personnel board: Sorley, herself, Sue, Stuart
Proctor, Pete Harriman, Andy Greegan, the names of a couple of
civilian indexers and the doctor who had attended the scene. And
someone called Maxine Hewitt. Stella crossed to where Mike Sorley
was setting up shop in a corner of the room half-screened by free-
standing soundproof panels. It gave him an illusion of privacy: his
office. She said, "Who's Maxine Hewitt?"

"Your second DC. She comes recommended as bright, tough, and
sharp."

"Sounds like an advert for Sabatier. Where did you find her?"

"She's local. Kensington. Eager to get on an AMIP squad."

"She's on her way, is she?"

"Getting something off her desk. Her DI guaranteed her by mid-
day."

"Okay. So I'll take Harriman with me to *Imago*. Has someone
been through her address book?"

"DC Greegan."

"Parents?"

"Different addresses."

"We'd better talk to both."

"Father's address is in Chile."

"You're kidding. Mother?"

"Richmond."

"I could send a couple of uniforms to bring her along," Stella
observed.

"No." Sorley had suffered bad press in the past. "Let's be sure."

Sorley lit the last cigarette from his first pack of the day. Smoking
is a thing policemen do, like footballers spit. Stella had given up six
months before, but wasn't a non-smoker yet. In the AMIP-5 squad
room, all you had to do was breathe.

She said, "Remember her passport was in her handbag?" Sorley nodded. "She was going somewhere: a trip."

"Where?"

"We haven't found her ticket. But it was abroad. She'd packed for somewhere hot."

As she was leaving, she remembered the coke; took it out and showed it to Sorley. "In her knicker drawer."

He smiled. "Where else?"

The wind had brought in a five-minute rainstorm, then swept it away. Now the sun was out, flashing silver on the leaves of roadside trees, on storefront windows, on the wet grass in the cemetery. The boy didn't sleep the night through and wake early like most children; he kept the rhythm of the dogs, sleeping when it suited him and waking to forage. Now was time to forage.

He took one dog, the big, brindled cross-bred hound, and set off between the rows of broken columns and blind angels. At night, the Strip that led up toward Kensal Rise was a neon river: fast-food places, minicab booths, wine stores, late-night mini-marts, bars. It was also an all-weather meat market where the girls stalked the curbs in micro-skirts and thigh boots, in crop-tops and PVC blousons, while the pimps watched from their cars. By day, things changed: the shop-keepers put stalls out in front of their properties and set up fruit and vegetables in neat tiers. Before they stocked the display units, they hosed down the night-time pavements. The gutters on the Strip were a tiny dark torrent carrying roaches and condoms and syringes and a thick, sour scum that might have been bad food or bad dreams or bad luck.

The shops were Iranian and Armenian and Greek and Italian and West Indian and Pakistani and English. The boy hadn't raided here for a while, so he hoped they wouldn't be expecting him. He crossed the road from the cemetery farther down from the Strip, so no one would see him until he turned the corner. Closer to the Strip, he broke into a run, then rounded the corner at speed, the dog loping at his side. He went down the shopfront displays taking whatever was within reach and easy to carry. By the time he'd got to the final shop, he'd been spotted. A shopkeeper came out onto the street to cut him off, but the dog moved fast, coming between them, its muzzle lifting back from its teeth. The shopkeeper pulled up, but the dog moved in on him, stiff-legged, snarling, until the man went back inside his shop. The boy kept running and, after a moment, the dog followed.

The shopkeeper called the police, but they would be no more help than before. No one knew the boy's name, or who his parents were, or where they lived. As it happened, neither did the boy. His story was simple: one morning his mother walked down the road away from the Harefield Estate and kept walking; she had left a bowl of Frosties and a carton of milk on the table. No one knew where she'd gone, but it was probably going to be a place where stimulants weren't hard to find. His father wasn't expected to be back on the streets for five years, but he barely knew of the boy's existence. Social workers went to call on members of the boy's extended family and heard only the sound of slamming doors.

The boy went into care, but was gone from the institution within a week. Now his face was one of tens of thousands on the Metropolitan Police missing-persons files. Although that was only a year ago, it was a face much younger than the one he now wore.

He went back to the cemetery. There was a tap nearby where people got water for the flowers they put on their loved ones' graves, and he drank a few mouthfuls from that before taking his haul down into the mausoleum. This was his food: sometimes he shared, but mostly the dogs found their own. In London, you're never more than twenty feet from a rat.

John Delaney stood in the shower. He had to adjust the angle of the shower-head because Stella had shifted it in her favor. He soaped his body slowly and thought of Stella.

When he got out, steam had clouded the mirror, restoring the face that Stella had drawn earlier. Delaney stared back at the downturned mouth. He reached out and put in two blob eyes that wept tears from the touch of his finger.

He said, "I know how you feel."

5

Post-mortems are about subtraction: the more you take away, the clearer things become.

Stella went down a flight of stone steps and along a passageway where the doorways were transparent plastic slap-flaps. She went through a lab with its stainless-steel glare, its row upon row of relics in jars, and came to the PM room. Even though it was halogen-lit and machine-rigged, Stella thought of it as the underworld. She wouldn't have been surprised to see the Grim Reaper standing silently in a corner waiting to take the dead before Hell's judge. In fact, the figure on the far side of the room wasn't at all grim: Sam Burgess, in green scrubs and ready to go about his business. He was putting some music on the CD player. Sam liked to work to music: usually something classical, though today it was some low, slow jazz. Jane Doe was full length on a steel table. Stella thought the woman didn't look any better than when she'd seen her last. In fact, she looked a lot worse.

Stella said hello to the morgue assistant and Sam turned to her voice. He was a small man with a monk's fringe of hair and a good, wide smile. His fingers were short and stubby: just right for the job of delving and dividing. He said, "Preliminary report suggests she died eight days ago. Hello, Stella."

"Hello, Sam. Not seven, not nine . . ."

"Eight, I'm pretty sure. The insects tell me; the little creepy-crawlies." Sam grinned as he approached the dissecting table; not a grin of malice: Jane/Janis was his stock in trade. Stella stared at the flesh bruised by its own blood. The gash in the dead girl's throat seemed wider now that she was under a harsh light; wider and dirtier. Stella knew that it was the grime of decay.

"There are things we need to eliminate, Sam."

"Was it a sex crime . . ."

"Or domestic," Stella said.

"Not a murder in the course of theft?"

"Nothing's impossible. He might have broken in to rob, found her on the premises . . ."

"There are multiple stab wounds," Sam said. "Not the usual sort of thing where robbery's the motive, is it?"

Stella remembered what Sorley had said: . . . *someone was playing with her.*

Sam stood over the body and gave Stella a smile. A small boom microphone was suspended over the steel table, just above head height. The assistant switched it on and Sam started to scrutinize the body, his hands moving delicately, like those of an archeologist who has just unearthed something rich and strange. Stella saw him lean over and put his face close to Janis's, like a lover about to close for a kiss. He tweezered something up from the corner of her mouth. When he had described everything that could be discovered by peering and probing, he turned to the bright instruments laid out ready.

Meat, Stella thought. Just meat and teeth and a hank of hair. Love and sorrow, laughter and loss, triumphs and disasters, it all comes down to this—something on a slab. After a while, she closed her eyes and listened as Sam began to describe what Janis had come to: a long, sad litany of corruption and decay.

6

Stella came out of a T-junction, winning a little chicken run with a Cherokee Jeep, and took her place in the pan-London tailback. The Jeep pulled in behind her, too fast and too close, another of the big-tire off-track four-by-fours that cruised the smooth byways of Belgravia and Kensington. She called Harriman on her mobile and he picked up at once, as if he'd been waiting for her. Which he had.

"Where are you?"

"Outside this magazine office, boss. *Imago*." He pronounced it two ways, not sure which was right. As it happened, both were wrong. "Where are you coming from?"

"The morgue."

"Okay. Stay off the Westway. It's solid."

It was an indelible part of the way Londoners communicated: Your mother's dying, oh, and by the way, don't even think about taking the A3. Stella drove a route that took her past tower blocks and town houses, past broken-down terraces and prime apartments. Two worlds, she thought. It was a simple division: those with lots of money and those with almost none; the oddity was that they existed almost side by side. It wasn't just a matter of some people owning the material world: a big house, a certain sort of education, long holidays in the sun, state-of-the-art living. Money bought more than that; it bought control. There were the rulers and the ruled; the judges and the judged; those who made fashion and those who followed it. These two groups understood one another, more or less; maybe they thought such inequalities were the way of the world.

But there was a third group, who had no understanding, no agreement, with anyone. They were people who would kill you for your money, for your car, for your mobile phone. They would kill you because you got in their way, or failed to show respect, or walked down the wrong street. They would kill you because they felt like it. Million-pound houses or hutches on the Harefield Estate; people with professions and people whose job it was to kick your door down and take what they liked and sell your kids crack at the school gate.

Stella's patch had all those people, all those lives. Two sides of the street. And Stella worked both sides.

Harriman was sitting in his car with the windows up. When he got out, a long billow of smoke came with him and was tugged away by the wind. He said, "Why here first? Why not the mother?"

"Sorley wants to be sure it's Janis Parker," Stella told him, "before we start bringing grief to parents. Maybe Sam Burgess will be able to make her presentable, I don't know."

"Give her a lick of paint," Harriman observed.

Stella smiled. Jokes were one way of making the job easier. Making it easier to face up to the dead.

Imago magazine was in a glass-and-steel-pipe office just off Portobello Road. The news that the visitors were cops went from reception to the transparent offices on the two upper floors at electronic speed. The wild flurry of activity as Stella and Harriman walked through made it seem that the entire office was tidying its desk or rushing out on an errand that couldn't wait. One or two were trotting to the loo. As Stella and Harriman approached, the trot quickened. It made Harriman laugh. He was still laughing as they were met by an anxious secretary and taken into an office, which was just a glass box, apart from one wall that was crowded with prints from photo shoots, publicity shots of models, and *Imago* front covers. "We should have told them we're not drugs squad," he said.

A woman came in behind them, as if she might have been waiting to hear that. She looked like the women pinned up on the wall, except that she was a little older, a little less tall, a little less thin. Not much, but it was crucial. She was dressed in clothes that left Stella feeling dowdy and hostile. She stood in the doorway, regarding them with eyes that seemed to have lost their blink reflex, then said, "Nina Groves," though she lingered on the threshold as if deciding whether or not to stay. Stella sat down on a small sofa by the picture-wall, so Nina crossed the room and occupied the high-backed leather chair behind her desk, then Harriman sat down on a small chair that stood at right angles to the desk. It resembled a series of moves in a complicated game of live chess.

Stella told the story and showed Nina the framed photo that Sorley had found. Nina seemed to have stopped breathing at the point when Stella had said "murdered"; her eyes were still wide. Eventually, she said, "Janis is in Morocco."

"We don't think she is," Stella told her.

"A few days' holiday; also looking at locations."

"We found a packed suitcase in her bedroom," Stella said.

"Marrakesh," Nina insisted.

"When do you expect her back?"

Nina lifted a phone, pressed a button, and paused a moment, then asked, "When does Janis get back?" The secretary was just beyond the door and her reply didn't need a phone. Nina passed it on anyway. "Should have been Tuesday."

"The day before yesterday," Stella observed. Nina nodded. "She didn't call in?"

"It's not like that."

"Not like what?" This was Harriman.

Nina answered without looking at him. "Not twenty-four/seven."

"What?"

"Not a job like yours," Stella told him. Then to Nina: "Tell me something about her."

"Meaning . . . ?"

"People in her life, what she liked, where she went, anything you think might be helpful."

"Her plane might have been delayed."

"We don't think so."

"Maybe she decided to spend a few more days . . ."

Stella gave a little sigh. Denial was usual, but it was a hell of a time-waster. She said, "The body of a young woman was found in the bedroom of a flat in Notting Hill. It's not easy to be absolutely certain that it was Janis Parker because she was killed seven or eight days ago and a week-old corpse doesn't look exactly like the person it once was, but the body was wearing Janis's watch and the hair color was right and since the flat in question was Janis Parker's and the bedroom appears to have been Janis Parker's, the odds are massively in favor of it being Janis Parker. I'm sorry." She paused. "Who's Stephanie James?"

"She shares the flat with Janis."

"She wasn't there. She hasn't come back." Stella was asking a question: *So where is she?*

Nina shrugged. "I don't know her that well. She works for a sales company, I think."

"Selling what?" Harriman asked.

Nina still wasn't looking his way. She shrugged. "I never talked to her about it." To Stella, she said, "She wasn't at the party."

"The party?"

"Janis's party."

It's like getting blood from a stone, Stella thought. "Tell me about the party."

"It was the last time I saw her, now I come to think about it. Saw Janis. It was her thirtieth-birthday party. A place called Machabo's. It's in Soho."

"Many people there?" Stella asked.

"No. Fifty, maybe."

Stella fell silent. Harriman passed a hand over his eyes, briefly. Fifty. They were thinking of the legwork. The paperwork. Eventually, Stella said, "When was this?"

Stella watched Nina as the woman thought it through, and saw the tiny wince that came with understanding.

"Eight days ago."

"Exactly?"

"Yes. A week yesterday."

"When was she supposed to leave for Morocco?"

"The next morning."

"What happened after the party?"

"We went to a club."

"Janis too?"

"No. Janis didn't even make it to the end of her own party. She got a migraine. Someone had to take her home."

"Who?"

"Guy called Mark Ross."

"He's . . . who? Janis's boyfriend?"

Nina's phone rang and she answered it. From the other side of the glass wall, her secretary said, "It's Pedro." Nina swiveled her chair, putting its back to the room, and started to talk to Pedro about skinny girls and heels and snakeskin panels. After a couple of minutes Stella leaned over and broke the connection.

Nina swiveled back, her face dark with dislike. She said, "Are you allowed to do that?"

"Not really," Stella said. "Mark was Janis's boyfriend, am I right?"

"No," Nina said. "Mark is Stephanie's boyfriend."

"So why did he—"

"She felt ill. He said he'd make sure she got back all right."

"Do you know where he lives?"

"Locally, I think. I'm not sure. Sorry."

"I'm going to send an officer round later. We'll need the names of whoever was at the party."

"You think I can remember all—"

"Just tell us about those you can remember," Stella said. "They'll name a few more, and so on." She got up to leave.

Nina said, "You mean it, don't you? About Janis being dead."

"Yes."

"And someone did it." She was avoiding the word "murdered." "It wasn't an accident."

"No. Someone did it."

"Who?" Nina asked the question as if no one else would have thought of it.

Harriman said, "We'll need to see her diary, search her desk, talk to her secretary. Eventually, we'll need to talk to everyone here."

Nina was still phasing Harriman out. She swiveled the chair, putting its back to him. "She'd been there a week—dead for a week?"

Stella nodded. "More or less."

"My God," Nina said, "she must have looked like hell."

Janis's secretary was in the mold: tall, thin, expensive all over. Her name was Petra. She told them that Janis was between boyfriends (and supplied the names of the last three), that she hadn't seemed worried or upset, was indeed prone to migraines, and that her tickets would have been waiting for her at the Heathrow BA desk, which explained the lack of them in her flat. She knew who Mark Ross was, but nothing about him except that he and Stephanie were an item. She'd met Stephanie but didn't know what she did for a living or where she might be found. She went on to say that Janis had no dark secrets so far as she knew, or enemies, or bad habits. She told them all this in a voice just above a whisper and ended by saying that it couldn't possibly be Janis.

"Why not?" asked Stella.

Petra shook her head. "How could it be?" she said. Her eyes were bright with backed-up tears. "It's someone else. Someone I don't know."

Before they left, Stella walked back to Nina Groves's office. Nina could see her approaching and was trying to decide what expression she ought to wear. The police make everyone nervous. She settled for a half-smile.

Stella stood in the doorway. She asked, "Where did Janis get her coke? Please don't say the vending machine in the lobby."

"What makes you think she did coke?"

Now Stella wore her own half-smile. She said, "The same place as you? The same place as your friends?" Nina looked away as if she was waiting for Stella to leave. "You can tell me," Stella said, "or I can sit here with you until they come with the dogs, a warrant, and someone who'll explain exactly what Class A means."

"I could get hurt."

"You could get busted."

"His name's Daz."

"That's it?"

"That's all I know."

"Tell me what he looks like."

"White, short, ties his hair back . . ." Nina paused to remember. "Earrings and a lip stud. Stupid nose."

"Stupid?"

It's sort of . . . too big for his face."

"Where do you find him?"

"The pub."

Stella said, "I know this is a bad time for you, and I don't feel good about having to come here and tell you that your friend's almost certainly dead, but please don't piss me about because I've got a lot to do and my mood can change."

"The Wheatsheaf. North Kensington, near the Saints. I can't remember the street."

Stella knew the Saints well. There were scag-dens and fuck-shops and gun marts, but very few wheatfields. Nina's phone rang to tell her that navy was the new black, and Stella joined Harriman, who was standing in the middle of the open-plan part of the office, regarding a series of posters that featured a model who was wearing a succession of top-label T-shirts, thigh boots, and nothing else.

"I wonder what she's selling," he said.

Stella went past him, heading for the stairs. "Whatever it is, you can't afford it."

The wind carried smells: petrol, McMeals, gutter garbage, incinerator smoke from the hospital. Harriman was trying a back-street route to the nick. "What do you think happens," he asked, "when someone at *Imago* needs a secretary and a fat girl with spots turns up for the job?"

"A fat girl with spots and cellulite."

"A fat girl with spots and cellulite and thick eyebrows."

"Spots, cellulite, thick eyebrows, and bad teeth."

"*Fuck!*" Harriman pulled up behind a line of cars. At the junction ahead, two vehicles had contested the grid and everything was locked off. Before they had started back, he'd gone to Pret A Manger and picked up lunch. Stella had already eaten her sandwich. Now Harriman pulled on the handbrake, sighed, and stripped the cellophane from his BLT.

"It's got to be domestic," Stella said. "If it's not domestic, it's drug connected." Following the train of thought, she added: "Guy called Daz who deals out of the Wheatsheaf over by Ladbroke Grove."

"That's where they get their stash?"

"So it seems."

Harriman gave it some thought. "I don't know him. I'll ask the locals."

"Not yet," Stella said. "News travels. I've got someone who might help."

"Whatever," Harriman said. He was watching a boy in charity-shop jeans and sneakers walking along a row of parking meters and pressing the reject-cash buttons one by one. The boy was wearing a filthy red blanket over his shoulders and there was a dog at his heel. The drivers in the back-up were leaning on their horns as if noise could break the gridlock. Harriman put his half-eaten sandwich on the dashboard and lit a cigarette. He said, "They get younger."

Stella looked at him. "What?"

"That kid." But when he looked again, the boy had gone.

Stella got out of the car. She said, "I'll walk back. Relax. Someone from traffic division will be along soon to fuck things up even more."

7

and marveled at the frailty of flesh. She thought of the girls in the *Imago* cover shots, their bodies sculpted by diet and light workouts, the perfect planes of their faces, the slick hint of cash, the electric sex of it. And here was Janis Parker, who had once been every bit as beautiful, but was now too ugly, too deformed, too corrupt to be looked at for long.

A voice behind her said, "More than fifty stab wounds." Stella turned. The woman was about thirty, pretty in a thin-lipped sort of way, and wore her dark-brown hair in a straight bob that fell to her jawline. She said, "DC Maxine Hewitt, boss."

Stella nodded and said, "Welcome," then added, "You're up to speed on this?"

"I think so. I read the SOC officer's notes and the initial medical report. I've seen the SOC video. I've talked to DI Sorley."

"And you've got Sam Burgess's preliminary PM notes."

"E-mailed over, yes."

"Which is how you know how many wounds."

"He could only be sure of fifty. It's probable that some hit the same spot; others go criss-cross."

"What's your guess?"

"Domestic."

"Why?"

"No robbery, no sign of a break-in. I mean, who knows? But it seems the likeliest choice. Things are usually what they seem."

"She was stabbed more than fifty times."

"Domestics are often the worst."

Stella nodded; she knew that was true.

Day one and the squad room was already littered with fast-food boxes, crisp bags, Twix wrappers, carryout cups from Starbucks and Coffee Republic. The ashtrays looked volcanic. Mike Sorley took a step or two out of his makeshift office while Stella briefed the team. Pete Harriman arrived in a rush, a man with a grudge against the traffic division. He saw Maxine Hewitt and checked her profile before finding a chair. Everyone had a cigarette going except Sue Chapman and Stella.

"We're pretty certain that the dead woman is Janis Parker, but we need confirmation. Dental records first, DNA if we're still not sure. Close-relative ID is going to be difficult. Even so, I don't think we're in any real doubt now. We know she was supposed to be in Morocco, which is why no one missed her, we found the suitcase in her bedroom. Hair color, the Rolex . . . Also," Stella shrugged, "you'd have to say the dead person looks like her if it looks like anyone. It's time someone spoke to the mother." She glanced across at Sorley, who nodded.

"Pete," Stella said, "you go—with Maxine." She nodded at the new arrival. "This is Maxine. There's a possible drug connection, and I'll follow up on that. At present, we need to find the flatmate, Stephanie James, and her boyfriend whose name is Mark Ross. So far as we know, he's the person last seen with Janis Parker."

"Which puts him in the frame?" Maxine asked.

Stella nodded. "Theoretically, yes, I suppose it does. Until we know more, or know better."

She ran through the evidence they'd gathered from Nina Groves and Janis's secretary. "So—other people who need to be contacted and talked to: the people who were at the party; the people who work at *Imago*." She looked at Sorley. "We're going to have to draft in some local help." Sorley nodded. "We've got her address book, appointments book, and so on, which means we know the name of her dentist. Forensic staff will get on to that. There'll be more to work with once we get the full post-mortem report, but as things stand, we're not treating it as murder in the pursuit of a robbery."

Sue Chapman asked, "You think she knew him?"

"Him or her," Stella said.

"Him."

"Why?"

"Fifty wounds," Sue observed. "It's obvious."

First the killing, then the discovery, then the paperwork. Everyone knew about the paperwork. Two words that are the key in any investigation: crime and punishment? No. Budget and paperwork. Stella wrote her report, gave it to Sorley, then made a phone call.

"Chis" is an acronym. It stands for covert human intelligence source. You might run half a dozen and you pick them for what they know and who they know; each to his own. Stella was phoning a chis called Jackie Yates. A childhood illness had left Jackie not just bald, but hairless; in reports, Stella referred to him as Badger. In the world of crime everyone has a nickname, but for a chis it's a mask; it's safety first; and no cop would ever ask a chis to go into the witness box or attend a line-up or even meet another officer. You made a date with your chis, but you didn't tell anyone about it. Jackie said he'd be at the corner of Bayswater Road and Queensway at seven o'clock.

There was a pub directly opposite the nick and most of the cops used it at one time or another. Stella liked to drink vodka there: just the one; maybe two. It was neutral ground: neither here nor there; not home, not John Delaney's flat. The vodka had to be over ice in a shot glass, and when she took that first sip and her synapses reacted to the booze she felt better. Not great, just better. It was a ritual that she shared with no one.

How long can this go on?

She sat at a table on her own and made a phone call to George, her voice smudged by the yelled conversations of office workers who were starting their evening with a few drinks, a few laughs, a few lies, perhaps, to whoever was waiting at home. Stella was telling a kind of truth: it involved Jackie Yates, but omitted other possibilities.

"How late?" George asked.

"I'm not sure." Which really meant: I'm not sure whether my next call will be to John Delaney.

George said, "I'll carry on working. If you don't get back, I'll have pizza."

George was a boat designer; he worked for himself but liked to keep office hours. Long ago, he had realized that the rhythms of Stella's life wouldn't match those of his own, and he'd settled for that. Stella's view of things was that George was a gentle man who loved her in an uncomplicated way and was able to make the compromises that would help keep them together. In truth, she knew that love is never uncomplicated.

A couple of office workers trading gossip sat down at her table. Stella got up. It was time to meet Jackie Yates, the first of two secret appointments she had to keep that evening.

8

Margaret Parker knew she had opened the door to bad news, but didn't realize just how bad. She said, "It's William, isn't it?"

Maxine Hewitt had rung the bell; Pete Harriman was standing a little way back, as if nasty shocks were women's work. The house was seven bedrooms, three bathrooms, and half an acre. Margaret led them through to a large room off the galleried hallway and composed herself to grief.

"William's your husband," Maxine guessed.

Margaret nodded. "We're separated. Eight years now. Tell me what happened."

"No," Maxine told her, "it's not William."

There was a moment, a few seconds, while Margaret looked from one of them to the other, trying to work out what that meant. Then her mouth went ragged and her hands started to shake. She said, "Janis . . ." in a voice so small that Maxine lip-read the word.

Maxine asked her to sit down. She wondered if there was a friend who might be telephoned. Margaret said, "No one. I don't want anyone. There's no need. Everything's all right."

Maxine started to recount what they knew; what they supposed. She hadn't said more than a few words before Margaret Parker stood up. She said, "Could you leave, now, please?"

Harriman said, "Mrs. Parker, we have to—"

Margaret stepped toward him and took his arm, shoving him toward the door. "No, you have to leave. You have to go."

"Perhaps it would be better if you called someone," Harriman said.

"No, no, that won't be necessary." Margaret turned toward them, one hand extended, ushering them out. She was smiling so hard that her eyes were slits and she seemed to be speaking on an indrawn breath. Maxine saw what was coming. She moved toward the woman, putting out her own hands to comfort or support. In the same moment, Margaret Parker fell toward her, deadweight, all her senses switched off.

Harriman called an ambulance while Maxine sat on the floor with Margaret Parker's head in her lap.

She said, "Don't ask me to show her the SOC photos."

The Golden Dragon was small and hot and noisy—a stir-fry roar from the open-plan kitchen, orders being called, waiters yelling for no apparent reason, diners crammed together at the tables and competing with one another to be heard; which is why Jackie Yates liked it: easy to be nothing more than a face in the crowd. Also, nearly all the customers were Chinese and many of them spoke no English.

One thing you can count on the Chinese for: they all smoke. Most of the Golden Dragon's customers smoked between courses, some of them smoked between mouthfuls. The noise, the heat, the stir-fry sizzle and steam, were wrapped in drifting layers of cigarette smoke. Meeting in the restaurant was Jackie's method for getting a little extra for the information he would give, because Stella was expected to pick up the bill. He ate like the Chinese, keeping the bowl close to his face, his chopsticks traveling the minimum distance.

Stella asked about someone called Daz.

"I know him," Jackie said. "Why do you want him?"

Stella laughed. "I can't tell you that."

"It's murder, right? We must be talking about murder, here, because that's your area of operations. Murder." Jackie filled his mouth, then chewed and spoke at the same time, spilling little gobbets of chicken and rice. "He's not the type, Mrs. Mooney."

"No?"

"Not at all."

"Why not?"

"Some people can, some people can't."

"Some people," Stella said, "think they can't until they do."

Jackie called Stella Mrs. Mooney because he thought it sounded funny. It certainly sounded funny to her.

"Geezer I used to know called Charlie Brown—" Jackie was still chewing, still talking, "—not really Charlie, you know, it was Arthur, but there's that kid in the comic strip, yeah? So he got called Charlie." Stella waited. Never ask a chis to cut to the chase; it's not the way to get results. "He liked it. Really liked it. Saw him glass a bloke once, no real reason, the guy had said something, laughed at the wrong time, yeah? Charlie stuck that pint pot in his face half a dozen times and you thought, okay, now he'll stop, but he didn't, just kept going with it, kept doing it to him, until the glass was down to just the base, yeah?, and Charlie's hand was cut up, he needed stitches in the end, but he kept going."

"Where were you?" Stella asked.

"Yeah," Jackie said, "I was there."

"No. *Where were you?*"

"Oh, you mean why didn't anyone try and stop him?"

"Yes."

"Don't joke. He'd got a head of steam up and a glass in his hand." Jackie lifted his beer. "You don't get in the way, yeah?"

Stella was eating, but keeping her eyes down. Sharing a Chinese meal with Jackie Yates wasn't a happy experience. Apart from Jackie's chew-and-chat routine, there was also his wig and his bald face. The wig was immobile and blond and sat on Jackie's dome like a nest. His face wasn't just hairless, it looked scoured: he had never grown stubble or raised an eyebrow.

He blinked lashless eyelids at Stella and said, "Not everyone's like Charlie, yeah? So if it's murder, don't bother with Daz."

"It's not murder, Jackie, it's drugs. A drug connection."

"Yeah, well, that would be more like it. That's why he's called Daz."

"What is?"

"Cuts his scag with anything handy."

"Washing powder?" Stella grimaced.

"Whatever he's got."

"I need to talk to him, Jackie, without causing a fuss. Without any echoes."

"He can't be seen talking to Old Bill. Think of his connections."

"His connections being . . . ?"

Jackie shook his head. "Who knows?"

Stella could see plainly that Jackie knew and that knowledge was a dangerous thing.

"Well," Stella said, "I need to have a chat with Daz, one way or the other."

"You mean you'll nick him."

Stella shrugged. "That's one way." It wasn't what she wanted to do. Sure, she could ask the drugs squad to keep Daz under observation, lift him when he was carrying, then turn him over to her so that she could offer some kind of a deal. It wasn't a good way to operate, though. Daz's connections, whoever they were, would sniff danger and find the shadows.

"What's the other?"

"Through you."

The cloth on Jackie's side of the table was a litter of food fragments. He kept his bowl at chin-level, but stopped eating for a moment to gaze at Stella; his smooth, pink face looked clammy, as if it had been skinned. "Not me."

"Through you," Stella insisted.

Jackie put his bowl down. He said, "Can't be done."

"I can't walk in on him at the Wheatsheaf." Stella saw Jackie's bald eyes narrow a fraction when she mentioned the pub. "Bound to be noticed; and that wouldn't be good for either of us—mostly not good for him."

Jackie swallowed some beer through the food in his mouth. Scarves of cigarette smoke drifted between them. He smiled and shook his head.

"A fork in the road," Stella said. "Think of it that way. You come to a place where the road divides and you make a choice. And you go down the road you've chosen—"

Jackie sighed. "Whatever," he said, "whatever. But it can't be done."

"—down the road you've chosen and the days pass and the scenery changes and pretty soon you couldn't hope to find your way back to the place where the road divided: not a chance."

Jackie had filled his mouth again. He was looking right and left as if bored, as if trying to find something that might pass the time while Stella told her story, but his real reason was that he didn't want to catch her eye, because he knew how the story ended. When he swiveled his head, the stiff strands of his wig lifted from his neck like a straw helmet.

"When we started out, Jackie, I had you cold. You were in the same bind then that you're in now—if you came clean you were in danger from the bad guys, if you kept quiet you could be charged with concealing evidence. In the end, I didn't need your evidence, but we did a deal. That was the choice; that was the road you took. You stayed out of prison and every now and then you and I meet for a chat."

"It was a while ago. That's all dead and gone."

"No, Jackie, it's not dead and gone, it's here and now. You're a chis; you're an informant. There are people in prison because of things you've told me. There's no way out of that. It's fact."

"You do it," Jackie told her, "you grass me up and you'd find all the doors and windows closing, yeah? No one will talk to you, not even to call you a cunt."

Stella laughed. "Be serious. I've got another five like you and I can pick up five more any day of the week. By and large, people don't want to go to prison, Jackie. By and large, people would sooner do a deal. As you know."

Stella was facing the street. The wind had fallen off a little during the day, but now it was stronger than ever. People were either leaning to walk, or were scuttling along as if being shoved by an invisible hand. The local stores had closed, leaving their garbage in the street for tomorrow's collection, and all the loose stuff was airborne. A cardboard box drifted past at head height, twisting and rising.

"Through me," Jackie said, "but you stay out of the picture."

"No."

"You tell me what you want to know, I talk to Daz, then I talk to you."

"No."

"Why would he talk to you?"

"Because if I have to, I *will* lift the bastard. My way, we can make a date, meet somewhere safe, no unpleasant surprises and no one need know."

Jackie put his bowl down and lit a cigarette. "I'll call you."

"You do that." Stella stood up and took her coat off the back of the chair.

"What about the bill?" Jackie asked her.

"Your turn," Stella said. "It had to come round sooner or later."

9

A fork in the road, both ways snaking off into darkness. The fairy story where one path leads to the peaceable kingdom, the other to Bluebeard's Castle.

"Everyone, every day," Anne Beaumont said. "Sometimes the choice matters a lot, sometimes hardly at all. And sometimes people find they can't choose, so they stand at the place where the road forks, waiting for a sign."

Anne was Stella's second secret meeting: secret because Stella had barely admitted to herself that she was seeing a shrink. She liked to think that each session would be the last.

"But the sign never comes," Stella said. "It's wishful thinking: an excuse for leaving things unresolved. Have I got that right?"

"Yes."

"So the person continues to stand at the fork in the road until . . . what?"

"Time passes, the roads become overgrown and, in the end, impassable. She can't go back, that road's closed to her. So she stays at the fork; which is, really, the last place she wants to be."

"I saw him today for the first time in a week."

"How was it?"

"Short. We didn't talk much. I had to leave. Someone graffitied his front door and hacked at it with a knife or something."

"That's why you went round?"

"No. I was in the neighborhood."

"Stella, you *live* in the neighborhood."

Anne got up and went out of the room. Stella was curled up in one of two armchairs that were arranged either side of the fireplace, which is how the two women always sat, as if one were telling the other a story. Stella realized that all Anne's clients sat with her in just the same way, but for some reason that was reassuring. Anne came back with two glasses of white wine. She had a slightly country look about her: tall, blonde, a soft complexion, but there was something sexy and unrestrained about her loose-limbed walk. Wind rattled the windows. Anne handed Stella her wine and said, "You don't often get weather in London. Not proper weather. I like it."

Stella would sooner have had vodka. Vodka had become her drink. "I know what I want to do," she said.

"Of course."

"But I don't know if it's the right thing to do."

"What makes you think there is a right thing?"

"That sounds like a standard shrink's response."

"You're right, it is. Guess why."

"Because my problem isn't anything new."

"Only to you."

"I've got an idea," Stella said. "You tell me what to do and I'll do it." Anne laughed and a silence fell between them. Stella sipped her wine and looked out to where streetlights were coming on alongside Hyde Park. She had known Anne Beaumont for more than a year: had been talking to her once, sometimes twice a week. It was the dream that had sent her to Anne: the dead-baby dream.

You learn how to keep your distance and most of the time you can. Being a cop, you see bad things all the time, you meet bad people, you hear bad news. Deal with it and move on is the advice that most police officers give themselves and most of the time that's exactly what they do. It was what Stella had always done, until the Bonnelli case.

Luca Bonnelli claimed that he'd found his wife's body when he returned from a drinking session with friends. The problem was that no one could really remember whether he'd been around when the pub closed; and the friends were just people he drank with, played pool with; he knew their first names but he didn't know where they lived. Luca and Stella sat in an interview room all night. She was pretty certain he'd killed his wife. They smoked and drank thin coffee from Styrofoam cups and went through the same list of questions, the same answers, until the next morning. Luca didn't confess, but he did keep asking about his kids: where were the kids, who was looking out for the kids? Stella didn't know, except, of course, that someone would be with them: a social worker, a relative, whoever had been upstairs with them while the SOC team had been going about their business.

People under interview get eight hours' rest in every twenty-four in accordance with the law, and Luca Bonnelli was almost asleep on his feet when Stella switched off the tape and sent him back to the cells. It was long past dawn. She sat in the squad room with her feet up on her desk and slept for a couple of hours, then made a call and arranged for a careworker to meet her at Luca's address. She needed to talk to the children: it's a good bet that, in a domestic murder, the children will give you most of what you need to know.

The careworker didn't show up, or else she showed up later. When Stella arrived the dream was waiting for her, all the details in place—every light in the house on, but a sense of darkness; the path seeming unnaturally long; an odd and undefinable stillness about the place. She might have been dreaming already. No one answered the bell, so Stella pushed the letterbox up, then crouched down and looked in. She could see the children's feet and, when she stooped lower, saw that they were hanging from the upstairs banister; two of them, a girl and a boy, but she couldn't see their faces: not until she broke a window and went in and stood in the little hallway looking up.

They'd found Luca's sister easily enough. All she could say was, "That bitch. That fucking bitch. She's dead now. They're all fucking dead." Several experts had decided that she was schizophrenic and the jury had agreed. Luca had put a slant on it later: "She come from the wrong family, you see? My wife. The wrong family."

Stella had been fine during the remainder of the investigation: charging the sister, dealing with evidence, getting the job done. Then one day she had got into her car and driven until she was too blind with tiredness to go on. She'd holed up in a hotel with no idea at all of what she was going to do next and spent her days behind drawn curtains and her nights dreaming of dead babies. George had found her, eventually, but the damage continued. Stella was pregnant with her own child and miscarried on the drive down to London.

She took the regulation sick leave, then went back to work. During her time at home, she had painted walls and worked in their tiny patio garden; sometimes she'd walk along by the river or in Holland Park. The days were dull and more or less okay; the days were like each other. Nights were dangerous, however late she went to bed, however drunk she might be when she got there. The dream was always there, waiting in the shadows. And there were not two dead children, but three.

Anne said, "Some people stand there forever: all their lives at the fork in the road."

"What do you think I'll do?"

Anne laughed. "How should I know?"

"You're the shrink. You're supposed to be able to second-guess things like that, aren't you?"

"Not how it works," Anne informed her, then added, "Time's up."

"Give me a hint."

"Time's up."

George was sitting at the kitchen table sifting through a pile of diagrams, his half-finished pizza pushed to one side. He said, "There's a snag to boat-building."

Stella kissed her fingers and pressed them lightly to his cheek as she crossed to the freezer for a real drink. "What is it?"

"The sea," he told her.

She took the vodka out and waggled the bottle at him: a question. He said, "Why not?"

While she poured, he talked about the pressure on hulls and how it might be withstood, but he was thinking about making love to her and she knew that.

John Delaney was browsing the news pages on the Internet: staying in touch with small wars, rigged elections, official lies, local murders.

He dialed all but the last digit of Stella's mobile and waited to see what he would do next. Nothing, it seemed.

More than one traveler; more than one fork in the road.

10

In the AMIP-5 squad room, a long pinboard carried the pictures of Janis Parker that the SOC photographer had taken: a couple of reels, this angle and that, close-ups and mid-shots, several that put her in context with the bedroom at large. In some of them you could see a forensic officer holding a hair dryer: an impromptu method for keeping the flies at bay. Nothing he could do about the maggots: a pale goiter.

Stella walked the length of the board like a visitor at an exhibition. She was holding Sam Burgess's notes, together with the forensic report and some information Andy Greegan had supplied concerning significant finds at the SOC. One was a fabric belt, freckled with blood.

The killer gagged her and tied her, Stella thought, then untied her and took off the gag. What was that about?

Maxine Hewitt was watching from her desk. After a moment she said, "The boyfriend?"

"What?" Stella didn't turn to Maxine's voice; she continued to study Janis Parker. The ex-Janis Parker. The one-time Janis Parker.

"The boyfriend's got to be favorite for it. Stephanie James's boyfriend."

"Yeah?"

"Last person seen with her, he took her home, you know—if it looks like an elephant and sounds like an elephant, chances are it's an elephant."

"Give me a motive."

Maxine shrugged. "Sex. Bound to be sex. He came on to her, she told him to piss off."

"So he stabbed her fifty times, then cut her throat."

"Maybe he's got a temper on him. You never know."

That much was right, Stella thought. In the business of human affairs, you never know. There was Maurice Fincher, for example. Maurice was eighty-three when he died. The scene of crime—a gimcrack flat on the Harefield Estate where Maurice lived with his wife, Mary—was a gore swamp: blood in the hallway, blood in the living room, blood in the kitchen where Maurice lay on the cheap lino with his brain spilling out of his head like yolk from a smashed egg. Mary had gone to get their pensions, she said, and found him when she returned. It seemed simple. This wouldn't have been the first time a pensioner opened the door to someone with a crack habit, no money and a single thought.

Then the oddities began to show up: blood in the bathroom, but only a speck or two; small but noticeable variations in Mary Fincher's account of discovering the body; forensics coming up empty-handed when they looked for evidence out on the walkway by the Finchers' front door.

It was the absence of any forensic trace beyond the flat that made Stella think; that, and Mary's reaction to her husband's death. A psychiatrist had diagnosed shock: the disassociation, the false calm, the denial of grief. He advised that she be watched carefully because reality, when it hit her, might be more than she could bear. It was what everyone thought.

Stella decided to think the unthinkable, and that was how she found the hammer, still clotted with blood and hair, that Mary had simply put back into the tool box. In the gap between killing her husband and calling the police, Mary had taken a bath and put her clothes on boil wash, but she'd simply replaced the hammer, as if washing clothes were a familiar task, but good maintenance of tools was a man's job.

Sam Burgess could never understand where she had found the strength for the job.

Maxine Hewitt was writing her report on the interview with Margaret Parker, which didn't amount to much, since Janis's mother was currently sedated and mute. "Either a temper," she continued, "or he started and couldn't stop. You know—got interested."

Got interested. It was a dark thought and it troubled Stella because it sounded right. It sounded true, like Mike Sorley's remark about someone playing with her. She said, "When we find him, we'll ask him."

"We've found him." This time, Stella did turn. Maxine said, "I thought you knew."

Stella glanced over to where Sue Chapman was logging reports. Sue looked startled. "*I* thought you knew."

"Before I can know, someone has to tell me. Where is he?"

"On his way," Maxine said. "The locals were interviewing people from the party. Someone knew his address and where he worked. Sue gave me the report, I told DI Sorley, you weren't around, so he sent Andy Greegan and Pete Harriman to fetch him in. Tried his flat; no good. Tried his place of work; there he was."

"And you thought Sue had told me?"

"Yes."

Stella looked across to where Sue was sitting with her hands poised over her keyboard like someone playing statues. "And you thought she'd told me?"

"I did, yes."

"Next time," Stella said, "why don't you both fucking tell me: all right?"

Maxine could feel the frost in the air. She smiled an apology, but she was thinking: Don't blame me. Where the hell were you when the news came in?

The answer was: sitting outside John Delaney's flat, trying to decide whether or not to go in, and feeling foolish. Which was exactly why Stella was tight-lipped and tetchy. She crossed to her desk and sat there to read the forensic report in conjunction with Sam Burgess's notes. The reports were exhaustive, so she picked out the principal points in pink highlighter.

FORENSIC

Blood splashes in the living room and the bedroom indicated that the victim had been attacked in both rooms.

The amount of blood and its distribution suggested that the attack had started in the living room and that the victim had finally died in the bedroom, though this couldn't be stated with absolute certainty.

Fingerprint elimination was barely possible. The surfaces in the flat, of course, carried multiple prints. Those of the victim had been eliminated, but that left a large number.

DNA samples had been taken from certain objects found in the flat: unwashed cutlery and dishes in the dishwasher, a glass in the sink, toothbrushes in the bathroom, hair samples found in both rooms during the forensic search.

There was one DNA sample of particular significance: a small number of strands of human hair were found to be plastered to the victim's wounds. These were not those of the victim. It was reasonable to assume that they were shed by her attacker. They had been sent for DNA analysis.

The dental records confirmed that the dead woman was Janis Parker.

SAM BURGESS

An analysis of insect infestation and the general state of decomposition of the body showed that Janis had died eight days before her body was discovered.

The digestive tract was full, so she had eaten not long before death. The food was listed by type.

There was a contusion surrounded by bruising on the side of the head, indicating a blow from a blunt object.

A residue of semen in the vagina was evidence of the fact that the victim had unprotected sexual intercourse shortly before she died. Semen traces were also found on the victim's underwear. The amount of semen indicated that sexual activity might have taken place on more than one occasion that evening.

There was no evidence found of sexual assault, though the body was in the initial stages of decomposition, which made it difficult to be certain on this matter.

The victim's wounds numbered fifty or more and though the smaller ones, taken cumulatively, might have proved fatal in the end, it was the wound to her throat that should be considered the cause of death.

Cuts to the palms of the victim's hands and forearms were likely to be defense wounds, indicating that she had fought her attacker.

Traces of adhesive had been found on the victim's mouth, cheeks, and chin. Forensic analysis (cross-referenced, here) showed them to have come from a proprietary brand of electrical tape.

Marks on the victim's wrists suggested that she had been tied at some point, though there were no rope or cord fibers at the point of examination and no deep scoring, which seemed to indicate that the bonds might have been fabric.

Prior to her death, she had been in good health.

She was in the early stages of pregnancy.

Mark Ross didn't look up when Stella entered the interview room; he was sitting like a gnome, fists to temples, hunched over and staring at the scabby surface of the table. She sat down opposite him, removed some ten-by-eight photos from an envelope, and slid them across: the SOC close-ups. Ross stared at them for a moment, as if not sure what they might be, then he closed his eyes and turned away.

"We've got dental records," Stella said, "but it would be good to have confirmation. We spoke briefly to her mother, but she's not in any shape to look at these."

"You think I am?"

"Someone has to." It was untrue, of course, but Stella wanted to judge his reaction.

Ross turned back and looked at the photos again, touching them lightly, squaring them up, putting them side by side, as if trying to find an arrangement that would make them more abstract. He said, "They look like her." *They* look . . . By referring to the photos, he made them more image, less Janis.

"The way I understand it," Stella said, "the way it was told to me, there was a party for her birthday at a place called Machabo's and you were there."

"Then I expect you also heard that she felt ill and that I took her home before the party ended. Do you mind if we put those away?"

Stella pushed the photos to the side of the table, out of Ross's direct eye line but still there to be looked at. "A migraine," Stella said. "She was prone to them, yes?"

"Yes." Ross looked to be about thirty, maybe a year or two older. He had most of the attributes of the Notting Hill rich: thin, attractive, designer this and that. His hair was soft mid-brown and looked good when he ran his fingers through it and let it flop forward: in this case, a gesture of distress.

"So you took her home . . ."

"I drove her home, she was feeling pretty dreadful and wanted to go straight to bed. She took some Migraleve. I left."

"What time was that?"

"I'm not sure. Somewhere around eleven-thirty."

"After that?"

"I went home."

"Not back to the party?"

"I didn't think it would last all that long once Janis had left."

"How did you get home: what route?"

He gave her a list of back-doubles to Elgin Avenue.

"And then?" Stella asked.

"Had a drink, watched TV for a while, went to bed."

"Can anyone vouch for this?" Ross laughed and shook his head. Stella asked, "Why laugh?"

"There must be hundreds of thousands of people who go home alone every night, have a drink, watch something on TV, and go to bed. Millions, perhaps. So why does it sound so unconvincing?"

"Does it?"

Ross glanced sideways again. "In context."

"What was on?"

"Sorry?"

"On TV. What program?"

"I don't watch TV for the content. I watch it because it's there." He paused. "A movie, I think; though that might have been another night."

"Where's Stephanie James?"

"I don't know."

"She's your girlfriend, have I got that right?"

"Yes."

"And you don't know where she is?"

"She's not dead." He said it with a little start of surprise in his voice, as if the thought had just occurred to him.

"How do you know?"

"I phoned her, yesterday evening." He paused, on the brink of something. Stella let him think it through. "We'd had a serious row. One of several, all serious. It looked like things were ending, you know . . . Steph disappeared; put herself out of touch. The idea was that we wouldn't see each other for a bit; then meet up and talk. She's been staying with friends, I expect. Not in London, anyway. I called to say, Let's talk."

"What was the row about?"

He shrugged. "Nothing." Stella believed him. All the most lethal rows are about nothing.

"What did she say?"

"Not much."

"Give me a summary."

"Not now. I'm not ready. Fuck off."

"Sorry?"

"You asked me what she said."

"You called her on her mobile?" Ross nodded. "You'd better let me have the number."

Stella switched off the interview tape and went out to the squad room, where Pete Harriman was typing with two fingers and a thumb: standard police issue. She gave him the number. "Stephanie James's. Call her and get her in. If it's switched off, send a text message."

In the interview room, Mark Ross had pulled the photos back and set them side by side. He asked all the right questions—Why? Who? When? How?—just as you would expect an innocent person to do. Now and then, he glanced at the tape, as if anxious to know that it was all registering: the shock, the outrage, the distress, the puzzlement.

Or am I just looking for it? Stella wondered. Cynicism: also standard police issue.

She asked Ross to let her know if Stephanie James called in; he said fine. She asked him for fingerprint and DNA samples—for elimination purposes; he said fine. She asked him to let her know if he intended to make any trips.

He said, "For God's sake, why would I kill her?"

11

The AMIP-5 squad had exchanged notes, compared theories, divided tasks, and to prove it there were enough cigarette butts to fill a bucket. Mike Sorley was in his makeshift office, silted up with paperwork. In any investigation, it was a constant: whatever happened, the paper kept on coming. Stella was sharing the space with him for a short while and thinking, as she did every day, about taking up smoking again—just defensively.

Sorley said, "What's it look like?"

"We haven't got a murder weapon, we haven't got a motive, and we haven't got a suspect. Apart from that, we're forging ahead."

"Everyone thinks domestic."

"Meaning you think that . . ."

Sorley shrugged. "Not necessarily. What about this guy Ross?"

"I don't reckon so."

"DC Hewitt likes him for it."

Stella allowed the merest hint of a pause before saying, "I know she does. She told me."

Sorley smiled. "Her boss tells me she's smart."

"That's good," Stella said, "because there's nothing more stupid than a stupid copper."

"Ross," Sorley reminded her.

Stella shook her head. "Not for me. He hasn't got the smell of it about him."

"Okay, if you say so. Just don't use the word 'hunch.' " Stella smiled, but the smile disappeared when Sorley added, "And don't lose track of him, either." He looked down at her report. "The mother's under sedation, the father's in Chile." He made it sound like much the same thing. "What's he doing there?"

"He's a mining engineer."

"And that's for sure where he is?"

"He was when I spoke to him. Now he's on the way home."

"So we've got Ross, though you don't fancy him for it; we've got a drugs connection; we've got the possibility that she surprised burglars, though it's unlikely, I agree; and we've got upward of fifty people who were at a party, to say nothing of her work colleagues, a wide circle of friends and neighbors, and a limitless number of passing strangers who might have taken an irrational dislike to her."

"So far," Stella agreed, "but it's early days."

Sorley didn't crack a smile. He said, "I'll tell you what I've got: a very small budget and a superintendent whose name is Tightarse Cheapo."

Sorley had left his wife because she liked to hit him: not just the occasional punch on the arm, but genuine attacks: hair ripped out, a tooth loosened, deep bruising. Another copper might have called it actual bodily harm. In some ways, Sorley found it ridiculous; husbands beat their wives and there were support systems and advice for those women, as there should be. But Mike Sorley was a bulky five foot ten and worked in a job where violence was always on the agenda. Why let her do it?

That had been Sorley's problem. He could either endure it, or go on the attack. And he was frightened about what "go on the attack" might lead to. So he left. He'd spent a few weeks sleeping in the office, living off burgers and beer and shaving every other Friday; it took a while before he shaped up, got a flat, arranged to see the kids at weekends. It was okay; a half-and-half existence. Then he got lucky in a way that few people do, and found a new sort of life with a new sort of woman who had slimmed him and spruced him and brought him down to two packs a day, but she hadn't been able to make him a cockeyed optimist. No one could do that.

"We're using local back-up," he said, "and lots of it. It's a different column, but it's all on the same fucking bill."

Stella's mobile rang and Jackie Yates came on to give a time and place: *Eight-thirty, Steadfast Cars in Kensal Rise, on your own.* She said "Okay," and closed the call.

"The drugs connection," she told Sorley. "Maybe that'll be value for money."

Stolen moments are sweet. You set everything aside for a short time— the people, the problems, the questions that don't have answers—and you let your mind take a walk: like gazing at clouds, like listening to the wind.

Stella sat in a booth in the pub across from the squad room and rolled a shot glass between her finger and thumb: vodka over ice, a cold kick. It was time out of time; no one expected her just yet; it was too late to make new plans for the evening, too early to make those phone calls to say, "I'll be late . . . I'll be later . . . I won't be there." She took half the shot and held the liquor on her tongue a moment, then swallowed, closing her eyes to get the best of it.

When she opened them, a man was sitting opposite her, lighting a cigarette. There was a bottle of beer on the table in front of him. He was in his early forties, well-built, a slightly fleshy face with a long jaw and the kind of stubble you have to tend. He had the sporty look that some plainclothes men favor: leather blouson, Levis, white socks.

He said, "DS Mooney?"

"That's right."

"DS Graham. Steve Graham. Local CID."

Stella could feel the chill in the air. She said, "Hello, Steve," in a voice that urged caution. He smiled very slightly.

"This is a request," he said, "just at the moment." He took a swallow of beer and then paused, as if thinking about the best way of saying what he had to say. "You had a meet yesterday with a guy called Jackie Yates. You asked him to help you out in certain ways. The problem is, if Jackie does what you've asked him to do he runs a risk and so do I. His risk is exposure. Mine is losing a chis."

"Most informants take an income from several sources," Stella said. "You know that. Sooner or later, interests clash. By and large, that's when a chis loses his usefulness."

Graham scratched his head with the hand holding his cigarette and a scroll of ash fell into his hair. "Yes, well, *by and large,* he's still very useful to me, so *all in all,* I'd be grateful if you'd cut him some slack. Getting a chis to run errands for AMIP isn't a terrifically good way of keeping him out of trouble."

Stella said, "I did the deal with Jackie that put him onside. If he's useful to you from time to time that's okay, but when he works for me, he does what I want."

Graham leaned forward a little, as if about to deliver a confidence. "There's something coming along that I'm going to need him for. Do me a favor. Keep him out of trouble."

Stella remembered Jackie's voice on the phone: *Eight-thirty, Steadfast Cars . . . on your own.* Too late, CID.

Stella gave DS Graham a willing smile. "I'll certainly do my best." She sounded as if she meant it, but the smile gave her away.

Graham, leaving, passed Pete Harriman coming in. Their shoulders knocked and Harriman turned, but Graham was already letting the pub door slam behind him.

Stella said, "Local CID, here with a message."

"You've rattled a cage, have you?"

"It's nothing," Stella told him. Harriman went to the bar and came back with a beer and another vodka. Stella let the drink lie; to-night was not a good night to take the edge off her reactions. She said, "I've made a contact. The guy that deals out of the Wheatsheaf. I'm seeing him later. Where are you going to be?"

"With you?"

"He'd disappear before we got close."

"Who is he?"

"I've got a name: Daz. It was in my report to Sorley."

"Yeah, I remember." Stella smiled. Harriman got round to reports in the end.

"So—you'll be—?"

He thought for a moment, as if some forward planning was going on. "Meeting a friend, getting something to eat, probably. After that, it depends."

"Keep your phone on, okay?"

"Okay."

"If you're likely to hit a bad reception area or thinking of going clubbing, give me a call first. And check-call me anyway . . . say ten-thirty, okay?"

Harriman sipped his beer, nodding at the same time. "Look, boss . . . If you think Janis Parker's a drug-related death, is it a good idea to get close to her dealer? He could be the one—she owed him, or she was over-buying, cutting the stuff again, and sell-ing on."

"He supplied Nina Whass-name at *Imago*," Stella said. "Doesn't mean he supplied Janis. Maybe she got her stuff from Nina. I just want to see if there's a trail—from Janis's little stash to the import warehouse. Find the warehouse. Go there. See who shows up."

"Ask the drugs squad to do it."

"We're not looking for the same thing. If I find something that they might want, I'll pass it on."

"And if you talk to this guy, whoever—"

"Daz."

"Daz, right, and you start to think that he's the guy who killed Janis Parker . . ."

"If that was likely we'd be going mob-handed."

"You're sure about this?"

"I got to him through a chis—someone who knows the street. If Daz had topped Janis, the chis would have got a whiff of that, for sure. Another thing: if Daz was the killer, he wouldn't be meeting an AMIP officer. He'd be long gone."

"So no worries, then."

"No worries."

"Which is why you want me to leave my phone on."

Stella decided to take just a nip of her vodka after all. She asked, "Any luck with Stephanie James?"

"I called ten times. No good. I left messages. I left a text. Want me to keep trying?"

"Not now: later. Try her at bedtime."

"Look," Harriman said, and took a photograph out of his pocket. It showed two people in a hot country sitting in the shade of a tree and drinking wine. Mark Ross and a tall, blonde girl, deeply tanned and wearing a thin, white cotton dress. The way she smiled directly into the camera made you like her right away.

"Stephanie James," Stella guessed.

"Got it from Ross after we picked him up. Jesus, I'd *love* to try her at bedtime."

"You went to his flat?"

"Sure. Just in case."

"Nothing?"

"Nothing. Nice flat, very neat, state-of-the-art sound and vision, no bodies."

The stolen moment was long gone. Stella drank the rest of her vodka and thought about making the first phone call. She said, "See if you can hurry the rest of the forensic tests."

"Science," Harriman said, "takes time." He was still looking at the photo. After a moment, he said, "You don't think she's dead, do you?" Genuine regret in his voice.

12

She pulled in to a filling station just off the Strip, parked in the grid reserved for shoppers, and got out her phone.

To George, she said, "I'll be late: someone I have to see."

"Late as in late supper, or late as in don't wait up?"

"More like don't wait up."

"Anyone with you?" There was nothing probing about the question; it meant, Will you be safe?

"It's okay," she said. "Nothing heavy."

To Delaney, she said, "Are you in later?"

"I'm at the keyboard. I'll still be at the keyboard when you get here. What time will that be?"

"Not sure." She looked at her watch. "Nine-thirty, maybe? Ten."

"I don't think I've got any food."

"I don't want food."

"No?" His voice had an edge of irritation about it. "What do you want?"

Steadfast Cars was a hole-in-the-wall minicab outfit on the Strip: just a narrow shopfront that let on to an office about the size of three phone booths. Outside, a yellow and black spinner—STEAD backed by FAST—was working overtime in the night wind. Inside, a guy covering the phone, a couple of chairs for waiting customers, three drivers sharing a spliff, but no sign of a white guy with earrings, a lip stud, and a stupid nose.

Stella walked past, went into ShopLate and almost bought a pack of Marlboro Lites, but settled for Doublemint gum, which she wanted a lot less than the cigarettes. When she emerged and walked back, Daz was leaning up against a T-reg Honda Accord with patchwork paint. He asked her if she'd ordered a cab and she wondered, briefly, how he managed to prevent his solid-silver tongue bar smacking up against the back of his top teeth.

Stella got in the back and let the window down a little: the mash of petrol, ganja, burger fat, and sour ozone coming off the Strip was better than the dark-brown smells leaking up from the seats of the Honda. The well between the seats was a litter of cigarette butts and tissue-trash that Stella didn't want to think about. The cab must have had a blow-out recently, because the jack and wheel-nut crank were under her feet.

Daz took them out on to the Harrow Road and started to go nowhere in particular. He said, "It's on hire, this cab. Doesn't come free. Neither do I."

They spent a few minutes haggling; it was likely to be the most expensive cab ride Stella had ever taken.

"I got this message you wanted to see me. Passed along the line, you know: like Chinese whispers. But I think it must have started with Jackie Yates."

Stella put a shrug into her voice. "I don't know anyone called Jackie Yates."

"No? Oh, okay." There was a moment's pause, then Daz gave a bellow of laughter, as if the punchline of an obscure joke had just registered. They cruised by the cemetery, a pool of darkness in a lake of light. Daz stopped the car and left the engine running while he got into the back seat alongside Stella. He said, "Take off your jacket."

"What?"

"Take it off."

Close to, Daz was a big presence and he seemed even taller sitting down. Stella was wearing blue jeans, baseball boots, a thin roll-neck, and a black cotton jacket: clothes to make you anonymous on the Strip. She took off the jacket and handed it over. Daz patted the pockets and felt into the sleeves for a wire. He came up with the envelope she had brought for him. He smiled, checked the money, then put it in his pocket.

He said, "Pull up your top."

"Are you kidding?"

"Or the ride ends here."

Stella pulled the roll-neck up over her bra: Daz felt the straps, looking for the same thing: a wire, a mike, the little black brick of a recorder. He felt her boots like a store assistant checking the fit, then patted the legs of her jeans, back and front, up to her crotch. She unbuckled her belt and part-unzipped while he ran his fingers round the waistband. He seemed almost disappointed to have come up empty-handed.

Back behind the wheel, Daz said, "Go on, then."

"Let's start by agreeing not to arse around with whether or not you deal. Because that's what my questions are about, so we'll have a tough time communicating if you're going to pretend that dope is just another name for idiot. Okay?"

Daz's silence said, I'm no idiot.

"It would probably be cocaine," Stella said, "but I suppose you might have had regulars for hash and maybe one or two for scag; but I'm guessing that most of the people I'm interested in do coke. We're talking about people in the fashion business, okay? About skinny girls who stay skinny by snorting not eating; men who park their Porsches outside the Wheatsheaf for a Virgin Mary and some carryout."

"I see all sorts," Daz said. "Everyone does drugs, didn't you know that?"

"Cash on delivery?"

"What?"

"Does anyone ever run a tab?"

"Not as such."

"Meaning?"

"You want to score, yeah?, and you're a bit pushed, you can get what you want, but there's a, like, premium."

"You charge interest."

"Right." Daz reached into the top pocket of his denim shirt and took out a spliff. His lighter hissed: a two-inch flame. He inhaled without taking the spliff from between his lips.

"People get into debt, sometimes?"

"Where's this taking us, police lady?"

"What happens if someone runs up a bill they can't pay?"

"Never happens." Daz sounded tense. Stella caught his glance as he shifted position to look at her in the rearview mirror.

"It must do."

"Never happened to me."

Stella let it drop. She said, "You're a street dealer. You get your supply after it's been imported and cut. Then you cut it some more. You're last in line before the drugs reach the punters: in theory, anyway. But some people buy from the people who supply you, am I right?"

"Your point is?"

"I've got a dead person, a young woman, she was cut up. She used cocaine and so do her friends. Some of them score from you."

"You think I killed someone?" Daz sounded calm, almost amused.

Stella was pretty sure he hadn't: not Janis Parker, anyway. She'd recognized Daz as soon as she'd met him: recognized his type. He was a street trader; he could probably handle himself in a ruck but his clients had to feel safe with him. Murder wasn't good for business. Of course, you could always hire someone to take care of problems for you: just run your finger down the B-list.

"No, I'm asking you if you heard about someone getting killed. Maybe she got in over her head."

"Over her head?" Daz laughed delightedly. "Hey, that's a fuck of a lot of nose-candy to be in over her head." The chuckles died away. "You say she was cut up."

"She was."

"You're thinking punishment."

"Something like that."

"Nah . . . Doesn't sound right. If someone wanted to top her, it would be just bang-bang, one to the back of the head, one to the heart, thank you, done and dusted. Punishment: that's another thing. With punishment, whoever it is—they have to live, otherwise where's the pain and distress factor?" When Stella didn't reply, he added, "Not only that, it's got to be a lesson to others, right?"

Stella had been only half aware of their route. Mostly, Daz seemed to have been driving in a circle. Now, he swung the wheel and started down a narrow approach road that led through a bleak little wasteland to the vast, gray tower blocks of the Harefield Estate.

"What are we doing here?"

"Cut through," Daz told her. "This ain't my cab, is it? The geezer's going to want it back."

Harefield was a fortress in a war zone. The low ground that separated it from main roads on all sides was a demilitarized zone thick with inner-city detritus: syringes, condoms, fast-food cartons, garbage bags, bike frames, rank mattresses, junked TVs, and fridges leaking CFCs. Apart from being home to people simply trying to live their lives, the tower blocks were a business address for druggies and dealers and muggers and gangsters. You could find shebeens and casinos and all-day/all-night brothels. You could find armories.

The place was a treble-racked, four-sided, high-rise layout with an open space in the center that locals called the bull ring. At ground level there was a convenience store, a bookie's, a launderette, an off-license, and a KFC. They all had pull-down steel screens that covered the doors and the windows; like every other part of the estate, the screens carried multicolored tags. Only the off-license and the KFC were still in business, but they were shuttered: blind eyes, like the rest.

Stella knew Harefield because she had grown up there. It had been bad then; it was worse now. It had its own laws, its own judges and juries, its own army. There were pre-teen warriors and pre-teen whores, there were dealers on every landing and high-stakes tables on every night of the week.

Daz drove into the bull ring and stamped on the brake. Stella cannoned forward, hitting the front passenger seat full on, then bouncing back and falling into the seat-well. Daz switched off the engine and was out before the car had stopped rocking. Stella got to her hands and knees, then turned to rest her upper body on the seat. She was trying to find a way to get air into her lungs, though they seemed to have emptied out and closed down; her throat was in spasm and her shoulders heaved. A strange image started up before her eyes like a glass wall slowly turning black and she realized she was passing out by degrees, then she made a sound like a buzz-saw as the air came back. She stayed where she was for half a minute or so, finding a normal rhythm to her breathing, then she got out of the car.

There was a man leaning up against one of the concrete pillars of the bull ring outside the KFC. Stella realized that they would have been waiting for the car: waiting for Daz to pull up and run. But there was no hurry. Where was this cop going to go? This bitch. This piece of live bait, piece of dead meat.

Not just him, Stella knew that. Not just this guy. Him and his friends. One behind her, maybe two, registered by a chill between her shoulder blades, by the skin puckering on her scalp.

In the bull ring, surrounded by the concrete cliffs and canyons of the tower blocks, there was no wind; and there was no sound, until the man by the KFC took a step forward, until he laughed, until he pursed his lips to blow her a little string of kisses *smack, smack, smack*.

John Delaney closed down his computer because his eyes ached and he'd had more than enough of corrupt politicians, voracious multinational crooks, and the wretched of the earth. He put a CD on the player, went across to the galley kitchen, and checked the fridge. The only things that seemed to add up to a meal were some eggs, a can of artichoke hearts, and some parmesan, but artichoke omelette had a contradictory sound to it. He opened a bottle of wine, drank some, looked at his watch. Nine-twenty. So give her half an hour.

The friend Pete Harriman had spoken of earlier was a redhead with a little ribbon of freckles over the bridge of her nose and a great laugh. Harriman was seeing more and more of her and they both seemed to like that, though no one had talked about what happened when they weren't together.

They'd had a drink and they'd eaten Thai, and now they were back at Harriman's place and he thought that this would be a good time to call Stella, just to check, just to avoid interruptions later.

The redhead poured two drinks and took them through to the bedroom. Harriman took his mobile with him. He had two backed-up calls to make: Stephanie James at bedtime; Stella in—what?—twenty minutes, he decided.

Or maybe half an hour.

13

Business before pleasure: that's the best way.

Go shopping on the Harefield Estate and you can buy most things. A passport, a respray, hash, flesh, white goods, hot goods, it's a buyer's market. And guns, of course. With guns you never miss.

They had guns, the guys who were watching Stella as she tried to decide what to do; they could have killed her at any time. They didn't, not because she was a cop: that would be a bonus; and not because someone might hear the gunshot: who would notice? They didn't kill her because they were putting pleasure before business: the thrill of the chase.

There was only one man behind her. Stella flashed a look over her shoulder and saw him walking toward her across the broken paving stones of the bull ring; he was wearing a new pair of white Nike trainers that seemed to glow in the half-dark and he wasn't hurrying. The guy by the KFC had detached himself from the pillar and was sauntering across, lips still pursed: *kissy-kiss-kiss*.

As a child, Stella would come down twenty-three floors to the bull ring to buy milk or bread or a chill-cabinet supper. She knew that there were just two ways out, and she also knew that KFC Man and Nike Man had them covered. The way past KFC Man led directly into the nearest tower, the other was a passageway that was a feeder to the maze of paths and alleys between the three southside blocks. The car door was open on that side and Nike Man was getting closer all the time, so it was the choice of no choice. Stella reached into the car and snatched up the wheel-nut crank from the floor, but kept her back turned. Nike Man had a heavy smell about him: dope and sweat and bad food; he laid a hand on her backside and said, "Hey, police lady."

Stella turned, swinging the crank. Nike Man saw it at the last moment and got his hand up, but the iron caught him on the wrist and he let out a yell—*Dah!*—and dropped his shoulder. She swung again, a short, hard, chopping motion, not much backswing, and laid the bar across his neck, just below the jaw. He stepped back, staring at her and already beginning to fall. He went a pace or two, knees bent, like someone trying to walk under a pole, then sat down hard.

KFC Man couldn't see all of this because the car was between him and Stella, but he heard the shout and he heard the meaty sound of the crank hitting flesh. He and Stella started to run at the same time, heading for the passageway into the maze, Stella having the double advantage of a thirty-foot start and a skyrocket adrenalin rush. Her disadvantage was that KFC Man was a hell of a lot faster. By the time she hit the passageway, her lead was twenty feet and dropping. She was running and thinking and trying to remember, from too many years ago, whether she turned left or right when she got to the T-junction at the end of the passageway; all she could be certain of was that one way led off into the maze and the other was a bin room. She hoped that left would take her into the maze, because that was the way she intended to go.

KFC Man was on her heels and laughing as he ran; he hadn't shot her because he was running too fast to get his gun out and, anyway, he was still having fun. She made the turn and the next alley was there in front of her. Two more, she reckoned, maybe three, and she would emerge into the demilitarized zone; then a flat-out sprint across the debris and dreck to the road, where Bruce Willis would be waiting, dressed in singlet and combat pants and hefting a belt-fed Bofors.

She wasn't going to make it, and she knew as much. He was too close and there was too far to go. In fact, there was less than six feet between them and he had started to reach out for her when she slammed round the next corner and immediately dropped into a crouch, folding like a stapler, her hands clutched across the back of her neck. She slid a couple of feet, taking the skin off her knees, as KFC came round at full tilt and had a milli-second to wonder where she'd disappeared to before his foot hit her ribcage and he went down on his face.

She came back into the bull ring looking rapidly left and right, but there seemed to be no one there. You could hear the distant crackle of television gunfire, but no one was offering the real thing. If she hadn't gone through so fast, making for the entrance to the north-side blocks, she would have noticed Nike Man sitting with his back to the car, staring into the gloom with sightless eyes. She ran into the concrete and steel lobby of the first block, its broken lights and tag-on-tag graffiti, then started up the stairs two at a time. On the fifth floor was the first of the walkways that cobwebbed the estate; she was headed for that. She had thought of simply knocking at a door, explaining, going in, making a phone call. It was tough to calculate the odds on that. Shebeens, brothels, casinos, armories . . . and, of course, the world's innocent, banged up behind their triple locks and hinge bolts and door chains, watching the news where worse things happen.

She kept running. Sometimes you knock and the door opens on to chaos.

Every floor has its landing, every landing its CCTV.

Stella went through landing five and out of the glass and wire-mesh door on to the walkway. She could see the DMZ from there and the road and the lights of cars. She shouldered the door on to the landing of block two and went straight across and out. A second walkway doglegged to the right and rose a floor: steep running. She took it, breathing hard now, and made the door to floor six of block three. Again she went straight through, taking the walkway that would bring her back down to five but on the far block, as close as she could get to the DMZ and the street.

She hadn't seen KFC or heard him, so she was beginning to think he must be tracking her at ground level. She broke her stride and looked down, but it was like staring overboard from a ship on a starless night. Only the string of streetlights and car lights beyond the wasteland were visible: a place of safety close enough to touch, too far to think about.

When she got to the final landing, the lift was ascending and there were feet on the stairs, so it was a multiple-choice conundrum: meet KFC on the stairs; pass a stranger on the stairs while KFC emerged from the lift; wait on the landing and join the innocents in the lift when it stopped; or stay put and watch KFC step out of the lift with a gun. The stairs seemed more of a rat-trap, so she thumbed the lift button and stood to one side, out of sight.

The lift whined to a halt and the doors opened. No one got out. Maybe he was waiting for her to move, just as she was waiting for him, but pretty soon the lift doors would close. Stella stepped into the open, expecting to see his face, his lips pursed, *kissy-kiss-kiss*.

The lift was empty, but the footsteps on the stairs had stopped.

She got in and hit the ground-floor button, terrified that the lift would stop at a lower floor—*Gotcha!*—but that didn't happen. She crossed the entrance lobby at a fast walk, then sprinted hard as hell across the DMZ to the road and flagged down a black cab. Her knees were bleeding: a seepage under her torn jeans, blood beads running down her shins. She folded her arms across her stomach and leaned forward, breathing fast, winded by the run and by fear. There was a sharp ache round her ribcage where KFC's boot had taken her.

When the cab stopped at a red light just fifty yards down the road, she looked back at Harefield, the great, gray slabs under a bruised sky, the pattern of lit and darkened windows like a crossword puzzle grid. You had to have lived there to know the geography of the walkways. You had to have spent time dodging the toughs on the landings who were looking for a kid just like you; you had to have walked your Shoprite bags up twenty floors when some drunk had kicked the lift doors crooked.

I outran him, she thought. I outguessed him.

But that wasn't what had happened.

KFC had come into the bull ring in time to see Stella make the passageway that led to the first tower block. He was halfway across the ring when it occurred to him to wonder how in hell she had managed to get there. She'd put the other man down somehow, sure, but where was he now? Then he saw the sneakers, clean white in the murky light, and he pulled up and went across to the car.

Nike Man had died on a stalled breath, the cry of pain and shock still locked in his chest. He was sitting, backed up to the car and gazing into the distance as if there were a horizon and he was trying to look beyond it.

A window had opened and closed on the second floor. A figure appeared for a moment at the end of the passageway to block one, then faded like smoke. What was happening down there in the bull ring was nobody's business.

KFC had said, "Oh, fuck, man," a whisper as he'd crouched

down and checked the eyes, checked the neck pulse. "Oh, *fuuuuck!*"
Then he'd taken out his mobile phone.

Stella saw a light on farther back in the flat. She called out "Hi!" and
he answered but didn't come out to meet her: still working.

She went through to the bedroom and eased off her jeans, wincing
as she rolled them over her knees. Two big ragged grazes were still
weeping blood. She stripped off the rest of her clothes, balled everything up and stuffed the bundle into the bottom of the wardrobe
where he'd never look, then collected a T-shirt and some warm-up
baggies and went through to the bathroom. She swabbed her knees
with antiseptic, saying *ouch-ouch-ouch-ouch,* then cut gauze pads
and taped one over each wound. She turned sideways to the mirror
and saw the big, bluish bruise from KFC's boot; when she palpated
the area it hurt, but she thought her ribs were probably intact.

She went into the bedroom and lay down, because her knees hurt
and her side hurt and she felt sick. It wasn't until George came in
with an offer of pasta and a glass of wine that she remembered
where she was supposed to be.

No one saw it happen, no one heard it, no one spoke of it.

KFC Man made the necessary phone calls. A kid who worked
as a mule for KFC's connections arrived and hot-wired the Honda,
then drove it back to the Strip. Daz took it from there and returned it to its owner. The owner drove the car out of London to a
wrecking yard and someone worked a late shift. A cab was waiting to take him back to town. Compensation had already been
arranged.

It took an hour. The car had gone.

Three guys left a card game on the sixteenth floor and came
down to help KFC with Nike Man. They bagged him and carried
him to the estate through-road and loaded him into a panel van.
The guys in the van didn't know who Nike Man was, and didn't
want to. They were a clean-up service; they'd already quoted their

price, including the premium for a night call. The body went to a place where the men could get to grips with it for a while: at a glance, you might have mistaken their workspace for Sam Burgess's little underworld of steel and white tile. Then the body moved again, though this time it was lighter and smaller and barely resembled itself at all. Two hours later, it arrived at a workshop near Mile End that specialized in reclaimed metals, where it soon became ash.

It had taken seven hours. Nike Man was gone.

In a flat on the eighteenth floor of block two, the women sat down with Nike Man's girlfriend and talked to her and cried with her and saw her through the night. In a nearby flat that doubled as a drugs warehouse, the men dipped into the dealer's shelf-stock and worried about what had gone wrong. Already, they had found someone to blame.

As for the lack of ceremony, the lack of farewells and fine words, both the women and the men were agreed that things couldn't really have been handled any other way.

She was running in the sky, dodging through cloudbreak. Then she was dragging her feet through tar on a mile-long walkway, passing a hundred doors, all of which had letterboxes that gaped wide open. Behind each door, the self-same tragedy. When the phone rang, she woke instantly, as if glad to be rescued.

George said, "Bastards . . ." but didn't lift his head. She had to reach over him to get to the phone.

"Did you switch your mobile off?" It was Harriman's voice; he sounded relieved.

"I'm okay," Stella said. "It's fine."

"Where are you?"

"At home. It's okay. Thanks for checking."

"Okay," he said. Then, after a pause, "Good. That's good."

Stella put the phone down and got out of bed. She went to the bathroom and checked her knees; the gauze was bloodstained, but the blood was dry. There was another graze on her left forearm, long and ragged, that she hadn't noticed before; it was beginning to scab over. She wanted to take a shower but knew that would rouse George, so she padded down to the kitchen for a drink.

She made herself a vodka over ice by the light from the fridge door. The blue LCD digits on the oven timer told her it was just past two A.M. A thought struck her: Harriman was supposed to call her at ten-thirty. But if he'd done that, if he'd called and got no reply, he'd have taken action, wouldn't he? Officer not responding.

She laughed. *You forgot, you bastard.* Not that it would have made a difference.

14

Sam Burgess looked odd in mufti: like seeing your dentist on the beach. He was wearing the last corduroy jacket to survive from the fifties and its close cousin, a paisley tie.

"I've got a training day here. Lots of fresh faces soon to turn green." He opened his document case and took out a folder. "I thought you might like this: the fuller version of my lab report. There are some DNA matches that might be important."

Sam stole a Twix from Sue Chapman's desk and popped it into his case, alongside the full-color catalogues of human decay, the videotapes of meticulous butchery. "They look like hell to you," Sam would tell his off-color rookies, "but they're a source of endless amazement once you get to know them." To show he had a sense of humor, Sam called his initial lecture "Gutless Wonders."

"There are a few late tests," Sam observed. "Short staffing, I'm afraid."

"Tests of what?"

"You know: scrapings, final analysis of the stomach contents . . . There was something in her hair."

"What?"

"A dried substance once of a glutinous nature."

"Semen?"

Sam shrugged. "Tough to tell. It'll be in the report."

"When it comes," Stella said.

"Yes, when it comes."

Stella watched Sam as he made for the door: a small man in his late fifties, a monk's fringe of white hair, the stooped back of the scholar. It was only in that warren of underground rooms that he seemed himself: white-coated and light-fingered, snaffling the secrets of the dead.

Pete Harriman came in while Stella was still reading. Without looking up she said, "You forgot."

"No, well, I called Stephanie James's number, then—"

"You forgot."

"Yeah. Sorry, boss." The girl with the freckles and the great laugh was still on his mind. She had been in his bed when he woke, and that was a first.

"Tell me about Stephanie James."

"Tried her four times. No answer." It was more or less true. He hadn't tried her at bedtime, but he'd tried her at two A.M. just after he'd called Stella, and he'd tried again three times that morning. "She's either underground, out of the country, or just not answering."

"Underground," Stella said. "There's a thought."

"Not a nice one." He prized the top off his coffee carton and read over Stella's shoulder. "What's this?"

"Lab report. Look." She pointed at the squared-off page where the chemical and technical analyses were listed. Against two of the SOC substances there was a red asterisk. "Everyone at the party gave a sample, so did people at the *Imago* office. There are two matches. The first is a match with DNA on one of the two toothbrushes in Janis Parker's flat." She turned a page and pointed to a list of names. One had been highlighted: Mark Ross.

"You'd expect it," Harriman said. "His girlfriend lives there."

"You're right. Except it's not the only match for Ross," Stella observed. "Of the two, both are his. The other is semen."

It was the principal subject for discussion at the mid-morning briefing: that and who had stolen a Twix. Mike Sorley had just come from a meeting where money had been the first topic on the agenda, and also the second. He'd been asked for a daily progress report, which meant that his paperwork quotient had just doubled. He looked at the lab report and shrugged.

"It's something. It's not much."

"DC Harriman's been trying Stephanie James's mobile on a regular basis. He never gets an answer."

"Maybe she's out of the country."

Harriman nodded. "That's what I said."

"You've checked with parents, other friends—"

"—people at her office, yes, all of that. The parents are trying to find a way of not worrying. They say she's unpredictable. Mark Ross says she's with friends somewhere, but if she is they must be very new friends."

"What do you want to do?" Sorley asked.

"Have him back and see what he has to say," Stella suggested. "He's been lying to us."

"Lying, or withholding the truth?"

"Same thing."

"There's nothing here to arrest him on."

"There's not," Stella agreed, "but maybe he'll supply what we need."

When the briefing broke up, people handed their reports on current activity to Sue Chapman, who logged them and made abstracts that she would pass on to Mike Sorley, who would add them to the pile. Homework. Stella's report was a few lines long and gave a heavily edited version of the previous night.

Sue looked up from her keyboard as Stella went past to the water cooler. She said, "This guy dumped you in the middle of Hare-field . . . ?"

"Stopped the car and legged it." The report said nothing about the two men in the bull ring: Stella's mistakes were her own affair.

"Which makes him interesting," Sue suggested, "this Daz . . ."

"Maybe. We'll talk to him again if we can find him. He doesn't like cops and he doesn't like being out in the open, but I don't think he killed Janis Parker."

"What happened?"

"I walked until I found a cab."

It was the same story she gave to Pete Harriman as they drove to the city bank where Mark Ross worked.

"So, do we have this Daz guy in, or shall we give him to the Drugs Squad?"

"I don't think we'll find him," Stella said. "Not for a while, any-way."

The traffic on the Embankment was moving at a record twelve miles per hour, everyone driving too close, everyone running the lights. In the spring sun, the vapor haze showed like a glass wall.

"No sign of rape," Harriman offered. "Didn't Sam Burgess say that?"

"He also said that didn't mean much, given her injuries. Think of the tape over her mouth; think of the marks on her wrists."

"So you think it's a possible motive. Possible factor."

"Not really. Her underwear also had semen stains."

"And so?"

"Not on the outside, on the inside. She put her clothes back on after she'd had sex. Put some of them back on, anyway."

"Maybe she had a quickie earlier in the evening. It was her birth-day: why not? On top of the desk at the office, or bending over a line of coke at the party."

"*Imago* has see-through offices and the party was held in a restaurant."

"So?"

There were clouds and gulls in the sky, white on white. Stella's phone rang, then canceled before she could answer it.

The bank had glassine lifts. They watched Mark Ross all the way down from the sixth floor and he watched them.

"Is it Stephanie?" he asked. "I've been trying to get in touch with her. Her phone's off all the time."

Stella nodded. "We know that. It's not Stephanie."

He was puzzled for a moment, then he saw the looks on their faces and sighed. They rode back to Notting Hill in silence, as if the cops were rehearsing questions and Ross second-guessing them in the hope of coming up with handy answers. Stella's phone rang and she caught it in time. It was Jackie Yates asking for a meeting. He sounded like someone who had run a long way and had a long way yet to run.

15

The interview room had a table, four chairs, an audiotape machine, and no windows. The heavy, sour smell was nicotine; it seemed to ooze from the walls, a thin brown stain. Harriman took one of the chairs to a corner of the room and sat there like an audience of one at a fringe drama called *Suspect*.

Ross glanced at him as if he might be the cop with something in reserve: a forgotten secret, the killer question. Stella didn't show Mark Ross the report Sam Burgess had turned in, but she did ask him if there was anything he ought to have told them; anything he might have forgotten. He said he couldn't think of a thing, so Stella told him about the DNA match. To her surprise, he shrugged.

"We were having an affair. Not an affair . . . a sort of on/off thing. It was just sex, you know? Not serious, not intended to last, no one got hurt."

"Not even Stephanie?"

"Steph didn't know. Doesn't know." He looked at Stella with raised eyebrows. "Needn't know?"

Stella smiled. "I can see you'd prefer that. When did it start, this on/off thing?"

"A couple of months ago. December."

"That's four months ago." Stella paused and let the tape run on. Then she said, "Janis Parker was pregnant, did you know that?"

Ross's eyes widened. Suddenly he seemed to be sitting unnaturally still. "No, I didn't know that."

"Was it yours?"

"If I didn't know, how could I tell?"

"What's your thinking on it?"

"My thinking? My *thinking* is I don't know what to think. I guess if it was mine, she'd have told me. On the other hand, maybe not. Maybe she was going to have an abortion. How pregnant was she?"

"Not very."

"There you go then."

"Did Janis have a regular boyfriend?"

"No."

"Did she have casual sex?"

Ross gave a little laugh, half-closing his eyes. "She certainly did with me."

"With others?"

"I expect so. Wouldn't you?"

"So, if you had sex that evening, Janis didn't have a migraine at the party."

"No. We just wanted to leave."

"For some on/off."

Ross winced. "If you like."

"And your relationship with Stephanie James . . ."

"Wasn't going well."

"Any idea why?" Stella asked; she wasn't expecting an answer. "So, she went away to think things through, you're not sure where she is, you called her mobile and spoke to her the day before yesterday but since then you haven't been able to get in touch with her, and neither have we, despite numerous calls and text messages."

"Perhaps she's still thinking."

"Perhaps. But I bet she'd respond to a text message from the police letting her know that her friend has been murdered, however hard she's thinking."

"Is this the point where I ask to speak to my solicitor?" Ross asked.

"If you like."

"Am I under arrest?"

"No."

"I can leave any time I like?"

"You can. I'd prefer you to stay. For a short while, anyway."

Ross nodded. "All right. It's a quiet day on the markets."

As Stella walked across the squad room, heading for Mike Sorley's office, she stopped off at Maxine Hewitt's desk. Maxine was sifting through yesterday's batch of interviews with office workers and partygoers.

"Anything I should know?"

"You mean because you've got Mark Ross in the interview room? Not so far, boss."

"Nothing that seems to link Ross with Janis Parker?"

"Link . . . ?"

"They were having an affair."

Maxine looked pleased. "Well, no one seems to have known. Or else no one's saying. In fact, everyone's telling the same story—party, migraine, the birthday girl left along with Ross, some people went on to a club about an hour after that." She smiled. "One or two have been anxious to point out that there were no class-A drugs on the premises, just in case we'd wondered about that." She grinned.

"They were having an affair and she was pregnant. I said it was him."

Stella shook her head. "Suspicion, no evidence."

"I've got him at five to one."

"There's a sweep?"

"He'll be shorter odds, now. You'd be lucky to get evens."

Andy Greegan was adding a diagrammatic layout of Janis Parker's flat to the whiteboard exhibits. He said, "I could give you fifteen to one on person or persons unknown. That excludes colleagues and friends."

"It's him," Maxine said, "trust me."

Sorley would sooner have had Ross at odds on. He said, "It's all negatives. No murder weapon, no motive, no witnesses."

"No alibi either," Stella reminded him. "And there's a hint of a motive."

"Is there?"

"He and Parker were having an affair. Sam Burgess found an early pregnancy. A DNA test would tell us whether it was his."

"What does he say?"

"He doubts it."

"Just doubts?"

"He didn't seem to mind all that much one way or the other."

"The pregnancy is a motive?"

"Not in itself, no. But it does mean there's something there that we hadn't factored in before: sex, passion, lies being told. Add to that, Stephanie James is missing . . . or, at least, she's not responding to calls and text messages. We've only got his word that he spoke to her on the phone."

"Let him go," Sorley said.

Jackie Yates was drinking like a herbivore at a waterhole, a sip, a quick look round, another sip: the fear of becoming prey. Stella joined him at the bar. She said, "What happened?"

"You know what happened."

"All right, what happened, yes, of course I know that. *Why* did it happen?"

"These guys are in business," Jackie said. "That's what I tried to tell you. Daz and the rest—local traders. What do you think it is round here—the economy? Where do the jobs come from? This boozer, the Kilburn Car Warehouse, the Paki shop on the corner? No. It's scag, Mrs. Mooney. It's Charlie. It's whatever you can inhale or inject or sniff or stuff up your arse." He took a sip and a quick look round. When his head swiveled, the back of his wig stayed put. "The only reason Daz cooperated was because he reckoned on getting busted if he said no."

"He didn't cooperate," Stella said. "He ditched me in the middle of the Harefield Estate. A couple of guys were waiting; it was a set-up. What were they going to do? Show me their business plan?"

"He's in shit, now," Jackie said. "We're both in shit. They're one down."

"What?"

"Over on Harefield. They're a man down."

There was a media input clash in the pub: a TV above the bar showing Italian football and some retro-country on the loop tape; the rest of the noise came from drinkers yelling to be heard. Even so, a silence seemed to fall between Stella and Jackie; a held breath.

"Who's down?"

"Two guys, you said. Yeah? You hit one of them with a car jack."

"It wasn't a jack."

"I heard a jack."

"I don't give a fuck what you heard." Stella spoke through clenched teeth: a sudden rush of anger. "What do you mean—'down'?" She knew what he meant; she was absolutely certain about what he meant.

"He's dead, Mrs. Mooney. You topped him."

The pub was filling up and Jackie was looking over his shoulder at the door every ten seconds or so.

He said, "Let's get out of here."

They walked down Portobello toward the Westway flyover, then headed for Ladbroke Grove where Jackie had parked his car. The sky was dull blue and pink and laced with vapor trails; one or two street lamps had come on in the early dusk, but Jackie walked like a man in a spotlight.

"I'm going to need some cover," he said.

"How much?"

"Witness-protection cover."

"That's a complete ID makeover," Stella said. "Name, social-security number, passport, location . . . Big budget." She was wondering how cost-effective it would be for a man with a bald face and a bad blond wig. "How would they know you were involved?"

"It was me spoke to Daz."

"Sure, but why would they get tough with Daz? Surely he was doing what they wanted—driving me down to Harefield, dumping me there."

"If things had gone right, fair enough. But they didn't. There's a dead geezer. They'll want to go all the way back: anyone associated. So they'll be asking Daz . . . if he hasn't bunked off already. They'll get to me, sooner or later."

"I'll see what I can do," she said. "Call me."

Jackie's car was parked less than fifty yards from John Delaney's front door. A red stripe went up toward Notting Hill Gate, roof bar flashing, siren whooping. Jackie followed it, as if staying close to the cops was a new way of life. Stella called Delaney's number and got a busy signal. She looked up at Delaney's apartment and saw that the light was on; he passed the window and seemed to be looking down, but maybe that was because he was using the phone. She had keys, but felt that, in giving them to her, Delaney had presented her with a challenge and that was a good enough reason to back off.

His new front door was raw wood with the apartment number written in marker pen. New door—new lock. She knocked and Delaney opened up immediately, holding gifts: a glass of wine and a shiny spare key. He said, "If you hang about in the street like that, men in cars will cruise by and offer to supplement your income."

"I tried to phone."

"I was getting another mystery call. Nothing said, just silence. I suppose obscene callers only target women, which is a shame because there's a distinct lack of obscenity in my life just at present."

"There's an outfit called the NCB—Nuisance Calls Bureau. They can put a trace on for you."

"If it goes on," Delaney said.

"It could be someone checking to see if you're in."

"A burglar, you mean."

"It's movie-time, theater-time, restaurant-time. People are out. The local kids make a few calls . . . Maybe they'll get lucky. They just need enough for an evening's clubbing, a few beers, a few Es."

"Sounds reasonable enough." He sipped his wine. "There's no food. There was no food last night either, but then you didn't turn up."

"I'm sorry. Things got complicated."

"Did they?" Something in her voice told him that "complicated" didn't do it justice.

She walked over and stood looking out of the window and he moved to stand behind her, but didn't touch.

Stella said, "I lie to George about where I am. I stand outside your door wondering what to do next. I go home and wish I was here. I come here and feel as if I ought to be somewhere else. I worry about what I'm really feeling, what you're really feeling, what George might be thinking . . . Sometimes I wish it was just me, you know? Me on my own, no involvements. Other times, I can't imagine anything worse."

He said, "Sometimes it's one thing or the other."

"Like a fork in the road?"

"Just like that, yes."

He turned her and kissed her very lightly on the lips: just a graze; she felt his breath on her face. He said, "What do you want to do?" and she knew he meant eat in, eat out, go home.

She said, "I'd better go. I think I should go," but she collected the bottle of wine from the counter and sat down, like someone getting ready for a night of it.

After a moment, she said, "I killed someone last night. Last night I killed a man."

16

Mark Ross sat at the blackjack table and got a queen and a jack for openers. He wagged a finger and the dealer, whose house badge said April, looked at the other players. The man on Mark's left tapped his cards, a nine and a seven, and caught the ten of diamonds. April was tall and black and wearing a dress that showed enough of her breasts to take the edge off the concentration of an all-male table, but that night Mark was gambling with the kind of recklessness that didn't require focus. It was hit or shit stuff. Just now, it was hit and he'd come over from the roulette table to spread his luck.

After leaving the AMIP office he'd gone back to work. Janis's murder and Stephanie's disappearance were known about so it was no surprise to his colleagues that Mark was spending time with the police. People were sympathetic. And very slightly curious. And just a touch excited. *What if . . . ?*

The markets were sluggish: that's what Ross had told Stella and it was true. Too many local wars, too many suicide bombers, too many riots. It was bad for business when the world wouldn't behave. So Ross and a few friends had walked away from their screens at about five and started drinking; then they'd taken a table at a calculatedly expensive restaurant and done a few high-grade lines in the men's room; now they were spreading out through the casino like a raiding party.

April looked at him, one eyebrow raised. An eight and a four lay on the baize. He tapped and she dealt a three; he tapped again and she dealt the six of clubs. Sometimes you try to coax luck along, sometimes she follows you around like a dog. He liked this half-and-half euphoria of narcotics and good fortune: it took the edge off things. April dealt him an ace-eight. As he backed it he felt the mobile in his pocket vibrate, but he ignored it until he'd played the hand: ace, eight, but then came another eight and he was left with one foot on the boat, one on the dock. He tapped. April turned him a five, which she offered with a winning smile.

The call had broken his luck. He took out the phone. There was a text message.

Whr R U? Steph.

"How do you know?" Delaney asked. "How can you be sure? You heard this from your informant, your chis, whatever you call him. You say he was reluctant to get involved from the off. Maybe he's lying; maybe that's his idea of fun."

"I'd like to think so." Stella was sitting at one end of the sofa, knees drawn up. "The problem is, he's scared shitless and can't hide it. He's asked for the witness-protection program. No one would go there who didn't have to. You give up everything and get very little in return."

"It was self-defense."

"You don't get it, do you? I didn't mention it in my report. Why not? Well, I fucked up and I wasn't eager to let people know that. I got in the cab and I let him drive me, I didn't watch where he was going, it was stupid. That was the first reason. The second reason was I didn't want coppers all over the Harefield Estate shoving sticks into holes, because if Parker's death was drugs connected, the people I need to talk to would be unreachable very quickly. It's difficult to backtrack on this. In fact, it's already too late."

"Has the death been reported?"

"I don't know. I don't think so."

"What's the worst that can happen?"

"In law? A manslaughter charge, I should think."

"But you don't think, do you?"

"I'm a cop," Stella said. "He was a gangster off the Harefield Estate, bound to have form, he'll have dealt drugs or girls or guns or all three. No, listen, I can hear the sound of doors slamming already. We protect our own."

"That's good," Delaney said.

"Yeah, that's good. Except I killed someone." She paused, remembering. "And when I killed him, I was up close."

"Does it make a difference?"

"I could smell him: dope and sweat. I hit him in the neck. I didn't know you could kill someone by hitting them in the neck." She shook her head as if to attest to the sheer effort on Nike Man's part.

Delaney took her glass away from her and held her and kissed her, which was more holding and kissing than they had done for a while. He said, "Stay here. Why don't you stay?"

Stella said, "For a while."

She slept as people sleep when there are things they want to forget: a kind of hibernation. She was sprawled across Delaney, so that when his phone rang, he had to slip out from underneath her, cradling her head, letting her go full length on the couch. When he lifted the phone and said "Hello," there was silence—more than just the absence of a voice, something deeper. He said, "Talk to me," then, "Who are you?" Instead of hanging up, he continued to listen, as if there were something to be heard, and the silence deepened and broadened, something vast and starless.

He was still listening when Stella's mobile rang.

It was Mike Sorley. He said, "Mark Ross and Stephanie James just walked into Notting Hill nick together."

She was tall, just as her clothes had indicated, and she was blonde, which is what the negative-check forensic analysis had said, and she was pretty, which had been evident from photographs supplied by Mark Ross and her parents. Just now, she looked as if someone had hit her in the head with an iron bar and she was still waiting to drop.

"If I'd gone home," she said. "If I'd gone back to the flat."

"Where did you go?" Stella and Maxine Hewitt were present at the interview. It was Stella who'd asked the question. Maxine was there to watch; not to learn, to *watch*. Now and then, Stella would turn her head or consult the case file she had in front of her: a moment when she wasn't face to face with Stephanie, when the blonde girl might drop her guard. Maxine was looking for the give-away blink, the averted gaze, the tic. Body language of the liar. It was standard stuff.

Stephanie had been sipping water since they'd begun; now she picked up the polystyrene cup to show that it was empty. Maxine said, "I'll get some more," then added, "in a moment."

"I went straight to Mark's place."

"Why not home?"

"I wanted to see him. It was the first thing to do."

"Why?"

Stephanie shrugged. "It's personal stuff."

"Someone's been murdered," Stella said. "Nothing's more personal than that."

"We were talking about breaking up. That's why I went away." She paused. "Okay, I was talking about breaking up. Mark didn't want that."

"And you went to him first to tell him—what?"

"Jesus . . ." Stephanie shook her head. "What has this got to do with the fact that someone killed Janis?"

"It's background," Stella told her. "Everything's background."

"I went to see Mark first to say that I was prepared to give it another go."

"Are you?"

"Yes." Stephanie looked into the empty cup again, looked at Maxine.

"So . . . Where have you been?"

"What?"

"People have been trying to get in touch with you. We tried."

"Yes, I'm sorry. Could I have some more water, please?"

Stella spoke a couple of sentences for the benefit of the tape, then motioned to Maxine, who shrugged and got up. While she was gone, Stella shuffled through the papers in the case file, avoiding Stephanie's eyes, because she didn't want the conversation to go any further: not while the tape was off.

"Mark said she was . . . whoever did it . . . they stabbed her lots of times. Is that right?"

"We'll come to all that later."

"She was . . . he said they cut her throat."

"We'll get to that." Stella fended her off, but the pain in Stephanie's voice was plain to hear. Stella put the papers back in the file and looked up. "I'll need to know exactly what Mark told you: as you remember it," then added quickly, "for the tape—later."

"Yes, okay." Stephanie hadn't cried yet, not in front of Stella, but it wasn't far off. "I should have been there: at the party and at the flat. I just . . . was so upset . . . about Mark and me. I had to go away somewhere. Otherwise I'd've been at home with Janis."

"Maybe better that you weren't."

Stephanie looked at Stella, suddenly registering the significance of what she'd said. "Oh . . . I hadn't thought of it like that." The backed-up tears were suddenly there, making her eyes shine.

"I wish there was a different way of doing this; an easier way," Stella said. Definitely something she didn't want on tape.

"It's not real," Stephanie assured her. "It's something from someone else's life."

Maxine returned with a full jug of water. Stella switched the tape back on and repeated her last question: "Where did you go?"

"A retreat."

"Where?"

"A place . . . it's run by nuns. I mean, it's a nunnery. You can go there, you help out, live their life, you get time to think—"

"No," Stella said, "I know what a retreat is. I said where." Stella had been brought up a Catholic; only her take on it was *no* time to think: thinking was a dangerous activity. *Faith,* that was the requirement: a mind locked off.

"In Surrey. St. Dymphna's."

"You didn't check your messages?"

"I didn't want to."

"Even when you left?"

"I got to Mark's place, he wasn't there, that's when I switched my phone on and called him. Didn't get an answer, so I sent a text. After that I picked up my messages."

"And . . ."

"I didn't know what to do. Then he called me from wherever he was. I waited for him to come home."

Stella said, "We need fingerprints and hair samples and a DNA match."

"Okay."

"I'd also like you to look at the scene-of-crime reports together with the still photos and the video."

"Video of what?"

"The flat, the way things looked when we found Janis. Scene of crime."

"Does that mean . . . Will Janis be there?"

"Not those shots. Just the flat, the way it looked, in case you see anything that might help."

"What would I see?"

Stella sighed. "I don't know, it's your flat, not mine. Maybe you'll know when you look. Maybe there isn't anything. It's a long shot, but why not?"

"Okay." She still sounded worried.

"You won't see Janis," Stella told her. "You will see some blood."

Stephanie nodded. "Okay." She tried to smile.

"There are one or two aspects of all this that we haven't covered," Stella said. "Things we'll have to get to later."

Like your boyfriend, the one you've decided to try again with, was screwing your flatmate, Stella thought. Like the fact that she was pregnant.

Stephanie put a hand over her eyes. She said, "We were really close, you know? Janis and me. Really close." She looked away, holding on to the tears. After a moment, she asked, "Is Mark still here?"

"Yes," Stella said, "he's outside."

Stephanie nodded, clearly reassured. "He'll understand," she said. "He knows how close we were. I can talk to him."

"You're right," Stella said. "You should talk to Mark."

17

London street crime is world class.

Up on Clapton Pavement a guy crossing the road with his girl on his arm is kicked to his knees by a couple of Yardies and executed. The traffic stops for it in the same way it stops for a red light. After the shooters have strolled off, the guy lies across the white line while smaller vehicles drive round him. It's a skirmish in a turf war; the bigger the patch, the bigger the sale.

In London Fields a twelve-year-old girl is knifed for her mobile phone.

In Fulham, a man is parking his car when two jackers get in and show him a gun. He drives three streets, just as they ask, then gives them the car keys, just as they ask, but they shoot him anyway. It's a three-year-old Saab: not even a class jacking.

A teenage drinker in a Stonebridge pub looks at a girl who belongs to a man in YSL shades. The kid doesn't know he's doing it: his glance has actually traveled beyond her to a guy he hopes is going to sell him some uppers. The misplaced look is bad enough, but maybe he would survive it if he didn't jog YSL Man's shoulder as he goes past. Again, he doesn't know he's doing it: the dealer's leaving the pub and the kid is in need. YSL Man follows the kid out and shoots him in the car park while the deal is going down. The kid was guilty of not showing respect.

In Harlesden, some nine-year-olds at a loose end find a boy on his own, douse him in petrol and set fire to him. They do it because he's black. No surprises there.

This is aside from the bloodless stuff: the phone jackings, the no-big-deal muggings, the bag snatches, the shop-lifting, theft from cars, theft *of* cars, steaming, dipping . . . It's a normal week's work for the teams involved.

During that week, AMIP-5 finished interviewing the partygoers and the office workers, shared the relevant reports, made compare-and-contrast abstracts, interviewed Janis Parker's father, dealt with his requests to have the body released for burial, waited for the results of Stephanie James's fingerprint and DNA matches, and continued to take bets on the likely outcome.

Mark Ross was slipping to odds on, with a side bet on Stephanie James as accomplice.

If you can make a living doing something you love, you're a lucky man, and George Paterson considered himself lucky in that respect, but sometimes you get a job that makes the bile rise. He was working late to get some plans finished. Finished and off his desk.

Stella had come home early and made supper while he worked: salmon steaks, Caesar salad, new potatoes; preparation time as long as it takes to open three packets, cooking time twenty minutes, tops. Stella knew how to cook, but she got bored easily. In the Eight-til-Late, she had come across a piece of new marketing and decided to give the product a try. It came with a little booklet that listed some mixes and Stella went for Wild Mule which added lime juice and ginger ale. She took two glasses into George's work room.

He sipped and looked startled. "What's this?"

"Absinthe."

"Are you serious?"

"That's what it says on the label." She looked over his shoulder as he added a couple of grace notes to his design. She said, "What you've got there is a mink-lined gin palace."

George corrected her. "It's a custom-built bawdy house."

"A fuck-barque."

"A shag-ship."

"It's also," she reminded him, "a stonking great commission."

He had this way of touching her cheek with his cupped hand as if holding something rare. She thought, I'll never get over you. I'm in love with someone else, but I'll never get over you.

Next morning, the reports came in.

Stella spent ten minutes with Mike Sorley, then they went back to the open office together. Cigarette lighters snapped and flared all round the room. Sue Chapman had typed a half-page synopsis of the new forensic information and printed copies, so everyone knew pretty much what Stella was going to say. What they didn't quite know yet was exactly what it meant.

"We now have the forensic report on Stephanie James's DNA and fingerprint matches, together with the final forensic reports on DNA traces found in human hairs stuck to the wounds of the victim and other DNA traces in the flat. If you cut to the chase, you'll see that the hairs are female, they're not the victim's, they're not Stephanie James's, and they don't match with any of the samples taken from women who were at the party or who work at *Imago*. There was also a cluster of palm-prints and fingerprints close to the bed—on the wall and on the bedhead—all of them partly obscured by blood and by each other. Basically, there are four sets. The victim's, Mark Ross's, and two other sets that we can't identify."

"Can't eliminate," Harriman said.

"That's right. They don't correspond to any of the prints that we've taken from friends, from colleagues, or from Stephanie James. So—two outstanding sets of prints. Now go to the DNA traces. There was an unidentified substance in the victim's hair. Tests show that it was saliva. Forensics looked for matches of the saliva and of the hair we found stuck to the victim's wounds. There are no matches. The hair and the saliva deposit were left by two different people, and neither of them are among those people we've sampled. Not Mark Ross, not Stephanie James, not anyone else.

"If we assume that the saliva was deposited by an attacker, and that the hair in the wounds was deposited by an attacker, then we have to say that Janis Parker was attacked and killed by two people whose identity we don't know." Stella paused. "Here's something else. The DNA analysis shows that the saliva is a man's, but the hairs came from a woman. They're head hairs. They must have been shed during the attack. Conclusion? She was killed by a man and a woman, acting together. And given the distribution of DNA, it looks very likely that the woman was the principal aggressor."

In the AMIP-5 sweepstake, person or persons unknown had just become the safe bet.

18

Mike Sorley looked mournful. He gestured at the piles of paper on his desk; the piles of paper beside his desk. Each pile represented money.

"We're starting from scratch," he said. "Starting from zero; nothing in the bank. They could be anyone."

"You'd have to think burglars," Stella said, "if it wasn't for the nature of the attack."

"Doesn't stop it being burglary," Sorley offered. "They taped her mouth, don't forget, and there were signs that she'd been tied up. That would have left them free to do the place first, then kill her. Druggies—druggies or drunks or dropouts. Hopeless task."

He was talking about the people who don't register. They don't register to vote and they don't register, either, when we see them in doorways, or asleep on the Tube, or gathered on benches in the mall passing a spliff or a bottle. They're not on any census, they don't have medical or Social Security numbers, you can't imagine them having a past and they sure as hell don't have much of a future. The city's invisibles, the no-names.

"Two weeks," Sorley guessed. "Two weeks before this is down-graded to an open file. No one wants to throw good money after bad." He sighed. "Unless we get a confession, of course; a couple of

scaggies with a sudden attack of remorse. That would help the fucking cash-flow."

"We've had eight confessions," Stella observed. "Five of which
came in over the case line."

"Anonymous."

"That's right."

"The other three?"

"One claims he beheaded her with a Samurai sword, another told
us she was a willing sacrifice to the Dark Lord."

Sorley nodded as if it all made sense. "What about the third?"

"Who knows? Probably took her immortal soul to Alpha Cen-
tauri for analysis."

"Two weeks," Sorley said. Then: "You're sure there's nothing in
the Ross-and-James theory?"

"She was at a retreat."

"Was she? On the day of the murder? You're sure?"

"I made a phone call."

"But you didn't go down there?"

Stella thought: the Mother Superior as accomplice? I'd give anything . . . But Sorley was clutching at straws. "I'll send DC Hewitt,
boss," Stella said. "She's a fan of the Ross-and-James theory, so perhaps she won't mind the trip."

Sorley looked at her sharply. "All right, DS Mooney. So what
would you do?"

Stella shrugged. "Charge the guy with the Samurai sword?"

AMIP-5 spent the next two days on paperwork. A couple of officers
spent time in pubs and clubs, but there was no word from informants, no word on the street. Stella talked to Mike Sorley about a
chis asking for the witness-protection program; she said he'd asked
a question too many and was probably right to believe his life might
be in danger; she didn't mention Nike Man. Sorley laughed. He said
he'd approach the right people, even though he expected to get the
wrong answer.

She asked Sue Chapman to log any deaths by violence in the area, anything at all, no exceptions. "Lone deaths," Stella insisted, "anything that might look drugs related. Harefield?"

Sue checked again and reported that Harefield had been death-free for some while. GBH, ABH, affray, four rapes, the usual rash of break-ins, but no unlawful killings.

Just before eleven o'clock, Stella went across to the pub. It would be an hour or so before the lunch-time drinkers would start to drift in, but there were a few disciples at the bar—men who looked as if they'd never been away, a couple of women who might have been returning from the late shift or on their way to an early start. Stella wondered about the degree of want that led to an eleven A.M. blow job. The degree of want on both sides.

She ordered a tomato juice with everything in it except vodka and took it to a quiet corner and called Jackie Yates. He said, "In a minute," speaking fast, and cut the call. She waited ten minutes for him to come back and when he did he sounded like a man in a hurry.

"No one called it in," she said. "No one reported a death on Harefield."

Jackie laughed sourly. "Oh, good. Now I can sleep at night."

"So where did he go?"

"Straight to heaven. No problem. What does it matter?"

"What was his name?"

"I don't know."

"What was his name, Jackie?"

"Did you ask about the witness-protection program?"

"What was his name?"

"You won't be able to get me on this number anymore. Don't try."

"I'm talking to people about protection. It isn't easy."

"You're right, Mrs. Mooney. It isn't easy."

"Where are you, Jackie?"

It was obviously the wrong question because he said, "Oh, please . . ." and cut the call.

There had been an echo to his voice: not something electronic, more to do with his surroundings, as if he might be calling from an empty house. A man on the run.

Don't get killed, Stella thought. For Christ's sake: one's enough. She was contemplating a not-quite-so-innocent tomato juice when she got a call from Pete Harriman.

He said, "There's another."

19

There are ways of keeping the worst of the city at bay. Don't use your mobile in the street. Don't wear a Rolex. Don't leave your car doors unlocked when you stop for a red light. Stay off Murder Mile and Killerman Corner. Don't use the underpass after dark. Live on a gated estate. They're good tips, but there are no guarantees. Delgarno Villas was a gated estate and Nesta Cameron was dead in a flat on the fourth floor.

Everyone arrived at pretty much the same time except the video man, who had been half a mile back when a panel truck overtook in the Hanger Lane tunnel and sideswiped a motorcycle. A nine-car shunt had blocked the tunnel and the approach roads were solid. Andy Greegan took the call from the guy's mobile and phoned for back-up.

Pete Harriman spent ten minutes with the uniforms who'd answered the triple-nine call, then put on a white pixie suit and made his way through the little crowd of death-workers trawling the flat. Stella was in the bedroom, standing with her back to the window while the doctor charted the body and made notes. She was looking down at Nesta Cameron and didn't look up when Harriman came into the room.

She said, "It's the same."

"Who spotted it?" Harriman asked.

Stella shrugged. "A computer match, apparently."

"It's a miracle," Harriman observed. Computer matches usually showed up too late or appeared when the investigating team had long since reached the same conclusion. He walked a couple of paces one way, then a couple the other: trying to peer round the doctor without getting too close. "Just like Janis?"

"Give or take."

Nesta Cameron's hands were tied with the belt from a dress, and Harriman could just see a little mustache of adhesive where the tape had been. He could also see the wounds all over her body, little raw mouths, and the gape where her throat was cut. She was lying on the bed as if she had fallen from a great height. Her hair was flame red, long enough to fall over her shoulders, and it was still possible, despite what had been done to her, to see that she had been beautiful, though not in a conventional way: her face a little too long, her mouth a little too wide. The creamy skin of the redhead made the wounds show particularly stark and raw.

The police doctor was crouching next to Nesta holding a thermometer and consulting his watch: death's calculus. Stella asked him how long.

"Well, it's half-past twelve now . . ." He nodded at a radiator under the window. "Is that off?" Harriman went across and touched it with a gloved hand. It was. "Okay, but I suspect she'd've had the heat on last night, so it must be on a timer. Depends when she'd timed it to shut down. The warmer the room, the faster the decay."

"Roughly," Stella asked.

"Ten-thirty, maybe eleven o'clock last night."

"Who found her?" Harriman asked.

"The cleaners: a team; they do ten other flats in the building." Stella was still staring at Nesta as if "dead body" were a new concept to her. "This was the eighth. They didn't expect her to be here, so they'd already cleaned half the flat before someone decided to make a start on the bedroom."

"Terrific."

"As you say . . ."

"What's that?" Harriman was pointing at the wall closest to the bed. An almost perfect hand-print stood out from the bloodsplash.

Stella shifted her gaze from Nesta to the wall. "I'm hoping," she said, "that it's a fucking great clue." She turned away, as if she'd looked at more than enough. "Let's leave them to it."

As they walked back through the flat and out to the stairwell, Harriman said, "What do you think?"

"I think there's a strong chance we're in shit."

They waited three days for confirmation which, even then, was partial, but it was enough. The fingerprints matched, so it was a short-odds bet that the DNA would match, too.

In those three days, everyone had been busy. Nesta Cameron's life had been turned over and scrutinized, but no dark secrets had been found. She worked for a lifestyle design company, she drove a Nissan sports, she bought designer labels but mostly warehouse, she was known at the local chrome and glass diner, she was Mrs. Normal or, at least, she was Ms. Average High Achiever, right down to the two grams of nose-candy in the drawer of her bedside table. There was nothing to link her with Janis Parker apart from the manner of their deaths. So far as anyone could tell—so far as friends and relatives of both women could say—they had never met, either socially or through their jobs.

The files and folders from Janis Parker's laptop had already been downloaded and transferred to Sue Chapman's computer. She had found nothing of use in any of them. Nesta Cameron's hard disk had been raided too, but Sue could find no obvious matches. If Janis Parker and Nesta Cameron had been connected, it must have been on the astral plane.

The fingerprint and DNA neg-checks isolated Nesta's friends and relatives. They isolated her estranged husband, who, in any case, was on a three-month secondment to Birmingham and could prove it. They isolated her boyfriend, who had spent the last week or more waiting for his mother to die; waiting with him were his father, his siblings, and a dozen family friends. Sorley asked for a comparison profile on Ross and James, but there was nothing to put them anywhere near the SOC, and no one really thought there would be.

The difference between Janis and Nesta was that Nesta's body had been found the day after her murder. Otherwise you could have made diagrammatic templates for the two killings and laid one atop the other and they would have shown the same pattern.

The hands tied. The mouth taped. The proliferation of small wounds. The cut across the throat.

Two days later, Stella was breathing the chill air of Sam Burgess's lab, with its overlay of formaldehyde and offal. She asked him the same question that Pete Harriman had asked of her: "What do you think?"

"There's no question," he said. "The DNA matches—and I gather the prints match?" Stella nodded. "So, two people," Sam continued, "a man and a woman, undoubtedly the perpetrators, inflicting a series of wounds with a thin-bladed knife or razor, culminating in a wound that severs the oesophagus and the carotid artery, with a resultant loss of life from shock or asphyxiation. The only difference between this death and that of Janis Parker is that everything was fresher. Not that we were particularly helped by that."

"The doctor at the scene put the death at about eleven the previous evening."

"Good guess," Sam said. "I'd agree. Maybe a little later, but not much."

The halogen lighting seemed to give skin a greenish tinge, as if everyone in Sam's subterranean world carried a touch of decay. He pushed his report across the desk to Stella. "Only one person attended the PM apart from yourself," he said, "as you know. My lab assistant typed up the report from my notes. Apart from the three of you and myself, no one's seen this." It was standard procedure in certain cases. Serial killing, for example: and Sam could see the possibilities. The press would get there sooner or later, but later was better.

Stella walked back through the slap-flaps to the outer door and the street. The wind was blowing in gusts, like a sea wind, but there was no salt in it to cut the grime.

Maxine Hewitt crossed her name off the circulation list and dropped the report on Mike Sorley's desk. Sorley was in a late meeting with the press office. One or two red-top journos were getting close to something remotely resembling the truth, which, in their world, was more than enough for a story.

It was almost eight o'clock and Stella was the only other person in the squad room. Maxine lit a cigarette as she walked back toward her desk, then paused to look over Stella's shoulder at the points-of-comparison chart she was working on: Parker and Cameron, Cameron and Parker. It was done in ballpoint on ruled paper. In the morning, Stella would give it to Sue Chapman, who knew about spreadsheets and color coding; a little later it would turn up at the morning briefing.

"It all fits."

"Yes," Stella agreed. "It all fits. Why are you still here?"

"Get in early, stay late, impress the bosses, then ask for references when my promotion board comes up." Stella smiled. "I'm going to a movie at the Gate. Meeting a friend. Still got half an hour to kill. You have to ask yourself," she continued, "how they got in."

"Delgarno Villas . . ."

"Well, yes, especially there because it's gated and you need a code to get in. But it was the same at Parker's flat—no sign of a break-in."

"We've ordered up the CCTV tapes from the Villas. Perhaps we'll find something there."

Maxine pulled up a chair and sat alongside Stella. Her cigarette smoke wafted across and Stella dragged in a lungful. Maxine gestured toward the comparison chart. "What have you got?"

"I'm still thinking about it."

"Okay."

Maxine pushed her chair back, but Stella held up a hand. "No," she said, "it's all right. Just . . . I *am* still thinking about it."

She pushed the chart across so that Maxine could have a better sight of it. "One death and you have a few facts. Two deaths and the facts start to make a pattern. Then you begin to think about what the pattern means."

She pointed to a column marked DNA. "The DNA traces in Janis Parker's flat . . . We started out by using them as eliminators, then we isolated the deposits at the murder scene, put them together with the neg-check on fingerprints and came up with two missing people. Two anonymous suspects. That was how we used it—as a sort of ID tag. But what I'm looking at now is something else. Not who it was, but where it was."

"Where it was . . ."

"DNA location at the scenes of crime. What it tells us about movement. Who went where and did what."

"There were traces all over."

"There were, yes."

"Mostly around the immediate scene: around the body."

"That's right. Not only there, though."

Maxine leaned over and looked at the chart, "Okay, in Parker's flat there were deposits in the hall, in the living room, in the kitchen, in the bathroom. Everywhere."

"Which you'd expect," Stella said, "with Stephanie James and Mark Ross, other friends and so on. But the killers went everywhere, too."

"In Parker's flat. Not so much in Cameron's."

"The cleaners had been more than halfway round the flat before someone went into the bedroom."

"Okay," Maxine agreed, "let's suppose it was the same in both flats—they went everywhere. Which means they spent time there. We know the victims weren't killed quickly. It tells us something about the killers' state of mind."

"It does, yes, but that's not what I'm talking about. There are DNA traces everywhere, and that includes the bathroom."

"Is that important?"

"I'm just thinking about these people. They would have been covered in blood."

"So they washed it off."

"Well, given the DNA placement—plasma, mostly—it seems they did more than wash: they took a shower."

"Yes, okay." Maxine thought about it for a moment, then she looked at Stella. "Janis Parker shared a flat with another woman. Nesta Cameron lived alone."

Stella nodded. "That's what I was thinking."

"So if the killers stripped off what they were wearing, took a shower, then got dressed again—"

"—they would have left the place in clothing that was heavily bloodstained."

"Unless they took some of Parker's clothes—some of Cameron's—and carried their own away with them in a bag or what-ever. In which case the man must have been wearing women's cloth-ing."

"Either that," Stella said, "or they stripped naked to do the killing."

20

KFC and a guy called Sparkler picked Daz up at about nine-thirty.

He'd dropped a punter in Kensington, then driven back to the call center because it was a thin time of night for fares and if you were on hand, you got the job. They were waiting by the STEAD/FAST spinner, looking up the road, waiting for him to arrive. Just for a moment, he thought to drive by: gun the engine, head down the Strip, try to make it to the M-way, find time to think. He blipped the accelerator and shifted down a gear, but then he registered the slow procession on both sides of the Strip as single men in cars trawled the pavements for the girls in lycra and crop tops. He'd never make it.

Sparkler gave Daz a wide grin. There was a diamond set in his left front tooth: it was how he'd got his name. The neon logo on a corner bar gave it an electric-blue tint. KFC opened the door like a flunkey to let Daz out and gestured toward a black BMW 3 Series parked a little way down the street.

He said, "Just for a talk, Daz. Someone needs to talk to you."

There were five guys crammed into the tiny call center, all watching TV, eyes fixed as if waiting for the last vital number in the midweek lottery. The guy who coordinated the calls was on the phone, trying to find a replacement driver. He glanced out into the street as Daz went past with KFC on one side and Sparkler on the other. He caught Daz's eye and lifted a hand, palm up, which meant *I'm sorry* and *Shit luck* and *What would you have done?*

Nobody spoke on the short drive down to Harefield, but Sparkler threw the locks and put a CD on the player, jacking up the volume so that the bass made loose fittings in the Beamer rattle. Daz looked out at people going about their business and wondered what it was like to be safe, to have nothing on your mind. He sat in the back with KFC, who seemed to be dozing: eyes half-closed, his head nodding sideways from time to time.

When they got to the estate, the two men prodded Daz into a lift, then flanked him along a seventh-floor walkway until they came to a door covered in steel sheeting. Daz had been here before, but under happier circumstances. It was a drugs warehouse. Daz got his supply from half a dozen places, but this was one of them, and he used it more than the others because the gear was good and the estate was well-defended: a no-go area for the local filth. You weren't going to get busted on Harefield unless you were unlucky enough to try to score on a night when SO 19 and the Drugs Squad were coming in mob-handed; but then it was more than likely that you'd know about that. The estate would know. The gear would have gone away for the night and the cops would have to scrub round for some hillbilly heroin and a handul of Es.

The guy Daz scored from was called Jonah and for all Daz knew that might have been his name. KFC made a call on his mobile phone and the door was opened by a boy of about twelve: a mule who was just leaving anyway. When Daz walked into the flat, KFC and Sparkler left. They'd done their job and Daz wasn't going to turn and run: that wasn't how things worked. Jonah was watching a TV quiz with a girl who was just a shade too fresh to be off the Strip; they were sharing a spliff the size of a log and the girl was concentrating hard on the quiz questions.

Daz said, "Can you help me out here, Jonah?"

The girl said, "Okay, okay, who starred in the classic 1952 Western *High Noon?*"

Jonah gave Daz a place to go to and a time to be there.

The girl said, "Hey, that was John Wayne, right?"

Daz said, "I brought her down here, I dropped her off. Jesus Christ, man."

Jonah advised Daz not to be late.

The girl said, "It was John Wayne." She nudged Jonah. "John Wayne, yeah?"

Daz had been told all he needed to know. Even so, he said, "I didn't say a thing to her. I didn't give her a thing."

Jonah repeated the place and time, just in case Daz hadn't taken it in.

The girl said, "Gary Cooper? Who the fuck is Gary Cooper?"

Daz got out of the lift and walked into the bull ring. The off-license was open, so he went in and bought a bottle of Scotch. The counterman asked which brand but Daz didn't seem able to focus on the question. His hands were shaking and there were tears on his cheeks.

The counter-man knew why Daz was crying. He said, "Listen, don't go," but Daz only shook his head and held out money for the Scotch.

"Don't go, man. Don't turn up."

Daz was trembling. The counter-man gave him a bottle of White Horse but didn't take the money; as if it were tainted; as if it would bring bad luck.

When he left the office there were some kids hanging out by the

KFC, a few others in the bull ring buying and selling, a boy circling on roller blades, his shoulders shifting along with the beat from his personal stereo. They paused to look at Daz as he crossed the ring.

A man with the goat-mouth on him.

After the Bonnelli case, when Stella started having the three A.M. dream, she had decided that the best thing to do was never to speak of it: not the dream, not the case. It was a technique that had worked well, apart from the days when she had to throw up a few times, and the days when she drank herself shitless before daring to go to bed, and the days when she'd be in the interview room with some lowlife and she'd just want to stop the tape and take the bastard down to a cell and stamp on his face till her strength gave out.

She had got through the first month, but couldn't see how in hell she was going to get through the second.

Then AMIP-5 was asked to focus on a series of pensioner rapes. For the most part, AMIP teams deal only with murder, but there are times when a string of serious crimes can be attributed to one person and the crimes cross several metropolitan boundaries, in which case an AMIP team is drafted in to conduct a coordinated investigation, rather than have different crime squads from different areas all colliding with one another, or getting territorial, or just plain pissed-off.

AMIP-5 could have been looking for an opportunist who went in to rob and stayed to rape, or it could have been a rapist who robbed as an afterthought. A DI called Don Robson was heading up the team and Stella had talked to him about bringing in a profiler. He agreed. The profiler was Anne Beaumont. It was how Stella and she had met.

The rapist was seventeen and had an IQ that barely stretched to double figures, which was pretty much what Anne had predicted. Once the case was closed, Stella took Anne for a drink. She talked about nothing for half an hour in a voice bright with inhibition until Anne smiled and stopped her and said, "What is it you want?"

After that, it had become a regular thing. George didn't know; no one knew. They talked about the three A.M. dream, although there were things that Stella still wouldn't own to: whether the child she'd lost had been a girl or a boy; the fact that she had given the child a name. Those were the details that made the dream so real, made it so terrifying. To know who it was hanging there beside the Bonnelli children.

They also talked about George Paterson and John Delaney and what Stella ought to do next. Or, rather, Anne let Stella talk about the fact that she didn't know what the hell to do next, and if Anne had any ideas she wasn't sharing them. Shrinks don't do that.

"It's like throwing dice," Stella said. "I might as well be doing that: six and below I go home, seven and up I go round to John's place. I never really know what I'm going to do or why the fuck I'm doing it. At least dice would make a pattern of things."

"You mean it would even out?" Anne suggested.

"No, I mean I'd have to do what the dice said. That would be the deal."

"Okay, get some dice."

Anne's consulting room was on the third floor of her house and faced the south side of Hyde Park. London's light pollution was a constant: the big hotels on Park Lane, the street lamps bordering South Carriage Drive, the Knightsbridge stores. Anne got up and pulled the curtains.

Stella said, "What is it I'm doing—as things stand? Going with instinct, is that what you'd say?"

"Sounds like it to me. Have you slept with Delaney yet?"

"Are you supposed to ask me that sort of thing?"

"Not really," Anne laughed. "I'm just dying to know."

"I haven't slept with him. He hasn't asked me to. But he wants me to. Does that mean he's a man in a million?"

"Definitely."

"Oh, good," Stella said, "that makes everything easier."

Neither woman spoke for a while. An emergency vehicle went down toward Kensington Gore and, after the sound faded, Stella could hear rain on the high windows. Her mind drifted to her other

life, Janis and Nesta dead, two people showering the blood off. After a moment, she said, "I think I'm going to need your help."

Anne misunderstood. "You come here, you talk, you pay. Sometimes I challenge you, sometimes I give you a lead. The best analogy
I know is that you're in a dark place and I've got a torch. That's as
far as I go."

"No. I don't want you to talk to Delaney or George or anything.
Not that." In truth, Stella would have loved it. George and Anne to-
gether; Anne and Delaney; working things out between them while
Stella took a break. "I've got two deaths—"

"This is a case?"

"Right, yes, two deaths, about twelve or thirteen days apart, both
victims are young women, apparently motiveless killings, not burglary, not rape, same MO, which involves a blow to the head followed by torture, no doubt about it being the same people—the same
killers, I mean—nothing to link the victims, nothing to indicate similarity of victim-choice except sex and age."

"You think it's serial?"

"Tough to think anything else; although we're not admitting it
officially yet. In fact we're not quite admitting it to ourselves."

"You said *people*."

"A man and a woman. That's what forensic evidence suggests."

"Suggests . . ."

"Like I said: no one's prepared to commit on this just yet."

"But you're sure . . ."

"DNA evidence. The pathologist is sure: two people unaccounted
for at the scenes of crime. The same people."

"And one's a woman."

"Yes."

"I've heard of it, but I've never met with it."

"I'm going to ask my DI to bring in a profiler. I'd like it to be you."

"You don't see a conflict in that?"

"I see a conflict because we're talking about it on my time, but
otherwise, no, I don't. Me the cop, me the emotional fuck-up: two
entirely different things."

Anne laughed. "You think so? You really need help."

. . .

Stella sat in her car on the Holland Park stretch of Notting Hill and watched the street life. She was exactly between home and Delaney's—halfway to, or halfway from. Neither here nor there.

Some kids rode by on bikes they'd just stolen, weaving in and out of the groups on the pavement, one hand to steer, one hand for the can of Red Bull. An ambulance went through, followed by a patrol car, sirens and lights hitting off walls and windows. Maxine Hewitt came out of the late-night movie with her friend, a woman of about her own age, maybe a little bit younger, and attractive enough to turn heads. They were trying for a cab and finally they got one.

The cab was for the friend. She turned and kissed Maxine on the mouth. They pulled apart a moment. Maxine's hand was on the back of the other woman's neck. They kissed again, lips parted, then the friend got into the taxi. Maxine stood arms folded, hugging herself; after a moment, she crossed the road in front of Stella's car, and looked down Holland Park Avenue for a cab to take her in the opposite direction.

21

It was after midnight, but the boy was awake and the dogs were awake. The waste bins on the Strip were full at that time of night, and the pickings were good; you just had to sort the sodas from the syringes, the kebabs from the Kotex.

About half an hour earlier, it had started to rain: a full spring downpour backed by a westerly wind, the kind of rainfall that could last all night, and the Strip had cleared a little, though the whores had put on hooded plastic shorties that provided a good view of the merchandise, and were still working the curb: the original wet dream.

Rain hissed outside the entrance to the mausoleum, a silvery curtain. The boy had an Eastpak that he'd stolen weeks before. He kept everything in it: his sleeping bag, a spare pair of sneakers, the baseball cap he wasn't wearing, the sweater he wasn't wearing, whichever jeans and T-shirts he wasn't wearing, a water canister with a screw top, a knife, a photograph of himself in a mock-silver frame. It was all stolen, except the photograph: the only thing he'd taken from the Harefield flat that had once been his home. He raided the rough sleepers, clotheslines, street stalls. When he was foraging, he emptied the Eastpak and left its contents with the dogs. Now he picked over the bin-bounty and divided it between the dogs and himself.

The pack circled and turned, waiting for its share. The brindle was the alpha dog. Now and then it nipped a shoulder or a flank, just to set precedence. The boy threw the scraps in among the pack, but fed the brindle by hand. The dog ate in big gulps, its head jerking forward, the scraps going down whole; then it turned and went to the broken rails of the entrance, its ears standing straight, its shoulders bunched. It was half-gazehound and could see, before the boy saw them, the figures coming through the cemetery, dark shapes that seemed to hang and drift in the long rails of rain.

Three men walking straight, one walking a mazy path as if he might at any moment pitch forward and fall. Daz had finished the Scotch and was certainly drunk, but his drunkenness was about balance and slur; it had done nothing to shut down his senses. Apart from his legs not working properly and his tongue getting tangled, he was terrifyingly sober. He knew where he was, he knew what was going to happen.

The men with him were not dressed for the weather: designer tracksuits and high-sided sneakers; they were very wet and they were very ill-tempered. The boy sat close to the broken railings and watched them troop past, then let a few seconds go by before he went out into the rain to watch. The brindled dog went with him and stood sentinel.

From where they were, boy and dog, it was like a shadow play; shapes in the downpour that seemed oddly unconnected with either the earth or the sky, a pall hanging across the dark, stony space of the graveyard, sometimes stained by hot neon reds or blues.

They stopped by a horizontal slab, scabbed and blotched with dirt, though you could still just make out that it was consecrated to the memory of Arthur Edward Stocker and his wife Sarah May. Daz lay down on it when they told him to. One of them took out a mobile phone and made a triple-nine call. When the operator answered, he gave a location, then said "Ambulance" and hung up. The mobile number would already be registered with the emergency services, but that didn't matter because the phone belonged to a clubber who was off his face on PCP and didn't know it had gone.

Calling the ambulance was a concession. Daz hadn't committed a capital crime, he'd just found himself wound into some action that had gone bad and someone had to suffer—Daz for now, because he had agreed to meet the lady cop; because he'd wanted to protect himself and his dealership; because a man had died. Jackie Yates later, when he could be found. No one would be calling an ambulance for Jackie.

They spread him, arms and legs, and one of them took a converted Brocock ME38 out of the zipper pocket of his tracksuit and shot Daz through both knees and both elbows. Then they walked back the way they had come. If they'd cared to look, they would have seen the boy and the dog, darker shapes on the rain's gray backwash, but they had their minds on other things: getting out of the wet, setting up a couple of lines, a couple of girls.

Daz had screamed when they shot him, but the weather muffled everything. The sound of traffic on the through road was damped down and even the high-pitched *whoop-whoop-whoop* of sirens was blunted.

He lay there, face up to the rain, unable to shuffle or shift. His cries seemed to come from a long way off and the paramedics took a while to find him. They gave him a shot of morphine, then lifted him on to a gurney, but the morphine didn't have quite the effect it should have, what with Daz's tolerance to opiates, and he howled as they wheeled him over the rough ground to the pathway.

A little later the dogs came out and sniffed at the last resting place of Arthur Edward and Sarah May Stocker. They licked the surrounding grass, which was dark and pungent where rain had sluiced blood off the stone. They had only a short time to do this, because soon there were more sirens, and lights, and men, and the crackle of radios.

The boy and the dogs went back to the mausoleum, where they circled, snuffling, then hunkered down in the dark.

22

Someone gets murdered, and it might be someone you love, someone you treasure, someone about whom you know everything, but once the word "victim" has been applied the police have a special relationship with that person. You might not hear it said, but the message is: *He's ours now.* Or: *She'll be all right with us.* You lose touch. No one tells you what's going on. Maybe they catch the killer; maybe they decide to close the case; you're likely to be the last one to hear.

Stephanie James called the squad room and got passed from hand to hand until Stella heard her name spoken and signaled that she would take the call.

"Is anything happening?" Stephanie asked.

"We're investigating."

"Yes. Have you . . . is there any progress?"

"We've got your number."

"No, I'm not at the flat. I couldn't. I'm with Mark: staying with him."

"We've got that number, too."

"Oh . . . Yes, right, you have."

"We're doing what we can," Stella said. "I can't really talk about the case . . . you know, the day-to-day."

"No. Okay." A pause then: "But you don't need us anymore?"

"Sorry?"

"Mark and me."

"Not really. Not now. Why?"

"We're thinking of getting away for a while. Going somewhere . . . You know, after what happened." As if Stella might care, she said, "Apart from anything else, it would be a chance for us to get things back. Back together."

Did he tell you? Stella wondered. That they were lovers. That she was pregnant.

Stephanie's next remark provided the answer. "He was fond of Janis, too. We were all friends. He was so supportive, you know? I don't think I could have got through it without him."

"It's fine," Stella said. "Go away. Take a break."

"The other girl . . ." Stephanie said.

"Other girl?"

"It was in the paper. They thought there might be a connection. Is there?"

Stella paused a moment. Then: "Leave us a contact number, okay? Just in case something comes up."

Sometimes it's a leak, sometimes it's clever journalism, sometimes it's luck.

Sorley handed Stella a tabloid folded back at page five, with the passage lifted in highlighter. "Apparently a journo talked to one of Janis Parker's neighbors and got a description of what the body looked like, then followed up with a call to the police doctor asking about Nesta Cameron as if he was a morgue assistant. He knew all the right names. I don't think he expected to find any sort of connection: just a crime reporter wanting more than his fair share. Then he saw the similarities and wrote the piece. No one else has picked it up."

"Yet. What have we done?"

"I talked to the editor. Muddied the water a bit."

"Any guarantees?"

"The guy stepped over the line, pretending to be someone he wasn't. I traded off that. We're okay for the time being." He shook a cigarette out of the open packet on his desk, and Stella felt a pang. The way her life was, she needed little compensations. A drink helped, but drinking without smoking had become a tough order. "Anyway," Sorley said, "who's saying it's serial? We have to look at the possibility, but it's too soon to settle on that."

"Is it? I know that as soon as we've agreed it's serial, we're into problems, but look at the forensic evidence. And there's no connections between Parker and Cameron, remember."

"None that we've found."

"You think they were part of a gang planning a second go at the millennium diamond and fell out with Mr. Big?"

"Don't fucking speak to me like that, DS Mooney."

A silence fell, during which Stella tried to catch the drift of Sorley's cigarette smoke. Finally, she said, "Sorry, boss."

Sorley wagged a hand in irritation. "I'm not prepared to say that we're looking at a serial. Not yet. I know about the DNA traces, but it could be—" Sorley spread his arms, a wide shrug, "—who knows? A punishment thing."

"So you'd have to connect them to crime. And like I just said: there's nothing there. Not singly, not together. One was a glamor-mag editor, the other designed wine labels and company logos, they earned more than you and me put together. It's not as if they were into gangster chic or running up unpayable bills at a casino; it wasn't their world."

"They both used cocaine."

"Everyone uses cocaine. It's your grannie's drug of choice."

He snapped her another irritated look. "They had to score it from somewhere. You went that route: it was the first thing you thought of."

"That was when it was just Parker. And it was all I had. And it was the wrong track." She didn't want to dwell on Daz and Jackie and her very sketchy report.

In the corner of Sorley's little screened-off space there were a couple of Tesco bags: new life, New Man. Stella remembered when he'd been bringing pizza and beer back to the office and sleeping between two chairs. She went away and came back a few minutes later with a coffee for each of them.

"Is this from the machine?" Sorley wanted to know.

"From here to the machine is by way of an apology," she told him. "Going out to Starbucks is exploitation."

"It's just around the corner."

"It's a step too far."

He smiled. "What do you want, Stella?"

"There's a profiler I've worked with before: Anne Beaumont. She's good. I'd like to put her on retainer."

"Yeah? Even this coffee's an unaffordable extra."

"Gang killings, drugs killings, heist killings, killing the wife because she forgot to video the match—they're everyday jobs, we know how to deal with those; one thing leads to another; there are connections—events connected to events, people connected to people."

Sorley knew it. "But serial killings aren't like that."

"No, they're not. Serial killers don't live in a world of crime and consequences. If this is serial—and I think it is—there won't be a chain of contacts and associates and bad guys we can squeeze. These people live in the shadows until the next time."

"These people you've just invented."

"I'd like an expert opinion now rather than later." She knew about the budget meetings, the progress meetings, and played a high card. "Let's be ahead of the game. It's good politics."

Sorley sipped his coffee and pulled a face. "By the hour," he told her, "and no fucking overtime."

Someone had once said of John Delaney that he liked the smell of smoke. That was when he was a war reporter: a pretty good way to earn a living because the world never ran out of wars, so you never ran out of copy. Its only drawbacks were the close-up view you got of butchery and rape and the murder of innocents. And the sight of psychopaths swaggering around in camouflage greens, opening con-centration camps and Swiss bank accounts in the same week. And the very real chance of getting killed.

Delaney had reported some of the worst wars and seen things he wanted to forget, but, if he was honest, there had been times when he'd been driving toward the gunfire, toward the smoke, and felt his nerves fizzing beneath the skin. He would never go back, not now, but there were times when his life seemed . . . well . . . just like anyone else's.

He'd been to see a movie. Although he'd been married once, he'd spent a fair amount of his life doing things on his own, and it was no hardship, though there had been a time when there were on and off girls between on and off wars. Now when he spent time alone he felt it was because he'd been put there. Stella's indecision left him not with a lack, but an absence.

He stopped off at an AllNite to buy a chill-cabinet pizza, a bag of salad and, for some reason that he couldn't fathom, a cigar. He hadn't smoked in years, and he certainly couldn't remember when he'd last smoked a cigar, but suddenly he could taste that richness, smell that fragrance.

When he stepped back onto the street, something happened that, in some odd way, was connected with buying the cigar. It was as if someone had pulled a thread in his spine. He knew the feeling, but couldn't connect it to anything for a moment; then he knew what it was and where it came from.

He'd been walking down a street in Sarajevo during a lull. The Serb farm boys in the hills would have been drunk on slivovitz since mid-morning, so any incoming would be mortars and grenades: stuff you didn't have to aim too carefully. The press were holed up at the Holiday Inn and Delaney had decided to drive down Snipers' Alley to the heart of the city and interview some of the citizens; just vox pop: how was your day, is your house still standing, any of your family die last night?

The word *snajper*—a warning, a promise—was scrawled on all four walls of the crossroads plain to see, but things were quiet and Delaney felt free to walk down this street in this war zone at this time, on his way to talk to the editor of the city's free news-sheet. He was past the four-way junction and out in the open with nowhere to go when he felt it: ice in the backbone; the sensation like a wet string being drawn; his legs suddenly losing the power to hold him; and he knew that somewhere someone was lining up on him, that he'd been picked out, and that the distance between him and that man was just as far as the bullet would fly.

He had wanted to run, but that was impossible. Instead, he found himself sitting down and then, because luck was with him that day, being able to roll sideways into a doorway. The bullet kicked up splinters from the pavement and he stared at the raw gouge mark and the way the sun struck off the chipped stone. The people who owned the house simply opened the door and took him in.

And now the same feeling. He went a few more paces, then pretended to pause before turning and walking back toward the AllNite as if he'd forgotten something. The street was crowded, but there was no one who looked much like a *snajper*.

Back in his flat, he ate the pizza and salad and smoked the cigar. The first long pull took him back: he was in a Jeep on a warm, bright morning crossing rough terrain. In the distance, a thin plume of smoke and the erratic crackle of gunfire. His driver was a crazy man called Josip. He swerved off-track, taking a direct line toward the action, and laughed, and handed Delaney a cigar.

It had rained on and off all day; spring showers. Now the wind was warm, but the pavements were still wet. Delaney stood at his window, rolling the cigar smoke in his mouth, and looked down at the street.

The phone went, but he didn't pick up.

Who are you?

They were having an evening in, Stella and George, George and Stella, and it was just as it should be: a simple meal, a bottle of wine, gentle talk, laughter. George had finished the design for the boat: they talked about that, the client's excess of money and sore lack of taste. Stella told a good Alzheimer's joke that she'd heard in the squad room: they talked about getting old as a theory, though neither of them could feel it yet.

After the food and the wine and the talk they went to the bedroom. George watched as Stella undressed, and saw the carapace of scabbing on her knees and the ripening bruise on her ribs. It wasn't mentioned because her work was never mentioned unless she took the lead, but she knew that he'd noticed because he was careful to take his weight off her when they made love.

Stella thought that George had fallen asleep: his stillness, the rhythm of his breathing; or maybe he was also awake, also listening to music from an upper floor tangling with the rumble of an aircraft bellying down toward Heathrow.

The evening in had been determined by a throw of the dice: she had bought a pair for just that purpose.

"I never really know what I'm going to do or why the fuck I'm doing it. At least dice would make a pattern of things."

"You mean it would even out?"

"No, I mean, I'd have to do what the dice said."

Earlier that day, she had cast them and they'd fallen two and three. Below seven: George; above seven: Delaney. She had no idea whether she would ever do it again, but that day she'd followed the dice.

She could count the differences between the two men, but it was a pointless exercise. He's this way, he's that; kinder or funnier or better looking. Choices weren't made that way. You might as well throw dice.

The differences were noticeable in other ways. She had told George a joke, but she hadn't told him that she'd killed a man.

23

The Kandy Kave was a short drive from the Strip, but in cash terms it was half a million away. Behind Notting Hill Gate in a street that was mostly antique shops and chic restaurants, its day-glo logo splashed pink and green reflections along the wet streets: a neon girl forking her legs round a pole that rose and fell, rose and fell.

Kandy Kave girls get close, really close, but you mustn't touch. Lap dancers, pole dancers, table dancers, they strip and spread and stroke, they lie back and do scissor-splits, they bend over and back up to you, they shake it in your face. It's dancing or it's gynecology. Either way, the girls don't mind so long as you find somewhere to lodge that twenty once your time's up. And if you write your phone number on the banknote, well, who knows? Everyone has bills to pay.

Her dancing name was Sindee, though over the past year she had dyed her hair black to be Jet and red to be Flame and platinum-blonde to be Silvie. It was good to be someone new, someone else.

She'd been up close and over backward more times that evening than she could count. By the time the club was closing, she could no longer tell whether it was her sweat or theirs that freckled her body and although no one had touched her, she felt pretty used up. But it was fine, it was okay, because she was going home that night with more than she'd ever earned in a week on the perfume section at Romilly's. And she would—yes, sometimes, she would—lean right in to a punter, straddle him, her breasts so close to his face it was like a butterfly kiss, and get down low enough to whisper *Okay . . . later . . .* because you could make an extra two-fifty that way and also, let's face it, get laid.

But not tonight. Tonight she would walk the short distance to the twenty-four-hour Ocean Diner and sit at the glass-and-chrome bar with a large glass of Chardonnay and think about nothing at all.

It was a typical Notting Hill place: smart, but you didn't have to be. The barman would call a cab for her and ask her how things were: he knew her, but he didn't know who she was, a characteristic of all good barmen. He guessed she worked the tables at the Kandy Kave because she was a looker, but she came in with her hair pulled back into a ponytail and her face carrying that pale, almost translucent gleam you see when the make-up has just come off. Sindee would tell him things were fine and drink another glass of Chardonnay before the cab arrived.

She had no one to go home to and the first glass of wine had made her pleasantly drowsy. The barman hung up the phone and said, "Twenty minutes, okay?" She nodded and pushed her glass forward slightly, asking for a refill. There was a long mirror behind the bar and, above that, thin neon tubing that spelled out *Ocean Diner* in red, white, and blue script and terminated in cocktail glasses that filled and tipped and emptied, filled and tipped and emptied.

Sindee rested her elbow amid the slop of reflection on the chrome bar top, cupped her cheek, and stared into the mirror. She saw a fake blonde with a shiny face and a hole in her life. The hole was the shape and size of a six-year-old boy called Nick, who lived with Sindee's mother. She saw him when she could; in the meantime, she rattled cages at the Kandy Kave, which meant a better life for both of them.

A night bus had tagged a badly parked car in the Bayswater Road and slewed across the street; you could hear sirens coming in from three directions. Her taxi had to detour and by the time it reached her, she'd had a third glass. It was two-thirty and she was tired.

Much too tired to notice the person who followed her out, got into a battered C-reg Fiesta, and pulled away in the same direction as the cab.

24

If you're robbing a house for the TV and video, or the stereo, or antiques, then you're going to find what you want downstairs. If it's jewelry or cash, it's a short-odds bet that they'll be in the bedroom. People have the small stuff there: as if the bedroom were the center of the house; the castle keep. Perhaps they like to have it close to them while they sleep.

Some people will go in while the occupants are still there. Mostly, they're kids, or else they're experienced men who know the territory, know what they want, and also know that the owners aren't likely to be away until the holiday season, and some things just won't wait. Then there are a few housebreakers who like the thrill of walking the house and taking their pick while people are asleep upstairs: you pop a lock and wait and no one stirs; then you go up and ease into the bedroom which is fusty with sleep-breath. You're looking for something straightforward: an ornamental box in the bottom drawer, a velvet pouch, an Innovations safe pretending to be a double socket. Easy. They're still asleep. Maybe it's a warm night and the wife is sleeping naked. Maybe your fingertips skate her shoulder as you leave. But mostly, of course, it's a mistake: houses are easier to burgle if they're empty.

With Gismo, it was a mistake.

Gismo's real name was Derek Sutton, but they all have their street names. For some, housebreaking is a matter of kicking down doors or knocking a window out of its frame. Gismo liked tools: lock-picks, glass-cutters, keyhole punches. He liked gismos. He'd been watching a row of houses in north Fulham for a week or so, working on the assumption that if a car was missing, so were the occupants. It was a pretty reliable indicator: tried and tested. He'd gone drinking in the local pubs, watched habits, listened to conversations. It was research, all part of his trade.

He identified the house owners by the makes of their cars; and he knew that the Audi Quattro couple were taking a long weekend. What he didn't know was that they had decided to leave a day late because Mr. Audi Quattro had been called in to an emergency meeting. Their car was loaded and, sooner than unpack it, they had borrowed garage space from a friend in the neighboring street. So when Gismo slipped in through a back window at three A.M. he wasn't too concerned about being silent. Not that he put on the stereo or slammed doors as he went from room to room, but he didn't care much about being lightfooted, which is why, when he opened Mr. and Mrs. Audi Quattro's bedroom door, he walked into a full-blooded swing from a baseball bat.

Luck was on Mr. Audi Quattro's side, because he was swinging low and missed Gismo's head, taking him on the upper chest instead, which was more than enough to put Gismo down. Had Mr. A-Q's aim been good, his life would have changed: aggravated assault, at least; possible manslaughter. You can fear and hate the Gismos of this world, but you can't kill them. Mrs. A-Q had dialed 999 a good ten minutes earlier, when she and her husband had first woken to the sound of someone working downstairs. Now they could hear the sirens coming in from both ends of the street. Gismo could hear them too. He managed to sit up and shuffle off a little, wanting to put his back to the wall. Mr. A-Q advised him not to try to run. Gismo looked at the man, but said nothing; he was having trouble breathing.

Three doors down, Sindee was a few seconds dead. The sirens, the rotating flash of roof bars, had hastened things. If the Audi Quattros had left as planned, if Gismo's research had been a little more thorough, she would have died less quickly.

Farther up the street, paramedics checked Gismo and pronounced him walking wounded. The cops advised Mr. A-Q that he might be charged with assault. Mr. A-Q advised the cops that he wished he'd killed the little bastard. Neighbors came out to watch events and suddenly the street was very busy.

It was an hour or so before Sindee's killers would decide it was okay to leave. An hour or so before they would feel safe. They sat with her body as if keeping vigil. One of them made a sandwich.

They put the TV on and settled down to wait.

Death brings a silence that has little to do with the absence of noise. It's the absence that issues from a failed heartbeat, a voice stopped forever, all senses shut down.

And there's a stillness in death that is more than arrested motion. It's deeper and more profound. It's the stillness of stone.

Sindee lay in her own blood, her body not quite as perfect now. In the kitchen, there were eggs broken into a bowl: the omelette she'd never made. There was bread in the toaster. There was dry coffee in a cafetière.

The shower was still beaded with water. Sindee had used it when she got in. Then, later, her killers had used it.

The little creatures, the tiny carnivores, scuttled toward her body and swarmed on it. Sindee was food, now; she was a habitat.

25

"The further you look," Sam Burgess said, "the less there is to find."

Sindee was under his hands, and about to unfold. He had checked the body surfaces, the hair, the crevices, the condition of cornea and retina, the seven external cavities that old religions held to be the way into the soul—little exits and entrances for the Devil.

Sam's was the new religion of science. This told him that if

Sindee's attackers had made a noise when they entered her flat, she would have been perfectly capable of hearing them, and if they had worked up a sweat of excitement, she would have smelled them. It also told him that she had not been penetrated anally, nor had she been forced to perform fellatio. If she had been penetrated vaginally, her assailant had left no trace.

Stella thought that what hadn't happened wasn't so much of an issue. She watched from a little way back—though not far enough, she thought, not nearly far enough—as Sam made the Y-incision from the point of Sindee's shoulders across to mid-chest and then down to the pubis. The fillet. There was no blood. Sindee had done her bleeding. A second pathologist was assisting Sam: a younger man, short, with broad shoulders and big hands, as if this getting into people, this gut-deep pot-holing, would take some muscle.

"Meet Giovanni," Sam said. Giovanni was holding an electric saw. He glanced at Stella over his half-mask and his eyes smiled, then he transferred his gaze to Sam like a musician, instrument ready, looking to the conductor for his cue.

Sam switched on the overhead microphone. "This is routine," he said. "I don't expect to find anything. She appears to have been a perfectly healthy young woman."

"She got plenty of exercise," Stella said.

"Yes?"

"She was a pole dancer."

Slim, flat-bellied, breasts full but high. Men had eyed this body that Sam was disassembling and seen only one thing. Sam saw many things. He made a second incision at the back of the skull and Giovanni stepped into the light. His saw was designed to cut bone but not damage soft tissue.

Sam took a scalpel to cut the cartilage between ribs and breastbone. This would let him into the chest cavity. Giovanni trepanned Sindee. Sam spent some time freeing up the large intestine. Giovanni cut the brain from its cranial attachments and set it aside. Sam lifted out the heart-lung tree. He used a long needle to draw off a sample of heart's blood.

Stella wondered whether anyone had ever said of Sindee that she was a warm-hearted girl. That she was good-hearted. That she had a heart of gold.

They were moving as a team, Sam and Giovanni: you go here, I'll go there. As they worked, they dictated their findings to the microphone, a low drone, two priests of the old religion muttering invocations over the chosen one.

Sam sectioned the coronary arteries but, as he'd predicted, there was no sign of abnormality. Each organ would contribute a sliver to the preserving jar. Each organ would be weighed. There was a specially sensitive set of scales for the smaller parts. Giovanni started the dissection of the heart. A little later he would slice the liver in much the same way, but Sindee was too young for those large glasses of Chardonnay at the Ocean Diner to show up, fatty and orange. Her lungs, however, showed the cost of living in London and dancing at the Kandy Kave: cadmium and exhaust fumes by day, one long secondary inhalation by night.

They lined up her bits and pieces for scrutiny, her sugar and spice, her oesophagus, pancreas, duodenum, spleen, kidneys, bladder. They suspended the cerebellum in preservative. They took specimens of urine and bile. Sam repeated his earlier remark as if it were a new thought.

"The further you look, the less there is to find."

Stella looked at Sindee: empty, now; hollowed out. The soul is what Sam was talking about. All this dark interior brought into the light, and no sign of the hand of God.

Sam scrubbed his hands and forearms while Giovanni returned everything to the body cavity: everything except the slices and slivers and driplets and drops that would go to the path lab.

He said, "Same as the others: Is that your thinking? Nesta Cameron and whass'name."

"Janis Parker," Stella said.

"Parker, yes."

"Is it?"

"Oh, I think so," Sam said. "A contusion to the cranium,

undoubtedly the result of a blow with something hard but not sharp, just like the others. Cause of death isn't a problem: throat cut, just like the others. Several other non-fatal incisions. Just like the others."

"She was tortured . . ."

"Just like the others. But," Sam added, "not to the same degree. So they were interrupted. Something stopped them."

"They. Them. You said, 'Them.'"

"Preliminary tests," Sam observed, "and nothing back from the lab for a while, but forensic reports indicate that there are certainly two errant traces of DNA associated specifically with the activity on and around . . . ah . . . this . . . ah . . . girl when she died." Sam pulled a laboratory sheet toward him: he was looking for Sindee's name.

"Amanda," Stella told him. "Amanda-Jane Wallace." Then, "You reckon . . . ?"

"It's likely to be identical. Apart from the DNA traces I'm sure we'll find, there's the trademark stuff: hands tied with a fabric belt, the tape residue round the mouth, cuts to the fleshy parts of the body with a razor or thin-bladed knife. I'm saying nothing official until tests are completed and on my desk, but I don't think there's much doubt, Stella. Unless you can find some sort of a connection between the three victims, it's serial and she's the latest."

"I can't," she said. "There's no connection."

He looked at her. "Lousy luck."

It had been three days before Sindee was found. Friends had called and listened to the ringing tone and wondered why the answerphone didn't cut in. After a couple of days, they'd started to worry, but no one did anything. A part-time boyfriend called a few times and got the same response. He went to the Kandy Kave expecting to find her there, but no one had seen her. Gerry Moreno, the guy who owned Kandy's, was someone else who had been trying to call Sindee: "Someone's a no-show, girls have to double—it's tough going, you know? A night on the pole, that's a real workout. Tell her to call in. Tell her there's a queue of girls for the job."

Sindee's mother called to remind Sindee that it was visiting day and Nick was waiting to see his mother. She called five times, then she left Nick with a neighbor and went to Sindee's flat and pounded on the door. She was more worried than angry, because Sindee never missed her Nick day. It was mid-afternoon and when Sindee's mother put her ear to the door she could hear an episode of *Butt Ugly Martians*. Later, the neighbors said they had been able to hear the TV playing night and day since the previous Sunday. They'd banged on the wall a few times and yelled and left notes under the door telling Sindee she was a bitch and a whore, but it hadn't occurred to them that anything might be wrong.

AMIP-5 had picked up the shout pretty soon, because the Parker case and the Cameron case had been logged under a single heading and notified to AMIP HQ. Stella, Pete Harriman, Maxine Hewitt and Andy Greegan had covered the immediate contacts: Sindee's mother and the part-time boyfriend, whose name was Dean. Stella didn't expect anything to come of those checks and she was right. The mother was only holding together for the child: without that responsibility, she would have been a basket case. So mother hates daughter for baring it all at Kandy's wasn't an option. Nor was jealous part-time boyfriend, because Dean was also part-time with a few other girls, one of whom had been with him at an all-night party when Sindee died.

Stella had gone into the bathroom of Sindee's flat, dressed in her pristine SOC whites, and looked at the damp shower tray. She had stood in the middle of the living room in Sindee's flat and looked round at the blood splash. On the TV was a framed photo of Sindee with Nick, heads together, smiling at the camera as if that was the way it had always been and would always be.

A forensic officer was dusting the TV for prints. The early evening news was on, and none of it was good.

"It's men who go there. It's men who stuff banknotes into the girls' garters and between their breasts and into their G-strings. It's men who sit close enough to lick and it's men who are getting hard under the strict dress code. You're a man. That's why you have to come with me. I don't think the Kandy Kave expects single women customers."

"You're a cop. You can go there any time."

"Officially. I want to go unofficially. At first, anyway."

Stella was driving back to AMIP-5 from the morgue, using her mobile phone on the hands-off earpiece, eating a chicken and mayo sandwich with her right hand, steering and changing gear with her left. When she stopped at the lights, a good citizen glanced across and pointed to his own ear: a note of criticism. Stella said, "Fuck off," then, "No, not you. Will you come?"

"It sounds as if I might."

"Funny. Will you?"

"Is this my only opportunity to see you, Stella? As a decoy at a lap-dancing club?"

"I could take DC Harriman."

"Why don't you?"

"Because he'd enjoy himself too much." She took a bite of sandwich and said, "Because I want it to be you."

They arranged a time and a place to meet. He said, "What if I find the girl of my dreams?"

Having made the one call, Stella had to make the other. He sounded distant, as if the phone was too far from his mouth. Then there was a dead pause, a sudden blank in the airwaves. She said, "George?"

"No. I'm here."

"I'll be late."

"Yes, I heard you. Okay. What time?"

"I don't know. I'm taking DC Harriman to a lap-dancing club."

"Are you? He'll enjoy that."

Stella felt she ought to say more. "Listen, why do men go there?" she asked. "What do you think it is?" Chips of sound came at her:

George's voice fragmenting. She said, "You're breaking up. I must be getting into a black zone."

"It's shopping," George told her. "It's mix and match . . ." He said something else—*wives* or *lives*—but the signal cut in and out for a moment more and then she lost him.

26

"I'll need everything," Anne Beaumont said. "Scene-of-crime reports, scene-of-crime photos and videos, autopsy reports, case notes, everything."

She and Stella were sitting on a bench in Hyde Park, close to Anne's office. Stella had picked up sandwiches and water at a local deli. Anne liked to get out for an hour when the weather held up. The room where she saw her clients sometimes seemed thick with pain. Just now, the clouds had broken; there were big, ragged patches of blue sky over London and there was a little warmth in the sun. Soon it would rain and the wind would take on a damp chill. Either way, the park was no refuge from bad air. They sat and ate, watching the people who passed.

Anne said, "See him?" One of London's homeless was going through the park, his hair matted into ropes, his clothes thick with filth. "It's likely that there are six to eight serial killers working in Britain at any given moment. He's not one of them."

"No?"

"No. *He* might be." Anne was indicating a man dressed in a blue suit and carrying an attaché case. "Though he's probably too old. Forty-five, would you say?"

"Around there."

"Too old," Anne confirmed, "though it's not a precise science. Also, we don't get that much practice. America has most of the world's serial killers."

"Why too old?"

"Serial killers are almost always young. Youngish. Not above forty usually, though it's foolish to generalize: leads to prescriptive thinking, which is dangerous. Your profile can mistakenly exclude the exception to the rule. And the point about serial killers is that they *are* exceptions to the rule."

"Because they're insane."

Anne laughed. "Christ, who knows what that means? They're all insane once they've been caught. Until then, they're likely to look and behave like Mr. Very Normal Blue Suit who just walked past."

"I'm taking Delaney to a lap-dancing club," Stella said. "In the course of business." Anne didn't reply. They ate their sandwiches in silence for a while, until Stella added, "I can't go on like this. I need some advice. Not instructions. Just an opinion would do."

"You're not booked in until Thursday," Anne observed. "Also, I'm on my lunch break."

"And theorizing about psychopaths, even though DI Sorley says no overtime."

"Psychopath is a loaded word. They're rare. With psychopaths, all bets are off. Forget the young/old thing, forget patterns, forget everything. Sociopath might be a closer bet, though we could be dealing with APD."

"What?"

"Antisocial Personality Disorder: none of these labels mean much in the end. Every case is different, every personality, too, even if the person in question is deranged."

"And we've got two," Stella observed. "One of them a woman."

"Which is really rare." Anne took a drink from her water bottle. "And I ought to point out that I can do what I like on my lunch break." There was silence between them for a moment, then she said, "A lap-dancing club because of the last victim?"

"Yes."

"Well, I guess it's all in a day's work. Let me know what it's like."

"Why?"

"I'm curious," Anne said, "aren't you?"

The wind picked up, shaking the trees and bringing the first small flush of rain. People in the park began to walk a little more quickly. Stella said, "Don't you ever tell people what to do?"

"Of course not. If I did that, they wouldn't need me. How do you think I can afford a house on the park?"

Stella said, "I bought the sandwiches. Give me a hint."

"Okay. Still got the dice?"

"Yes."

"Make a life decision."

Stella looked at her. "On a throw of the dice?"

"Okay," Anne said. "Don't."

The girls didn't take long to get naked. Stripping wasn't the issue; teasing wasn't the issue; getting right down to the Brazilian wax and doing airborne splits, that was the issue.

The girl doing it for Delaney was called Lola. She swayed and bucked and humped a few inches from his nose then turned her back, bent down slowly and looked at him through her spread legs. He pushed money into her suspender and asked Stella if it was an allowable expense.

She spoke without looking at him. "We're on a tight budget."

There was hard, hot music and smoky-soft multicolored lights. There was a smell of perfume and sweat. There were cocktails that cost more than the girls. Lola hoisted herself on to a pole and turned turtle, feet to the ceiling. Her breasts didn't change shape. Delaney swiveled sideways on his stool to take the dance area and the poles out of his eye line.

"Why are we here?" He had to speak in a controlled shout to get above the music. "What do you expect to find?"

Stella shrugged. "I'm not sure. I just wanted to get a look at the place before coming back as a copper. Of the three victims, Mandy Wallace was the one most likely to have weirdos on tap. I wanted to see this place up and working."

It was Sindee's mother who had told them that Sindee was Amanda-Jane and Amanda-Jane was really just Mandy.

"Weirdos?"

"Look around. What do you see?"

He shrugged. "A few lads out on a spree. Tourists. Business-men."

Stella recalled Anne Beaumont's observation in the park—not the down-and-out you walk round to avoid, not the wide-eyed loonie who talks to himself on the Tube; no—the guy in the business suit, the guy with the smooth shave and that attractive little flop to his hair.

Or that guy over there in the cheesy matching shirt and tie, his gaze fixed on Lola as she straddled the pole and dry-humped it. Or that guy with the moon face and the silly little blond goatee beard under his lower lip, smiling, breathing hard, getting a lap dance from a girl who was standing between his legs and leaning in, her breasts close enough to catch the dew from his breath.

"They have CCTV, don't they?" Delaney and Stella were in his flat, looking into the fridge. He poured two drinks and added, "There's a Pizza Heaven two doors down."

"Okay." She added ice to her vodka. The fridge had only ice. "Yeah, we'll take a look at their surveillance tapes, but they're usu-ally pretty low-grade: sometimes deliberately. Better if the faces of the judges and top cops and cabinet ministers are a bit blurry," De-laney was drinking Scotch. She wondered if he kept the vodka just for her. "What do you think when you go to a place like that?"

He shrugged. "I don't go to places like that. Did you imagine I might?"

"No, not really. But what did you think tonight?"

"I thought these were strong, empowered women who were choosing to exploit God-given resources to beat an otherwise un-avoidable socio-economic trap."

"I'm sorry I asked." After a moment, she said, "Okay, how do you think other men might see them? The lads on a spree. The busi-nessmen."

"I think they think they're snatch."

"You do have a way with words."

"American Hot, Marguerita, Four Seasons . . . ?" He had picked up a takeaway menu from a rack on the counter.

"You mention the CCTV," she suggested, "because logic dictates that other people would guess it was there . . ."

"And so wouldn't go to the club to select a victim."

"Someone selected Mandy Wallace."

"So maybe he found her somewhere else."

"*They* found her."

Delaney looked up. "Yeah . . . That's an odd thing, isn't it?"

"Team Killers. That's what they're called."

"Sounds like a spectator sport."

"Yes," she said, "I imagine that in some ways that's exactly what it is." When he looked at her, puzzled, she added: "It's my turn, so you watch. Now it's *my* turn, so *you* watch."

"You think it's like that?"

"I don't know." She took a sip of her drink and suddenly felt weary to her bones. She said it again, "I don't know," though this time it meant something else. She put her head in her hands and realized that she was close to tears.

Delaney crossed to her and held her. They stood for a moment, Stella with her arms turned in and her face covered. Then she lifted her face to him and they kissed one another, a brush of the lips, then something more.

She said, "I give in."

She took his hand and covered her breast with it. He let it smolder there for a moment, then took her hand in return and started to lead her out of the kitchen.

I give in, I give in.

But when her phone rang, she barely hesitated before answering it.

"There's something missing here," Anne Beaumont said, "and I can't decide what. There's a picture, but it's not complete."

"You're looking at the SOC material?"

"That's right. And I'm looking for similarities that lie beyond the signature."

"The what?"

"The signature. Which, in this case, is the method: multiple wounds, then a final slash to the throat. It's a power thing: a control thing. Heard of John Wayne Gacy?"

"American serial killer."

"Yes. He liked to take his victims to the point of death, then haul them back so he could torture them some more. He used to ask, 'What's it like—knowing you're going to die?'"

"But that's not what you're—"

"I just feel I haven't got all the information. Some sort of pointer . . . I don't know. Did someone check the personal belongings of the victims?"

"Routine check, yes."

"Was anything reported missing? I don't know if it's that, but sometimes it's part of the pattern that sadistic killers will take something away with them."

"What sort of a something?"

"An item of jewelry, a photo, something that the victim would have had close to them, something intimate." Anne paused for a moment. Stella looked at Delaney, who was leaning against the counter reading that day's paper. Current affairs, she thought. Anne said, "Sometimes they take a piece of the victim. *That* intimate."

"Not in this case," Stella said. "I was at the post-mortems."

"No . . . If they did take something away, whatever it was will tell me something about them. What they value; how they see the victim; maybe what makes them choose one person over another. Look, I'm not at all sure I've got this right, but the way the crime sheets read, the killings seem oddly impersonal. This kind of murder is very personal. I run the thing in my head like a movie—possible scenarios, possible scenes—and it's as if the sequence is incomplete."

"Okay," Stella said, "we'll try to find out. Stolen items."

"Trophy-hunting," Anne said, "that's the technical term."

"It's always good to have the technical term."

"Are you ever so slightly tetchy?"

"Not at all."

"Are you with Delaney?"

"Yes."

"Ah . . . I'll let you get back to it, then."

"To what?"

"Whatever you were doing. Whatever the dice said."

Delaney spoke without looking up from the paper. "You might not know this, but the greatest threats to global longevity are Third World debt, population movement, and environment degradation. Also, retro-chic is a thing of the past."

"I have to go," she said.

"Of course you do."

"The phone call . . ."

"Yes. Absolutely." He allowed her the lie. "I'll come down with you."

They stepped out into the street. One A.M. and the neighborhood was busy. The rain had held off, but the wind was back, rattling street signs and shifting garbage. Delaney turned toward the snappy neon logo of Pizza Heaven. Turned his back. Stella started her car and put the radio on loud: sounds of the seventies, that nothing decade.

She undressed in the dark. George felt her get into bed. She was hot, as if she might have a fever. She lay facing out for a while, then turned over and he could smell the booze on her breath.

She tried Anne Beaumont's technique of running in her mind a film of the murders, two killers with blanks where their faces should be, one using the belt to tie her hands, using the tape to close her mouth, that would be the man; the other watching, taking out the knife, the razor, that would be the woman; or maybe the man carried the knife, maybe the man started things with the knife; but then, no, go back, first things first, they were taking their clothes off, making a neat pile of them, the woman taking his hand and laying it on her breast.

Delaney's face showed up in the dark and Stella shook the dice. She was asleep before she could see how they fell.

27

Amanda-Jane Wallace, aka Mandy, aka Sindee, is sitting on the floor, her mouth taped, her eyes wide. Because her hands are tied behind her back, she is using her legs to move away: knees up, shuffle-push, knees up again, trying to get a little more leverage with her bound hands by pressing them to the floor, but it isn't very effective. She can't get far and she can't go fast.

She isn't looking at the camera. Her eyes are fixed on Donna as she moves into frame. The trick is to get the tape tight across the mouth, sealing the lips, because they can't make much of a noise that way, can't go much beyond a kind of shrill mooing, and Sonny has done just that. He's good at that.

Donna is taking her time, she's choosing her moment. You can hear her laughing as Mandy kicks out at her. She circles and Mandy tries to circle with her, but there's no way she's going to be fast enough, and even if she were, she's naked and Donna has the knife. Of course, Donna's naked, too, because of the splash factor. They always have to allow for the splash factor. That's part of it, the being naked; it's a part he particularly likes.

Donna comes in from behind and her hand moves fast. You can see the tendons stand out suddenly on Mandy's neck, you can see how her whole body convulses.

"That's nothing," Sonny tells her, his voice close-to because he's handling the camera. "That's nothing. We haven't got going yet. We've hardly started."

There's a bit more of Donna moving and cutting, of Mandy arching, her legs thrashing, then you hear the sound of sirens outside in the street and everything is still for a while, except for Mandy shaking her head; mooing and crying and shaking her head. Then Donna speaks, but it's difficult to catch what she says: *Finish. Better finish.* She moves behind Mandy and takes her under the chin.

It had been a disappointment. The others had lasted much longer: the girl who looked like a model and the woman with the flame red hair.

Sonny rewound the tape. He wanted to get right to the beginning: to the moment when he and Donna were first inside the flat. He wanted to see the shock of surprise on Mandy's face when she first began to realize something was wrong: the slack look that came with the first rush of fear. He played it a couple of times, holding her in freeze-frame to get the best effect, then got up and closed the curtains because the early-morning sun was striking in through the window and bringing errant reflections to the screen. He released the freeze-frame and let the tape play.

When Donna came into the room, Mandy was in close-up, Sonny taping her mouth, kneeling on her arms, paying no heed to her feeble kicking. He and Donna were both fully clothed at this point, but it was still a good moment. Mandy was dazed from the blow, but not unconscious and it was there in her eyes: the knowledge of everything that was yet to come.

Donna stood by the door and watched with him for a short while, then she asked: "Where were you last night?"

"At the pub."

She sauntered across and sat on the far end of the sofa, her long legs stretched out. Donna was tall and slim and had heavy, shoulder-length hair that was usually glossy black, though she hadn't bothered to treat it for a while and the nondescript brown had begun to grow back in. Men who walked behind her in the street saw that height, that slender back, the long jet hair that swayed, catching the light, and would turn to look. It happened all the time, a backward glance followed by glazed indifference. The figure was great, but Donna wasn't pretty. The men saw the sloping chin, the hooky nose, the thin lips and they dropped their gaze; she was a disappointment to them.

"In the pub?"

"That's right."

"In the pub until nearly three A.M.?"

They watched in silence for a moment: Mandy Wallace kicking out, traveling backward on her haunches, Donna moving round her with the knife like an artist surveying a painting in progress, adding a touch here, a touch there.

"Was it three?"

"I heard you come in."

Another pause. Mandy swiveling, turning away to protect her face and getting it across the shoulder, across the arm. Donna said, "You went back."

"No, I didn't."

"You went back to the Kandy Kave. It's on your clothes."

"What?"

"On your shirt, on your jacket. Perfume. Where they got close to you. Had a lap dance, did you?" Sonny went to freeze-frame. He was staring at the screen. "We don't go back," she said. "We agreed that we wouldn't go back."

"Back to the places where they died."

"Also not back there. Not back to that club."

"Who would know me?"

Donna said what Delaney had said: "They have surveillance."

"I'm just a face in the crowd."

Donna sighed, then gave a little laugh. "Of course you are, you stupid bastard. That's the problem."

Sonny released the freeze-frame and Mandy's torment came back to life. When it was over, Donna straightened up and smiled as Sonny came in for a close-up. Then there were just some domestic details: Sonny in the shower, Donna in the shower, Sonny mugging for the camera, Donna getting dressed. She was wearing the same jeans and sneakers that she had on now, but this morning she had chosen a Disneyland Paris sweatshirt.

She said, "I thought you would. I thought you'd go back there. I saw the look on your face after the first time."

"You should have come. You'd've liked it."

"I don't think so."

"Just to choose, Donna. Just to look and choose."

"Don't go there again."

"Okay."

She looked at him, unblinking, but he kept his face turned to the screen. "Don't go there again, Sonny."

"I won't." After a moment, he said, "Do you want to do something?"

"I don't know."

"Come on, Donna. Let's do something." He ejected Mandy and took the Janis Parker video out of its slipcase. "Come on."

Donna kicked off her sneakers and pulled the Disneyland sweatshirt over her head. "Don't go there again," she said.

Sonny nodded. "I promise." He turned to her, his moon face shining. His moon face with a silly little blond goatee under the lower lip.

28

Sue Chapman had logged eight calls that morning from people wanting to say how much they had enjoyed killing Amanda-Jane Wallace, and how and why. The "how" brought eight warped imaginations to the fore, each with its own particular techniques and quirks, each with its own black versions of pain and the response to pain. The "why" was depressingly similar: she was a bitch-whore, a whore-bitch, a filthy diseased whore-bitch, a diseased filthy bitch-whore. The permutations were limited but they certainly made the point that Mandy had deserved to die.

Sue filed the call sheets along with those from the previous day, and with the calls relating to Janis Parker and Nesta Cameron. All in all, it seemed that the three women had been murdered by twenty-seven different people. Well, not people: men. She turned the fresh calls over to Maxine Hewitt, who scanned them before putting them on Stella's desk with a note that said, *All nuts.* Stella took copies of them for Anne Beaumont, because *nuts* was a good, brief description of whoever had killed Mandy and Janis and Nesta.

Pete Harriman came over with a crime report and a note from Stella that he couldn't read. Stella told him it was "trophy" and maybe he should get an eye check. "Take Maxine," she said. "We need to talk to all the friends, all the relatives."

"All the friends?" Pete was thinking of the fifty people who had been at Janis's party.

"Close friends."

"Jewelry and photos," Pete said, looking at Stella's note.

"Jewelry and photos and ornaments and fluffy toys . . . anything personal, anything that ought to have been in the apartments but wasn't."

"What's the point?"

"Trophy hunters are a special breed. Might give us a better idea of who we're looking for."

"Who?"

"Okay, not who—what type."

"Our profiler says." There was a hint of impatience in Harriman's tone. Stella looked at him and he shrugged. "I know all that stuff. They say it's probably a white possibly unemployed male most likely to be between the ages of twenty and forty, either married or single, who might have hated his mother and is almost certainly impotent, and we're supposed to find that helpful."

"Profiles have been accurate in the past."

"Looks good after the event. Conventional police work gets you to a white thirty-year-old who lost his job a year before and can't get it up and the profiler says, 'There you go.'"

Stella laughed and gave him the victims'-known-contacts list.

"Do it." He handed her the crime report by way of exchange and she glanced at it. "What's this?"

"Same night Amanda-Jane Wallace was killed, same street, some middle-class hero took a baseball bat to an intruder, cracked his sternum, made a triple-nine call. The street was full of response vehicles and uniforms and paramedics, this was the early hours of the morning . . ."

"About when Mandy died."

"The call was logged at three-fifteen A.M. Sam Burgess put Mandy's death somewhere between then and three-forty-five. Pretty accurate. So, yes—about when Mandy died."

"It's why they stopped," Stella said. "Why they killed her before they'd gone very far. Uniforms all over the place, lights, people waking up and rubbernecking. They had to end it."

Harriman nodded. "Looks right."

"Let me have a report," Stella said, "as soon as you've done the trophy check."

Harriman glanced across to where Maxine Hewitt was sitting at her desk, arms raised to the ceiling, fingers locked, in a full-length yawn-and-stretch. It was a position that advertised the curve and loft of her breasts. He said, "Do you think Maxine does a turn?"

Stella smiled encouragingly. "How could she resist you?"

The mail went both ways: an out-tray of confessions from nuts *to* Anne Beaumont, and an in-tray of catch-up and theories *from* Anne Beaumont. Sue brought the incoming to Stella's desk along with a cup of coffee.

If you've stopped smoking, there are some times that are more difficult than others: the first coffee of the day; the mid-morning cup of coffee; lunchtime coffee; the coffee that comes after dinner. Any cup of coffee. As she read through Anne's notes, Stella drank her coffee and cocked her head toward Andy Greegan's desk, because Andy was smoking one cigarette while a second, forgotten, smoldered in his ashtray.

Stella: here's some basic stuff on serial killers. Homework. Not nice. This is for starters.

Anne.

BACKGROUND
Women serial killers (Keheller typology)

I'm listing all types here because, as you'll see, there's often crossover. These categories are not exclusive one from another. Forensic evidence indicates that we're dealing with TK types (see below), but you might find other connections. Anything's helpful.

Black Widow: marries, kills her husband, marries again, kills that husband, marries again and so on until she gets caught. Also kills relatives. Generally thought of as a gain-related crime, though BWs seem to kill anyone with whom they have a strong personal relationship.

Angel of Death: usually works in a hospital/nursing home/hospice/geriatric care unit. It's a power thing. Typically, the AoD has the choice of who lives, who dies. She has the means, of course, being a nurse or carer. Most often, her victims will be old/frail/ill and close to death anyway, so she feels less guilt than she otherwise would. Which, generally, is none.

Sexual Predator: speaks for itself. Rare in women, but documented. Like their male counterparts, SPs are usually early middle aged and tend to be mobile. Work off fantasy, fueled by deep ontological insecurity. "Seduce and kill" is the motto.

Revenge Killer: most RE killings by women are one-offs, so this category also rare. REs often start with family members, then grow more ambitious—which makes sense: payback killings center on parents or older siblings who made life hell. Deep and unmanageable anger the spur here. Victims often lookalikes for original tormentors, or people in positions of power.

Profit Killer: female PR killers also rare, though it's thought many go undetected. Contract killings by women almost un- heard of, but more domestic activity has been documented. Fam- ily murder a factor (where family wealth involved), also scams and cons set up to cheat victims of their assets before murdering them to keep them quiet.

Team Killers: okay, this is us. Not uncommon. TKs are a third to half of all female serial killers. Brady-Hindley, Fred & Rosemary West, others in the USA. Various combinations: male/female, male/male, female/female, family teams. Most often male/female. Female/female rare, although I read of a crossover case where a lesbian team were also Angel of Death killers who murdered to enhance their sexual activity, which I suppose also puts them in the SP category—a grand slam. In most instances of male/female TK, the man leads. It's usually a sex-based crime, though the vic- tims are often robbed. (Was this so with our three? I'm not talk- ing about trophies: was money taken?) Also, sadism is often a factor. As it is here.

Sadism

Almost invariably sexual. Usually occurs periodically, and after overheated, long-term sexual fantasizing. We know our TKs are sadists from the consistent wound-patterns on the victims. There's a difference here that you ought to consider. We were talking about psychopaths the other day. Psychopaths tend to have no sense of their victims' suffering: they blank on it; it doesn't register. Sadists love it: it feeds them.

Did you say that forensic evidence—the distribution of DNA in this case—tended to show that the woman was the more ac- tive? That's very unusual if true.

Sadists often select their victims for specifically personal rea- sons. They remind them of, or they represent, someone the killer wants to punish. Which is why the aim is often to humiliate and degrade the people they torture. Torture itself, of course, is a form of degradation.

Bondage (our victims were all tied) might be a way of rendering the victim helpless, but that also contributes to the killers' sexual excitement (bondage being a fairly common if mild sexual perversion. Ever try it?).

By the same token, the tape over the mouth is certainly there, I'd think, to prevent the victim from being heard, but in many cases it's the killers' way of maintaining the victim's anonymity.

Many killers of this kind need to think of their victims as a "thing" and to keep any exchange between them, especially verbal, to an absolute minimum. This is not so much because their better nature will be appealed to if the person they've chosen is allowed to represent him/herself as an individual—mother, brother, someone someone loves—sort of thing. Our killers don't possess better natures. But if the "thing" becomes a "person," then whatever fantasy the killer has used to overlay the encounter begins to break down.

Notes: may be useful/strike a chord/remind you of something
Often present at SOC: (1) Signs of ritual, (2) Signature—elements that always appear. This can be wound pattern, as with our three cases, but also has to do with means of control (hands tied, mouth taped), or certain word patterns (this will only apply if a future victim survives to tell the tale). It can also manifest itself in the way the body is "arranged" by the killer—left in a certain pose, perhaps, or maybe the killer will have written something on the dead person or on the wall (often in the victim's blood). There's also trophy taking: we've talked about this.

My thoughts so far center on the basic characteristics displayed by SKs together with the signature relating to the three cases.

1.   These people are intra-species predators, impossible to pick out in a crowd. They look like you and me. Well, not you and me, perhaps, but they look pretty ordinary. They know how to adapt their behavior patterns to the norm. However, they're also likely to be risk-takers: impulsive. They're easily tempted.

2.   They are incapable of love. In fact, incapable of affection and feeling of any sort. But they know how to act it so it looks real. Feels that way, too, I suspect, if you're the object of attention.

3.   They are very likely to come from broken homes. Lack of a father figure is a common factor.

4.   They will have practiced on animals. Sorry if that sounds gross. Somewhere in their backgrounds you'll find maimed cats and mutilated dogs . . . or something of that sort. I'm pretty sure of it. There is also likely to be evidence of other destructive behavior—arson being high on the list.

5.   They will be easily bored.

6.   They will be manipulative; also accomplished liars.

7.   They like to play games. Don't assume that all your supposed crank calls are from cranks. They might enjoy taunting the victims' relatives, too.

8.   They might well return to the scene of the crime. Re-visiting excites them. They often come to think of the sites of their killings as something akin to holy ground.

SKs talking about themselves: just background
"What's one less person on the face of the earth anyway?"—Ted Bundy.

"I had no other thrill of happiness. I was killing myself, but it was the bystander who died."—Dennis Nilsen.

"It's like being in a movie. You're just playing a part."—Henry Lee Lucas.

"Human nature is a nuisance. It fills me with disgust."—John Haigh.

"I was cleaning up the streets."—Peter Sutcliffe.

"Clowns get away with murder."—John Wayne Gacy.

Get the picture? One thing to remember, though: these "authentic" voices could be fake. Like I said, they're consummate actors and game-players. You might be hearing what they want you to hear; thinking what they want you to think.

Hope all this helps. More when we meet. You might want to circulate this to AMIP-5.

Stella took a copy of Anne's report in to Mike Sorley, who lobbed it on to the far side of his desk.

"Just what I need. More paper."

By way of exchange, he handed Stella a note from the press office, which was attached to a note from a tabloid. The tabloid editor was confirming that his paper intended to break the news that a serial killer was at work in London. It spoke of the public's right to know. The note from the press office asked Sorley how he wanted to play things.

"I'll make a statement," Sorley said. "Minimal stuff. Which won't keep it off the front pages, of course. I want you to talk to the press people. See if there's anything we can do: anything clever."

"Like?"

"If I knew, I'd be doing it. Ways of keeping the press out of our hair but also getting what we want from them. Talk to the profiler, too. The people who killed these women read the papers, don't they?"

Looking for news of themselves, Stella thought; a strange combination, to be famous and anonymous.

She wondered if she was famous down on the Harefield Estate: the cop who killed Nike Man. Sorley was looking at her, waiting for a response, and she opened her mouth to say, "I killed a man. I didn't report it. It was self-defense, but I didn't report it." Instead she said, "I've got a couple of contacts in the press."

29

Anne Beaumont was looking at a map of west London.

Stella said, "Apart from the fact that they're all local, there's nothing to get from location. Frankly, there aren't enough. Three killings, three venues: it forms a triangle, but it doesn't allow for triangulation, if you see what I mean. One by Notting Hill Gate, one up toward the Saints, the third off North End Road. It doesn't mean they're living in the neighborhood."

"It doesn't mean they're not. They might like the idea of being close to where they kill, living on their hunting ground. A thousand people walk past those flats every day, along those streets. Your killers might well be among them: getting their shiver of recollection, getting their thrill of pride. Who would know?"

"It's going to break in the press; probably within the next couple of days. Is there any way we can spin it that would help?"

They were working on their lunch break again; it had to be that or after Anne's last client of the evening. Serial murder was something on the side, but sad people were a way of life. They were down in Anne's small conservatory-kitchen, where she had made spaghetti with a supermarket sauce and opened a bag of salad. She poured two glasses of Chardonnay, then put the bottle back in the fridge, as if she were wine monitor. Although signing Anne on to the case had been her idea, Stella was uneasy about being there. The kitchen seemed off-limits, the food made things oddly casual, and the talk wasn't about her.

"It's a fair bet that they'll enjoy reading about themselves," Anne said. "They're egotists, that's part of the make-up, but it's not the egotism of the movie star or the sports hero, it's more like the egotism of the child. If people are pathologically self-centered, it's often because they don't know where their center lies: can't locate it. You might try seeding some false information that other papers will pick up on, something that they'll want to contest or correct. A way of getting them to make contact. Writing to the papers or taunting the cops is often part of the pattern."

"What sort of false information?"

"No one knows they're team killers, am I right?"

"Yes."

"Say the murders are the work of a single individual. If they're thrill killers, someone's going to feel left out."

"Set them against each other?"

Anne shrugged. "It's just an idea. Don't forget, they don't know that you know there are two of them, any more than the public at large knows. It's your one ace in the hole." She sipped her wine. "Talking of aces in the hole, what happened after I called you?"

"What?"

"Cards, dice, Delaney."

"I went home. Why?"

"There was something in your voice."

Stella ate in silence for a short while; Anne waited. Silence and patience were part of their usual rhythm. "It was close, if you want to know."

"Of course I want to know."

"It was close and I hadn't used the dice."

"That's close."

"Do you know how weird this feels—pasta and wine and being down here and talking like this?"

"I could bill you for it if that would make you feel better. How was the lap-dancing club?"

"I have to go back."

"That good?"

"No: back as a copper. Frankly, it was odd. Girls doing the splits in Delaney's face and all I could think about was my last smear test. He was looking at the girls as if it was part of his undercover cop routine, I was looking at the punters and trying not to be noticed." She paused. "It was sort of sexy at one remove, does that make sense? Watching the men watching the girls, knowing that they were all nursing hard-ons."

"Were they?"

"I suppose so."

"Was Delaney?"

Stella laughed. "Is this gossip or analysis?"

"There's not much of a difference."

The wind had shifted and the weather had become erratic, bruised clouds with sunlight behind them. The glass bevels in the conservatory projected fragments of rainbow.

Stella said, "I'm working on the assumption that they'll have done it before."

"For sure."

"The question is, where? There's no record of anything in London that replicates these killings."

"And they might not always have been a team," Anne said. "Think of that."

She walked across the park, a long diagonal to bring her out at the top of Bayswater Road. The clouds had backed off toward the east and the park was crowded. The wind was picking up again, making the trees lift and swirl; the leaf-roar was an echo of the traffic on the parkside roads.

Stella realized she was half-looking out for Mr. Normal Blue Suit, as if some sort of prescience in Anne had singled him out; as if he might be her man, one of a killing team. They were all normal, she thought: the office workers with their sandwiches and Coke, the cyclists, the joggers, the young mothers with babies in buggies. Normal was the problem.

A man and a woman were walking across the grass, hand in hand, chatting to one another. Stella looked at them and thought,

Why not? Partners in blood, talking about who next, where next. Discussing their infallible plan for foxing their victims into opening their doors, saying, "Hello. How are you? Come in." Reminiscing about how it had been, how it had felt with Janis and Nesta and Mandy.

The couple passed, suddenly silent, as if Stella's thoughts had come to them on the wind. Her phone rang and it was George: just checking. Late nights were what he expected, but, who knows, maybe tonight they'd have the chance to eat together, share a bottle of wine, ask How was your day?

"I'm not sure," she said. "It's tough to say."

"I could make a meal. That's what I'd thought of doing. Or we could go out."

"I'll call you," she said. "Is that okay?"

"That's fine," he said. "Make it if you can."

"Yes, I will. I'll make it if I can."

A touch of annoyance in her voice, driven by guilt. The dice in her pocket, waiting to be asked.

30

Stella and Maxine Hewitt went to the Kandy Kave at five, an hour before the club opened for business. With the house lights up full, no music, no girls on-stage and the tables empty, the place had a sad, stale air about it. Gerry Moreno sat in his office and bitched about the inconvenience.

"These girls double and overlap," he said. "The music's all set up. They each have their own tunes, you know? They've timed their routines to that music. It's a well-oiled machine. They have to be in costume and ready on time. Six o'clock."

Stella thought that "double and overlap" sounded like pole technique. "Amanda-Jane Wallace was murdered," she said. "We're investigating and you're cooperating, okay?"

Gerry leaned back in his chair and looked at the ceiling. A muscle ticked in his jaw.

"We'll be talking to the girls," Stella informed him. "First we thought we'd speak to you."

Gerry lifted his hands like someone surrendering. "It's lousy that she's dead. I'm upset. What can I say?"

"You have a surveillance system," Stella said. It wasn't a question. Four screens set into the wall of Gerry's office gave a fishbowl view of the club. Bar staff were setting up and the guy who worked the lighting rig was running through his spot sequence. "How long do you keep the tapes?"

"We don't."

"Why not?"

"They're on in case of any trouble: over-eager punters, drunks, whatever. If nothing happens, what's the point?"

"You record over?"

"Sure."

"Keep the tapes."

"Say again?"

"From now on, I want you to keep the tapes. I'll send an officer over for them each morning, okay?"

"You're not saying a punter killed her? Someone who'd seen her in the club?"

"You think that's impossible?"

Gerry sighed heavily. "Will you be telling the girls this?"

"We'll have to. It's going to break in the press pretty soon, anyway."

"It'll spook them."

Maxine asked, "Where do they think she is?"

"Working at Spearmint Rhino, I expect. Girls come and go." He was looking at his watch. "Could we get on with it? We open in less than an hour."

"What we're going to need from you," Stella said, "is your employment records, notes on your current staff, notes on anyone who once worked here but has since left, notes on any casual labor, bar staff or whoever, any regular punters you know about, any party bookings or corporate-entertainment evenings."

"That's a lot of men," Gerry said.

"Men and women," Maxine told him. "Everyone. Ex-dancers included."

"You're kidding me," Gerry said, "aren't you?"

They were called Raven and Topaz and Opal and Belle and Pepper and Toni and Kelly. They assembled in the club and sat on a banquette looking lost and overdressed. Stella told them that Mandy had been murdered, but that was all she said. Nothing about how, nothing about the other deaths. All the girls asked the same question: could it have been a punter? They all got the same answer: it could have been anyone.

Stella and Maxine took two groups, separating them and getting down to the bare essentials: real name, how well did you know Mandy Wallace, do you sleep with the punters, did she sleep with the punters, was there any single punter who asked for her a lot, has anyone hit on you recently, did she leave alone on the night she was killed?

The answers were: quite well/not well at all/only through the job. Sometimes/never. Yes/not sure/don't know. Don't think so/never noticed. Yes/no. Who knows?

The girls went to work with a few minutes to spare and Stella and Maxine sat at a back table in the club comparing notes as the early-evening punters came in, the house lights went down, the music started up, and Topaz and Kelly came out and kicked into their pole routines.

Stella raised her voice to a half-shout to get over the music. "Only one who's worried about a punter: one of yours, Belle, otherwise known as . . . what's her name?"

Maxine was watching the stage. "Karen Cooper."

"Right . . ." Stella was reading Maxine's notes. "She'd lap dance for him five or six times a night, he didn't like it if she danced for other men, asked her to go home with him, she wouldn't, she thinks he's followed her."

Stella said, "I think I need to know more about this guy."

"Okay." Maxine was watching Topaz as she worked the pole, crouching, knees angled wide.

Stella got up. She said, "Wait here. Enjoy the show."

The dressing room was mirrors and flesh. Wherever you looked, naked girls or the reflections of naked girls. Mirrors facing mirrors. A tits and arse kaleidoscope. Stella sat in a corner with Belle while the other girls got into their working clothes, made up, talked about nothing in particular. Mandy Wallace, it seemed, was on the taboo list. Except for Stella and Belle.

"What do I call you?"

"It doesn't matter. Karen."

"Tell me about this punter. The persistent one."

"He's not a bother. Big tipper."

"How long has he been coming here?"

"About a month, so far as I know. It's a month since he started asking for me all the time. I wouldn't have noticed him before that. They all look the same, you know? They're all types."

"What kind of types?"

"Business types, city types, laddish types. Same suits, same hair, same tongues hanging out."

"You told my colleague that he's followed you."

"A couple of times, yeah. I think it was him."

"And he always asks for you. Tries to monopolize your time."

"As long as he pays . . ."

"You don't mind?"

Karen shrugged and made a slight grimace. "Yeah, well, he's a bit freaky. Nothing he does, really. The way he looks. The things he says."

"The way he looks . . . ?"

"He just looks at my face. When I'm dancing for him. Stares at me, you know."

"Just your face?"

"When you lap dance for a bloke, he's getting a mega-close-up of the business, isn't he? With most of them, it's eyes everywhere. This one looks at me, you know? Not at my tits and the rest. *Me*."

"But he's not a bother, you say. You don't feel threatened?"

"I didn't, no, not till I met you."

"Not even when he followed you?"

"If it was . . . I think it was him. I just got into a cab. It wasn't a problem."

Karen was smoothing oil on to her legs. She moved up to her arms, her breasts. Stella remembered Gerry Moreno's remark: a well-oiled machine.

"He's asked you to sleep with him?"

"Half of them do."

"And . . ."

"No, not often. Now and again, if the guy looks okay."

"What, good-looking, young . . . ?"

"Rich."

"But not this guy."

"No."

"Not rich?"

"Don't want to encourage him. He's taken a fix on me, you know? I'm the star of all his dirty dreams. If you're going home with a punter, you want it to be nice night, thanks a lot, here's the dosh, see you around."

"The ones you sleep with, do they come back?"

"Oh, yeah. That's all right. You get a handy tip. If they want another go, you tell them once is enough. They move on."

"And the things he says . . ."

"What?"

"A moment ago, you said something about the way he looks and the things he says."

"Oh, yeah. Most of them just sit still and watch. Don't say anything. Some tell you what they want to do, no surprises there. They think they're being ever so exotic. If only they knew how many times I've heard it before. This guy doesn't go in for any of that. He makes a proposal."

"What sort of proposal?"

"No, a *proposal*. He says he wants to marry me. I'm on in a couple of minutes."

"What does he look like? How would I recognize him?"

Karen gave Stella a description. She'd been dancing in the guy's face on and off for the last month, so it was pretty accurate. "He hasn't been in all week, so he won't be in tonight. It's a pattern. Next week, he'll be here." The description nudged something at the back of Stella's mind, but the connection faded as soon as it was made.

Karen got up and went to the wall of mirrors and repaired her make-up, leaning in with no hint of bulge or sag. She had a body straight from the Barbie box: silicone, collagen, botox, lipo.

Stella wondered what it felt like, being sculpted for men.

She gave Maxine the description. "The story is he won't be in for the rest of this week. He alternates."

"He works a night shift," Maxine said. "One week on, one week off."

"It's possible."

"You want someone in here every night?"

Stella nodded. "Until we eliminate him."

"Is that what you expect?"

"He sounds like a sad type to me. There must be a lot of men who get obsessed with the girls, wouldn't you think? Men with wives and kids and crappy jobs. Men who'd like to go back twenty years and start over. I expect he's one of those."

"I'll stay for a bit if you like," Maxine offered. "No problem."

"Sure, why not?" Stella smiled. "Don't ask for a dance. The budget won't run to it."

She could feel Maxine's eyes on her back as she left.

31

Delaney was reading through Anne Beaumont's notes, which, strictly speaking, was against the law.

He said, "I'm not a reporter, Stella, you know that. I'm a features writer."

"You know reporters."

"I know some. And one of the things you can rely on is that they've got a pretty good nose for being set up."

"Someone'll go for it. A hot story, and the chance to be ahead of the pack."

"A hot story's one thing. Most people prefer it to be an accurate hot story."

"When you say people, do you mean journos? Because my experience of them has been that they don't give a flying fuck for accuracy."

"You might be right. But if they're going to run a dodgy story, they at least like the dodginess to be of their own manufacture. They wouldn't take kindly to having a copper lead them by the nose."

"How would they ever know? Would they be likely to find a connection? Do you talk about us?"

"Stella, I don't even talk about us when I'm with you."

"I need to draw these bastards out, John. Mostly, with coppering, it's battle lines drawn. Crooks over there, us over here, little excursions into no man's land. And the signs are usually plain to see. If it looks like drugs, then it probably is drugs. If it looks territorial, it'll show. Someone does a bank or a wages van, well, you look at the area, look at the method, you're already halfway there. The unsolved stuff is petty crime; that, and anything that comes out of left field: anything without a history."

She was lying full-length on his sofa, eyes closed, her hands clasped behind her head. She looked pale; her eyelids were veined with blue, dusty blue shadows under her eyes.

"But then, even muggings have an MO and some sort of overall pattern. Kids jacking mobile phones, old folk having their pensions lifted. It's tough to deal with, but you know about the black spots, the incidence of truancy in the area, that kind of thing. With killings like these, there are no connections. No gangs, no dealers, no informants, no fixers, minders. I need an edge."

"What do you want said?"

"That it's the work of a man. That no one else is involved. Imply that the police are at a loss. Don't go into detail about the way the women were killed."

"I thought you said the journo that called forensics had all that detail."

"He has. Not that it's two people, let alone that it's a man and a woman, but he knows about the multiple wounds. I'm going to try to get the press office to put pressure on him not to reveal the MO on the grounds that it could be prejudicial."

"Who is he?"

"Larry Stubbs."

"Yeah, freelance, a chancer, he'll sell to the highest bidder."

"He's already sold it. We're negotiating with the editor."

"Lots of luck."

"The important thing is to get our version into the press."

"I can see why you want to say that you're clueless—"

"They feel safer, more inclined to take risks—"

"—but why make it seem that it's the man?"

"For one thing, it helps weed out the cranks: all those sick creeps who are so eager to confess. They won't know it's a team. It also means that we can tell the real thing if we hear it."

"You mean one of the killers might phone?"

"You read Anne Beaumont's report. They're risk-takers and game-players. But there's another reason: maybe we'll manage to annoy the woman. Prick her ego. Make her want to bring herself into the picture."

"You really think she'll want to do that?"

Stella turned sideways on the sofa to take the light out of her eyes. "We think she's the team leader."

"What?"

"She's the instigator."

"You mean, she does the killing?"

"She's certainly not in the background, the DNA traces tell us that. If the press story cuts her out of the picture . . ." She paused. "Who knows? It's all guesswork."

He asked, "What do you want this to be: reliable source? Police spokesperson? Who shall I quote?"

"Quote me."

Delaney made a few notes, then got up and poured himself a whiskey. He said, "Stella, do you want a drink?" but she had gone to sleep almost as soon as they'd finished talking. He walked over to the sofa and watched her while she slept, her lips slightly parted, the blue stain under her eyes deepening. He took a lock of hair off her cheek and bent to drop a kiss, undetectably, alongside her mouth.

What am I going to do with you?

Maxine Hewitt clocked off at ten and flagged down a taxi by Campden Hill. She called her friend, the one Stella had seen her kissing a couple of nights before.

She said, "Know where I've been tonight?"

"Wherever it was, your phone was off." A pause, then: "Police work. Bad-guy business."

"I was in a lap-dancing club."

"Without me?"

"Well, you're right—it was police business."

"Silicone city."

"Some of them, not all. Pretty . . . *toned*, you know."

"Sounds as if you had a good time."

"Well, I was certainly thinking about having a good time. Having a good time was definitely on my mind."

"Where are you now?"

"In a taxi."

"Come over. I want to hear all about it."

"I gave the cabbie your address."

"Good thinking."

Maxine switched off the phone and lounged back in her seat. She liked the solitude of taxis. The club had been weird: sitting alone, watching the girls, watching the punters . . . and the punters, some of them, watching her, wondering what she was doing there, a girl on her own. Waiting for someone? Waiting for anyone?

A few had come over and offered to buy her a drink, to keep her company, to take her home, if that was her game. Maxine had smiled and said, No thanks. She said it in a way that made them think that she hadn't found what she was looking for. And she hadn't. The man she was hoping to see hadn't come into the club, hadn't been asking Belle for dance after dance, hadn't glanced at Maxine and thought, *Maybe* . . . If she'd seen him, she would have known him at once from Belle's description.

Round face, a touch overweight, bright blond hair, so yellow it must be dyed, and a silly little blond goatee beard. He sounded like a real loser.

She woke up and he was kissing her. Kissing her awake. He was definitely off-limits, and she laid a hand against his shoulder, saying, "I have to go. What time is it? I have to go," but he didn't give her an answer, just moved her hand, gently, and kissed her once again, then twice more, and she moved toward him, holding his arms, then framing his face with her hands, kissing him just as he had kissed her.

He undressed her, piece by piece. He could feel that she was trembling and he said, "All right? Are you all right?"

She told him she was fine, really fine, and smiled at him as he lay down with her.

The dice were in her coat pocket and out of reach.

When the phone went, she woke in the crook of his arm, but didn't open her eyes. She felt him reach out and the ringing stopped. He said, "Hello?", then said nothing.

Stella sat up and looked at him. He handed her the phone and she listened. There was a silence, burdened only by a faint electronic backwash, a black astral surf, almost musical.

32

Pete Harriman and Maxine Hewitt were working head to head at the same desk, compiling lists from the names that Gerry Moreno had supplied, collating and comparing with the names of acquaintances, friends, and relatives from the Parker case and the Cameron case. When they'd found that there were no overlaps, they would allocate groups of the new names to the on-loan uniformed officers, though they would visit a few of the contacts themselves. You papered everything, every step forward, every step back. If nothing happened, you papered that too.

Stella came in late, carrying a treat-yourself cappuccino. Mike Sorley looked at her as he went toward his boxed-in space, carrying a cup from the squad room machine.

He said, "I was expecting a morning update."

She said, "Doctor's appointment."

Their voices clashed. His next remark came clear: "I've talked to DS Harriman. He'll fill you in."

Harriman had caught the encounter. He said, "Apparently he can't hold the papers off any longer. You were supposed to be seeing the press office. They haven't heard from you."

"It's done. I've organized a leak. What we wanted. I'll tell him."

"He's about to phone the SIO: budget review."

Stella grimaced. "I'll tell him later."

Harriman handed her a message slip. He said, "You know some-one called Badger?"

"Yeah." She took it, but didn't look. "Anything on the scene-of-crime case files?"

"Not that I can see. We went back and asked everyone concerned whether there were items missing: anything that could have repre-sented a trophy. No luck. There's only one similarity: they seem to have taken cash. Most people have a few quid in their wallets, don't they, or lying about the house? It seems our victims didn't. Oh, we haven't been able to get in touch with either Mark Ross or Stephanie James."

"She called. Said they were going away for a while—to re-build their relationship." Stella gave a sour laugh. "Something like that. She was supposed to leave a contact number."

Harriman raised his hands, palms uppermost: not with me. He said, "You didn't tell her?"

"No."

"That her boyfriend had been sleeping with her friend?"

"No."

"That she was pregnant by him?"

"No."

"Why not?"

"Would you have told her?"

"Me? Jesus, no. But I'm wondering about you."

"You wouldn't have told her because it's blokes together, but you think I might have wanted to shop him—female solidarity."

"Something like that."

"We only found out because we were investigating a murder. It wasn't a factor. Basically, I prefer to get out of other people's lives as fast as I can. And, as far as possible, I like to leave things as they were."

"When you say people, you mean civilians."

"Someone you know gets murdered," Stella said. "Everything go-ing along as normal, then someone close to you gets killed. Think of

the damage. Enough's enough." She started down the office, snaffling a Twix from Sue Chapman's desk to go with her coffee. "Anyway, she'll find out."

"How?"

"Not about him and Janis, necessarily. Just about him. It's only a
matter of time. Always is."

She was speaking to herself and she knew it.

There was a note on her desk from Maxine. It said, *He didn't show.
Report later. Do you really want someone at the Kandy Kave every
night?*

Stella brought up the computer folder on Janis Parker and went
into the case file. The cross-referenced information was in the general folder that was on everyone's database, but she had kept a copy
of her own notes under a separate heading. There was a sub-section
for Stephanie James but no record of her mobile phone. She went
back to the general file and ran a search under Stephanie's name and
found the contact almost at once. Stephanie had phoned it through
to the squad room and Sue Chapman had logged it. Stella made a
note of the number, but didn't make the call. Instead, she looked at
the message that Jackie Yates had left: a street address, nothing
more.

She went to the women's room, taking her coffee with her, locked
herself in a stall and took out of her bag the prescription she'd just
picked up. The morning-after pill was called "Plan B." She took it
with a swallow of coffee, then sat on the loo and put her head in her
hands.

So how was it?

How was what?

Don't start with me . . .

*It was good. Actually, it was terrific. But then, it's always terrific,
isn't it? New sex. New person. New excitements and discoveries.
New horizons.*

New what?

Horizons.

You mean a future? New future?

I mean that it's a kick-start. You think about yourself in a differ-ent way. You've stepped outside.

Outside of what?

The life you've been living. You can see new things, new possibil-ities.

Jesus Christ, all this from a one-night stand?

Was it? I've known John Delaney for almost six months. We just hadn't made love, that's all. Do you think meeting, talking, being with each other, acting like a couple, is any less intimate? More, I think.

Acting like a couple, except for the lies and deceit. What about George?

I don't know.

You think that's the next move—the new horizon?

You can see it; you don't have to go there.

You seem to like the view, though. What about George?

I don't know.

So, what is this? You're in love with John Delaney?

If it's not that, it's something very like it. There's something I connect with. Something I haven't come across before.

Define it.

I can't. But I can offer clues.

Go ahead.

He knows about the three o'clock dream. He knows about the Bonnelli children and my breakdown and the baby I lost. He knows I killed a man on the Harefield Estate. I told him—as if he had a right to know. A right to me.

Put it a different way—does he love you?

I think he must. If he didn't, he'd have gone away long ago.

Does he know about the pact you made with yourself?

Pact?

That you would never be pregnant again?

No.

So he doesn't know everything.

I wouldn't tell him that anyway.

Why not?

Because it might not be true.

Don't say that.

I have to say it.

Don't say that!

Look, we've just gone for Plan B, okay? Oestrogen mega-dose wipe-out blitz-bomb. Get down off the bars of your cage.

Okay. So what next?

I don't know.

You'll continue to see him?

What do you think?

Continue to sleep with him?

That seems likely, wouldn't you say? Things being what they are.

What's going to happen?

I don't know.

What about George?

I don't know.

33

If you're a cop, there's no such thing as ex-directory. Stella made a call or two and found that there was no listing for Yates at the address he had given. No listing for Badger, either. In fact, it seemed that the address didn't have a phone.

Stella went over to the desk where Harriman and Maxine were fighting paper. To Maxine she said, "Every night, yes."

"Isn't this supposed to be his week off? Isn't that what Belle said?"

"Even so. Draw up a rota."

"All expenses and take a friend?"

"Take a friend . . . ?"

"Cover. If you look at the clientele, there are some singles, but not many. And no single women. They were hitting on me last night at the rate of one every five minutes. Apart from being annoying, it drew attention."

Without looking up, Harriman said, "I'll go alone. I'll drink tap water. Okay?"

Stella said, "Put the bills through me, not straight to the DI. One Coke per hour."

Maxine shrugged. "Costs the same as their fake champagne."

Stella pointed to a pile of cassettes on the floor by Maxine's chair. "What are those?"

"CCTV from Delgarno Villas and the Kandy Kave. Add to that, there are tapes from streets and malls round about the locations of all the killings . . . but since we don't know what we're looking for, I don't know whether it's worth viewing those."

"Everything," Stella said. "Share it out. Take turns."

"They're time-coded. So we just watch around the times of the murders, right?"

"These people are likely to have revisited the scene: that's part of the profile. Sorry."

"It's a hiding to nothing, anyway," Maxine observed. "If we can get crystal-clear shots of men repairing space stations, why are CCTV tapes like watching ghosts in a snowstorm?"

Stella gave Jackie Yates's address back to Harriman. "This is where I'll be. I'm going to see someone."

Something in her voice made him ask, "Want some company?"

"It's a chis."

Harriman nodded. "Oh, okay." He glanced at the piece of paper and took in the postcode. "Where the hell are you?"

"Whitechapel, isn't it? Stepney. The far east."

"And a long way off-patch. Do you want me to get in touch with the locals: tell them to expect you?"

"Don't bother."

Harriman looked at her. Letting another district know that they could expect a visitor wasn't just polite, it was a requirement.

Stella said, "It's a chis, Pete. I don't want it known that he's over there."

"Okay, boss."

Harriman remembered a moment in the pub: the local CID man leaving, a tight look on his face, Stella saying, *Keep your phone on, okay?*

He asked, "Is he at risk, then? Your chis?" And when she didn't respond, "I could be there. Stay in the car. Be on hand."

Stella shook her head. "You know how it is."

"How will you get there?" The London question, the question everyone asked. What's your method for routes, road repairs, diversions, one-way systems, black spots, stand-still tailbacks?

"Down the Embankment?"

Harriman pursed his lips. "Mid-morning build-up."

"So give me another route."

"Stay away from London Wall," was the best he could offer.

Mike Sorley was on the phone, but he beckoned her in.

"I'm on hold."

"What about the budget?"

"Also on hold. What about the press?"

"There'll be a leak today or tomorrow."

"Are we getting anywhere?"

Stella knew it was a leading question, so she gave the answer he was expecting. "Not very far, no. Not far at all. These are serial killings. You know the problem. Luck is a bigger factor than detection."

"They say people make their own luck."

"We're following certain leads," Stella said.

Sorley smiled wanly. "I always feel that sounds promising."

He looked away to consult a report, his attention shifting, but Stella didn't leave. She wanted to say, *I killed someone. Down on the Harefield Estate. I whacked him with a wheel-nut crank and something happened. I don't know what it was, but he died. Someone knows about this. His people know. Tell me what to do. The* impulse was so strong that she almost thought she'd started to speak, that the words had left her mouth, unrecoverable.

Sorley's call came back to him: money management, time-scales. He turned and hunched over the phone, a man digging in.

Harriman had been right, the Embankment was a close-formation crawl.

The river was high and the wind was helping the current. It was a fast river and a lethal river. Most people who went in drowned: the suicides, the drunks, the victims of random violence. Of course, many were already dead and the river was a method of effacement—features blurred by immersion, picked at by fish and rats and gulls—but it was also a method of distribution.

Think of a body dumped upstream and traveling through a dozen postcodes before it hits a weir, before a current leaves it high and dry for someone's dog to find. Whose case is that? Where did the victim die? Where does the murder team start to look for its killer?

And think of the reverse, Stella said to herself. Not the victim traveling, but the killer. *Same effect.* She reached for her phone and it went off in her hand. She took the call even though the LCD display said Home.

"Where are you?" George asked. It was a good reception; his voice sounded close. She told him.

"The Embankment's always bad this time of day."

"I had no idea."

He laughed. She laughed too, just as if nothing had happened.

She hadn't been so late the previous night; the phone had woken Delaney at ten-thirty—a silent call—and she'd gone home almost immediately: showered and dressed and kissed him and hit the street just like any practiced cheat. Even so, George had been in bed when she arrived home and the bedroom was in darkness. She hadn't made it back for the meal or in time to go out, and she hadn't called, either, but police work was demanding and unpredictable and often secretive, and how could he argue with that?

He hadn't argued. That morning, he had been in his work-room when she woke and she'd called out to say good-bye, but he might not have heard her. Now he said, "There's a displacement problem."

Stella's mind went to absences and a cold feeling started up in her gut. Then she realized he was talking about boatbuilding.

"I'm bored," he told her. "I've started talking to myself."

"Everyone does that."

"I know. But I'm so bored I've stopped listening."

She laughed. "I'll be early tonight."

"Early?"

"No, okay, normal time. Sort of."

"That's good. I'll look forward to that."

She said, "Maybe we could—" then stopped, because there was a deadness on the line that meant no one home. She checked the signal, but it was fine: he'd hung up.

She speed-dialed the squad room and got through to Pete Harri-man. "Listen to this," she said. "It's a fair bet that they'll have killed before. That's what the profiler said."

"Then it must be true."

"Look at it this way. Say you've got a killer who's a long-distance trucker. Picks up hitch-hikers, kills them, throws them out of the truck. Say he carries freight from the Channel ports to Scotland. Say he kills ten people in the course of one trip—lobs each body out wherever it's convenient. To him, it's just a random strip of motor-way. To the cops dealing with each murder, it's their patch—different counties the length of the land. A different police force in each case. If they never look beyond their own area, they're never going to find a pattern. In fact, there's no reason why they should ever realize they're dealing with a serial killer."

"You think they travel?"

"It just came to me."

"What do you want me to do?"

"We need to find the same MO but somewhere else."

"Like?"

"Could be anywhere. Everywhere. Nationwide."

"Oh, good," Harriman said. "For a moment I thought this was going to be difficult."

She dialed Delaney's number and he answered just as a motorbike courier went past her on the inside, flicking her wing mirror.

Delaney said, "Fuck you," and hung up.

She redialed. "It was me."

"You didn't speak. I thought you were my breather."

"A bike messenger was in a chicken run with me. Ride or die. I was concentrating."

"Did you get him?"

"Missed."

"That's a shame." A pause. She started to speak in the same moment as he asked, "How are you?"

"I'm fine." Another pause, then: "Did you speak to your man?"

"It's done. He was happy to get the story." He sounded suddenly businesslike.

"Is there a central archive?" she asked. "A news archive for the country?"

"Of a sort. What do you need?" She gave him the truck driver theory. He said, "You think they've got a secret history?"

"I do, yes."

"Who knows—we might get lucky."

"John," she said, "I've been asking myself if it was a mistake. If I made a mistake."

"Did you?"

"No."

"That's good."

"It took me by surprise. It wasn't what I'd intended. But I'm glad it happened that way."

"What had you intended?"

"Something else."

"So I was Plan B . . ."

She laughed: a sour note. "That's right. You were Plan B."

.   .   .

There was a lick of rain in the wind, now, the sky lowering.

She wondered what it meant: George saying: *That's good. I'll look forward to that.* Then the phone going dead.

She fished in her pocket for the dice, rattled them, cast them sideways out of her hand onto the passenger seat. They fell three and five, favoring Delaney. She called George back and he picked up straight away.

"Seven-thirty," she said. "My turn to cook."

34

There was a terrace of red-brick houses, fire-damaged and boarded up. Counting down from the far end of the row, Stella identified the tenth house as having the street number Jackie had given, but the door space was blocked and blind. She pushed at the board with her foot. It was screwed to the frame. The windows were boarded from the inside.

She walked to the end of the row and looked down the cross street. Each house had a yard, each yard had a fence. An alley ran down between the terraces and on either side of the alley was a lock-up garage. She counted her way to the back of what ought to be Jackie's house and stepped through a break in the fence into a yard cluttered with the rusting hulks of white goods, abandoned bedding, bottles, syringes. The back door was boarded. All the windows were boarded save one on the ground floor: a single open eye in a row of sleepers. The pupil in that eye was Jackie Yates's face. As soon as she saw him, he disappeared.

The window was small and there were still shards of glass in place. Stella was wearing a padded cotton windbreaker which she took off and laid across the lower edge of the window, then edged through, finding a sink on the far side on which to brace herself so that she could keep her torso above the sill. She was still halfway through when she realized that the sink was doubling as a lavatory: the stench made her eyes smart. She jumped clear and retrieved her jacket, retching.

She called, "Jackie?"

He had gone upstairs. When she called, he came out as far as the landing: the edge of his territory. She went out into the hall and he was standing there, looking down, his arms folded across his chest.

"Jackie?"

He turned and went into one of the bedrooms. Stella took out her mobile phone and dialed the AMIP-5 number but didn't press "send"; then she went upstairs.

The fire must have taken the whole terrace. It wasn't so apparent from the street, but inside the evidence was plain to see: charred wood, blackened walls, and even now the thin, stale smell of smoke. The banisters were skinny cinders, knobbled like a spent match, and when Stella went upstairs she was careful to put her weight on the treads where they met the wall.

Jackie Yates was sitting on the far side of the room, his arms still folded. There was something odd about him that Stella couldn't place, then she realized it had to do with his wig. It was lumpy and matted and the weave from the back of his head to the nape of his neck stood up in a stiff, filthy crest. Oddest of all, though, it was askew; he seemed to be both looking at her and looking away; his eyes holding hers while his head seemed to be half-turned toward the wall.

"Jackie?"

"Why are you talking to me?" he said. "Why talk to a dead man?"

His voice was hoarse, as if he'd been shouting. Shouting for help.

"What's happened?"

"You heard about Daz? Did you hear about that?"

Stella was standing in the doorway. She walked in and sat with her back to the wall, the width of the room between them.

"Tell me about Daz." She thought it might be the last thing she wanted to hear.

"They shot him."

"He's dead?"

Jackie shook his head. Stella could see that his clothes were stained and stiff, his face seamed with grime.

"Elbows and knees. They crippled him."

She closed her eyes for a moment. "Couldn't you find somewhere else to be, Jackie?" The room was empty apart from a clotted heap of bedding, which seemed to consist mostly of old carpeting and a floral curtain, rings still attached.

"Somewhere else . . . Where?"

"A friend . . . ?"

Jackie laughed, then started to cough. Finally, he said, "Think of all the things I haven't got. Friends are top of the list." He laughed again, louder, and there was an edge to it that made Stella jumpy. Jackie's arms were still folded. She wondered if he was cradling a weapon. After a moment, Jackie said, "I wanted you to come here—" then stopped, as if he'd lost track of his thoughts. He shifted his position slightly and Stella thought it must be a cat in the crook of his arm. He stroked it, nose to tail, and laughed again. "I wanted you to come . . ."

Stella realized that it wasn't over-use that had cracked his voice and left it weak. He was ill. She said, "I asked about the witness-protection program. I'll ask again."

"The what?"

"Witness-protection."

Jackie shrugged. He said, "I asked you to . . . I need some things."

"Okay."

"I need money."

"Yes, okay." She said, "Get away, Jackie. Go somewhere. France . . . I don't know."

"I just need some money."

"You can't stay here."

"It doesn't matter where I am," Jackie told her. "It doesn't matter where I go. It doesn't make any difference, that's the point."

"I'll take you somewhere," she said. "Anywhere you want to go."

"It's the same wherever I am," he said. "That's the point." He started to laugh again, the wig slipping stiffly forward as he bowed his head to get breath. He said, "That's the point. That's the point," laughing, bringing his knees up as if the laughter hurt.

Stella opened her wallet and took out what she had: it was sixty-five pounds. She got up and walked across the room. Jackie's head was still bowed. She nudged him and held out the money. "I'll come back with some more." He didn't respond, so she dropped the notes into his lap and he gathered them one-handed. The other hand was stroking, stroking. Stella crouched down. She said, "I'll come back tomorrow. I'll ask about witness-protection."

Jackie looked at her and smiled. "That guy you whacked over at Harefield. He must have been connected. He must have been a top man."

It wasn't a cat, it was a piece of fur: a sleeve, some sort of offcut. He held it in the crook of his arm, stroking.

Stella said, "I'm sorry, Jackie."

He looked at her as if he hadn't heard; as if she had just walked in. He said, "That's the point. Somewhere else makes no difference."

Stella went back down the stairs, remembering to tread close to the supporting wall. She took out her phone and canceled the number.

She could hear Jackie laughing. Laughing and crying.

It wasn't early when she got home and it wasn't the normal time, either. It was almost nine o'clock and she was carrying the gourmet selection for two from the local Indian restaurant.

"Sorley called a late catch-up meeting," she said, "and I had a skip-load of paperwork and we're never going to catch these bastards anyway."

George was opening his second bottle of wine. She noticed that it was a couple of notches better than the New World table wine they usually drank: as if he'd been saving it. He smiled at her and fetched another glass. "What bastards?"

"The bastards who are killing people all over my patch."

"I thought it was bastard, singular."

She realized how little George knew about what was happening in her life; how much Delaney knew. "There are two," she said, "a man and a woman. But that's classified."

"Who would I tell?" Then he said, "A man and a woman?"

"There was DNA residue. Team Killers."

"That's the technical name?"

"Sadistic Team Killers."

"What makes them do it?" he wondered. "What makes them *want* to do it?"

"There's a profiler working with us. Anne Beaumont. She's very good."

"Does she have a theory about why?"

"She has several theories. They're all off the peg."

It was a sign, and Stella knew it. Even to mention Anne Beaumont, to bring her into the conversation, to flesh her out, was the first hint of a desire to confess. The way cheaters mention their lovers. The way the best lies are mostly truth.

He helped her put the food on to plates. She said, "I'm sorry, George. I tried to get away."

He shook his head. "It's fine."

"And it's a bloody takeaway."

"Also fine." He took a forkful of food and tested it. "Tepid to cool . . ."

While he transferred the plates to the oven, Stella took her glass of wine out into their ragged little patch of garden and called Stephanie James's number. She was about to hang up when Stephanie came on, sounding breathless. Stella asked her about trophies.

"I packed up," Stephanie said, "my stuff and Janis's. There had been some money in a purse, not much, a few quid. We called it the house purse. Money for milk, stuff from the corner shop, you know. That had gone."

"Nothing else?"

"I don't think so. Not from my things. I can't really be sure about Janis's. What do you mean—trophy?"

"Something that would remind them of . . . their victim. Something personal."

"Christ, that's horrible." Stephanie paused. "I don't know. Nothing I noticed, anyway. It was strange that the television was on."

"What?"

"No, you're asking me about . . . was there anything missing and I was thinking my way round the room and I remembered the television. It was on."

Stella tried to picture the room: the forensic crew, Sorley in his white paper overalls, blond wood minimalist chairs, the sound system, the Bang & Olufsen TV showing *España Viva*. She asked, "How do you know?"

"You remember you asked me to look at the photos and the— scene-of-crime video, you called it—to see if anything seemed odd, or whatever."

"Yes."

"So the television was on. It occurred to me at the time."

"You didn't mention it."

"I did. I mentioned it to the guy who interviewed me afterward— after I'd looked at the tape."

"DC Harriman."

"Was that his name?"

"So . . . the TV was on and that was odd. Why?"

"She had a migraine. That's why Mark took her home. She didn't watch television much anyway, but never when she had a migraine, it made things worse."

Stella said, "Who knows? Perhaps she began to feel better. Perhaps it was something she needed to watch."

"I don't think so," Stephanie said. "Mark told me that when they got back, she went straight to bed."

She did, Stella thought. That's right. But not alone. She thought the temperature in the garden might have dropped, or else the chill she felt had more to do with being a woman and a deceiver talking to a woman who had been deceived.

Stephanie said, "But look, if I remember anything, I'll call you."

Stella said thanks and goodbye; said it too quickly, maybe.

It was almost dark, except that the city is never dark.

A 747 slipped down the flight path, so heavy overhead, so slow, so low, so threatening, that you could almost believe in a Heathrow cargo cult.

George brought the bottle out to her and topped up her drink; he leaned over and kissed her; she kissed him back.

"Come and eat."

You couldn't imagine, as they sat there with their good vintage and their spread of tin-foil cartons, that there was anything between them but love and openness. George had solved his displacement problem: a design thing. He explained it to her, using an empty jalfrezi carton with some rice as ballast. She told him about her serial killers and how Peter Sutcliffe had been picked up for a driving offense and that Dennis Nilsen was caught because his drains smelled.

"Luck," she said. "Not detection, luck."

She didn't say too much about Stephanie James or Mark Ross, about cheats and liars, but she had a few good lines about lap-dancing clubs. Which sent her back to the scene of crime at Mandy Wallace's flat. Which stopped her in mid-sentence.

She said, "I have to go out."

35

There were five VDUs up and running in the squad room, shedding a blue-white glow. Stella switched on the main lights, opened the file drawer in her desk and took out the crime report on Mandy Wallace. The photos and bullet-point paragraphs matched her mind's-eye reconstruction: the blood splashes on the walls, a photo of Mandy with her son in a frame on the television, a forensic officer dusting the TV for prints, a newscaster speaking of "tension" and "outrage" and "hotspots."

She checked the file on Nesta Cameron: the report and the stills photos. The TV had been switched off. She checked the file on Janis Parker, but she already knew the answer.

Anne Beaumont answered her call on the end of a laugh. Stella said, "At two scenes of crime the TV was on when we got there."

"Stella, I'm off duty. Off duty as an analyst, off duty as a profiler."

"I just want an opinion."

"Can't it wait till morning?"

It could have waited, of course: all of it. She could have stayed with George, talked some more, opened the third bottle. But she needed to know; needed to check the SOC reports, to be sure, or how else would she have slept? Wasn't that it? It had to be. Because the only alternative was that she had wanted to be somewhere else; that, in a limited sort of way, she was on the run.

"You remember that Nesta Cameron's cleaners had been in? They'd been through three rooms before they found the body."

Anne said, "I've got someone with me."

"It's entirely possible that they switched the TV off, wouldn't you think? Their assumption being that Nesta had gone to work and forgotten about it."

Anne sighed. "It's a theory."

"In which case, all three TVs would have been on. Why?"

"Because the three victims had been watching TV when their killers arrived on the scene. Why not?"

"It seems likely that Mandy Wallace was killed before they'd had their full quota of fun. There was a break-in down the road, the burglar was caught on the premises and there was a good deal of police activity as a result. The killers decided to finish Mandy, but probably waited for a while before leaving: until the street cleared."

"And they watched TV while they waited. Callous, but so what? These are not people with better natures."

"But here's another thought. Another theory. Suppose it was the killers who switched on the TV."

There was a silence on the line. Finally, Anne said: "You mean, for a purpose?"

"Yes, for a purpose."

"Where are they now, those televisions?"

"I'm not sure. But if you ask that question, you know what I'm thinking."

"You're thinking they might be tuned to the video channel."

"Yes."

"You're thinking that the killers videotaped their work, then played it back when they'd finished."

"That's the way they stay close to their victims. A video. That's the trophy."

Stella left a message for Pete Harriman, who was either out or not answering his calls. Then she went to her car and started the engine, as if she knew what she would do next. The dice were in her pocket, but she'd already cast them once that day and there were rules to be obeyed.

"I've got someone with me," Anne had said. Stella realized how little she knew about Anne's life. Not a fair trade. Hers was an open book.

She made a couple of circuits, going nowhere, then stopped off at a bank and drew her daily limit out of the cashpoint. Tomorrow, she would draw her limit again and take the money down to Jackie Yates. As if it might help him. As if five hundred pounds would buy him his life back.

George was reading when she got home, lying on the sofa, book in hand, a glass of wine from the third bottle on the floor at his side. He listened to her while she told him what she'd found: that the killers might have videoed their victims as they killed them; as they tortured them; and sat down afterward to watch a rerun of what they'd done. George set his book aside to listen, but didn't offer any comments.

When she'd finished he said, "I'm tired, aren't you?" He picked up his book and marked his place, then went to the door. As he left the room, she heard him say: "Tired of all this."

She sat alone at the open kitchen door, looking out on to the clumpy grass and uneven patio flags of the garden, and finished the third bottle.

City-glow, fractured patterns of lights in tower blocks, sirens on the cross streets, a voice raised in anger. The night was still and cool; you could taste jet fuel. Stella was thinking about damage. It was the word uppermost in her mind. The damage she had caused; was still causing.

She thought about Nike Man dead in the Harefield bull ring, about Daz crippled as punishment, about Jackie Yates in the burned-out terrace holding his scrap of fur. She thought about Delaney and George, and the fact that one of them would have to come to grief.

She thought about the damage she was doing to herself.

36

The TV was on, but only Sonny was watching. He'd flipped through the channels and found a movie that was set in some cold place or another, Canada or Alaska; anyway, there was lots of snow. Sonny had never seen snow: well, a thin covering perhaps, but not this thigh-deep stuff that went from horizon to horizon. He liked the look of it. More than that, he liked the look of the female lead. She resembled the girl who danced for him in the Kandy Kave. Belle. She had the same dark eyes, the same long, glossy hair. The film star was dressed for the cold, but Sonny knew exactly what he would see if she took off all those clothes. He would see Belle.

Without looking away from the screen he said, "Let's go hunting."

The on-screen girl had gone into a small cabin where a log fire was burning. A man came in from another room and the girl seemed surprised to see him. They looked at one another, as if not knowing what would happen next. In Sonny's mind, the man was Sonny.

"Let's go hunting, Donna."

The man and the girl crossed the room toward each other and kissed. His hands were on the small of her back. She kissed him more deeply, and one hand moved to the back of her neck. She couldn't have escaped if she'd wanted to. Next came an exterior shot, pulling back to show the cabin in a vast snowscape, the light from its window fragile in the surrounding darkness. In such a place you could scream but no one would hear. You could scream all night long but no one would hear.

He said, "Donna, let's go hunting."

She was sitting at the table looking at a road atlas. After a moment she said, "We ought to move on. One more here, then move."

"I like it here."

Donna looked up from the atlas for a moment. "Are you fucking stupid, or what?"

"I used to live here. This is where I grew up."

"If we move, we're okay. If we move, no one gets close to us."

"We need money, Donna."

"I know. I told you: one more here." Her voice sharpened. "Are you listening?"

He nodded. "Okay."

Donna went to the window and looked out at the street. Out at the Strip. Her eyes were dark, almost black, so that the pupils merged with the iris. She saw neon pools, the girls working the curbs, the pimps watching from cars, the minicab office with its slowly turning sign: STEAD/FAST.

A car stopped for a girl in pink lycra. She bent down low to the window, giving the tariff, showing the goods.

A man came up out of a basement shebeen and got down on his hands and knees to puke. When he was done, he went back downstairs.

A boy went past wearing a red blanket streaked with grime. A brindled dog walked at his heel.

Donna said, "Just one. One more." Suddenly, she sounded greedy.

Later, Sonny went out to get beer and pizza: they never had delivery. He walked along the Strip feeling good about himself, feeling powerful, as if he could reach out and snap anyone who went up against him. One of the whores offered business, and he let a smile be his answer. If only you knew, he thought; if you realized who you're talking to.

You never had to feel small if you could run that kind of thing in your head: the Janis Parker video, the Nesta Cameron video. It gave you a look. It gave you an aura. He could start it up in his head with a little *Click-whirr* like an old-fashioned movie projector, and it would start to roll.

He placed his order and sat down to wait. It was hot in the pizza place, so he cracked a can of beer and a little spurt of foam leaped up and hit his shirt. A guy opposite saw it and laughed.

If only you knew.

Sonny closed his eyes and leaned his head back against the wall. *Click-whirr . . .*

37

It was front-page news everywhere, but the tabloids had made the best of it. SADIST SLAYS THREE told the story pretty well, so did SERIAL FIEND TERROR, but MONSTER ON THE LOOSE took the prize for the most succinct method of raising panic. The press office had delivered the morning's papers to Mike Sorley and he took them to the morning briefing. The AMIP-5 officers didn't have to be instructed to say nothing to the press, but he told them anyway.

"If you read these pieces, you'll see that there are two crucial aspects to the case that aren't reported anywhere: the fact that the victims were tortured, and the fact that we're dealing with male/female team killers. You know why. It sorts the loonies from any genuine contact we might get from the killers.

"We've given a number that the public should call if they have any information that might have a bearing on the case. Okay: we've obtained permission from the families to release pictures of the victims. Tomorrow's papers will carry them. I'm asking for additional help with phone-manning, because we're asking anyone with information about the victims' movements on the evenings they died to call in. Or with information about the company they kept, random sightings, secret lives.

"But that phone number is also going to be used by cranks and time-wasters. It's a dedicated number, there are four extensions, and they're all clear lines—none of them have any service features like call-minder or whatever, which means the Nuisance Calls Bureau can get a trace straight away, so don't fuck things up by trying to dial one-four-seven-one. It's a penny to a pinch of dog shit that most of the crank calls will be made from payphones. If they're not, I want those bastards nailed, but don't forget that any call you take might be the real thing. Think that way. Make that supposition. There's a fair chance our killers will phone. They like to leave messages. They enjoy game-playing.

"Most of you know the routine, but I'll say it again. As soon as a confession call comes in, as soon as you take it, press one on the dial-pad. That puts the trace in. Then try and keep them talking for as long as you can. Ask questions, ask for clarification of what they've said, keep an even tone and speak softly—pretend you're a fucking Samaritan, let them do the talking. Don't say anything that might seem as if you're trying to draw them out. Play second fiddle. Don't say anything to lead . . . I mean don't ask them to describe the scene of crime, the location, the MO, anything like that.

"Even if they are phoning from a call box, we can triangulate that, we can find that. Just keep them on the phone. Sound interested, sound as if you believe them. If they've given you a name, use it; use it a lot; but don't *ask* for a name. Sure, the chances are they'll all be nuisance calls but, like I say, I want those assholes taken out of the equation. They're as dangerous as if they were giving the real killers help and assistance. Which they are. I want them arrested and I want them charged and I want them out of my fucking way."

He dropped the sheaf of papers on to Sue Chapman's desk. "Look at these and take a note of the names of the journos who wrote the features. You might well find them in your faces over the next few days."

They had made an early start, which was good news for anyone below the rank of DI. Murders usually meant long hours and plenty of overtime, but if you're DI and upward, you're putting in the hours for your promotions board.

There were coffee cartons and bagels and croissants. Andy Greegan was eating an egg and bacon sandwich, smiling round at the others and enjoying every calorie. Pretty much everyone was smoking, including those who were eating. Not Stella or Sue Chapman, of course, AMIP-5's token non-smokers. Sue was standing near a window, trying to get at least a one-to-five mix of fresh air and smoke. Stella stood up when Mike Sorley sat down, her head wreathed in blue.

"Okay, we've reached a certain stage. It's called having three bodies not one. After the first two it looked like serial, now we know it's serial. The press has got it. Things have changed. We might have to draft in more detectives and we're certainly going to have to ask for large-scale local-uniform help with the legwork.

"You'll have read my report and the notes I made late last night. You'll also have received the profiler's document. The trick here is to amass as much information about these individuals as we can, try to build a picture of them. We already know certain things. They're sadists: they torture their victims before they kill them. They probably strip naked to do their work, then use the victim's shower after the event. Obvious reasons.

"We don't know how they gain access to their victims. On each occasion, these murders took place in the victims' homes. Were they waiting for them? If not, how did they manage to put their victims at ease? What did they say that got them into those flats?

"Read the profiler's report if you haven't already. The question she asks is: Why did the killers pick these women? These young women. One theory is that it's something to do with revenge: a grudge against a certain type of woman because of some event in the killers' past. Or it's a power thing. Or it's sexual. There's been no evidence of sexual activity at the scenes as yet, at least none that proves itself to be forensically significant, although that doesn't mean it hasn't taken place.

"We need to know as much as possible about these people in order to improve our profiles of them. Their obsessions, the way they think, the way they see the world, every fact we have goes some way to providing a clue to their backgrounds, their histories. As children, they will probably have been cruel to animals: killed them, tortured them. There's the possibility of abuse in the family background: it's true that the abused abuse in turn. We need to put all these factors together. We need to make two and two add up to something useful.

"We need to try to imagine . . . how they think. Why they make the choices they make. What they do when they're not killing people. Do they have jobs? Do they sign on? Do they sit by cashpoints with their hands out? Do they sell the *Big Issue?* Are they on drugs? If so, where do they score? Are they local, or did they arrive recently? We need to check records for people with previous convictions for malicious wounding, stalking, that sort of area. We need to widen the search. Are they working to a geographical pattern? If I'm right about the video, is there a professional connection? Have they got a plan? What comes next? It's called projective thinking.

"We think that, maybe, they videotape their work and then play it back at the scene of crime once the victim is dead. It's a form of trophy-taking. All these things help, all these things go to a sort of mental Identikit.

"DNA traces tend to make us think that the woman is more active—or, at least, *as* active—as the man. By active, I mean aggressively involved in what happens to the victim. If true, this is very rare. If true, it's one of the defining factors of the case.

"Everyone has a job to do. There's still house-to-house going on. Broaden that. Take the photos of the victims further afield. Cover the patch. Use the local assistance we'll be getting. If we can come up with even the sketchiest description of these people, we're a lot further ahead than at present. Anyone new to the area, anyone watching the girls' flats, anyone behaving oddly.

"I want another round of interviews with close associates: sorry, but we know a little more, now, so there are new questions we can ask. Keep watching CCTV tapes from the streets and the immediate areas where the crimes took place. We know that serial killers like to revisit the scene. I want the CCTV from the lap-dancing club checked every day. Don't save it up for a girlie bonanza, view it when it comes in." She looked at Pete Harriman and got the laugh she played for when she said: "And no freeze-frames or replays."

Stella put down her notes and asked for questions and suggestions.

Colin Proctor asked what "forensically significant" meant when applied to sexual activity at the SOC.

"We know that Janis Parker had consensual sex not long before she was killed."

"Meaning she wasn't raped."

"Well, that's the problem—it's tough to be sure. Normally, you'd see evidence of coercion in the shape of bruising and so forth, but the torture wounds might well have covered that."

"The other victims?"

"No evidence of semen, but rapists often use condoms. They've heard about DNA."

Maxine said, "The videos. You say that the killers film what they do then sit down to watch it after they've murdered their victims."

Stella shrugged. "It's a theory. We need to talk to Nesta Cameron's cleaners . . ."

"I'll do that," Maxine offered. "But what if they actually take tapes to the scene with them?"

"What tapes?"

"Tapes they've made before. Tapes of their previous killings."

"Why would they do that?"

"To show them to the new victim."

Stella stared at Maxine, unable to speak. Finally, she said, "What put that sick idea into your head?"

"Protective thinking," Maxine said. "What else?"

Stella nodded. "I believe you."

Maxine intercepted Stella as she was making for Sorley's cubicle.

"The CCTV from Delgarno Villas won't help us. The doctor had the death between ten-thirty and eleven. Sam Burgess thought a little later, but not much. That was a Thursday. What we've got is a time-coded camera that started to re-record at midnight. It gives us the gate and forecourt activity for Friday. Well, as much of Friday as it recorded before we seized the tape."

"No other cameras?"

"That's what I was hoping. Good security on an estate like this would give you a three- or five-camera option. The cameras work on a rotating basis through a multiplexer, so you can refer back as many days as you have cameras. There's a digital system that gets everything for you and doesn't need tapes, but it's new technology and not many CCTV set-ups have it."

"And Delgarno had just the one camera and just the one monitor, so it tapes over the previous day?"

"That's right. Basically, tapes are only saved if there's been an incident. There was, of course, but no one knew."

"Great. Anything from the Kandy Kave?"

"Girls with their tits out, guys with their tongues out."

Stella said, "Okay. Keep looking," and started to move on.

Maxine said, "It was you, wasn't it? Parked up the Gate. I'd been to a movie with a friend. I was crossing the road, looking for a taxi."

There was a slight smile on Maxine's lips. Stella noticed her lipstick, a soft red to complement her dark-brown hair. She said, "It was me, yes."

"Some people know, some people don't. Coppers, I mean; colleagues. No one here knows, except you. It makes no difference to me one way or the other. I thought we should just acknowledge the fact that you *do* know, and that I know you know."

"It makes no difference to me, either," Stella told her.

Maxine said, "I noticed the way you were looking at me in the Kandy Kave. I should have said something then."

"You mean a gay woman watching strippers . . ." Stella shrugged. "No, look, I don't suppose you want to sleep with every attractive woman you see."

Maxine laughed. "A fair number of them, actually." Then, for some reason, she added, "It's a new relationship: the girl you saw me with. I'm nursing it along. I'd like it to last."

"Good luck," Stella told her. She thought of something: "Did Pete Harriman hit on you?"

"Oh, yes."

"What did you do?"

"I flirted with him."

"Why?"

"It was fun."

Sorley had his own set of morning papers. He said, "You get a lot of coverage."

"My tame journo asked who to quote. I told him to quote me, because he's my contact: I might have to go back there, leak more, leak less, correct a few misapprehensions, try to get a certain angle promoted. All in all, I'd sooner have given your name."

"The press office already have. I've asked for a liaison officer, but I'm not going to get one."

Stella didn't envy Sorley. Serial murders were a hot press issue and a good story caught readers. If the press pack found out that the killings were sadistic and that a woman was involved, they would make barracudas look like tidy eaters.

Sorley said, "The SIO has approved a cautious revision of the budget. That means more officers for legwork and manning phones. I might even draft in some civilian staff for the phones if uniforms are in short supply. I'm getting a DS for bagman work, but I don't know if I can get any more staff for you."

"I've got five, some doubling, but only two are real street coppers: Harriman and Hewitt."

"I'll try," Sorley told her.

He'd taken his phone off the hook to find time to talk to her. The cigarette pack on his desk was down to three. First of the day.

38

Stella took Pete Harriman with her to Mandy Wallace's flat. There were flowers on the cellophane on the pavement outside, and more stuck between the tall railings that surrounded the estate.

"Get the foot patrols to get rid of these, for Christ's sake. We'll have spooks and ghouls and rubberneckers all over the place." She shook her head. "When did we start doing that—leaving flowers for people we didn't know?"

Stella took the lift, Harriman the stairs. Different approaches, different points of view. They met on the second floor.

"On the other hand," Harriman said, "and because loonies like to go back to the scene, they might think that leaving a bunch of daffs along with all the other sad bastards is a safe enough thing to do."

"You mean we ought to organize flowers outside the other scenes and post a photographer to take snaps of everyone who adds to them?"

Harriman heard the wryness in her voice, but chose to ignore it. "You have to make it a possibility." He paused for effect. "Check with the profiler."

Stephanie James had packed up the contents of the flat she shared with Janis Parker. No one had told her she shouldn't. Nesta Cameron's TV had been off.

Mandy's flat was just as it had been. Someone had washed down the walls but the stains were still clear, gouts and dribbles and star-splashes. Stella could hear a radio playing somewhere; she heard someone shout in the street outside. She imagined Mandy tied and taped, trying to fend off her attackers; she thought of Janis and Nesta—the time it took for them to die. And people in the next flat, the flat below, the flat above. People within a few feet of what was happening to the victims. The door-to-door reports stated that no one heard a thing. Well, a bump, maybe, but so what? Something falling, but so what?

She found the TV remote and switched on to *This Morning*. She had brought *Titanic* with her—a sell-off that she'd got for George as a joke birthday present. She pressed "play" and watched as the ship broke up and bodies cascaded into the sea in a triumph of special effects: the place where George had switched off.

"Video channel," Harriman observed. "Good guess."

The contents of the flat had been catalogued: items taken away for further tests, items left *in situ*. Apart from the stripper's wardrobe, it was a banal list. A few airport books, poster-prints on the wall, Habitat sofas, a brass bed. Bathroom cupboards full of make-up; fridge full of fast food. There were snapshots of Mandy with the part-time boyfriend.

Stella and Harriman took a room apiece, then switched. In the kitchen were three brightly colored recycling bags in metal frames to keep them upright, each stenciled in black Playbill: Paper, Glass, Tin. In the bedroom, a scrapbook dedicated to Mandy's son, Nick: holiday photos, postcards, birthday cards with badly drawn crimson hearts, each sending love in a childish hand that improved over the years. In the living room, among papers on a dresser, a membership-renewal form from Oxfam. The unguessable details of people's lives.

Janis Parker's flat had an entryphone system. Nesta Cameron lived on a gated estate with CCTV security. Mandy's flat had a simple bell on the street door, but, even so, the killers had to find a way to get in.

She tried it out on Harriman: "How did they get in?"

"No sign of forced entry, was there?" It was a rhetorical question. "Not here, not at the other scenes."

"No. Okay: so how?"

"They were waiting when the victims got back, or else they arrived sometime after their victims returned. Either way, they'd have to blag their way in."

"In two cases—Janis Parker and Mandy Wallace—it was very late. Well past midnight. Nesta Cameron died at eleven or thereabouts. What gets you into someone's flat at that hour—what do you say?"

"Give up. What do you say?"

"Think your way into it," Stella told him.

She pressed "eject" and collected the tape. On *This Morning* a designer chef was doing something fey with aggressively mismatched ingredients. Stella watched for a minute. When the word "art" was mentioned, she switched off.

Margaret Parker opened the door to Maxine Hewitt just as she'd done before. And just as she'd done before, she invited Maxine into the large room off the hall. There were flowers in vases and the room was full of their scent. A photo-portrait of Janis hung on the wall; a second was framed and stood on a sideboard. They were among the shots Stella had found in the portfolio in Janis's flat.

Margaret smiled at Maxine, but nothing lay behind the smile. She said, "We weren't told that the flat should be left as it was. Stephanie told us she was never going back there. I asked her to arrange to have Janis's things sent to us."

"It wasn't your fault," Maxine said.

"The police took quite a lot of stuff away with them."

"It's just second thoughts. Something that's occurred to us."

"About the television?"

"Yes."

"I had everything put in the garage. It's going to a resale shop. I couldn't keep it, you understand?" Margaret looked at Maxine anxiously, as if selling her dead daughter's belongings might seem a betrayal. A denial.

They walked out of the house to a double garage. Janis Parker's belongings were neatly piled: a lifestyle stacked and abandoned. The television was sitting on a sofa, its own couch potato, and the remote was taped to the top. Margaret Parker found an extension lead and Maxine plugged the TV into a power source by the garage door, then switched on and inserted a video. It played.

Margaret said, "What does that mean?"

"We're checking something," Maxine said.

"Checking what?"

Maxine was thinking quickly. "No, it's . . . it's just . . . it helps us to determine what Janis was doing that night. Maybe she rented a video. Maybe someone from the video shop remembers her. Maybe someone followed her from the shop."

"I see." Margaret looked unconvinced.

They walked back to the front of the house. Maxine had parked in the driveway. On either side of the drive there was a long, neat, curving lawn, edged with spring flowers; at the roadside edge of the lawn, flanking the gates, were a birch and a rowan; the gates were supported by pillars topped by stone dogs.

The two women paused by Maxine's car. The house was a three-story Edwardian red-brick, with some fanciful turrets and tall chimneys: fifteen rooms, Maxine thought; maybe more. For some reason, she heard herself asking, "Do you live here on your own?"

Margaret's answer came after a beat or two, as if she'd had to think about it. "I do, yes." She smiled a dead smile. "It's the family home."

39

Stella dropped Harriman at the squad room, then drove through Chelsea to the Embankment and on to Stepney. The wind was carrying rain and there was a low build-up of black cloud that seemed to hang at rooftop height, although the sun was still out, standing at the very edge of the cloud-wrack. By the time she reached the burned-out terrace, fat drops were hitting the pavement with a soft *thock-thock-thock.*

She parked on the cross street and went through the fence, making her way between the clutter and dreck to the back of Jackie's chosen house. This time there was no face at the window. She called a couple of times, but only succeeded in setting a dog barking somewhere. The rain came full on in a sudden rush, with the sun shimmering through it: silver pillars of rain, pillars of silver sunlight. Stella took off her coat, as before, and used it to protect her hands and knees from any glass shards there might be in the broken window. She remembered not to reach down to the sink for support.

She called his name, but there was no reply. No one came out to the landing as she climbed the stairs. The room he'd been using was empty, though the stained mess of curtains and carpeting was still there. She walked over and stirred it with her foot. Rats were nesting there. A big doe ran out and scuttled to the center of the room, then looked back, a line of fur on its back raised in a spiky ridge. A little stew of hairless, pink bodies, thumb-sized and blind, squirmed in the tangle of material.

The roof was holed and rain was thwacking on the bare floorboards, the fall even harder, now, the sky darker, the sun covered. Stella started back toward the door and immediately felt the floor begin to give beneath her feet, boards cracking and shearing off. At first, she forgot to move—only heard the noise it made, before there came an awful moment of weightlessness as everything opened up; then she tried to step back, but there was nothing to step from, no purchase, and she fell, her shoulders hitting the wall and driving the breath from her lungs.

She folded over her own arm, whooping, fighting for oxygen. When she looked up, she was sitting on the edge of the caved-in section of floor with a clear view down into the back room. She pulled her legs away from the drop. Jackie Yates's bedding had fallen through and was draped over the sink. The big doe ran to and fro on the other side of the gap, her claws tapping the boards.

Stella went on her heels and hands, as close to the wall as she could, pushing her legs away, then pulling her torso after them, knees raised, the catch-and-gather method of a caterpillar on a fragile leaf. One hand was almost at the drop and she could feel the boards moving as she inched away. When she was six feet clear and near a corner where the supports would be stronger, she got to her knees, then stood up. The whole floor seemed to move.

She crouched down, then sat, then half lay on the floor, wanting to distribute her weight. To get to the rats' nest, she had crossed the room from the door. She'd gone half a wall's length back, so still had a wall and a half to traverse before she made it to the door. She moved as she had before, heels and hands, but things shifted beneath her again, so she stopped. The doe was running little, agitated circles, quite close, almost seeming to dart at her. There was a jolt as the floor shunted down a couple of inches: rotten joists giving way at the wall. She made a slow lateral movement, easing forward on her elbows. Another jolt. She could hear debris falling into the downstairs room. Shuffle and slip wasn't going to do it.

Stella looked across to the door and tried to calculate how many steps she would have to take to reach it; she reckoned four if, instead of edging round the room by the walls, she took a curve that would keep her out of the center of the room, but also cut the remaining corner. She was being rained on, her hair plastered across her face. She pushed it out of her eyes, put her back to the wall and slid upright. Things rocked beneath her. She put her palms flat against the wall and pushed off, looking only forward as she stepped long and light toward the door, arms outstretched.

It was like walking on air, the boards falling behind her, almost no foothold ahead of her. She got purchase for the first three steps, then there was nothing to tread on, but her momentum took her on and she stepped down on to the solid threshold, then out on to the small landing as the rest of the floor fell away in a rush.

She went downstairs at a run, ignoring the danger of loose treads because she could feel the partition wall shaking.

Outside in the garden, she looked back as if expecting to see Jackie's face at the window after all. Or her own face.

She had stumbled through splintered boards and foul-smelling plaster to get to the sink, then lifted the curtain and carpet bedding aside carefully in order to climb back out. *Why carefully?* The rat litter was unharmed, pink and seething. *I should stamp on them.* But she didn't. The doe would have survived—gone into a wall cavity or slipped along a roof beam. Rats could walk through fire. They sought out war zones. They lived off plague spores.

The rain clattered on the backyard scrap and a broken-backed peal of thunder rolled through the cloud base. Stella stood in the drench not moving. She stood there for a long time and when she finally walked away, the rain seemed to walk with her.

40

"They've got it wrong," Sonny said.

"They always get it wrong."

Like DI Sorley, Sonny and Donna had all the morning papers. The story was set to run and run. The next day's editions would carry pictures of flowers laid in the streets for Janis and Nesta and Mandy.

"They think it's just me," Sonny said.

"They think it's a man. Not you. They don't say it's *you*."

"They just put stab wounds."

"What do you want them to put?"

Sonny thought about it. "I don't know."

"They'd never understand," Donna said. "They'd never get it."

"This DS Mooney. The lady cop."

"Ladycop," Donna liked the sound of it. "Ladycop. She'd never get it."

Sonny laughed. "Let's go hunting, Donna."

Donna was sitting in a chair, legs drawn up, her face hidden in the fall of her hair. She had recently dyed it to bring it back to the glossy black sheen that matched her near-black eyes. Behind her, the windowpane was curtained by water. She said, "It's different for you."

"You like it. You *love* it."

"It's different."

The flat was two small rooms and a bathroom over a launderette; the pale smell of damp linen seeped up to them night and day, but there was a washing machine in the bathroom and they did their own laundry, just in case anything had splashed or spotted.

You could hear televisions and bass-beat music and voices from all sides. Sirens and car horns in the street. At night pub bands and disco sound systems.

"I'm on late shift next week," Sonny reminded her.

"One more," Donna said, "just one. Then move on."

The road atlas was open on the table: a land of opportunity. They could go anywhere to find their little helpers, their bit-part players.

Sonny went into the box-kitchen and fetched two beers from the fridge. Donna switched on the TV. "Play a tape," she said.

He chose Nesta Cameron for her red hair. You could hear Nesta saying, "Don't hurt me. Don't hurt me," but it was softened and muffled by the tape-gag; you had to know what she was saying. Donna knew. Nesta's eyes were big with fear as she watched Donna undress. Sonny was pretty good with the camera, panning back and forth between them. Pretty good with his close-ups of Nesta and the knife; the knife and Nesta.

After they'd been watching for a while, Donna went into the bedroom and came back with a belt from a woman's dress. It was made of floral fabric with a gilt buckle; it was frayed slightly along the seams and the buckle was tarnished.

"Come on," she said.

Sonny turned and let her tie his hands behind his back. He was wearing a T-shirt and boxers; Donna left the T-shirt on him.

He said, "Don't hurt me."

Donna slapped him on the cheek, hard but not too hard.

"Don't hurt me." He managed to look scared. He managed to get a shake into his voice.

On the TV, Nesta Cameron said the same, crooning with terror behind the tape-gag—*Don't hurt me don't hurt me don't hurt me*—like a ventriloquist with laryngitis, and Donna watched for a moment as her screen self moved in, cut, moved back, up on her toes like a dancer.

Now she turned back to Sonny. She slapped him again, harder. She started to undress.

Later, after Sonny had gone out to score some drugs, she fell asleep and dreamed. In the dream, she was awake but she couldn't see and there was a strong smell that made her throat sore. She couldn't see and there seemed to be no sound, as if she had been struck deaf on a starless night; except that there was no night breeze, no freshness on her face. She might have been in a black box.

Then, suddenly, there was a light, a ball of light in the dark, and a shape began to flow from it, began to coalesce. It was a face, forming there against the surrounding dark. A hand reached down, disembodied, and lifted her by the hair. A voice told her what would happen next.

She woke, startled, but the images scattered along with the memory of the dream, and she was left with nothing more than a vague sense of being troubled. She got up, feeling unsteady, as if she had woken to illness or the onset of a hangover. The bathroom had just a dim yellowish center light and the plastic shade threw thick, lacy patterns round the walls and across the mirror above the sink.

Donna was naked still. She leaned forward toward the mirror, putting her elbows on the sink. In her right hand she held a sharp, thin-bladed knife and she drew it, lightly, across the underside of her forearm. For a moment, it seemed that she'd only fetched a graze to the place, then a line of blood sprang up, welled a little, and ran in beads to the edge of her arm. She watched as the drops cascaded into the sink and made a thin track on the china, then she cut again, oh, so delicately, and sent a second line to chase the first.

In the thick light the mirror gave her back a shadowy reflection, but anyone watching would have noticed the little web of criss-cross scars on her forearms, on her breasts, on her belly, on her legs; a map of pain.

She cut again. Her face bore no expression.

41

Even with the fan full on and the vents down, the windows in Stella's car were fogged with condensation. Threads of steam rose from her saturated clothing. She squelched when she changed gear. A call came through and Stella plugged her phone into the hands-free mike, even though she wasn't on the move: London stops dead in the rain. Maxine Hewitt told her that Nesta's cleaners were closet fans of *This Morning.*

"They weren't too keen to admit it at first. They'd cleaned eight flats when they got to Cameron's, so they decided they'd earned a rest. They're just agency cleaners, time doesn't matter. They sat down with a coffee and a biscuit and watched for half an hour. That was after they'd flipped through the channels."

"But Janis Parker's TV was definitely tuned to video?"

"Definitely."

"Did you go to Cameron's flat?"

"Sure. It was because the TV wasn't on video that I asked the cleaners—"

"Okay. Were there flowers outside?"

"You want them cleared away?"

"I want them left."

She called Mike Sorley and asked for either CCTV or police photographers at all three scenes of crime.

"For how long?"

"A week?"

"Make it photographers," he said, after she'd told him why. "We'd have to subcontract CCTV anyway, and you'd need someone there to watch the monitor, or what's the point?"

The storm had brought down a false twilight. She was walled in by cabs and trucks, exhaust fumes floating through the downpour, a blur of tail-lights one way, a blur of headlights the other. She dialed again and got Pete Harriman.

"Where are you?"

"On my way to *Imago*. Back-up interviews." He sounded as if he planned to enjoy it.

"It was a good idea of yours—to leave the flowers. Sorley has authorized photographers at the scenes for a week. Give *Imago* to someone else and set it up. They'll have to find vantage points, so be charming to the neighbors; and make sure the photographers have got a note of your mobile and mine as well as the squad room number."

"I could manage *Imago* as well."

"Get the photographers in place."

"I'm just around the corner, boss. Be there in five minutes."

"Who is it?" Stella asked. "Nina Groves, the mentally challenged ice queen, or the secretary, whass'name?"

"Petra."

"Aha!"

"They like it," Harriman told her, "murder squad, nasty details, it makes their hearts flutter."

"Save it. Organize the snappers. Do Petra later."

Finally, she put in a call that was long overdue.

Brian Fairweather had worked with Stella for a little over a year and they'd been friends with no complications. He'd moved over to Serious Crimes and taken a promotion on the way. He came on the phone sounding like a man with a schedule.

"There was a shooting on the patch," Stella said. "Punishment shooting, elbows and knees."

"What's your interest, Stella?"

"None, not really. It was mentioned in another context. I'm elim-
inating possibilities."

"Get back to me if you find a connection?"

"Of course."

"It was a guy called Damian Connors. Sometimes he was called
Daz. A dealer, but not a real player. They shot his knees and elbows.
He clanks when he walks and he can only do that on a frame."

"Have you got anyone for it?"

"Sore point."

"Do you like anyone?"

"Got to be a drug connection. We've been down to Harefield and
interviewed the usual blind mutes."

"Where did it happen, Colin?"

"Where? Kensal Green cemetery."

"Exactly where?"

"They laid him down on a grave. You know: a horizontal stone
with the bodies buried underneath. Why? Does it make a difference?"

"No, not really. I like to get a picture."

42

Anne Beaumont laughed when she opened the door. She put Stella's clothes in the
dryer while Stella took a shower, which, Anne assured her, would
come at no extra charge, nor would the time taken be subtracted
from her session.

"You like making those jokes," Stella observed.

"What jokes?"

"Off duty, time's up, by the hour."

"Do I?"

"I think you feel bad about charging people who need a wise friend."

"Yeah? I've just installed a credit-card machine." But there was a briskness about the way she said it.

"These women," Stella said. "These women they killed . . ." It was what she'd come to talk about.

"I've looked. There are certain obvious factors, but nothing out of the ordinary. All attractive, all young, all independent, none of them in a relationship—"

"Janis Parker."

"I'm calling that a fling."

"She was pregnant."

"And—?"

"Okay, go on."

"Two lived alone but one shared, no common birthdays or astrological signs, a rough geographical link—Notting Hill and adjacent areas—but that says more about the killers than their victims."

"Says what?"

"That their method of choosing has something to do with location."

"Ah. I think we'd figured that one out."

"You asked. I told you. Two of the women were sociological A/Bs, the other not; the list of contents tells us that you could pretty well switch Janis Parker and Nesta Cameron in cultural terms, but there isn't that much difference when you come to look at Mandy Wallace's videos and CDs and so forth. Cultural choice is fairly homogenized these days."

"But Mandy Wallace looks the odd one out."

"No, I don't think so. Not really. The similarities are more significant: pretty, young, *female*."

Which caused Stella to ask another question. "What about her—the woman?"

"Yes, I've thought about her a lot. Normally, I'd type her in a certain way because the man would be the instigator, she would be the follower. Even the bystander, perhaps. I suppose that might still be the case, because the DNA traces can't be relied on to tell a full story. I mean, what if the man makes her do what she does? Forces her."

"Against her will, you mean?"

"I'm not sure that notion applies. Against her nature, perhaps. Not against her will. She wants to be there and she wants to be there with him. If she does it because he tells her to—orders her to—it's part of a game she needs to play; even if she plays at a cost to herself."

"And if the DNA is telling the right story?"

"Then I can't fathom her: hands up. But I suppose I'd have to apply the sort of profile I'd give to a man under the same circumstances. A history of abuse; childhood trauma; the torture of small animals; inability to connect with the world most of us claim to live in. You know this stuff. No idea of conscience. Indifference to the suffering of others."

"You've seen the SOC videos and the PM reports."

"Oh, yes. I think pleasure in pain is guaranteed."

"Fifty cuts," Stella remembered, "before the cut that kills. Fifty or more, wasn't that what Sam Burgess said?"

"The Innuit have fifty names for snow," Anne observed. "These people have fifty different names for pain."

"Two of the TVs belonging to the victims were tuned to the video channel. The other might have been, we can't know for sure. My guess is it was."

"It's a perfectly credible theory," Anne told her, "videos as trophies."

"Tell me more."

"They watch them, they re-live the moment, re-live the excitement, re-live the victims' fear. Little home movies of pain and death, and they're the stars." Anne fetched Stella's clothes. She said, "Whoever she is, she won't stop."

It was the expectation of being followed, Delaney decided, that made him feel as if he was stepping in someone else's shadow. He hadn't

seen the red BMW again and if he turned, quickly, in the street, there
was no one jumping back into a doorway or suddenly deciding to
cross the road. Turning in the street was becoming a compulsion; he
had to hold himself against it, as if he had a hand on his own shoulder.

He turned. No one. A kid on a skateboard; couples bound for the
movies; someone hailing a taxi. People going about their business.
He crossed the road and no one followed him. It wasn't a ploy: the
restaurant where he was meeting Stella was on the other side of the
street.

She had taken the day's reports to the pub and ordered her shot
glass of vodka, then she'd read the reports, then she'd asked for another vodka, then she'd made some notes on the reports, then she'd
written herself a couple of reminders. Displacement activity. Then
she threw the dice. Then she made her phone calls. It wasn't the dice
she was avoiding, it was the calls.

Now she sat in le Piaf, at a table as far from the street window as
she could get, although it wasn't an AMIP hangout and she'd never
eaten there with George, and she wasn't expecting anyone she knew
to walk in the door except for John Delaney.

The dice had fallen double six: no contest.

He kissed her, then glanced over his shoulder before sitting down.
She said, "There's no one there."

It's me," he laughed. "I'm there."

"Watching yourself."

"Watching us."

"What do you see?"

"I see a woman who isn't sure and a man who is."

Before the waiter could arrive, she asked: "Do you love me?"

He said, "I do, yes, I do love you." Said it at once, without pausing for thought, and she got up, quickly, and went to the women's
room, because it was impossible to stop the tears.

When she came back they ordered their food and talked about
nothing for quite a while. "Nothing" included murder. He told her
that he'd made a cursory search of two archives at newspapers where
he was still welcome, but hadn't come up with anything that seemed
to match.

"It might not look like a match. Or else it will, but you won't find it reported that way. Not initially, anyway. First reports often with-hold information."

"Or give misinformation," he said.

"You did a good job. The public is thinking what we want it to think; more importantly, the killers don't know what we know. The archives," she asked, "how far back are you looking?"

"A year."

"Make it five."

He smiled. "Okay, well, I've nothing else to do with my time."

She held up a hand in acknowledgment. "If I put a copper on the case, there'll be journos looking over his shoulder."

"It's okay," Delaney told her. "My deadlines are hours away."

"What *are* you working on?" She realized, suddenly, that she didn't know. He hadn't talked about his work and she hadn't asked, maybe because it was the wrong kind of intimacy: casual, quotid-ian, unrushed—a kind of luxury. Except he was hip deep in *her* day-to-day.

"Urban pollution," he told her. "Very unoriginal, very necessary."

"Who do you blame?"

"Politicians, mostly. They talk shit. Where there's shit there's methane."

"They should bottle it. Export it to the Third World."

He smiled and held her hand across the table, just briefly, as if they were on a first date.

"What about you?"

She nodded. "Me too. I love you."

They ate in silence and paid the bill and left.

The weather was coming up from the west. Either the storm had cir-cled and come back, or one storm was chasing another.

Stella lay in the circle of his arm, damp with her own sweat and his, watching rain sluice the windows. It ran orange and sulfurous yellow: city backlights. She thought about going home and wondered what she now meant by that.

The phone rang and Delaney got up on an elbow to answer it. Apart from "Hello," he said nothing, though he continued to listen.

After a moment he held the phone out to her.

"It's for you," he said. "It's George."

43

The crank callers were sad and dull, the friends and relatives remembered even less second time round, the house-to-house was either a shrug or a false lead, and no one with a moon face and a silly tuft of hair under his lower lip had turned up for a walk-on part at the Kandy Kave, but Pete Harriman's idea had paid off.

Stella fetched a cup of AMIP coffee and grimaced while she drank it. Her hair was scraped back into a stubby ponytail, her eyes carried shadows, and she looked like someone who was wearing what had come to hand.

Andy Greegan was pinning a series of photographs on the squad-room whiteboard; Stella had her own set: mid-shots, close-ups, the man approaching to lay his flowers, standing a moment as if in sentinel grief, then walking away. At Delgarno Villas he had wedged his bunch of arum lilies into the bars, just as others had done with their tulips, their irises, their roses. One of the shots showed him walking away, backed by a wall of blooms.

He was wearing chinos, a beaten-up denim jacket, and a baseball cap with a long bill that set his face in shadow. Stella tried to make a comparison with Belle's description of her stalker. He seemed the right weight and his face was pudgy, but his hair wasn't yellow and he didn't seem to have a beard. She looked across to Maxine Hewitt, who was having the same thoughts.

"Men shave," Maxine observed.

"So we've got him three times," Stella shuffled through the photos, "one at each scene of crime."

"Keep looking," Greegan advised.

She went through again, separating the photos into piles. There were more shots of the street outside Nesta Cameron's flat. She compared the time codes. "He's been back."

"He has. If you look—" Andy was talking to everyone in the room, "—you'll see he's been to all three, but twice to the Cameron flat."

"Which means he might well go back to the others," offered Maxine.

Harriman said, "Which means we can nick him. We'll need extra bodies."

"We'll get them," Stella said. "Since we became the tabloids' choice, the budget seems to have expanded. Nothing like public outrage and alarm for loosening the purse strings." She held up the photos. "Has everyone got copies of these?" Everyone had. "The time codes tell us that he's visited the scenes between twelve-thirty and one, in all four cases."

"He's on his lunch hour," Harriman said.

"Looks like it. Three teams, firearm issue."

"SO 19 will want to be there."

"Not a chance," Stella said. "Tell them we've got guns of our own."

She sat in the car with Pete Harriman and watched the approach to Mandy Wallace's flat. To begin with, Harriman had done all the talking, then he gave up on it. "Are you okay?" he asked.

"I'm fine. What's the problem?"

"With me? Nothing."

"I've got a hangover. Perfect bitch. Wasn't too bad earlier, but it's just kicked in."

"Okay." Harriman was entirely sympathetic to the notion of hangovers, their implication and aftermath; also their cure. "Full English breakfast is the only real solution." He looked round.

"Must be a caff somewhere. I could get you an egg and sausage sandwich."

"You bring it in," Stella told him, "I'll throw it up."

She put her head against the window and closed her eyes. The glass was cool against her cheek. She had been drunk, of course she had, but not nearly drunk enough, and if she looked rough it was less to do with booze than with having had no sleep. That and guilt. And misery. And pain.

People came and left flowers. Others just walked by with a look of curiosity. Stella thought maybe she ought to stop them all, question them all, why not? She made a mental note to get uniform to take a couple of random street interviews: Do you live locally? Do you normally take this route? Did you see anything suspicious on the night of . . . ?

Luck, she thought. That's how it worked with most serials. Anyone might be holding the clue. That man with his smart suit and document case: Mr. Normal. That woman with her pedal-pushers and heavy make-up: Ms. Lip Gloss. Maybe we should leaflet the city, she thought. A helicopter drop. Maybe we should give up.

George had asked, "How long?" And she'd told him.

He'd asked, "Is it serious?" And she'd told him.

He had stared at her, motionless, speechless, his eyes clouded with hurt.

44

It was like clockwork: twelve-forty-three, almost exactly splitting the half-hour. Maybe killers have schedules, Stella thought. The photographer was the first to spot him, but then he had the advantage of a long lens.

Mr. Lily. He was wearing the same chinos, the same jacket, the same baseball cap: as if he didn't want to be mistaken for anyone else. He walked down the short pathway that led to the street door of Mandy Wallace's flat and turned to the handspan of lawn, now crowded with flowers still in their cellophane wrappings. He stooped and laid his lilies there, then stepped back, as if in momentary reverence. Stella had been watching for three hours, and it was what everyone had done: ten people in that time, each with a bargain bunch, each stepping forward, setting the flowers, then stepping back, head bowed. For someone they had never known. What were they mourning, Stella wondered.

Mr. Lily turned and walked back to the pavement and Pete Harriman picked him up, clean as a whistle. Stella was out of the car and ready to back him up. She was wearing a Glock 17 in a harness holster but she hadn't drawn it, because her first look at Mr. Lily told her that he was going to be a big disappointment.

"What makes you think that?" Maxine was eating a late-lunch chicken and mayo sandwich and collating the third batch of second-round close-contact interviews. She added, "Where is he?"

"The interview room—with Pete."

"You haven't started?" Maxine had already made it plain that she would like to take a crack at Mr. Lily. She took a bite of her sandwich and pulled Stella's arrest notes toward her, catching a blob of mayonnaise in her free hand. "What's his name?"

"Mr. Lily," Stella confirmed.

"So he's not talking . . ."

"Not talking, not moving, I'm not convinced he's actually breathing. I thought I'd give him a little while to acclimatize."

"If he's not talking, how can you be certain he's a waste of time?"

"I don't know. When I saw him I thought: this isn't him."

"Feminine intuition," Maxine said. "An invaluable policing tool."

Stella smiled without looking in any way amused. She said, "Mind your fucking manners, DC Hewitt."

Mr. Lily looked at Stella from the opposite side of the interview-room table, while the tape spooled on in silence.

She had called Anne Beaumont before going in and asked for a key that might unlock the door. "We've got this guy who has been visiting the scenes of crime, laying flowers . . . he won't speak. Nothing."

"You think he's the male member of the team?"

"I doubt it. Don't ask me why."

"I wasn't going to."

"However, there's a good chance he's nuts."

"Disturbed."

"That's what I was going to say."

"Was he carrying any ID?" Anne asked, then immediately: "Okay, yes, you would have thought of that."

"A fiver and loose change, a door key, pictures of flowers outside the victims' flats that he'd cut from the papers. George knows," she said, completely without meaning to. "He found out."

"So now things are simpler."

"You think so? What in hell should I say to him?"

Anne suggested that talking to George was a task for Stella. However, she did tell her what to say to Mr. Lily.

. . .

"We know you did it," Stella said.

Mr. Lily smiled a secret smile. He nodded, but didn't speak; he was still wearing the baseball cap and the bill nodded with him like a demented bird. He might have been forty or forty-five, perhaps; he had a heavy beard-shadow but no growth; his gut started a long way above his belt.

"We know you did all of them."

Mr. Lily's smile broadened and he gave a little clap of the hands as if to reward Stella for getting him so completely right.

I did it. I'm the Fiend. I'm the Monster on the Loose.

"But we don't know why."

Mr. Lily looked upset; he looked agitated.

"And we don't know who you are."

Which proved the key. After that, he talked for an hour, giving them the how, the why, the ins and outs, the bits and pieces, not least his assertion that he materialized in the women's flats as a figment of their own darkest desires. Stella liked it as a metaphor, but as courtroom evidence it seemed a little flimsy.

One of the uniformed leg-men turned up a local GP who knew Mr. Lily. Stella spoke to him on the phone. He agreed to notify Mr. Lily's caseworker, who would arrive eventually with Mr. Lily's medication.

"What medication is that?" Stella was making notes for her report.

"I'm not sure what they've got him on. One of the neuro-leptics. Thorazine, I expect."

"What does that do?"

"Stops the voices and the visions. Well, more or less."

"It makes them better?"

"It makes them . . . different."

Stella hung up and wrote the end of her brief report on Mr. Lily. Wrote him off.

Voices and visions. Did team killers hear the same thing, see the same thing? Did they dream the same dreams?

She handed her report to Sue Chapman and asked for a transcript of the interview tape to be given to Mike Sorley.

"And circulated?" Sue asked.

"Two-line summary to let people know what happened. Recidivist time-waster, referred to psychiatric social worker, prosecution not recommended. There's enough paper in this fucking office."

Sue had already noticed the hair pulled tightly back, the barbed-wire body language. She thought of asking Stella what was troubling her, but all she said was: "You're right."

Stella found that day's surveillance photos on her desk, with a note from Sorley asking whether she wanted to keep the photographers in place. Mr. Lily had shaken his faith; hers too.

She leafed through the shots: Mr. and Mrs. Anyone bringing flowers or walking past, each wearing the odd, abstracted look of people in close-up who don't know they're being observed.

Donna in her pedal-pushers and too much make-up.

Stella tossed them into her waste bin.

The rest-room mirrors gave back the image of a woman in her early thirties who needed sleep, was close to tears, wanted more than she deserved. She put on some mascara, a smudge of rouge, a dab of lipstick, nose to nose with herself, and asking why.

George standing with his hands flat on the table as if unable to support his own bodyweight, his head hanging, his tears falling straight down like rain. He was saying, "You ought to go. Don't you think? In the morning. It seems to me that I'll be better on my own."

Delaney watching her as she put her clothes back on, turning away from him in sudden embarrassment. He was saying, "Will you be all right? Do you want me to come with you?" And, as she was leaving, "You have a key. Don't forget that."

Voices and visions.

45

"Let's go hunting."

"Have you found someone?" Donna was drinking brandy and water; there was something wrong but she couldn't put a name to it. She felt light-headed and there was a little lick of pain behind her eyes that came and went like a guttering flame. She hadn't eaten all day, she just wanted the brandy. The brandy and maybe a line or two of coke.

"Yeah. Someone . . . I've been looking at."

"Not from the lap-dancing club?"

"Of course not. We don't go back: you said that."

Except when the feeling gets too strong and you have to pay a visit, just a walk-by, just a way of reliving the moment when you stood outside and everything had yet to happen. My rules, Donna thought, and I can break them. I can go back. Sonny can't. He's too stupid, too much of a risk.

"Who is she?"

"Jean Halliday. That's what her credit card says."

"You think she could be the chosen?"

"Yeah. The chosen. She looks right to me."

"The chosen" was how Donna liked to describe them. It sounded special. It conferred status.

"What's she like?"

"Blonde hair, but I think she colors it. Quite tall. I like her."

"She's pretty?"

"Of course she's pretty."

"When do you see her?"

"Now and then. Sometimes in the middle of the week, but most often on a Friday."

"She's a regular?"

"Comes in on her own with a book and has a coffee or a white wine, but she isn't waiting for anyone. Once or twice she ordered food: Caesar salad. I think there must be something she does, something she goes to, a class maybe, and she comes in when she's finished."

"What time?"

"About ten-thirty or eleven."

"That's early. Early for us."

"No, it's all right. She stays: reads, drinks. She hangs around. She's there when my shift ends. I think she's looking to be picked up."

"She could get lucky," Donna said.

Sonny laughed. "Could get lucky, yeah." He laughed long and hard.

Donna liked planning, she liked the anticipation, the mind pictures; as she and Sonny talked, the fine hairs on her forearms lifted and prickled. She gave herself a splash more brandy: not too much, because she might be driving back tonight. If they got lucky. If Jean Halliday stopped off for a coffee. It didn't always work, of course. All the planning could be for nothing if the chosen didn't live alone after all, or the place looked wrong, or someone saw them going in.

"She's local, is she?"

"Off Bayswater Road: one of the squares."

"Sounds rich."

"So she might have some money lying about. We need money, Donna, especially if we're going traveling after this."

The pain behind Donna's eyes flickered and spread, a light touch. "How many times have you been over there?"

"Three. I followed her three times. She went in on her own, there were no lights on, no one went in after her. Once she went to the Eight-til-Late and got some shopping; it was all stuff for one, you know? Small carton of milk, small Special K, a chilli chicken, and some rice."

"She didn't see you?"

Sonny shook his head, eagerly. "No, I was . . . I bought some stuff too, I was right behind her at the checkout, I was close enough to touch her. She was just shopping, you know? She didn't look at anyone."

All part of the build-up, all part of the excitement. Sonny spotted them, Sonny sized them up, Sonny tracked them and waited and watched. Sonny the Great White Hunter. Anyway, Donna liked the surprise she was going to get: like a child being taken to a mystery destination for a special treat.

"Will she be there tonight?"

"It's the right day."

"But she's not always there?"

"Not always. Usually."

"I hope she's there tonight," Donna said. "I'm ready for it. I'm up for it. Aren't you?"

She gave a little shiver: bright-eyed, feverish.

46

Stella was looking out on to a cobbled mews just off the Saints. Most of the flats in the mews were studios of one sort or another and the area was coming up despite its reputation. You could get a goat curry or a wrap of cocaine within a three-minute walk and there were half a dozen armorers nearby who'd rent you anything from a Mach 10 to a Glock 17, but the city traders and private-investment genies were colonizing the blocks to the south and west. The bad hoods and hardmen weren't moving out, but the mix looked good.

The studio belonged to a man who was about to go abroad for a couple of months. He was currently in north Cornwall spending time with a client, would come back, touch base for long enough to pack, then fly to the Caribbean to fit a boat. He was a business friend of George's, and Stella knew just how fine an irony it was that she should have lucked in to the flat that way. It also let her know just how eager George was to have her go: he'd fixed it for her in a couple of hours and was out when she called after work to collect a few things.

The flat was bachelor luxury: glass-and-chrome bathroom, enormous living space, leather furniture, an untouched kitchen; a lot nicer and a hell of a lot more expensive than the flat she shared with George. Had once shared with George. It was pretty much central in the AMIP-5 patch, and she'd lived there all her life, but she felt like a stranger in a strange land.

There was no point in throwing the dice. She called Delaney. His answer machine said: Not here, leave a number, beep.

Sonny was making food sculpture. It was his speciality. When the salads went out to the customers, there would always be one little centerpiece to catch the eye: almost too clever to eat. Except people didn't go to the Ocean Diner for the food. The most they might want would be the hamburger or the chicken satay or maybe the pasta. No, they came for the cocktails and the atmosphere. The Ocean Diner was cool. You could go in after the movie, drink, talk, make a relationship or break one, wait for that crucial phone call, cruise, schmooze, and still be there when the morning papers came in and the menu was coffee with eggs.

Now and then Sonny would go to the door of the kitchen and look through to the bar. He was waiting for Jean Halliday, who usually had coffee or white wine and sometimes a Caesar salad. It was a little early just yet, but he was longing to see her.

Donna walked round the room a couple of times, touching objects, touching surfaces, restless and a little breathless. The pain in her head had grown dull and spread, but it didn't worry her: she felt light and energized.

Sonny would do it well. Sonny would get it right. Ever since they'd started, he had wanted to please, his moon face looking up at her, his eager smile, his eager hands. He loved what they did, but for him it was all raw excitement, all adrenalin rush. Donna had more at stake than that.

Noise hemmed her in: music, TVs, engines and mad laughter from the street. She went to the window. It was a mild night, no rain in the air, and the breeze had dropped to almost nothing. A group of cabbies stood outside the Steadfast office waiting for a call. The turnstile whores were waiting on corners or walking the curbside. She watched the girls as they got in and out of cars. Any of you, she thought, any of you would do if the conditions were right: somewhere private; no interruptions; time to work.

She chose a video and slipped it into her bag: a record of the time they'd spent with Janis Parker. She went to the bedroom and fetched a fish-gutting knife in its long, solid scabbard, and put that into her bag as well, then went back to the bedroom and stripped off the pedal-pushers, her sneakers, her Sloppy Joe top. The twelve-by-ten room was furnished with a plain, slat-based bed and a flat-pack wardrobe. She took out a dark skirt, a light-blue shirt, and a light cotton zipper jacket, all of them recently washed and ironed. From the drawer at the bottom of the wardrobe she took a pair of sheer tights; some dark-blue court shoes stood by the bed.

There was no need for it, but she took off her underclothes. Then she went back to the living room and retrieved the fish-gutting knife and returned to the bedroom, where she stood in front of the cheap mirror on the wardrobe door. The pale web of scars stood out against the flush on her skin. She was sweating slightly; her body felt clammy as if someone had turned up the heating. A savage little percussion had started up in her temples and now it leached down to her cheekbones.

She put the blade of the knife to her breast. She said, "Don't hurt me."

She held it to her stomach and to the meat of her thigh. She said, "Don't hurt me."

The blade was cold, though her body was hot. She pressed it to the plumpness of her buttock, turning so that she could catch its glint in the weak bedroom light. She said, "Don't hurt me."

Her cheek. "Don't hurt me." Her nipple. "Don't hurt me." The boss of her arm. "Don't hurt me."

She slid the blade slowly between her legs. "Don't hurt me, don't hurt me, don't hurt me."

She put the knife back into its sheath but didn't get dressed. She lay down on the bed, naked, a little light-headed, being careful not to disarrange the clothes she had laid out. The light hurt her eyes so she turned it off and lay in the dark. Outside on the Strip there were shouts and car horns and music with a meaty bass, but she could hear none of it.

I'm ready, Sonny. Give me a call. Tell me she's waiting.

Stella's new home had a good hi-fi, original art, a wall-mounted plasma-screen TV. Bachelor Boy was in the money: he wasn't a de-signer like George, with stabilization problems and questionable marketing skills; he supervised big refits for rich clients who moored their Bluewater 60s and their Passoa 54s in the Cayman Islands and the Seychelles. The place reminded Stella of Janis Parker's flat and the comparison, when she thought of it, made the skin on her shoulders pucker.

She watched TV for half an hour without knowing what was on: voices and visions. She switched off. There was a different re-mote control to dim the lights. It was quiet in the mews: when res-idents came and went, she could hear their voices; she could hear doors being closed and double-locked. She was sitting in a big black-leather and blond-wood armchair with a foot-rest: it was op-posite the TV, set up for solitary viewing, and her face was re-flected, dimly, as if the screen were a window to a farther room, where her twin sat watching and waiting to see what would happen next.

I'm not wild about this place.

It's somewhere to be, her twin told her. *And you need some-where to be.*

There are plates and pans in the kitchen and linen in the airing cupboard and clothes in the wardrobe and none of it belongs to me. There are books and videos and a computer and none of it belongs to me. There's a wine rack with vintage stuff in it. The freezer is full of gourmet meals. None of it belongs to me.

What do you want? It's a palace.

That's why I can't live here.

You're unsettled. Your life is upside-down. Of course you feel strange.

There are condoms in the bedside cabinet. The bathroom is full of men's stuff. Bachelor Boy cosmetics.

All right, I know what you mean. Go to Delaney's.

Delaney isn't in.

He'll be back. Leave him a message.

I could have done that; I could have gone there. He asked me to. He said, "Remember you've got a key."

But you won't go there . . .

It's not right. I ought to be nowhere, no man's land. A land where no man is.

Somewhere in between: neutral ground.

That's it. But this place makes me edgy.

Find your own place.

I will. That's what I'll do.

In the meantime, crack a vintage and defrost a gourmet meal.

Fuck it, Stella said to her twin, *why not?*

But she didn't do that. She went out into the mews and slammed Bachelor Boy's door behind her. Back in the flat, the phone started to ring. Her twin called her back, but she shook her head. *That'll be a rich client with a bulkhead leak.*

She walked out to Ladbroke Grove and up to the Harrow Road, then turned left to Kensal Green cemetery. Colin Fairweather hadn't been able to tell her exactly where Daz had been taken, though by following the path nearest to the road she found three horizontal stones and guessed it must have been one of them. Too dark to check for bloodstains. She sat down on the middle stone and set a picture in her mind of Daz being brought down the path, the men with guns, wired up and anxious to get the job done. She didn't know about the rain that night, or that Daz had been drunk, but her mind's-eye image wasn't too far from the truth.

Something moved behind her and she got to her feet, turning in fear, but it was only a dog, trotting through the grass between the graves. As it reached the path it was joined by another, then another, both seeming to come from nowhere, visible for a moment in the light from the street, then gone again.

Further back, hidden from Stella by broken columns and ivy-crusted crosses, Dog Boy stood by the gate to the mausoleum and watched her. She was sitting on the stone that he had come to think of as the butcher slab and her head was down as if she might be crying. He wondered if the man they'd shot had been related to her in some way; whether she had come to look at the place to get a sense of his pain. The brindled dog's ears lifted as the three others came toward the mausoleum; his big eyes scanned the dark and a growl, just audible, started low in his throat. When he scented them, his ears dropped again and he looked away. They stopped close by and flopped down. Hunger had made them restless. Soon the brindle would lead them into the darker reaches of the cemetery and they would hunt the rat holes and rabbit holes back by the old plague pits.

The boy continued to watch for a while, then grew bored and went down into the shelter of the mausoleum. The woman was no threat. She wasn't searching for the living.

47

People move on, people die.

Jean Halliday knew this for sure, because in the last couple of months her partner of three years had traded her in for a tall, cool blonde and her father had died. Neil had been good about it—that's how it was seen, anyway, handing over the flat and its contents, handing over the car. Being good about things was very close indeed to being guilty about things and, in any case, he could afford it. The blonde wasn't going to last and she suspected Neil knew that, but as interim lovers go she was pretty tall and pretty cool. Jean's father died just six weeks after that. He'd been ill for a year, but fighting; then there came a moment when the cancer caught and spread like a fire in dry scrub.

The odd thing was, Jean didn't feel so bad about any of it. Neil had begun to bore her; sex with Neil had begun to bore her; life with Neil . . . She felt betrayed and she felt a hint of failure, but a real sense of loss was more difficult to find. Her father's death left her slightly stranded, but not too far off-course. She wished she could have known him better, but since he'd never encouraged that it was difficult for her to feel genuine regret.

At the funeral, her mother had watched, dry-eyed, as the coffin slipped out of sight behind the velvet curtain. As she and Jean walked back to the car, she had said, "Who was that man? Do you know?" They had been married for forty-three years.

Now Jean and her mother both lived alone. Once a week, often on a Friday, Jean made the short trip to her mother's house in Kensington and they talked in new ways. It was as if they had been recently introduced and had liked each other on first meeting. They laughed together, they told stories, they exchanged ideas, and they rarely reminisced.

Jean valued those evenings; but she was also doing the things that people do who are supposed to think that they've been left with half a life—except that the Tai Chi class, the two movies a week, the theater trips, the concerts didn't at all leave Jean depressed or resentful. She felt more as if she'd reclaimed the half of her life that had gone missing.

Calling in at the Ocean Diner was part of her new life. It was a good place to be. It was very likely that she wouldn't be the only singleton in there and, even if she were, it wouldn't matter. If a guy hit on her, it would be done in a casual, oblique, unfussy way, and she could simply look up from her book and smile and shake her head and no one felt any the worse. Jean didn't mind. And anyway, maybe she wouldn't always look up and shake her head; maybe one time she'd have a feeling about the guy, about his un-English good looks and his wry smile and the way he'd glanced at the book she was reading, and she'd say, sure, thanks, white wine would be nice.

Until that happened, or if it never happened, she liked to call in at the Ocean Diner if she wasn't feeling too tired, or didn't have a heavy schedule next day, or it was a Friday. She would get there at around eleven, when other bars were closing, and stay until the streets emptied and grew quiet, until the rhythms of life seemed to change and places you thought you knew well were scarcely recognizable for being empty and unsmudged.

The red, white, and blue neon piping above the bar flashed like a beacon, though the rest of the bar was dimly lit by swan-necked lamps fixed to each table. At that time of night, the music would be blue-note or classic Ella. Jean had a vision of herself sitting at her usual booth, near the window but off to one side, reading her book in a pool of lamplight by Edward Hopper, and around her—little unguessable psychodramas—the other nightbirds leaning on the bar, or speaking softly and intensely to one another, or holding hands in silence.

It was Friday and she was a little later than usual because her mother had cooked for them: she enjoyed trying out some of the more complicated and exotic meals that her husband would have refused to eat. Jean parked at the upper end of Holland Park Avenue and walked back.

The booth she most liked was free. The drink was white wine. The book was *Madame Bovary*.

48

Donna seemed to be shedding a glow. Her neck ached, now, along with her head, but she was still on the denial side of illness, and a couple of lines of cocaine were helping her belief. Once or twice she had fallen asleep and the black-box dream had begun, but she had told herself she mustn't sleep and she'd come to almost at once, the dream dissolving before she was properly awake. She was hot and cold; when she got up to answer the phone she left a damp outline on the bed, but her teeth chattered.

Sonny said, "Come now." It was enough.

She dressed in the clothes she'd laid out, then made a contents check on her bag: Janis tape; video camera, loaded and charged; a play-cassette that would hold the smaller film-pod from the camera; the fish-gutting knife; a few capsules of amyl nitrate. Then she went out onto the Strip.

It was a busy night: the whores whoring, the dealers dealing. Donna was in a hot, bright tunnel of lights and noise where the smell of fast food rose and floated atop a low, thick layer of diesel.

She caught a bus to the Gate and started to walk down toward Bayswater Road. There was plenty of time. Jean Halliday was home, now, and wouldn't be going anywhere.

. . .

The surfaces in Bachelor Boy's kitchen winked and sparkled aggressively, the utensils gleamed unusably. Stella had come home
with a little bag of ready-made from the Eight-til-Late: houmous,
bread, a seafood salad. She had no worries, though, about opening
the drinks cabinet, which had everything you could possibly want
and a few bottles more. She had lifted the phone and listened to the
dial tone, which told her that it was working just fine and, by the
way, there were no messages. She ate without wanting to and drank
with a will, then fell asleep in the black-and-blond armchair.

When she woke it was two A.M. and the phone was still silent.
She dialed her home number and hung up before it connected. She
dialed Delaney's number and call-minder cut in after a few rings.

Bachelor Boy had a pepper-flavored vodka that would make any
girl drum her heels on the floor.

Jean Halliday came round to a white moment, a blank moment,
when she could remember nothing of what had just happened to her,
and had no understanding of what was about to happen. Her mind
went to the way her mother had smiled at her as they'd talked; the
image lasted for only an instant, but it was the last time in her life
that she would be happy.

Then what was happening became blindingly clear and a great
wave of fear swamped her, making her head swim. Sonny was taping
her mouth and her hands were tied. She was naked. They were all
naked.

She said, "Don't hurt me." From behind the tape-gag her voice
sounded small and far away. "Don't hurt me."

They all said that, Donna thought. She smiled and asked, "How
does it feel?"

"Don't hurt me."

Sonny turned Jean so that she was facing the TV screen and
lodged her shoulders against the sofa so that she wouldn't miss
anything. Then he put the Janis tape on the video and they all
watched it for a while. Jean was shaking and crying, then she

passed out. They often did that. Donna rooted in her bag for the amyl nitrate while Sonny rewound the tape and took out the camera.

Jean said, "Don't hurt me."

Donna said, "How does it feel?"

Sonny backed off a little to get them both in frame. He knew that, in a minute, Jean would start traveling, start backing off hard and fast using her legs, her eyes fixed on Donna but her whole body in motion. The chase. The pursuit.

Donna moved in and cut.

Stella said, "Where have you been?"

She was still in the designer chair, a glass of straight Absolut resting in her lap. The TV was tuned to *News 24*; with the sound turned off, the bomb-blasts and fields of fire looked just like the movie she'd been watching when she fell asleep.

"Having a night of it," Delaney told her.

"Good for you."

"Not like that. My car got trashed."

"Sorry?"

"Someone trashed my car. Are you okay? What's this number you're at?"

"How badly?"

"Well, first he took a baseball bat to the lights and bodywork. Someone called the cops and they rang a few bells until they found someone who knew the car. Then they found me. I made a statement, or whatever you call it, and they went away. It was too late to call—"

"Where was it?"

"Outside. Just down the street. So it was too late to call a garage. I went to bed. Then the guy came back and set fire to it."

"Did what?"

"Set fire to my car. Are you all right, Stella? Where are you?"

"You're saying 'the guy'—he."

"Okay, she."

"Or they."

"Yes, or they." Neither of them spoke for a moment. "What's happening?"

"I'm in this flat that belongs to a friend of George's, this rich guy. It's the sort of fully equipped mews loft space that markets for upward of a million, it's got a Star Wars kitchen and a walk-in drinks cabinet, it's a bit like living in a style mag and about as two-dimensional. What happened—the fire?"

"The fire brigade turned up and put it out, the cops came and got me again, we all stood round looking at the mess. The cars either side of me were damaged: paint blistered, glass shattered, tires done for. That's where I've been. What do you want me to do?"

"To do?"

"Stay here or come there."

Suddenly she felt very close to tears, which was odd because she'd been wanting to cry all night but hadn't been able to manage it. "I don't know. I don't know what to say."

"Jesus Christ, Stella."

She told him to hold on. She put her glass down, then went into the bedroom and found her coat. The dice were in the pocket and she had to roll them best of three before they came up seven.

Donna was coasting at 103 degrees, eyes bright, heat coming off her skin, a sweat running down between her breasts that mingled with flecks and flobs of Jean Halliday's blood. She stepped back, panting with effort. Jean was making noises; she was threshing; her feet were kicking spasmodically and she was shaking her head like a clockwork toy.

Donna took the camera from Sonny. She said, "Go on."

He turned Jean over so that she was facing the camera: put her on all fours, her hands still tied back, and knelt up behind her. He said, "Have you got me?"

The camera was shaking in Donna's hands. She tried to steady it, holding tightly, but the fever was stronger. She said, "Do it."

.   .   .

By the time Delaney found a cab, got across to the mews, and rang the bell, Stella had gone back to sleep, so he called her on his mobile. She opened the door looking more tired than drunk, but as he walked in her knees gave way and she fell on him.

She cried and talked for an hour and then they went to bed because there was no reason not to.

It went on past all ability of flesh to endure.

Donna stood over her victim, her hand snaking out, moving, then stepping back and savoring that, then moving again. She was shivering, her teeth chattering, though she smiled and smiled and smiled. Sonny moved from side to side to get all angles, trying not to let Donna's stooping form obscure the action. He was after effects, the glint of light on the thin blade, the glisten and welter of everything. He would zoom in for a close-up of Jean, trying to get the eyes in focus; then for a close-up of Donna, her endless smile. Jean had stopped saying, "Don't hurt me." She was beyond speech.

It went on past all ability of the mind to comprehend.

Then there came a point of exhaustion for everyone, Donna hanging there, one hand braced on a chair, her long frenzy spent. She knelt up behind Jean just as Sonny had, but for a different purpose, one hand cupping the woman's chin, the other holding the knife just under her ear.

She said, "How does it feel?"

Sonny showered first, then Donna. The hot water was more than she could bear, but the cold chilled her to the bone. Suddenly weak, she leaned against the wall of the shower and watched the dark rivulets as they ran off her and tracked toward the drain, turning the water pink. She washed her long hair and a fresh fall of blood sluiced down her back and across her face. When she was finished, she toweled off then folded the towel to take it away with her, just as Sonny had done. At these times she usually checked herself in the mirror but the fever had her now and she wanted to get away and lie down.

When she returned to the main room, Sonny had brought a couple of chairs in from the kitchen—nothing in the living room was clean, now—and arranged them in front of the TV.

The room carried a silence that was unlike any other; it flowed from the body of Jean Halliday as she lay naked and heavy on the far side of the room. Normally, Donna would have wanted to stay and savor that silence before sitting down to watch the drama of Donna and Jean, Jean and Donna, but she said, "Let's go."

Sonny looked puzzled. "The video."

"Let's go," she said.

"But the video . . ." He was rolling a spliff.

"Let's go," Donna said. "I feel like shit."

Stella lay awake as Delaney slept. Her hand rested on his chest and she could feel the rise and fall; his mouth was slightly open, as a child sleeps, and his breath fluttered between his lips.

George hadn't told her how he knew and she hadn't asked because it was his secret and he was entitled to it; it gave him the drop on her. But the fact was he *did* know: he knew Delaney's phone number so he probably knew Delaney's address, and she tried to manufacture a mind's-eye picture of George with a baseball bat swinging at the car, George with a can of petrol and a soaked rag. It was a pretty clear picture and seemed authentic. She hadn't seen George with that look of anger and despair on his face before, but she understood why it was there and she couldn't bring herself to blame him for it.

Delaney stirred and rolled under her hand, putting his back to her. He was hard-muscled and she realized that he must have a workout routine. How little she knew about him. She moved with him, wanting his warmth, and after a few minutes drifted into sleep.

In her dream, she stood close to George, guiding his hand as the baseball bat swung in a fast, wide arc and slammed into the neck of Nike Man who went down, as he had done in life, folding at the knees, the light leaving his eyes.

As he had done in death.

In the Harefield bull ring, he sat propped against the car as George torched it. His limbs ignited and, as the fire shrank his sinew and cranked his limbs, he got to his feet again, scarfed in flame, and walked forward on stiff legs, ready to follow her to the ends of the earth.

49

On a fine Sunday, there are lines of cars headed for green spaces or for the coast. They get there very slowly and return at half the pace. Those who aren't fooled by one day's sun stay at home with a beer and try to find a scrap or two of good news in the weekend broadsheets.

It was the first really warm day of the year, a clear blue sky, no breeze. People in T-shirts and shorts were standing shoulder to shoulder on pub riverfronts, and cafés had put tables out on the pavement. The grass of the private garden-square opposite Jean Halliday's flat was a designated dog-shit-free zone. Giles Baker had taken a camper chair out there and was all set with his paper and his Becks and his Raybans. The grass had been recently mowed, there were spring flowers in the borders, there was even a trill or two of birdsong floating through the throb of engines and the sound-stew of radios and TVs.

From time to time, as Giles turned the page, he would glance up at the windows of the flats: he was waiting for a wave from his wife to let him know that lunch was ready. It wasn't an unfair division of labor, this Sunday it was her turn to cook. Of course, she could have called him on his mobile, but the wave pleased them; it came from a different era: women calling men in from the fields.

Each time he glanced, he noticed something strange, but only really registered it at the back of his mind. Every window in the block was silvered with sunlight except one on the first floor, which remained dark. It wasn't until he got the wave, swallowed the last of his beer, folded his paper and started across the road, that he looked more closely at the window.

At first, he thought someone had hung a blackout sheet: someone easily woken by early light, perhaps. Then he saw that the curtain was moving: not being drawn, but rippling as if a draft had caught it.

Then he saw that the curtain was flies.

The cars were moving against the major traffic flow, but still had to balk and weave. Their siren lights ran out on a wire and were clamped to the side of the roof. Pete Harriman and Maxine Hewitt were driving together and every time he rode two wheels on to the pavement or slalomed round someone on a cross-street, her braking foot slammed into the seat-well.

Jean Halliday was dead, they all knew that, but the fear was that uniform would tramp all over the scene before the professionals got there. Uniform were aware that detectives thought this way, which is one of the many reasons why they, along with criminals, sometimes referred to plain-clothes officers as "the filth."

The call had come in to the AMIP-5 crew fifteen minutes earlier and had been automatically patched out to Mike Sorley, who had called his officers. Maxine knew that Harriman lived in her area, so she'd called and asked for a lift. "My friend left five minutes ago with my car."

He came down from eighty to twenty on a crowded intersection, found a space that allowed him through with just a nick to the wing-mirrors, and went up through the gears again.

"Your boyfriend went off with your car?"

"Did I say that?"

"You said 'friend.' " Maxine was silent on the issue. "Is this a permanent friend, or more a pass-in-the-night sort of a friend?"

"Does it matter to you?"

"No, not at all." He went through a light that had been red for a count of three. "Let's change the subject. Are you vegetarian?"

"Vegetarian?"

"That's right. Do you eat meat at all?"

Maxine laughed. "Yes, I do."

"Because I sometimes go out for a hamburger."

"Do you? For a hamburger? Ever go out for something three times as nice and four times the price?"

She pointed to the two uniformed men standing either side of a section of pavement cordoned off by blue-and-white crime-scene tape. Harriman flashed his headlights a couple of times as a cursory warning to the oncoming traffic and pulled over to the far curb. Andy Greegan showed them where to change: the lobby had been screened off so that only the stairs were accessible. They put on white paper suits and latex gloves and joined Mike Sorley in Jean Halliday's flat. Maxine walked in, then walked out again.

"Where's DS Mooney?" Sorley asked.

"Be on her way, boss."

"I don't think so. She didn't respond. No answer from her flat, mobile taking messages."

"No signal? On the Tube, maybe?"

"Keep trying her. If she doesn't call in soon, send someone round there." He looked toward the door. "Where's Hewitt gone?"

"I asked her to check progress on the door-to-door."

Sorley smiled. "If she throws up, it had better be away from the clear path."

They were not looking at each other, they were looking at Jean Halliday, at the gore-splash round the room, at the sheer spoilage of it all. The forensic team in their white coveralls were reflected dimly in the TV screen: a row of little gnomes, heads down, searching for fairy gold.

"Was that on?" Harriman asked.

"No."

"So there's a difference."

"Or they switched off this time. Anyway, it's only DS Mooney's theory."

"And the profiler's."

On the facing wall, where the blood patterns were most violent, a further decoration stood out just above the loops and star-splashes; a handprint done in blood, half the palm, the heel of the hand, four fingers and the side of a thumb: a forensic gift. Harriman remembered the print on Nesta Cameron's wall and walked across to tell the stills photographer to frame it up several different ways. Then he went out to find Maxine.

She was sitting in a corner of the stairwell while uniforms rang doorbells. When Harriman walked over, she looked up at him and smiled. Her lipstick was lurid against the dead white of her face.

"I've seen them before, but not like that."

"Don't worry."

"I'll be okay in a minute."

"Go back to the squad room. Take the initial reports with you and get on the computer."

Maxine shook her head. "I don't think so. I've heard enough of that 'What do you expect, she's a girl' stuff."

Harriman shrugged. "It's not a test."

"I think it is. It is for me."

Harriman went back in and Maxine followed him a couple of minutes later. Together they checked the bedroom and the kitchen. There was a spare room that Jean had used as an office. Harriman made a note for the computer files to be checked, though he doubted they would be of much use.

"Why?" Maxine asked.

"This killing is the same as the others. It might not be random, but I don't think these people are business contacts or new friends. Check the bathroom. I'll go through things in here."

Maxine stood in the bathroom. She remembered the MO that Stella had drawn up, the evidence of showers after the event. She reached out and touched the strip on the sliding door to the shower. Her fingers tingled.

What does it take?

Mike Sorley came in and told her to raise DS Mooney.

50

Pretend everything's all right, pretend everything's in the past: George's pain and my guilt and the sheer fucking mess of it all. Pretend this is our flat and we actually like the way it looks, its cool untouchability. Pretend we've been living here for a couple of years now and we woke late—*Christ,* really late—and we made love and I didn't cry and he's in the shower and we've got a good plan for the rest of the day.

Pretend that.

She was still pretending when the doorbell went, and there was nothing to do but go and answer it because when she looked out of the window she saw DC Hewitt standing back to get a perspective on the studio's domed windows with the plantation shutters.

Maxine said, "You didn't answer your mobile, so Sorley sent me to your place. The guy there gave me this address—your husband?"

Stella shook her head. Then she said, "I think my battery's low." It sounded like a report on her state of mind. "I'll get dressed. Where is it?"

"Bayswater."

"The same as the others?"

"The same." Stella opened the door a little wider, then hesitated. Maxine said, "I'll wait in the car."

She saw the handprint before Harriman could point it out to her.

"The TV wasn't on," he said.

"You put a video in?"

"Yes. It's on the right channel."

Stella made a tour of the flat. Like Maxine, she stood in the bathroom and stared at the shower. Something about them being naked; something about the commonplace intimacy of that.

She went back to the living room. Jean Halliday had gone. Sorley had gone. The forensic team would be another hour or so. Stella said, "Let's get out of here." On the first really warm day of the year, a room full of blood was no place to be.

Sonny watched the Jean Halliday video on his own with a spliff and a can of beer. He watched naked. Every so often, he replayed the tape, then stopped it, and closed his eyes to relive the moment. He teased himself, making it last.

The pleasure soured, briefly, when he remembered that he hadn't used protection. He'd forgotten; and then, when things had started, he'd been too excited to wait. He dismissed the thought. He would never go with the whores on the Strip or call one of the numbers pasted up in call boxes: those girls carried everything known to man. But Jean Halliday wasn't like that, he was sure of it. None of them had been like that.

He let the tape run, then rewound to find himself again. He liked watching Donna moving and turning—her knife hand slipping out like a striking snake before she pirouetted away again, arms raised like a dancer, so graceful—but even more, he liked watching himself.

And here he was, moving into frame, the hunter with his prey. He watched; he closed his eyes; he watched again.

Stella called Anne Beaumont and said, "I need to talk to you."

"I got your message. Did you get mine?"

"Saying you wanted to visit the scene of crime . . ."

"That's right."

"I did. I need to talk to you about all sorts of things."

"Business or pleasure?"

"Was that a joke?" Stella asked.

"Of course it was a joke."

"What are you doing?"

"Now?"

"Yes."

"I've got a client in half an hour. After that, nothing until this evening."

"In two hours, then." Stella gave her the address.

You notice the lack of a body, because everything else is still in place—pain and cries and hatred, terror and delight, and desire—the sheer black energy that crackles in the room like a force field.

Anne Beaumont stood by the wall, not wanting to go further; not wanting to be caught up in those terrible echoes. She felt Jean Halliday's absence, as if her bodyweight still lay in the room, displacing shadows. It wasn't possible to clear the room of flies and there was a heavy smell that seemed to stick to everything it touched.

Stella said, "This is bad. This is a particularly bad one."

"Thanks for telling me." Then, as an afterthought, "Listen, I asked to come."

Stella took her on a tour of the flat, of the bloodstained walls and floor, the bloodstained furniture, the bloodstained pictures and curtains. They went into the bathroom and, like Maxine, Anne put out her hand to touch the handle on the shower door.

Stella spread SOC photos on the worktop in the kitchen: Jean Halliday, butchered. Anne stared. Sunlight through the window cast glossy reflections on the images, and she shifted the photos to get them out of the light.

"The handprint," Anne said.

"Matches the handprint we found on the wall at Nesta Cameron's flat."

There was something in Stella's voice that made Anne ask, "And . . . ?"

"They were made by the person who did most of it. Most of the cutting. The blood splash tells us that." A moment's silence, then she added: "It's a woman's hand."

"She was the instigator," Anne said, "as we thought."

"The executioner," Stella said, "yes."

The knowledge was one thing; the bloody evidence was another. A hand put out to steady someone dizzied by effort; dizzied by pleasure.

In the car, Stella asked whether being there had made any kind of difference. Anne told her that it had.

"Not my thinking about them, the killers, but my feelings about the victim. I want them caught. Anything I can do. *Anything.*"

"It's personal," Stella suggested.

"In a way."

"Don't let it be." She said it, even though she felt the same way.

Anne laughed. "When it comes to emotions, I'm the professional, remember?"

Stella started the car. "I'm living on my own for a bit," she said.

"Are you?"

"Just for a bit. Neutral ground."

"That's good," Anne said. "That's the right thing to do."

"Delaney's been round."

"I expect he has."

"George found the place for me. A friend of his." They drove in silence through the park toward Kensington Gore. Stella said, "He looked at me—" but didn't know how to continue; she didn't have words to describe the look. After a moment, she said, "I wonder if I'm in the process of getting everything I want, or losing everything I have."

Anne was trying to listen, but she was still in Jean Halliday's flat. Those echoes; that smell.

51

Donna had been in bed for two days and Sonny had been sleeping between two chairs, because the bed was wet with her sweat and she moved constantly, as if she were trying to get out of her own way. Despite the dope and the beer, he felt edgy without Donna to tell him what was coming next. The next move had been *move*, but she was too ill for that; most of the time she slept, or half-slept, her face glistening wet, the room filled with her feverish cries and protests. When her eyes were open, they appeared unfocused.

After he'd finished with the video, he put on some sweat pants and a T-shirt. It was the day after the hunting and the papers were scattered round on the floor. He picked one up and looked at the picture of the ladycop. DS Stella Mooney. While Donna had slept, Sonny had written Ladycop a note. He guessed that Donna might not have wanted him to do that, but he knew it wouldn't bring them to harm and he wanted to feel his power.

I know you, but you don't know me.

He had written notes before—different places, different times, different cops—and nothing had come of it. He looked at Ladycop's face. She was pretty, but she had tough-lines round her mouth and her jaw was set. She was looking straight at the camera; straight at Sonny.

I know you, but you don't know me. Ha-ha-ha. Hee-hee-hee.

He fetched an empty plastic sports bottle and filled it with water, then went into the bedroom and placed it by her side. He said,

"Donna, I'm going out." Then, after a moment, "I'm going out. Will you be okay?" Then, "You'll be okay, won't you?" She seemed to look at him, but he couldn't be sure; her eyes were tinfoil-dull, like the eyes of a dead fish.

In the bathroom he stripped and made a triangular wash, armpits and crotch, and shaved carefully to avoid nicks. He used deodorant and aftershave, a dab and a splash, all the time singing quietly under his breath, then went back to the bedroom and fetched clean clothes.

Donna's hair lay damply on her forehead; her eyes were closed. She had kicked the thin quilt off to find cool air and lay with her legs spread and her arms out, breathing rapidly. Sonny took his clothes out into the main room and dressed there. He didn't love Donna, he loved someone else, but she compelled him. Without Donna there would be no killings, because Donna led him to them as a lost soul is led into the light. She gave them to him as the weak are given strength. He felt that wherever they went, he and Donna, they had a purpose: they were traveling toward new excitements, new discoveries.

No one knew who they were or what they could do. He took a hundred pounds from their stash. They'd found two hundred in Jean Halliday's wallet: a good haul. If anyone had asked him why they did what they did, Sonny would have said, "To get money." It was where things had started: killing for money.

He put on a black, tailored leather jacket and a shirt with sharp sleeve-creases from the launderette below, one of the garments he could take there because he never wore it when they went hunting. The jacket was from a street-market rack and the shirt was from Buy-Rite. He combed his yellow hair. He put on a pair of wrap-around shades with yellow lenses.

He was ready. Man of mystery.

Sonny on the Strip: moving among the lights, the big-bass music, the fast-fry, the tough hombres, the whores painted and powdered like Blow Job Barbie. Sonny walking under the iron bridge on Ladbroke Grove, kicking aside the boxes and black bags left by the daytime shopkeepers, kicking aside the piss-stained down-and-outs scavenging the bags, kicking aside a brindled dog, its haunches up, its head low as it tugged at the black plastic, and getting a growl-snap in return before a boy called its name and put out a hand to soothe. Sonny flagging down a taxi and feeling better, much better, once he'd told the driver to take him to the Kandy Kave.

And Sonny pinned to his seat as Belle stripped for him, close-up, her hips weaving, her breasts rolling with the beat, wetting her fingers and stroking herself and leaning in to smile, to pout, her scent wafting to him, not perfume but the scent of herself.

"I love you," he told her. He was looking at her face even though his eyes were at the level of her waist. "I love you, Belle."

"Do you, darling?"

"Come home with me."

"I can't do that."

"Come away with me."

"I can't do that, darling."

"Marry me. I've got money."

"Have you, darling? That's nice."

"I'll tell you my secrets if you tell me yours."

"Yeah? Go on then, darling."

"Tell me yours."

"I haven't got any."

"Everyone has secrets."

"Not me. Not interesting secrets."

The music only lasted so long. Belle leaned over, making globes of her breasts; she flipped her hips to the last few beats.

"Again," he said, but she told him she had to move on. Later. She would be back later. He held her wrist and she looked down at his hand, her face frozen. "Sorry," he said. "Sorry." Then: "We could be happy."

She turned away and a drop of sweat flicked from her to him, catching his cheek. He put out his tongue.

52

Mike Sorley was in the best possible position for the worst possible reason. His Senior Investigating Officer had just doubled his budget and tripled his manpower. Fresh deaths, fresh thinking. The press was working all the scare-words: MONSTER, RITUAL, PSYCHOPATH, GHOUL, PANIC, TERROR, *AT LARGE.*

"What it means," Sorley told Stella, "is we have to find the bastards. These are not 'case unsolved' investment levels."

AMIP-5 was now a unit inside a capsule. Stella was working with the same people, but getting more information and covering more ground. She secretly wondered whether the information was to the point; she also thought that the ground might carry too many footprints.

"You look tired," Sorley informed her.

"Yeah, I'm tired."

Sorley was a man who had looked for a new life and found one. He seemed to remember it was an uphill trip. He said, "Are you all right?"

"I'm fine, boss." "Boss" made it official. It said, *Don't ask. Maybe later.*

"I'm sorry it's always you." Sorley was talking about the postmortem. He never went, he never even looked at the PM photos if he could help it. "We've got other detectives on the strength, now, if you want to offload it."

"I'd better go," she said. "Continuity."

As she left, she stopped by Sue Chapman's workstation to let Sue know where she would be. Her mobile wouldn't have a signal in Sam Burgess's underworld.

"You look tired," Sue said.

Stella smiled. She said, "Sex and drugs and rock 'n' roll."

"Very good indeed," Sue offered.

Sonny's letter lay among fifty others on her desk. It sounded just like all the rest, apart from one detail. One word. Sue would read it, but she wouldn't spot it.

Sam still had Giovanni as his assistant. Sam had taken to calling him "My right-hand man"; this was because Giovanni was left-handed. They worked on Jean Halliday like fine-fingered gardeners: the lung-tree, the seed pods, the pale blooms, the dark tubers.

Sam said, "He forgot this time, or he didn't bother."

"What?" Stella was a few feet away. As usual, Sam was working to music. Today it was something sweet and slow, Stella didn't know what it was called, but she'd heard it.

"A condom," Sam said. "Forgot or didn't care."

"You think it was the same with the others?"

"The same?"

"He had sex with them."

"I expect so. I'd think so, wouldn't you?"

"So what was different this time? Why no protection?"

"You're the detective," Sam said. Giovanni looked up for a moment and smiled at her, as if in encouragement.

"A condom means he doesn't leave his semen: doesn't leave DNA."

Sam shrugged. "Listen, these people leave DNA traces all over the place. They don't expect to get caught. I don't think it was that."

"Fear of infection, then."

"More likely."

Stella tried to picture someone who tortured people and raped them and then killed them, and took a videotape of it all to watch later, and thought of the victim as a potential threat.

"Apart from that," she asked, "anything new?"

"Nothing new."

Sam removed Jean Halliday's heart and handed it to Giovanni, who carried it in cupped hands to the scales and weighed it, as if he might calibrate the weight of sorrow that lay there, or guess the freight of dreams.

Forensics sent an initial report, along with a terse note saying that they were backed up. A full report would be along soon and would have been sooner if people weren't so anxious to do violence to one another. Some things were easier to deal with than others. They came back on the palm-print. It matched. They came back on the DNA, which, even though it was scrambled with the victim's, was distinct enough to compare with that from other scenes of crime. It matched. That much now, more later. It seemed a formality, anyway, because Jean Halliday's was a signature killing that no one could mistake. Sam Burgess was right, Stella reflected, these people didn't expect to be caught.

She was walking back through the last set of slap-flaps before Sam's dark kingdom gave way to a realm of light and air. The light was murky-pearl and the air was rich with river smells. When she walked up the concrete stairway to the carpark, her phone caught a signal. The LCD display read "Office," which meant nothing, because all her colleagues were in the memory under their names, and the squad room would come up as either Chapman or Greegan. "Office" was her code for Delaney. No need for codes, now.

He said, "I've got something for you. Marie Turnow."

"Who is she?"

"Who was she. She's dead."

"I don't need more dead women."

"Dead and gone. A year ago, in west Somerset."

"You're going to tell me it's the same MO."

"That's right."

"This came from a news archive?"

"Several consecutive reports in local papers, only two in the nationals. I found the nationals first and didn't pay much attention because it was the same story in both papers: copycat reporting. They just mentioned stab wounds, but made it clear that the motive was robbery. Then I happened across a feature in one of the tabs—the usual sort of "Slashers and Slayers Since Jack the Ripper" thing. It mentioned the killing and seemed to give a different slant. So I went to the locals and got the full details. It sounded like a replica . . . well, a few differences, perhaps, but essentially the same. Death of a thousand cuts, ending with the throat. This victim was raped, though."

"So were the others."

"I thought not."

"New evidence. When exactly?"

"Eleven months ago. But Stella—"

She had reached her car and unlocked it, now she leaned against the driver's door, her head turned from the hazy sun. "Anything about it being a team?"

"No, that's the point—"

"Name of the Senior Investigating Officer?"

"Yes, it's all there, but listen, Stella, the point is, they got someone for it."

"What?"

"They arrested someone. A guy called Carrick: Albert Carrick."

"He was convicted?"

"He was, yes."

"Can you send me the cuttings?"

"They're in your e-mail."

"What e-mail?"

"It's on your card."

She remembered giving him the card: a pain-in-the-arse journo whom she wanted to keep at a distance; fax, e-mail, voice mail.

"That goes through to Sue Chapman."

"So it's in her e-mail. What time do you want to eat this evening?"

"Are we eating?"

"You have to eat. I have to eat. I thought we could eat together."

"I'm tired, Delaney."

"I make a world-famous smoked-salmon pasta. I've hired a car. I could come to you."

"Yeah, okay." She got into the car and slammed the door. "Whatever you like."

She snaked round the rows of cars parked head to head, driving too fast over the speed bumps so that her head tapped the roof and the suspension whacked the axle. Close to the exit, she pulled over and dialed him back. She said, "It would be great if you cooked. That's a nice idea. Thank you."

She felt happier with herself for having said it.

53

Sue Chapman had printed out the e-mails and left them on Stella's desk under an A4 sheet carrying a message that Maxine Hewitt needed to speak to her. Normally, Sue would have left the message on a Post-it note, but the A4 sheet was there to conceal the endearment that Delaney had added to the e-mail.

Stella went across and said, "It's a new thing. It's a secret."

Sue smiled. "I thought it must be."

"Why didn't Maxine call my mobile?"

"She did, only five minutes ago. It went straight to message."

"Oh, right." Out in the AMIP carpark, Stella had taken a call from a detective whose name she didn't know, but who knew hers. The team was now three teams. He told her that Jean Halliday's mother was under sedation and couldn't be spoken to for the time being. Stella didn't think they would learn anything from her anyway.

She read the salient facts of Delaney's e-mail as she was going down the plain concrete steps to the basement.

Body of Marie Turnow found in a terraced house in a village near Taunton . . . local beauty queen, later owner of antiques

business . . . multiple stab wounds to the body . . . throat cut . . .
motive thought to be robbery . . . local man Albert Carrick arrested . . . tried . . . convicted . . . I know things are lousy at the
moment . . . I love you . . . hold on.

The basement was where they kept the video set up for the CCTV
film. Maxine was leaving as Stella arrived. She said, "The desk called
to say you'd come in, boss. I was on my way to fetch you."

"You found a candidate . . ."

"I found *the* candidate. Fat face, yellow hair, silly beard."

"He was there last night?" The tapes came in on a daily basis.

"That's right."

Maxine had locked the tape at the point where Sonny walked on
to camera: the moment that he entered the club. He got a drink. He
sat down. He waited for Belle to come on. The girls worked the
poles, but his eyes were on the curtain at the end of the catwalk
where the new dancers entered. His table was close to the stage, and
when Belle walked out she must have seen him at once because
she walked past and looked down and gave a little shimmy.

When she used the pole, she was acrobatic and fast, turning and
spreading, lifting herself up and wrapping herself round. When she
danced for Sonny she was sinuous and slow, open like a book. She
smiled a hard, professional smile.

It was the same smile she gave to Maxine and Stella when they arrived at her apartment an hour later. Through the smile, she asked:
"How did you get my address?"

"We asked your boss."

"Gerry Moreno isn't my boss; I'm freelance." She spoke as if it
mattered to her.

The flat was dark, blinds down and curtains drawn: a night-
worker's habitat. Belle was wearing the T-shirt she'd slept in and a
pair of jogging pants that she'd dragged on to answer the door. She
offered coffee and, instead of drawing the curtains, put on the lights.

"Why didn't you call us?" Stella asked.

"I didn't know he was that high on your agenda. He's just a punter with a one-track mind. Nothing too unusual about that."

"We'd like to talk to him. So here's what you do. Next time he's in, dance for him, make it special, then promise you'll dance for him again later. Find a phone. Call us."

"He's a creep. I've had them before."

"You said he was following you."

"I think. Maybe."

Maxine said, "Remember Amanda-Jane Wallace . . . ?" Belle looked blank. "Sindee."

"It's not him," Belle said. "Trust me."

Stella asked, "What happened? Last night."

"I danced for him, he told me he loved me, he asked me to go home with him, he asked me to marry him, I danced for him again— same routine."

"Did he follow you last night?"

"No."

"How can you be sure?"

Belle hesitated. "Last night, I went home with a punter. Belgravia. Big tip, small dick. I could use some sleep, you know?"

"Next time," Stella reminded her. "Dance, smile, phone."

As they were leaving, Belle said, "It's always special." Stella looked puzzled. "What you said earlier. When I dance, it's always special."

They were driving down an avenue of London planes, pollarded to let the light through to upper windows, their trunks patched with impetigo, their knobby, raddled limbs reaching up like the arms of famine victims. The sun was shining through a light, greasy rainfall.

"He's just a long shot, anyway," Maxine observed. "Poor sad bastard's probably got a wife and three."

"Take mug-shot prints from the tape and circulate them, city-wide to begin with but especially west London. Put some of our extra bodies on door-to-door in the area. He might be a long shot, but he's all we've got."

"Okay, boss. Send it to the papers and TV newsdesks?"

"Not yet. He thinks he's faceless. Our advantage."

They kept silence for a while, then Stella asked: "Your new friend, the one you went to the movies with that night . . ."

Maxine looked at her. Stella was driving and had her eyes on the road. "My new friend, yes . . ."

"Are you faithful, or is it just now and then?"

"You think that's the way it is with gay women," Maxine wondered, 'just now and then'?"

"It's not a gay question. It's a people question."

"How long were you with him?" Maxine asked. "Your bloke."

"Six years. Does *everyone* know?"

"Yes," Maxine said. "Everyone knows."

Stella pulled into the bus lane, came up on the inside at a left filter, then laid some rubber to get across the intersection. It was London driving, but a little more so.

With all the back-up available to her, Stella could have given the job of checking lookalike killings to any one of ten, but she gave it to Andy Greegan because he wouldn't get impatient, wouldn't get bored, wouldn't miss a lead. She handed him Delaney's e-mail, the source deleted along with the last couple of sentences.

"Anything similar in the same area," she said. "Anything similar in nearby areas. Anything similar in the west country or any other fucking part of the country. It won't be easy because the crime sheets won't be categorized in the same ways, but give it a try."

"Getting anyone to read the faxes I send," Greegan told her, "that'll be the main problem."

She handed Sorley another copy of the e-mail, with the SOI's name in orange highlighter: DCI Bill Stephens. Sorley took a moment to read, then looked up at her. "It says they got someone for this."

"I know, boss."

Sorley sighed. "You want me to ask for the crime sheet, is that it?"

"That, and I'd like to make a visit."

"Oh, Christ."

"If I'm wrong, I won't go. But from this angle, it looks the same."

Sorley lifted the phone. "They won't want you," he said. "I wouldn't want you."

54

The darkness came in waves, riding with the fever. She was in a place she knew, though she could see nothing. The smell was cleaning fluid or white spirit and it hurt her throat. As before, no sound. As before, no movement in the air. She pushed out with her arms, wanting to shove the darkness back.

Sometimes, if she listened carefully, she could hear the sound of the TV or a voice calling and Dilly barking. Dilly was a terrier; she barked for food and she barked to be taken out and she barked if you ran away from her. Dilly might come to the cupboard door and snuffle at the crack, but Donna knew better than to make a sound.

I'm only a child, she thought. Why doesn't someone come to help me?

She couldn't remember what she had done, or why she had done it, or how long she had been in the cupboard. She was hungry, but worse than that she was thirsty. The dryness in her throat made the rasp of the white spirit worse. She had wet herself several times, mostly from fear, because she knew what was going to happen, and each time she had tried to find somewhere dry to sit, but that was difficult because inside the cupboard it was black, heavy black, no chink of light anywhere. She couldn't see what was around her and she couldn't see herself. The smell of her urine bonded with the chemical smell.

The fever rocked her and she couldn't tell whether she was a woman dreaming of a child, or a child dreaming she was a woman. Both woman and child were waiting for the moment when the door would open and the light would blind her eye. She would smell a perfume like flowers. Then a face would come slowly into vision, a woman's face, a beautiful face. Her hair, backlit by the overhead hall light, would be filaments of fire glowing like a halo. The face would be dark, but the hair bright.

Don't hurt me.

At night there is always something to break the darkness: starlight or moonlight; lamplight, streetlights, the lights of cars. The darkness in the cupboard was nothing like the night. It was solid. It pressed on her, making her breathless.

Don't hurt me.

There are more viruses than names to give them, and Donna's virus was a wicked strain that doctors call mutative, which is about as accurate as a shrug of the shoulders. Her core temperature was 103 and rising, and she was mildly delirious. Donna's infection came with its own very special set of images and smells, together with a terrifying creature who inhabited the blackest recess of the fever's deepest nightmare. This creature was called the Mother.

Don't hurt me.

Donna tossed in her own sweat, her body slick and shiny. The dark was very frightening, but the light was worse, because that was when she would smell the flowery perfume and see the Mother's face falling into focus, would feel a hand taking her by the hair and dragging her out. Donna felt it. The child felt it. One part of the punishment over, the next about to begin.

March upstairs to the big bedroom, with Dilly scampering on the stairs. *Don't hurt me.* Stand in front of the tall mirror. *Don't hurt me.* Hear a voice telling you how evil you are, how wicked. *Don't hurt me.* Hear a voice telling you that you have to learn. That you have to be taught. See the knife in the mirror: a fish-gutting knife, its slim blade curving, catching the light. Your mouth taped, your hands tied with a belt from one of the Mother's dresses. Close your eyes. Feel the terrible sting, the single drop of blood pearling on your thigh and running down like a tear. Hear a voice asking you how it feels.

Don't hurt me, don't hurt me, don't hurt me.

Just a mumble from behind the tape.

How does it feel? the Mother asks. *How does it feel?*

She woke to more darkness and rain beating the windows. There was a pulse in her temple that quickly became a pulse in her brain. After a moment, she recognized it as a bass-beat coming from somewhere out on the Strip. Her skin was electric, throwing sparks and static shocks; her head was a Chinese lantern.

She got up and walked naked to the kitchen, needing water. The lights in the flat were cheapskate low wattage and threw soft-edged shadows. She stood holding her sports bottle until the water ran cold. When a drop or two splashed up and struck her skin she fancied she could hear it hiss.

On the way back she noticed Sonny, who was standing by the window, waiting for the rain to ease. He was wearing his black leather jacket and staring at the way the downpour silvered the glass and gave him back his own reflection along with the lights of cars and the neon swill. When she moved to stand behind him, her own reflection swam up alongside his. He turned and she balled her fist and punched him. Although she put everything into the blow, it was barely enough to turn his head.

She swayed and took a half-step forward. "I can smell it on you," she said, "on your jacket. You went back there." She took another swing and he caught her arm, sending static shocks up to her shoulder.

"No one knows us, Donna. We know them, they don't know us."

"You were going there tonight."

"I am."

"No," she said. "No you're not."

"You don't know what it's like to be in love."

Donna looked at him a moment, wide-eyed, then started to laugh. The laugh grew before cascading into a gravelly cough, grit and heavy fluid in the lungs. Her body shook, racked by laughter and coughing and fever. She put her hands over her face, as if looking at him made the laughter worse, then raised her arms above her head and turned circles in the middle of the room, naked and pale, a little dance to celebrate the joys of love.

Her hands descended on whatever was near: a glass, a plate, a cheap print in a frame, and hurled them across the room. Spinning and moving, lighting on the flat's street-market bric-a-brac, a vase, a carriage clock, a cloudy-pink fruit bowl, a mug-tree, throwing them left and right. Turning and turning, catching up what she could—the telephone, the gimcrack dining chairs, a pile of CDs, the CD player—pitching them at his head, and all the time screaming at him, until she fell, dizzied by the dance and by illness, her body slamming into the wall on the far side of the room.

Sonny stood by the window, which now carried a long diagonal crack, the debris piled round his feet. Donna was panting like a dog, her knees drawn up and circled by her arms, her head bowed, her long hair masking her face. She said, "You went back, Sonny."

"I'm sorry, Donna. We can move on. Let's move on."

She laughed. "I can hardly walk."

"Maybe you need to see a doctor."

"You think so?" She laughed.

"Maybe you need antibiotics."

"Don't be a stupid fuck."

"You'll be better soon. Then we'll move on." He went over and helped her to her feet and she leaned on him. Her nakedness and the heat coming off her made his blood race. He said, "Let's do something."

She pushed him off and took a couple of steps toward the bedroom, then sat down on the sofa. "Where's my water?"

He found the plastic sports bottle amid the rubble. She drank it off, so he fetched her some more from the kitchen, then went back to the window. The rain was easing, now; soon it would stop. He made for the door.

"Sonny," she said.

"I won't go there."

"Sonny."

"I'll go for a drink, that's all. I'll go down the Wheatsheaf."

Her teeth chattered and sweat-beads were running between her breasts, tracking down over her belly. In the dim light, she glistened.

After he'd gone, she went to the bathroom and stood over the sink and looked at herself in the plastic-framed mirror. Her skin had a yellow tinge to it and her eyes were smudged with black, as if she'd been bruised. The hard, risen knobs of her cheekbones gave even more shadow to her face. She wasn't beautiful like the Mother.

She was shivering, but could feel the heat of her illness and noticed how her body was patched with red, as if a dozen little fevers were building inside. Her shoulders and breasts were a rash of goosebumps and her nipples were stiff.

Illness, it was all illness and filth.

She picked up the fish-gutting knife and drew a line on the boss of her shoulder, watching red spring up amid the web of old, white scars.

Phlebotomy, an old remedy for sickness in the blood; the old wives' method for spilling sin.

Holding the knife delicately, *delicately,* between finger and thumb, she let the blade graze her breasts, her ribs, her belly, each cut a little shock of surprise and joy. The blood drizzled down. In the dim light of the bathroom, it looked black.

"George, it's me."

"I know who it is."

"I thought . . . we ought to talk."

"Go ahead."

"Not now. Not on the phone."

"Why not?"

"Better face to face."

"People make love face to face," he said. "I've had enough of face to face."

She didn't know what to say to that. The line between them carried a great weight of silence.

He said, "I miss you."

"I miss you too." It was true. She felt lost.

"Are you coming home?"

"I don't think so, George. Not now."

"Not now but sometime, or not now that you've left?"

"I wish I had the answer."

It was a lie and he knew it. Stella listened as George replaced the phone, gently, as if closing a door.

She went from the bedroom to the kitchen, where Delaney was making his world-famous smoked-salmon pasta and had brought a likeable chaos to what had been tight-arsed order. He poured three ounces of Bachelor Boy's Glenmorangie into the cream sauce.

"It says so in the recipe," he told her.

"Good recipe."

"Cooking burns off the alcohol."

"It's the thought that counts."

He poured them both a drink from the Glenmorangie bottle. "Are you seeing him? What did he say?"

"He asked me if I was coming home."

"And what did you say?"

"I said no." Which, strictly speaking, was the truth.

He folded her into his arms and kissed the top of her head. She put her arms round him and locked her hands.

He was thinking of how things change, how life changes.

She was thinking of the dice.

55

The Wheatsheaf had a sports screen, five fruit-machines, a big backwash of voices and laughter, and a small, dark pool of silence where Sonny sat at the bar with his whiskey chaser. Or, at least, it seemed silent to Sonny, who was deaf to everything except a whispered conversation between himself and Belle in which they spoke to each other of love and regret.

He would do as Donna said. They would move on, as they'd planned, and Belle would stay behind. His dream-plan could never have worked: Donna and Sonny and Belle. It could only be the two of them, the two hunters. He would never see Belle again, not even to kill her, though that would be better than losing her.

Sonny sometimes thought that he had spent his life hearing women say No. He'd wondered whether he was sufficiently careful about personal freshness. He'd bought books on how to make friends and stay popular. It wasn't for lack of effort. But something about him made women say No. They sometimes said No and turned away with a laugh. Or they said No and turned away with a grimace.

It was okay with prostitutes, who were paid to say what he told them to say, but the lack of feeling in their voices had made him cringe. Then he'd found a way that helped. It was called being in control and the control factor was fear. The first had been a neighbor: she had asked him to help with a plumbing problem. Sonny couldn't fix taps but he pretended. When they were alone in her flat he told her to say what he wanted, to do what he wanted. The control mechanism was a kitchen knife. It was all very satisfactory, and the event had gone unreported as many such events do.

After that, he ranged a little farther. He bought a ski mask and a pair of handcuffs to go with the knife: his basic equipment. He was living in London at the time and was briefly famous as an artist's impression. The press were eager to stress the violence involved in Sonny's activities, as if it were a form of bad manners. For Sonny, it was part of the event; control, fear, punishment.

He became a traveling man, and the opportunities were greater. The women said what they should and they did what they should and everything proceeded from fear. Fear was the key.

When Sonny met Donna in west Somerset he found a like mind. She was happy to play his games, but she had games of her own to offer. Control, fear, punishment, *death*.

A hand came out and nudged him. He was at the bar, between a sports fan and his view of a bantamweight contest on the big screen, and the guy had laid a hand on Sonny's shoulder to ease him back. Most people at the bar were standing, so they could jostle to find a clear view. Sonny looked at the hand, then at the guy, who was lightweight himself, though the arm reaching out to Sonny was muscled and there was a flinty look in his eye.

Sonny hunched over his drink, but that was no good to Sports Fan. The only way it would work was if Sonny got up and stood with the rest of them. The arm flexed, the hand pressed harder—move back; get out of my light—and Sonny shifted slightly, turning to dislodge the hand. The bantamweights squared up to one another, fast and furious, quick on their feet. One slipped a left lead and countered sweetly, bringing a roar from both screen crowd and pub crowd. Sports Fan used the heel of his hand to jog Sonny's arm just as Sonny was bringing drink to lip and the glass rapped his teeth, sending whiskey on to the bar.

Sonny got off his stool, turned, and hit Sports Fan flush in the mouth. It wasn't so much a response to being jogged as a matter of reflex: he was miserable and the misery had crystallized and become anger. The fight was short, just a few exchanges, but the energy levels were high and there was blood on the floor and on the bar. On the screen, men with gloves and a set of rules; in the pub, men with bar stools and bottles and no way back.

Sports Fan took a hit with a bottle. It didn't break, but it struck him alongside the cheekbone and connected with his temple, and he sat down hard. Sonny moved in and kicked him twice but not accurately, once on the upper arm, once high on the head. Someone grabbed Sonny from behind and he shook the hands off, then aimed another kick as Sports Fan was trying to rise. It caught his man on his upper chest and made him grunt. Then there were four people holding Sonny and soon the cops from the red stripe who had taken a call just two streets from the pub were threading their way through the bar, their adrenalin rising. Both had unsheathed their batons. Sonny held up his hands to say, *It's over, all over now, no need for you guys,* but that just made it easier for them to get the cuffs on.

56

The press had run features, the victim pictures had appeared in tabloids and on TV news, Mike Sorley, powdered and tidied, had appeared on *Crimewatch,* but no one had come forward with information worth a damn. The only noticeable effect of the exposure was to increase the misery of the bereaved, who were forced to confront the faces cut from holiday snaps or garden groups—smiling faces; loved faces.

The cranks, however, were having a hell of a good time.

Sue Chapman had logged them and filed them; she'd read the letters and read the transcripts of phone calls. So far, only two of the nuisance-makers had been lifted. Sorley wanted to have them burned at the stake, but they got police bail, which fell a long way short of dry wood and a good, red flame. What Sue needed was a computer system a lot more sophisticated than the micro-byte basic at her disposal, but she cross-referenced as best she could and invented sub-sub-sub-headings for the reports. It was a lot of paper and a lot of words.

She was making a time-log for the phone calls when one of the words floated up at her, blowing trumpets and waving flags. It was the same word she had failed to notice on the crank letter that had come in a week or more ago. Normally you'd call it a little word, a *tiny* word, but this time it damn near filled the room. She took it down to Stella's workstation and laid it on her desk.

The word "we."

The time of the call was logged at seven-fifty P.M. two days earlier. Stella beckoned Maxine Hewitt over and showed the report to her. Sue had picked the word out in highlighter.

"A phone booth," Maxine said.

They looked at the notes added by the detective who'd taken the call. *Male, probably under thirty, definitely under fifty, sounded agitated or excited.* There was a batch number for the tape. Sue went to fetch it.

"This is the day Belle's secret admirer went to the Kandy Kave," Maxine observed.

"It's seven-fifty. He's on his way to the club." Stella pointed to the NCB location fix. "He's in Notting Hill. He wants us to know he's out there, having fun."

"So where's she—the woman?"

"Who knows?" Stella said. "On her way to a Chippendales gig."

"It's thin stuff," Maxine said.

"I know that."

Sue brought the tape and they found the spot. Sonny's voice was breathy and fast, a slight south London tang, laughter behind the words. They could hear the sound of a siren swelling and falling away.

"Detective Sergeant Stella Mooney?"

"She's not here. Can I ask who's calling?" The detective has late-shift lassitude.

"Those women. Janis Parker and the rest? We killed them. We cut them up."

Now the detective's voice changes. Trying not to be brisk, trying not to be offhand. He would have dialed *"one"* already to activate the trace. *"Did you? When was that?"*

"You know."

"DS Mooney's due back pretty soon. She'll be here soon. You can talk to me till she comes."

Sonny laughs. *"No thanks. Another time. Just tell her—"*

"Do you want me to see if I can find her?"

"Just tell her she doesn't stand a prayer. We'll be gone soon."

"Talk to me about it," the detective says. He's doing as good a job as anyone could. *"Talk to me about Janis Parker and the rest. I'll listen."*

"Tell her what I said," Sonny says, and the phone goes down.

Stella was sitting with her head in her hands and her eyes closed. She said, "Again."

They listened twice more, then Stella turned to Sue. "Get copies made and circulate them. Bring me the first copy. I'll give it to DI Sorley myself."

Pete Harriman had come into the squad room while they were listening for the second time and had stood still to hear that and the third play. He said, "It's him, isn't it?"

Stella turned to him. "You heard all of it?"

"Yes."

"Why do you think it's him?"

Harriman had heard it right. "He said 'we.' "

Sorley listened, leaning his jowly face on one hand. He said, "They had a tape of the Yorkshire Ripper. Except it wasn't. That was a ton of manpower down the drain."

"This *is* him. One of the killing team."

"Because he says 'we' . . ."

"No one else has said that. We've had forty-eight calls and nine-teen written communications, and none of them has said 'we.' Why would he say it?"

"Perhaps he's a member of the royal family." Sorley liked the idea and started to laugh. Stella waited until he'd finished.

"Anne Beaumont says he'll probably call back. Call several times. It's not unusual. They like to play games. We can get voice-prints, but I'd know him without that. I'd know him from the tape."

"Sure," Sorley said. "Do it." He took an e-mail off his printer tray and handed it to her. "You wanted a trip to west Somerset. Here it is. Can you do it in a day?"

"There'll be people to talk to," Stella said. "I'll get Sue Chapman to set things up for me. Better make it two days."

"I've got something to say."

"Okay, boss."

"Don't piss anyone off. The DCI who spoke to me was just a bit on the chippy side of welcoming. They know that serials have a low clear-up rate, so they'll assume we're desperate for a result. They closed the book on this whass'name—" he looked round on his swamped desk for his notes.

"Albert Carrick," Stella reminded him. "Victim was called Marie Turnow."

"—Okay, Carrick—a year ago and they won't want you in their faces telling them they made a bollocks of it. That's what I wanted to say. That's the official line."

"Straight from the SOI."

"Straight from the SOI," Sorley agreed.

"Is there an unofficial line?"

"Yes, there is," Sorley told her. "Bunch of hayseeds. Fuck 'em."

It was a long time since George Paterson had packed to travel light: basic clothes, wet-weather gear, a hip flask. It was a long time since he'd sailed Cape Horn, but that was the next move: it hadn't been difficult to find a boat needing crew.

Stella's stuff was all over the place: make-up in the bathroom, shoes under the bed, jewelry in little plush-lined boxes, clothes still hanging in the closet. They had the look of things abandoned long ago.

He pulled plugs out of their sockets and emptied the fridge. In his workroom he wrote an e-mail to a client who was about to be disappointed, then closed down the computer. He laughed at himself: running away to sea. But it was what he needed, he assured himself, a few weeks away, being busy among people who didn't know him. He remembered how it was to be out of sight of land, where the only noise was the noise of weather.

Early morning and, in the sky, red streaks laid across a delicate aquamarine backdrop. He noticed everything: a dog trotting past, its legs seeming to scissor as it took a long diagonal across the empty road; the sound of shutters going up; a radio giving out bad news. He closed the door of the flat behind him and it echoed.

Then the echoes stopped.

John Delaney dropped Stella's bag into the boot of her car. She was taking enough for an overnight.

She said, "You can't stay here." At Bachelor Boy's.

"I know. I'll tidy up and go home." He kissed her as she was getting into the car and she started slightly as if taken by surprise.

The red in the sky was a flush, now, fading a little as she came up on to the M4 approach road, driving with a light touch and flashing the fast-lane cruisers. Like George, she was traveling west toward the sea.

57

Don't confuse slow-talking with slow-thinking. DCI Bill Stephens had a farmer's accent and a raptor's eye. Stella had been kept waiting, no coffee, no apology, then Stephens had come by in a rush and she'd followed him into his office trying to keep her sense of irritation under control. She knew the technique: it was body-language for *You are a big pain in the arse.* Her response was to take longer than necessary over closing the door, so that when Stephens sat down, she was still standing. She waited until he gestured her toward a chair.

He was short and not quite gray, a solid shape that was starting to blur round the edges. He took out a plastic nicotine-placebo and put it on his desk, as if intending to treat himself later.

"You read the crime sheet?"

"I did, yes." She smiled winningly. "Thanks for sending it."

Stephens had brought his coffee with him. He made an issue of stirring it, as if waiting for Stella to speak. Finally, he said: "Albert Thomas Carrick, a known criminal with previous convictions for theft, taking away and driving without the owner's consent, fraud, issuing threats, etcetera etcetera, fingerprints and DNA at the scene, admitted to having been in the company of the deceased on the night of the murder, confessed during interview, confession later withdrawn, motive theft, opportunity obvious, no alibi, conviction a unanimous decision by the jury. What are you doing here, DS Mooney?"

"As I recall," Stella said, "the previous didn't add up to much. The theft was some pretty amateurish shoplifting for which he got a year suspended, the taking-away charge was said to be a misunderstanding, the threats were a two-way affair in a pub . . ."

"Your point is?"

"That he had form, sure, but it didn't make him much more than a nuisance. And there certainly wasn't any record of violence."

"Which has no bearing on the fact that he killed Marie Turnow, was arrested and tried and is currently serving a life sentence." Stephens took a pack of B&H out of his desk drawer and lit one. The placebo went back into his pocket.

Stella said, "I read your crime sheet. Did you read mine?" He looked at her until she said, "Sir."

"Multiple stab wounds. And Turnow suffered multiple stab wounds." He shrugged. "How many murder victims over the last two years have suffered multiple stab wounds? Want to make a guess?"

"There's a difference between multiple stab wounds and the way Marie Turnow died—there's a pattern."

"Who says so?"

"A man called Sam Burgess."

"The pathologist." Someone had prepared an abstract of the crime sheets on Stella's victims; it lay on Stephens's desk, but he hadn't needed to look at it to recognize Sam's name.

He's done the work, Stella thought. Which means he's worried.

"That's right."

"Backed up by a profiler." The word came with a wry smile which Stella ignored.

"It's not so much the way they died, Turnow included, although there is a discernible pattern—wound distribution, hands tied, mouth first taped then the tape removed after death, sexual assault, the fatal slash to the throat—it's the time they took to die." Stella paused, then said again: "The time they took to die."

"It's over," Stephens told her. "It's in the past. You're here to tell me we've got the wrong man. We haven't."

"I need to talk to a few people," Stella said. Then, "Sir."

"I don't think that's going to be necessary."

"The arresting officers, others on the case, the officers who interviewed Carrick." She looked at her notes. "DC Morgan, DC Harris, DS Child, have I got that right?"

Stephens was shaking his head. He said, "I can't help."

She indicated the video image of Sonny that was part of the

crime-sheet package on Stephens's desk. "I'd like the investigating officers to look at that."

"I'll circulate it."

Stella took note of the way he dropped the summary on top of the IDK printout. It was what he'd intended. She said, "I gather there's an appeal."

"There's always an appeal."

"You won't mind if I talk to the solicitor . . ." She asked because she knew he couldn't stop her.

Stephens drank his coffee. He turned slightly in his swivel chair and peered down at the High Street traffic. There was a slight flush to his cheek and the muscle was bunched at the point of his jaw.

Every story has its necessary omissions: the moment-by-moment stuff, the inessentials. Stella sat in a pub with a lunchtime sandwich and a beer and re-read the story of Marie Turnow. Re-read the crime sheet with its bald facts and bullet points.

- Marie-Ann Turnow, generally known as Marie. Divorcee.
- Owner of The Attic, a small shop selling antiques and bric-a-brac.
- Found murdered at her premises situated on the first floor of the same building. Time of death subsequently fixed at between midnight and twelve-thirty the previous evening. Body discovered by shop assistant next morning.
- Multiple stab wounds characterized by the police doctor as "a frenzied attack."
- Murder in the course of theft: contents of the till and the shop safe stolen, together with certain items from stock, including the murder weapon.
- Albert Thomas Carrick, intimate associate of the deceased, a known offender, questioned and released on police bail.
- Fingerprint analysis reveals Carrick's presence at the scene of crime. Carrick had already admitted to being with the victim on the evening of her death.

- Carrick questioned further, during which time he confessed to the murder of Marie-Ann Turnow. Carrick arrested and charged. Confession withdrawn two days later on the advice of solicitor, Thomas Allen (Allen & Poole).
- Case file submitted to DPP who found clear grounds for prosecution. Albert Thomas Carrick convicted of murder and sentenced to life imprisonment with a recommended tariff of twelve years.

The summary listed the names of the investigating officers, the police doctor, the pathologist, the coroner, the counsels, the trial judge. DCI Stephens was given as Senior Investigating Officer. Morgan, Harris, and Child cropped up again. It was noted that an appeal against the conviction was pending.

There was nothing between the lines but a faint whiff of brimstone.

Thomas Allen was forty, short, skinny and spoke in a light, rapid voice as if anxious to get things said. He read through the summary of the four crime sheets that Stella had brought with her: the sad stories of Janis Parker, Nesta Cameron, Amanda-Jane Wallace, Jean Halliday.

"Four of them," he said. "Four." As if two would have been enough. "How did you find Albert Carrick?"

Stella had made an appointment with Allen, but he'd had to break it. Now it was almost eight and they were in the near-deserted bar of Stella's hotel: clearly not a popular place and Stella was glad of it because the only alternative was her room, and two strangers in the presence of a bed doesn't make for an easy exchange of views.

"Basic MO," Stella told him.

"How close are you?" He meant to an arrest.

"Not very. Not close at all."

"Serial killings," Allen said. "If you're right and Marie Turnow is part of the pattern, my man walks, no question. Can I have copies of your crime reports?"

"For the appeal hearing?" He nodded. "Eventually," Stella said. "Not just yet."

"Or find the killer," Allen suggested, "and get a confession: that would do."

"He confessed—your man."

"Yes, that's right, he did." Allen handed the summary back to Stella. "Guess why."

"You're going to tell me it was beaten out of him."

"That's right. Sorry."

"Why sorry?"

"You're the police. It's not something you'd want to hear."

Stella was silent on that. She said, "What's his story?"

"Pretty straightforward. He was having a relationship with Marie Turnow. She sounds like a pillar of respectability—antique-shop owner. The fact is that it wasn't so much antiques as high-class junk, if you see what I mean, and I don't think she asked too many questions about the stuff that went through the shop. The police knew that. Another thing: if you look at Albert Carrick's record, you'd take him for a bit of a lowlife. Not so; not really. Middle-class background, red-brick university, couldn't settle to a job, liked booze and dope— an all-round hopeless case. He and Marie Turnow were a match: no surprise they found one another. He saw her that night, they had sex, he went home at about eleven, swore he didn't go out again. His prints and DNA were all over everything, including her, but then why not? It was the confession that sank him."

"It was convincing?"

"Very. But then, it would be, given that the interrogating officers had attended the scene of crime and read the pathologist's report."

"How do you know he didn't do it?" Stella asked.

"He told me so. I believe him." It was a good answer.

"If he didn't, who did?"

Allen shrugged. "It was a robbery, I'm pretty sure about that. The police never recovered the money—certainly not from my client, though the jury didn't seem to set much store by that. I don't think the idea was to kill Marie and that taking the money was an afterthought. Other way about."

"For an afterthought, they made a pretty good job of it."

"They?"

Stella covered the slip. "Whoever did it. The killer."

"That's why it wasn't Carrick," Allen observed. "Not in his nature. Also, he had a sort of alibi."

This was news to Stella. "He did?"

"He lived in a small block of flats about three miles from the High Street where Marie Turnow had her shop. The flat was over the shop—"

"I remember," Stella said.

"Carrick had been drinking—with Marie Turnow and then, later, when he got home. My guess is he was good and drunk. He was playing music. A neighbor called him and complained."

"They spoke on the phone?"

"At the time of the murder, or thereabouts. The neighbor had been woken up and Carrick was pissed, so neither was able to give an accurate account of the time. It wasn't much of an alibi, but it was something. The neighbor was able to bracket the time and it seemed to put Carrick three miles from the scene at the time of death. The pathologist's report was reasonably precise. It was all arguable, of course, a bit vague, difficult to establish."

"The jury didn't go for it?"

"The jury didn't hear it. Carrick gave the information to the police. They never told the defense."

"Didn't Carrick tell the defense?"

"That's the issue. He'd forgotten. His memory of the evening was pretty vague, especially as to time. The cops found out when they were doing a standard house-to-house—in the hope of finding someone to say he wasn't in all night, I expect. Instead of which, this neighbor pops up with a story about Elton John coming through the wall at midnight . . . if that's not too grotesque a notion."

"When did Carrick tell you?"

"After sentencing. I guess the idea of a life sentence concentrated his mind."

"That's the substance of your appeal?"

"By and large. Thin stuff, but our own."

Stella hadn't been surprised by the story. Angered, but not surprised. "What did they say when you challenged them on it?"

"The police?" He smiled and looked away, as if avoiding a confrontation. "They said the notes had been lost. What do you think?"

Stella nodded. She had nothing else to say on that. "Who found the body?"

"A girl who helped in the shop. Local girl." The case notes were in his briefcase; he took out the file and poked through the papers for a minute. "Donna Scott." He passed the file to Stella. "I could copy these for you in the morning."

"Yes, please."

Stella read Donna's account of getting to work that morning, opening up, wondering where her employer was, checking the upstairs flat . . . She had given a brief statement to the police concerning her movements the previous evening, just as everyone else had who was in any way connected with Marie Turnow: a drink at the pub with her boyfriend, Leo Martin (vouched for by Martin and pub crowd), then home for more drinks (vouched for by Martin and a few of the pub crowd who went with them). It was a normal enough account of a normal evening: one of fifteen or twenty statements made by Marie Turnow's friends, acquaintances, business contacts. She showed him SOC photos of Janis Parker and Jean Halliday, but he'd never seen Marie Turnow dead. She showed him the picture of Sonny they'd lifted from the Kandy Kave videotape, but Allen had never met Sonny.

"Person or persons unknown," Allen observed. Then, as he handed back the photos, "Imagine what she felt when she went in and found the body. Donna Scott. Scarcely anything of the poor woman that wasn't cut: foot soles, back of the head. Think of the blood. You'd never forget that, would you?"

58

"What did you expect to find?" Delaney asked.

"Nothing," Stella said. "Nothing positive, anyway. It's more about whether Marie-Ann Turnow is one of ours, so to speak."

"Is she?"

"She is."

"You're sure?"

"I am."

"Go on . . ."

"They kicked a confession out of him. Carrick. He retracted it, but the damage was done. Juries are sometimes fickle, but more often blinkered. Apart from which, it's a carbon copy of Parker and the rest."

"Could be a story," he observed. "Miscarriage of justice."

"Be my guest. There's a DCI called Stephens who could use some bad press."

"Why don't I join you?"

"I'll be home tomorrow. There's follow-up to be done down here, but I think I'll send Harriman."

"What are you doing?"

"In my room. I had room service."

"Okay?"

"Crap. I could have had dinner with a pint-sized solicitor, but there was something about the way he suggested it."

It was late. Stella was drinking vodka over ice and looking out of an open window to the country-town high street. It had been raining, but the midnight breeze was cool, not cold: fresh and untainted.

Delaney asked, "What's it like there?"

"Fields, cows, sheep. Strong smell of bullshit."

She helped herself to another drink, a *final* drink, then looked through the photocopies of Thomas Allen's notes and compared them with the crime sheets supplied by DCI Stephens's office.

She read the SOC officer's notes and the pathologist's report. She scanned the witness statements and interviews with Marie Turnow's social and business contacts. She barely registered that Donna Scott referred to Leo Martin as "Sonny." She read the accounts of DC Morgan, DC Harris, and DS Child, all written in standard cop-lingo. She gave herself another drink—*and fuck it, why not?*—then lifted the phone and called George.

To say, "How are you?" To say, "What are you thinking?" To say, "How strange this is."

She listened to the ringing tone for a minute, two minutes, three . . .

The night-time silence was almost as constant as the London night-time noise. She could sleep with a background of planes and cars and music and drunks, but a lone car on the street woke her, or a single shout of laughter.

Or a knock on her door at one A.M., light at first, then heavy-handed. She was sleeping in just a T-shirt. She dragged her jeans on, thinking this couldn't be anything but bad news.

He was standing close, dominating the space between them as she opened the door: a copper's technique. He showed her a warrant card, but too fast for her to read it or tell whether the picture matched the man: broad across the shoulders, fleshy-faced, his hair cropped to take attention away from the thin widow's peak. She was stepping back to let him in but he pushed through, catching the door with his shoulder to jog her aside. Stella noticed the sheen of sweat on his forehead.

"Morgan or Harris or Child?" she asked.

He was drunk, though the slight clumsiness as he crossed the room, the quiver in his speech, were a mix of anger and anxiety. There was no chair in the room, so he sat on the bed, putting out an arm to brace himself, his hand in the patch of warm where Stella had lain. She pushed the door to, but didn't close it.

He said, "I'm going to be nice about this." A slur to his voice, his eyes not holding hers, as if he already knew that he was making a mistake.

"Morgan, Harris, or Child?"

"It's just a matter of letting it drop. You came down here looking for a connection—you didn't find one." He took some time over lighting a cigarette, glancing at Stella, glancing round the room, as if looking for an advantage. She folded her arms, conscious of her breasts, loose under the T-shirt. "You didn't find one, did you?"

"I think you're Child. DS Child, is that right?"

"He confessed. His brief made him retract. That's all. A piece of game-playing. The jury said fuck off."

"Were you one of the interviewing officers?" Stella asked. "Did you lay hands on him?"

"Jesus Christ . . ." He shook his head in disgust. "A bleeding heart." He ran the words into each other and took a long drag on his cigarette, as if that might help to steady him.

"Albert Carrick wasn't guilty, DS Child, and you know that. The fact that you're here asking me to say something else is proof itself. Whoever killed Marie Turnow is still out there and still killing. When I report to my SIO, that's what I'll be saying. What happens after that is up to him. And I wonder if your boss knows you've come to see me. Because if he doesn't, you're in trouble; and if he does, you're both in trouble."

He came off the bed, fast, and crossed the room to stand directly in front of her, his breath sour, his eyes slightly unfocused. "Leave this alone," he told her. "Let it go." Then, "You're so fucking lily-white, are you?"

Nike Man taking the wheel-nut crank across the side of the neck, going down, his legs buckling, the shock spreading on his face.

Stella put a hand on the man's chest and shoved him back: a

challenge. He took hold of her wrist, hard, then let it fall. She moved to the door and opened it.

"You've made a mistake," she said. "You've been drinking and worrying and thinking about the best way to handle this, and you chose the worst."

"Let it drop," he said again, but his voice had changed, the anger smudged by anxiety.

When Stella held the door a little wider he crossed to the bed, hawked up from deep in his throat, and spat on to her pillow.

As he left, she gave him a broad smile. "Goodnight, DS Child. I imagine the night porter let you in. I'll get his name in the morning: just for reference."

She threw the pillow into a corner and sat cross-legged on the bed, trembling slightly. She wasn't frightened, nor had she been, but the high-adrenalin reaction to threat would take a while to ebb. She found her phone and half-dialed Delaney's number, then pressed "cancel."

Nike Man propped up against the car, his eyes wide open and lightless, the breath stopped in his throat.

She went to sleep sitting up, and the image bled into her dreams.

Next morning, before she drove back to London, she sent a note to DCI Bill Stephens, saying that the murder of Marie Turnow demonstrated an MO that was too close to the murders she was currently investigating to be coincidental and that she intended to proceed with that in mind. She also said how much she had enjoyed her meeting with DS Child. Or Morgan. Or Harris.

Her hands light on the wheel, her right wrist carrying a faint blue bruise where he'd gripped her. Beside her on the passenger seat, the file Thomas Allen had given her, with the names of Donna Scott and Leo (Sonny) Martin noted and already half-forgotten.

She was walking into the squad room when her mobile phone rang: one of those bizarre moments of synchronicity, because Maxine

Hewitt was making a call at the far end of the squad room, looking down at something on her desk, and when Stella answered her phone it was Maxine who spoke to her.

She said, "I'm here."

They met halfway, Maxine carrying a print-out of the delayed forensic report on the Halliday scene of crime with its lists of dust and detritus, blood types and secretions, palm-prints and body fluids.

Maxine said, "There." She was jabbing the top sheet with a finger.

From the blood-cake in Jean Halliday's flat, from that unspeakable mire, forensics had taken many samples, among them a single hair which could without doubt be said to be a man's beard hair or pubic hair. The forensic examiner had opted for beard hair, since it had been dyed with a proprietary brand named "Blondie" that could be bought across the counter from any chemist.

"You bastard," Stella said. "It's you."

59

There are many ways to make a living on the Strip, but none of them offers a pension or Medicare. You can hook, deal, fence, mug, or dip. You can run guns, run girls, run porn shops and shebeens. You can set up a basement casino and take the house percentage home each night. That's for the locals, the homeboys. That's if you live and work on the Strip. The other way to cash in is to be a raider; to come in from the badlands farther west, mob-handed, carrying lots of firepower, and take what you can find. Bandit raids on the Strip weren't frequent because the locals had a pretty good intelligence network, but they happened.

Another way to make a living would be to rob the robbers. No one had ever done that, which is why it was at the planning stage with Marcus Lucio and six of his friends. Marcus lived on the Harefield Estate, where he'd come up through the educational system called gang warfare. Now he was twenty-three and a graduate. Marcus had Spanish coloring and the muscled, thickset build of a sprinter, and he was a dozen IQ points brighter than any of the young men there with him in the fifteenth-floor apartment, but that was okay because what he needed was weight of numbers; the brainwork he could manage. He was talking tactics that were simplicity itself, even for those who had started the day with a light spliff.

Harefield was many things—factory, bazaar, warehouse, whorehouse—but it was also an operations center, and Marcus had his own intelligence network. He knew that a casino on the Strip had been targeted and he knew that a four-handed team would make the hit.

"Four," he said, "and they won't be expecting us. They call themselves the Crew. They're nothing."

Street-gang names seemed to trade off limited choice. Cool Crew, Hard Crew, Rude Crew. The Crew were a back-to-basics bunch.

"We watch them go in, we watch them come out, we do them, and we take the money. No one knows who the fuck we are. They'll know the guys who jacked the place because they'll be out of it, but they don't know us. No comeback."

The fashion-wear for the upwardly mobile of Harefield was a ski-mask and a Hilfiger leisure shell. Your accessories were a MAC-10 or a 9 mm automatic. Marcus was pleased with his plan because it was simple and simplicity was the key to success; it also had the considerable advantage that someone else would do the dangerous stuff. Marcus's motto for the gig was go there, fuck the bandits, go home richer.

It was a new casino run from a basement under a Chinese restaurant, and it was doing such good business that the Chinese freebooters who had set it up were thinking of buying more restaurants with basements. Marcus had heard about the raid from someone who was too stoned to remember ever having boasted about it. Sometimes life simply plays your way.

. . .

Stella sat with Mike Sorley in his screened-off space and listened while he first said "No," then tried to soften it with reasons.

"Hayseeds, you said," she reminded him. "Fuck 'em. Wasn't that it?"

"This isn't coming from me, Stella, you know that."

"They've got a man banged up for a crime our team committed, and apart—"

"There's an appeal pending."

"—and apart from that, I didn't speak to witnesses, to the dead woman's contacts and friends, to the arresting officers, to the guys who kicked him round a cell until he confessed—"

"And that's the problem," Sorley said. "That's the problem, right there."

"It's not in my report, but one of them turned up at my door in the small hours, pissed and angry, telling me to let it go."

Sorley looked at her in surprise. "What happened?"

"He made a lot of noise, then left."

"Threatened you?"

"Intimidation was the idea. Sad bastard."

"You want to take it further?"

Stella shook her head. "I want DC Harriman to go down there and do the follow-up, that's all."

"They've closed the door," Sorley said. "This guy Stephens. Closed it and thrown the bolt. The only way back would be a full blue-on-blue investigation and that's only likely if the appeal succeeds."

"Some chance."

"I've been told, Stella. I've had the official memo. People of rank talking to people of rank."

"It's them," Stella said. "Turnow is down to our team killers; we ought to be treating it as another unsolved—God knows what we might find. You saw the forensic report—I've got this bastard's picture. I gave it to Stephens, he's supposed to be circulating it."

"I've faxed him the picture again, along with a note saying that this might be one of the team killers."

"It's him," Stella said.

"Maybe. One hair. Try it in court."

"I won't need to. There's more than enough DNA evidence waiting for when we catch him. He did Marie Turnow, I know it."

"You know it, but Stephens isn't having it."

"And in the meantime, Albert Carrick is serving life with a tariff of twelve years."

Sorley shrugged. "He had form anyway. If it's not one thing, it's another."

60

John Delaney had got back from Bachelor Boy's loft to a freshly graffitied front door and a set of key-stripes on the curbside bodywork of his shiny Hertz rental. His answer-machine carried a series of silences.

Stella said, "I hate to think about your insurance rating." She was full-length on the sofa making notes from the notes she'd made in Somerset.

Delaney said, "I tried to call George."

Stella couldn't see the connection for a moment, then she sat up, frowning. "You think George did it?"

"I don't think it was the Keyring Fairy."

"You're wrong." She sounded more disturbed than angry, though anger was a makeweight.

"Okay, I'm wrong. I'd like to ask him, though."

"I don't know where he is. I've been trying him myself."

"Well," Delaney said, "if you reach him, ask him to call me. I know he's got the number."

A frost in the air; a distance opening up.

Delaney at his keyboard, Stella doing her homework. Later, she would go back to Bachelor Boy's place, that was the deal. Too easy for them to start living together by default; too easy to find that early habit had made their decisions for them. They had cooked together and stacked the dishwasher together and avoided all mention of George until now, but he'd been sitting there at the table with them, the uninvited guest.

Stella walked over and dropped her papers on Delaney's desk. "There it is, if you want it."

He took a few minutes to read through. "I want it," he said. "Are you going back?" She shook her head. "Someone from your team?"

She wasn't going to tell him that she'd tried to send Harriman and been knocked back; who'd want to be first reserve? "Not now. Not right away. The cops I know I need in London, the ones I don't know I don't trust. Wrongful imprisonment is a touchy issue."

"Extracting a confession under duress, withholding evidence . . ."

"You'll meet a lot of opposition, so don't go looking for it."

"Meaning?"

"Don't breeze into DCI Stephens's office telling him that you're there to fuck his life up."

"Are there any cops I *can* talk to?"

"You can talk to whoever you like. If you want my opinion, I'd avoid it. If you decide to be confrontational, you could try to get to one or all of the interviewing officers."

He checked her notes. "Morgan, Harris, and Child."

"Yes. They'll see you as the enemy, but anger can cause tongues to slip. Make it a last resort."

"Which one was it—in your room?"

"Child, I think. It's a guess. There's a description of him in the notes I've given you, but don't take it to heart. He's a frightened man."

"Good." He paused, looking at her. "Isn't this odd for you?"

"You mean, because I'm the police too?" He nodded. "There are straight coppers and bent coppers. We're not on the same side. Some people think there's a gray area in between. I don't."

It was almost true. More or less true. What she needed was someone working for her on the Marie Turnow case.

He got up and circled her with his arms. It never failed. Everything in her quickened and she wanted him at once. She kissed him and stood back a little so he could undress her.

At least, it hadn't failed yet.

She drove as if she didn't know where she was going, making circles, taking wrong turns, and arrived at her own front door. At first she hardly recognized the place: as if she'd been away for years. Where did that picture come from? Where does this door lead?

Into the bedroom, of course, with its drawers and closets full. She thought a few of George's clothes might be missing, a few of his belongings, but how to tell for sure? She took a few things she needed: clean clothes, shoes, a shoulder bag, and went through to the living room. Who bought this CD with the bluesy sax? Where do we keep the vodka?

In the freezer, of course. With the music on low and the dimmer switch down, she poured a double shot over ice and lay on the sofa, just as she had earlier at Delaney's place.

Shut your eyes. Where are you? Where do you want to be?

The hall was littered with junk mail, the fridge was empty, the tape on the answer phone was blank. The drawing board in George's workroom carried no plans, no specifications, no thumbnail sketches of ships in sail. Who chose those plantation shutters? Where do we leave notes for each other?

Pegged to the board by the back door, of course. More ice and more vodka before she slit the envelope.

> . . . gone away for a while. Don't worry . . .
> . . . he called and hung up one time. I dialed 1471–3 and heard his voice. I thought someone who'd take a risk like that must have a lot at stake. I didn't do anything for a while. I thought you'd tell me. I thought you would be bound to tell me . . .
> . . . could feel myself diminishing in your eyes. And I felt so sorry for you, knowing how you hate deceit . . .
> . . . feel different, but not toward you . . .
> . . . for now. But I'll have to come back sometime . . .

It was folly to spend the night there, but she would definitely drink more, and vodka and sadness make a volatile combination. She went into the bathroom, stripped, and got into the shower. Delaney's smell was on her skin; she felt blurred, an off-center version of herself.

She sat on the floor of the shower, knees to chin, a refugee in a downpour.

61

Donna could have walked on water, could have floated from high windows. She was light and thin-skinned. The fever had almost left her, but the dreams wouldn't stop. Even in her waking hours, the images flocked round her, darkness pierced by light, the Mother's halo of hair, the mirror and the knife, Dilly's frantic *yip-yip*.

The best times were when the Mother went away and Donna was left alone. There were pictures of the Mother all round the house. The Mother was beautiful. The largest pictures were of the Mother in a swimsuit and sash: Carnival Queen, Miss Dairy Products.

Donna ate food from tins and drank water from the tap. The dog nipped her when she fed it, but that was okay because no one was there to watch when she kicked it or threw stones at it.

She could leave the house and walk round the streets. She could stay out until after dark and pretend she would never go back. Sometimes she would go into the cupboard and pull the door to behind her and sit in the dark for a while, then step out to an empty house. When the Mother came back, the darkness was different.

She heard Sonny on the stairs to the flat, heard him laughing as he came in. She could eat, now; in fact, she seemed to be hungry all the time. He put a pizza down on the table, still laughing, and went to fetch a knife.

She said, "A couple of days. Then we can move."

"Okay."

"How much money have we got?"

"Some. What we took from the last one. I got some stuff down at the Wheatsheaf."

"What?"

"Coke. Some good grass. We can get off our heads." He laughed. "Right off our fucking heads."

He cracked a can of beer and stood by the window, a slice of pizza in his hand. From there, he could see the payphone where he'd stopped off to leave a message for Ladycop.

I know you, but you don't know me. Ha-ha-ha, hee-hee-hee.

This time it was the woman herself. DS Stella Mooney. She had wanted to keep him talking, but he wasn't stupid.

"Tell me. I want to hear. Tell me about Jean Halliday."

"I know you—"

"Tell me about the others. What were their names?"

"—but you don't know me."

"You phoned up to talk, didn't you?"

"Just to say, we'll be back."

"You might be a time waster. How do I know you're not wasting my time?"

"We'll be back, Ladycop."

"All right, look, there are things you want to tell me, aren't there? Okay, I'm listening. Whatever you want to say. You can say anything to me."

He laughed. "Goodbye for now, Ladycop. Goodbye. Goodbyeeeeee . . ." He was still laughing as he hung up.

They did a few lines and watched a video in which they both starred; their co-star was Nesta Cameron. Donna was wearing a cotton bathrobe. While they watched, Sonny untied the robe and pushed her back against the arm of the sofa. She drew her knees up for him and watched the video over his shoulder. The cocaine sharpened everything: the white of flesh, white flesh laced with red, the whites of eyes, a red handprint on the white wall. Afterward, she dozed. The tape rewound and replayed, the images on the screen seeming to merge with the images that mobbed her.

That was the time the Mother was gone for several days. That was the time she spent more and more of her day on the streets. That was the time Dilly had snapped at her, going through the leg of her jeans and drawing blood from her calf.

That was the time she locked the dog in the cupboard, leaving it there despite the scuffling and clawing at the door, despite the barking that became a trembling whine after a day or two, Donna opening tins for herself, finding beer that the Mother kept in her room, going out to walk where she chose for as long as she chose, going home in darkness, knowing Dilly was still hungering and thirsting in the cupboard, waiting another day and a day after that before standing in front of the mirror in the Mother's room backcombing her hair to make it fluff up, putting on the Mother's lipstick, putting on the perfume that smelled of flowers, then going to stand outside the cupboard door.

That was the time when she took Dilly's collar and led her back upstairs to the mirror, the fish-gutting knife in her hand, a roll of duct tape from under the kitchen sink in her pocket. She took a belt from one of the Mother's dresses. Dilly was weak, but Donna tied her anyway, and taped her muzzle, because tied and taped was the way things should be.

That was the time when she darted in and out with the knife, cutting through the short fur, watching the gashes open up, watching the blood start.

Dilly screamed. The tape held most of it back, but she seemed to be saying, *Don't hurt me. Don't hurt me. Don't hurt me.*

Donna snicked and snagged, her eyes wide and bright, the knife good and sharp.

How does it feel?

62

Stella had the transcript in front of her. An ARV had already been to the payphone and lifted a sixty-two-year-old Chinese male who spoke no English. Maxine Hewitt was reading over her shoulder. "At least he stayed on long enough for the trace. Except . . ."

Stella completed the sentence: "If he called from there he doesn't live there."

"Probably not. If we manage to get a trace next time, we'll have a better idea."

"You're sure there'll be a next time?"

"This guy's got a taste for it."

Maxine pointed to a moment on the page. *Ladycop.* Then again: *Ladycop.* "He thinks he knows you."

"But I don't know him. Yet. It makes him laugh."

The video-lift of Sonny's face lay next to the transcript: she had laid them side by side, putting a face to the voice.

"You bastard," she said, "it's you. I know it's you."

Andy Greegan came over at speed and handed her an identical picture but rougher round the edges: one of the faxes he'd sent. Someone had faxed it back with a note. Stella read the note twice, then looked at Greegan who grimaced and said, "I know."

"They had him on affray and actual bodily harm?" There was a note of despair in her voice. "They *had* him?"

"He was refuse-charged."

Sonny and Sports Fan would have been spoken to separately and asked if either of them wanted to make a complaint. They didn't.

They would have been detained while CROs were checked to discover whether either of them was wanted by other forces on other charges. They weren't. After that, the duty officer would have signed them out under whatever names they'd given, no details recorded, no addresses taken. Refuse-charged.

"They couldn't have known, boss."

The cover note with the fax gave the source as Ladbroke Grove nick. Greegan pointed it out to her. "Looks like he called you from home ground."

"Send someone over to Ladbroke Grove to talk to the arresting officers and the duty officer: anyone there who spoke to him. See if we can trace the guy he clouted." Greegan laughed at the idea. She said, "I know, it's a long shot: he didn't bring charges which probably means he doesn't like the police, but let's try. We've got the man-power, so let's do a house-to-house right through the area, take the video picture, go back to places where there's no answer first time round, do shops and offices and pubs—starting with the Wheat-sheaf."

She talked to Mike Sorley about releasing Sonny's face to the press. "We might get a name, we might get a good location. He doesn't know we've got this picture. We've got him operating in a very small area: the Wheatsheaf, the phone booth . . . I'd rate the chances of getting a positive ID from house-to-house plus press and TV coverage pretty high. We could poster the area, too."

"He sees himself, he goes underground," Sorley suggested.

"He's underground now. He's never going to stay on the phone until we get there. At this stage of the game, it might be better to know who he is—which might tell us who *she* is. We've tried the other way. If it does have the effect of sending them to cover, at least that means they'll be less likely to kill."

"Or they'll leave our patch and start killing somewhere else," Sorley said. Stella wondered whether "leave our patch" was the more important consideration. "Okay, do it," he said. "Tell the press office."

.   .   .

The squad room was full of new faces. Greegan and Harriman and Maxine, together with Sue Chapman and Stuart Proctor, the exhibitions officer, worked as a unit inside a unit.

Does everyone know? she had asked Maxine, and the answer had been, *Yes, everyone knows*. But no one had mentioned it, although Pete Harriman had been looking like a man with something to say, and when Stella had given Sue Chapman a note of her temporary address and her mobile as the only phone contact, Sue had nodded and looked up, expecting more. Stella wasn't ready for that. She wondered if the new faces had the gossip, too.

She had almost fallen asleep amid the steam and drumming water, but eventually the shower had run cold. She had slept on her side of the bed. Next morning she had eaten a biscuit and drunk water, as if coffee and toast would have been a sort of home-making.

Next morning traffic had been building to a standstill in the North End Road, so she'd cut through the Harefield Estate as anyone would who knew the back-doubles, the rat-runs, the exact place in the bull ring where X marks the spot.

63

You'd know them, but you wouldn't know their names. The drunk who slept in your shop doorway each night so you had to sluice the piss and puke away each morning; the whore with the cherry earrings who once, just once, you'd taken into the store room after you'd pulled the shutters for the evening; the freelance cabbies who sat in their cars and played the music stations; the guy with the yellow hair and freaky little beard who came in for a pizza, extra toppings.

It wasn't just the guy at the pizzeria who knew Sonny. Half the Strip knew Sonny, but they didn't know where he lived. Stella interviewed a few of them herself. He was local, they told her, they'd seen him around.

Ever with a woman?

Sure.

What was she like?

Well, she was fair, dark, tall, short, heavy, slim, pretty, and plain. And she had long hair, they all agreed on that. No, they'd seen him, but they hadn't seen her; not for a while. And, hey, couldn't the police do anything about the kid who stole fruit from the street display? The kid was a pain in the arse and his dog was a killer.

Then Maxine Hewitt and Pete Harriman found someone who could get them closer than that.

Frank Cattano had been forty or so when he'd climbed a scaffolding ladder with an angle joist on his shoulder. He'd done it many times before, but on those occasions the ladder had been roped to the planks. No one was likely to take the blame, because Frank had dropped three stories to hit the ground on his back and people standing twenty feet away heard the sound in his spine, like a mallet driving a post. Frank's world shrank to a wheelchair and whatever you could do with a life from the waist up. A lot of the time, he watched the street from his window.

"That row of shops," Frank told them, "but I don't remember which door." On one side of the launderette was the Eight-til-Late, on the other a Chinese restaurant; either side of those were a bookie's and a place that heeled shoes and sold locks; between each shopfront was a narrow door that let on to a flight of stairs and at the top of the stairs was a landing that gave access to two small flats. The layout didn't vary."

Four doors, eight flats.

"He eats a lot of pizza," Frank told them. "Bright yellow hair and a little stringy beard the same color." There was a girl all right, but Frank hadn't seen her for a while. He thought maybe they'd split up.

Stella called Greegan and organized a team of four to trace the owners of the flats, but it was late in the day and offices were closing. "A lot of those places are let on the fly," Greegan told her. "Rents paid but not declared. Not only that, it's a fair bet that some of the premises will be used for illegal activities."

"Tell the owners we're looking the other way. We just want names and descriptions of tenants. Reassure them. Tax avoidance, a crack factory—we're looking the other way."

"Okay, boss." As an afterthought, he asked: "Are we? Looking the other way?"

"No," Stella said. "Of course not."

She stood in Frank's living room, which was also his bedroom and kitchen, and stared out at the Strip. She wasn't needed, because there were three surveillance teams already in place, but she had wanted to talk to Frank and she'd wanted to get sight of the location.

The temptation was to go in, now—just make a guess—but eight-to-one was long odds. The best option was to go in to all eight, but for that you needed paper. That kind of raid, that kind of manpower, eight doors down and only one of them the right door—that took a lot of paper, a lot of signatures. Then there was the possibility that Frank had got it wrong: not that row of shops, but another. Four different doors, eight different flats. One reason for doubt was that Frank was seventy, now, and slept in his chair a lot of the day; another was the half-dozen empty Scotch bottles alongside the sink.

"He's not making it up."

Stella and Harriman had been sitting in a parked car two streets off the Strip while the surveillance was set up.

"No, he's seen our man, all right," Stella agreed. "It's when and where."

"He thinks the girl might have gone."

"Maybe they've both gone. He got nicked, after all. Refuse-charged, but enough to make them edgy, wouldn't you say?"

"Frank's pretty sure he's seen him since then."

"Frank was pretty sure he'd left his glasses by the bed. They were round his neck."

Stella was being negative because she was hoping for the best: don't expect to get lucky and you might throw a seven.

She left Frank's without having had sight of Sonny and went back to the squad room. She'd pulled the house-to-house, then called Sorley and asked for SO 19 to be advised. If it was going to be a gun-squad operation, they'd want their own surveillance officers in place. She asked for a police helicopter to be put on standby and she asked for police drivers with local knowledge. When she got back to AMIP-5, Andy Greegan had whiteboarded one end of the room and tacked up building plans and large-scale maps of the Strip and the streets that surrounded it.

Stella was running the briefing, but Sorley's was a voice to be heard.

"SO 19 will want at least a day's surveillance and a day's set-up. If possible, they'll want to find a similar location and run some trials. If they're involved, they won't want AMIP-5 officers to be issued with firearms; in fact, they would oppose gun-issue even if they weren't part of the operation. You know how it is. Largely speaking, I agree with them."

"We could lift the man," Harriman said. "He's likely to make an appearance sooner or later, even if the woman's gone."

"What if she hasn't?" Stella asked him. "Take one and lose the other doesn't sound like an option to me. So far, we've only traced ownership of three of the eight flats. You'd be surprised how many property transfers relate to those houses. One of the flats carries documents for sixteen sub-lets, none of them to the people currently living there. Either we watch him leave, keep tabs, then watch him back in—which would narrow things down to two flats—or we turn up at eight front doors asking to read the meter with ten guys waiting on the stairs. The other option, of course, is to turn up at eight front doors with a Hatton gun."

Sorley's sour laugh said, Don't even think about it.

"It's not an easy area for surveillance," Stella said. "Lots going on, much of it illegal, which means it gets a lot of police attention. No way round that."

No way round, because a change in temperature causes the creatures of the night to sniff the air. But there was another reason. Ask for a new procedure-pattern and you have to say why—and news travels. Maybe one of the eight flats was a drugs warehouse, maybe another was a porn factory. Maybe money sometimes changed hands to buy security. A cop's pay doesn't buy many extras. It's why SO 19 officers are given their objective at the last minute and only after all mobile phones have been accounted for.

"He'll show," Sorley said. "If he's in there."

Stella nodded. "But if he's not we're wasting a lot of resources and time."

"Do it this way," Sorley told her. "Give it a couple of days. Maintain surveillance on the row and set up a team to follow him out and back. Narrow it to two flats. Then—if you still don't have ID for the occupants—jump in."

Maxine Hewitt asked, "If he doesn't come out, boss?"

"He'll come out," Sorley said. "He likes pizza, he likes a beer at the Wheatsheaf."

Sonny and Donna, each in technicolor dreamscape. Stella and Frank, either side of the window, looking down on the Strip with its non-stop nightlife.

Are you there? Stella wondered. *Almost within sight. Almost close enough to touch.*

It had been a clear spring day and there was still light in the sky at eight o'clock. The whores were doing good business, just shadows in doorways until a punter pulled over and they came to the curb, drenched in neon, to brace a hand on the car roof and give the tariff. There were crack deals going down in the side streets. In a basement casino beneath the Chinese restaurant a punter let his bet ride on eight black and the wheel of fortune stopped just for him.

.   .   .

It wasn't until noon the next day that Sonny shook off his coke dream and cracked a beer and decided he felt hungry.

Stella had been away and come back, getting negative reports from the three surveillance units. She had watched the early-morning sweepings and hosings, shutters going up, pavement displays being set out: it was a different world by day. A boy with a big, brindled dog at his heel had played nip-and-tuck with the shopkeepers, taking a haul of fruit while the dog made snaky circles, looking for attacks from left and right.

She saw Sonny a moment before the first surveillance team called in: Pete Harriman's voice. "He's heading toward Kensal Rise. We're on him."

"I can see him," Stella said.

A car pulled away from the curb, traveled to the next side-street junction and made the turn. An officer got out; two others stayed in the car. If Sonny changed his mind and walked the other way, a second car would cover that.

As it happened, no cars were needed, and no officers. Sonny went into the pizzeria and placed an order, then sat down to wait. It wasn't necessary, either, to watch his return: Stella had seen him emerge from the door between the launderette and the Chinese restaurant; only two flats were involved and a two-to-one shot didn't require too much paperwork.

64

An hour later, Maxine Hewitt brought it down to no-bet. The launderette was registered with the local Chamber of Commerce to Thomas MacIver at an address that had never existed. No one was going to walk into the launderette and show a warrant card to the women who worked there: you might as well roll up to the door in an ARV. Maxine had gone through the phonebook MacIvers and the ex-D MacIvers without getting lucky, so she stopped to think about Thomas MacIver, who owned a launderette—probably owned several, along with other ventures—but didn't want to be too closely connected to them.

She had him down as a big guy, a heavyweight, although a pretty small deal in the world of organized crime. Inevitably, his friends, his "business acquaintances," called him Big Mac. He was fiftyish and the weight was more flab than muscle. When his hair had started to go, he'd opted to have a close crop. He wore gangster Armani or Hugo Boss and his wife didn't complain about the girls because the girls didn't live in an eight-bedroom house in Surrey or have accounts at Harrods or Harvey Nicks.

None of this need be accurate. It didn't matter whether Maxine had got it right about his size, his clothes, his wife, his nickname. She was guessing a lifestyle and the picture helped. He would pay himself a salary. He would drive a company Merc. He would have the mother of expense accounts.

She called Companies House in Cardiff and found that the personal address he'd given was the same as the nonexistent location on the local register. The address of his registered office was that of an accountant's offices in Pimlico. Maxine made the trip and met a man called Laurence Hall, whose natural tendency to say little became a determination to say nothing once she'd shown him her ID.

"I can't possibly give you client details of that sort without a court order," he told her. "Even then, I'd probably seek advice from a solicitor."

It was unfair of Maxine to take against him because he had thin, sandy hair and a prim mouth over a weak chin, but it helped her to find the tone she wanted. "That's fine, that's okay. But let me tell you, we're investigating a series of killings and we just need a little information from Mr. MacIver. We don't intend to look into his affairs, or check his cash flow, or ask Customs and Excise to go back over his VAT returns. We're not even going to ask why his business is registered to a nonexistent address, or why he gave the same false information to Companies House. None of that. And we're not going to ask any other police division to look into the fact that you represent such a client, or ask about other clients you might have on your books who also give false addresses and might have questionable accounts. All we need is a little cooperation."

"I think I'm going to seek legal advice on this," Hall told her. "If you wouldn't mind leaving now."

"I need to know about the occupants of those two flats," Maxine said. "If I go away from here without that information, all the things I've just mentioned will happen."

A glint of moisture had sprung up on Hall's lip. "You're threatening me."

"No, I'm not. This would be a threat—telling you that I'll come to your house mob-handed, acting on information received from a source I can't name, kick the door down, and roust your family into the street while we search for the high-grade cocaine that we would be pretty sure to find." She paused. "Would be absolutely certain to find."

Hall noticed that she was standing much closer to him than before. He backed up a little and Maxine filled the space he'd just vacated. He opened his mouth to speak, then went to a VDU on his desk and tapped in some details.

"Numbers 34 A and 34 B. Above the launderette." Maxine waited. "It can only be 34 B. 34 A is unoccupied. It's used for storage."

"I won't ask what he stores there."

"If that's all." He was standing up, moving to his office door.

"Almost all," Maxine said. "All except that I want you to know that if anyone—MacIver, the people at 34 B, anyone—gets a whisper of this and as a result the operation we're involved in is compromised, I will personally see to it that you are fucked, your business is fucked, and everything you value and hold dear is comprehensively fucked. I hope you're listening closely. It will happen."

She went to her car with a smile on her face. There are too few real enjoyments in life. When Stella took her call, she could hear the lightness in Maxine's voice.

·   ·   ·

There wasn't much room to maneuver in Frank's tiny flat and there wasn't a lot of privacy. Frank took his dump of the day and there were few secrets involved. He wheeled back into the bedroom-sitting-room-kitchen, trawling a heavy miasma of vegetable decay, and made himself a cheese sandwich. He wondered whether Stella would like one; she said that was kind of him, but she wasn't feeling terribly hungry.

She went back to the squad room and briefed Sorley and asked that SO 19 be kept out of things. "We know that these people are dangerous, but they're not gangsters and there's no evidence that they'd be carrying firearms. SO 19 set-ups can take a while. We need to move quickly. I think the woman's in there and I'd like to pick them up sooner rather than later. It's an operation we can handle."

"You think the woman's in there?" Sorley was having lunch: a white-bread BLT, a Carlsberg, a cigarette. "You can't even be sure this guy is one of our team killers. Maybe he's just a sad fucker who falls in love with lap dancers."

"The forensic evidence. The beard-hair dyed blond. The fact that Amanda-Jane Wallace worked at the Kandy Kave and this guy's on their security video. Also, he's been sighted with a woman companion. What more do you want?"

"It's more what I don't want: wrongful arrest, for instance." When Stella didn't respond, he asked, "When do you want to go in?"

"Tonight."

They would wait until the small hours if they could, until lights went out in the flat and it was a reasonable bet that the occupants were asleep. Anyone sprung from sleep by violence experiences a frozen moment, a failure to read events. It's the moment when you find a gun at your head and the plastic handcuffs cinching up round your wrists.

"Weapon-issue?"

"Yes."

"Okay. Anything from the owners?"

"We know which flat."

Sorley brightened. "You sure?"

Stella shrugged. "Pretty sure. It came from a frightened man."

Sorley was making notes. He asked, "What are we calling this one?"

All operations had names for identification purposes. Harriman had offered one and it had stuck. "Operation Chop Suey," Stella said.

Sorley looked at her, said nothing, wrote it down. As she was leaving, he asked, "Where's this?" He was pointing to the circulated copy of Stella's temporary-address notification that was on top of a sheaf of papers held together with a vast fake clothes peg, labeled "NB."

"Over toward the Saints."

"Okay," he said, then: "Are you all right?"

"I'm fine."

He nodded, still looking at her. "If you feel like a drink some night." Sorley was remembering his own drama, his nights in the office with fast food and too much beer, nights spent sleeping between two chairs and waking with a thick head wondering whether things would ever get better.

Stella nodded. For the first time since George had left, she suddenly wanted to cry; not just cry, *howl.* Her eyes filled with tears and she raised a hand, *Thanks,* then walked fast down the office and out into the car park.

Kindness can bring you down.

65

When they killed Marie Turnow, one of the things they stole was a small silver locket, which opened out to a miniature of a small girl on one side and a twist of hair in the cavity on the other. It was the one thing they hadn't sold. There was no chain, but Donna kept it in a pocket, or sometimes pinned it to whatever she was wearing, which, on this occasion, was the cotton zipper jacket that she'd worn when they called on Jean Halliday. Sonny was folding clothes into a nylon tote bag, his and Donna's. They traveled light; sometimes, they wore each other's things: jeans, T-shirts, socks. He collected their set of videos from under the TV and put them in a small shoulder bag along with some duct tape, the video camera, and the fish-gutting knife. He did it with care, just as a good workman handles the tools of his trade.

He slipped something else into a side pocket of the bag when Donna wasn't looking: a newspaper that carried his picture on one of its inside pages. He asked, "Are you ready?"

Donna was sitting down, head in hands. "I'm ready."

"What's wrong?"

"Headache. Pain in my head." She added the rider as if it were a useful distinction. "Get me some water, okay?"

He brought it and she drank, but didn't get up. "It was a bad flu," she said. "It was crap. I'll be all right in a minute."

They had decided to travel north, maybe up into Scotland. They would play safe and ditch the C-reg Fiesta, then take the Tube to Docklands and find a trucker who was offloading one cargo and loading another for the return journey. They would offer money for the trip, and that always helped, but truckers covered many thousands of miles in a year and they liked company: someone to talk to when they were past their legitimate mileage for the day and they could feel sleep tugging at them. It was a good, anonymous way to travel. In the dark, up there in the high cabs of trucks, passengers are just shapes, just voices you'll never hear again.

Sonny laid out a line of coke on a coaster and sat down beside Donna. "Go on," he said, "your head's fucked, you need some of this."

Donna snorted it and waited for the hit. She rubbed her gums with the dusting left on the coaster, then lay back on the sofa for a moment. "I'll be fine," she said. "Give me ten minutes."

Sonny put the TV on reflexively and found a news broadcast: small wars spreading across the globe like bush fires, politicians smiling and telling lies, celebrities talking about each other. Sonny and Donna watched disinterestedly—news, quiz show, sitcom, it could have been anything.

When Sonny's face appeared, there was a beat or two before either of them registered it, then Donna turned, slowly, to look at Sonny as he sat beside her gazing at his own image, hearing the newsreader telling anyone who saw this man not to approach him, but to call the number on the screen.

Neither of them spoke. The newscaster ran through the headlines; a pretty blonde weathergirl forecast rain.

Sonny said, "I'm sorry, Donna."

She put her hand out, fast, and he flinched, but all she did was brush his hair back from his forehead. The look on her face seemed one of concern, as if he'd crossed the road without looking or gone too close to a sheer drop.

"I told you not to go back."

"I'm sorry, Donna."

"The lap dancer. They would have put someone in the club to watch."

"I'm sorry, Donna."

"You should have thought of that."

"I'm—"

"Why didn't you think of that?" She switched off the TV and they sat in silence for a while. "We'll move later," she said, "after dark. Really late." She went into the bedroom and lay down fully clothed. She felt light-headed, her skin sensitive to the touch of her clothes. Her fever dreams still hung in the room, clinging to shadows. If she closed her eyes she saw the Mother, saw Dilly squirming, saw her own image in the mirror.

Don't hurt me.

Sonny put the TV back on: a comedy show he'd seen before. The room filled with stale laughter.

66

Each of the punters in the Chinese casino had a system, but luck has a system, too. It works like this: you can be lucky on Monday, but on Tuesday it'll be someone else's turn. Luck is democratic and luck has a lot of people to favor. Don't expect your turn to come round again for a long time. As for the roulette wheel or the fall of cards in the blackjack deck, luck has nothing to do with it, it's all percentages. Luck will be working for someone sometime, but percentages work for the house every time.

Percentages also convert to cash and the Chinese casino had a method for moving their takings. Since the place operated without a license, there were no permanent structures in the basement—no cashier's cage—so at certain stages through the night, the excess would be strongboxed and moved to a small room near the back door. This door opened on to a yard and a fire escape that gave access to the restaurant. The boxes were then taken to the restaurant kitchens and stowed in steel cabinets. Even after the restaurant closed, the cash-traffic continued until the casino dealt its last hand, threw its last dice and spun the wheel for the last time that night.

Marcus Lucio and the Crew had made the same calculation: when the Chinese restaurant was getting ready to close at about one A.M., most of the night's takings would be in the kitchens.

Stella and Frank, one either side of the window like old folk at the hearth. She had an open line to the surveillance units, but so far things were fine. The blond man had returned with his pizza and hadn't come out again. The curtains in the flat were drawn across and a faint glow from the room lit the edges of the window.

It was difficult to police the rear of the building, and the fire escapes that zigzagged up and down the back walls of the terrace were a worry, but there was no reason to expect that the individuals would leave that way.

Individuals. It was police talk for killers, rapists, robbers, muggers, all-round bad guys. These two are individuals all right, Stella thought. Never been anyone like them.

It was after midnight and there were two five-man units drawn up several streets away, each issued with weapons and body-armor, all of them drawn from the extended manpower of AMIP-5. SO 19 had been informed of the raid and had registered their objection. Officially, this said that SO 19 felt that such operations were best left to the experts. The unofficial line was that giving firearms to the filth was about as safe an activity as swimming with sharks and as far as the gun squad was concerned Stella's team could all get shot shitless.

A third unit was ready to take up position in the street of houses that backed on to the Strip. It would be impossible for anyone to make an escape by that route without going through one of the facing houses, but desperate people do impossible things. A fourth unit had a vantage point in one of those houses and was watching the back of the Strip with night-vision glasses.

This was all overkill. This was all better-safe-than-sorry. The man and woman would be inside and asleep when the team went in.

Donna woke from dreams of death and went in to Sonny. He'd been watching a video. Now he took it out of the VHS player, restored it to its carefully labeled box and put it back into the shoulder bag—Jean Halliday.

"It's time," Donna said.

Sonny lifted the tote bag, Donna carried the bag containing the videos, tape, camera, knife. Their worldly possessions.

He said, "I'm sorry, Donna."

Down on the Strip, there was a single gunshot. This was followed by a long burst from an Uzi that would have emptied the clip.

. . .

The air was full of voices screaming. Some belonged to the boys of the Crew, who were down with gunshot wounds; others were riding the airwaves between police walkie-talkies and mobile phones.

Stella's was one of the voices. "What in *fuck* is going on?"

Harriman came back to her. "It looks like a robbery in progress."

"I don't believe it," Stella said. But when she looked down on to the Strip it was all too believable. Marcus Lucio plus six in ski-masks—five on the street, one in a high-sided Suzuki Jeep. On the ground two of the Crew, one flipping in agony and holding the back of his thigh where a burst of fire had caught him, the other lying very still. As she watched, one of the Ski-Mask Six approached one of the Crew, who was holding the only strongbox that hadn't already been loaded into Marcus Lucio's Jeep. He waved his machine pistol in a tight arc, hitting his man's chest, hip, and knee, then scooped up the box and sauntered away with it.

The night-life had vanished. The whores, the pimps, the dealers, the punters, the night-time vagabonds, together with any civilians who might have happened to be passing and found themselves walking face-first into a firefight. The Strip was deserted, apart from the foot soldiers: three down, one gone, and to the victors the spoils.

"Do we give chase?" Harriman wanted to know.

Stella looked across to the window of 34 B, drawn curtains edged with the pale light from a TV or a weak lamp. No one could have failed to hear the gunfire.

I'll lose them. Maybe I've already lost them.

"Take out the Jeep," she said. "Send the second unit into the flat."

But Marcus Lucio was already clearing the lower half of the Strip, passing the sidestreet where AMIP- 5 had its second surveillance unit and running a red light on the Harrow Road. The AMIP car gave chase blind, not knowing which way Marcus had turned. Stella could hear sirens coming up from Notting Hill.

67

The TV still playing, the lights still on, plates and glasses unwashed in the sink. A beer can on the small table by the sofa. In the bedroom, drawers open, the bedclothes thrown back, the pillow carrying the hollow dent of a head. The window still open where Donna and Sonny had got out on to the fire escape.

Stella checked with the officers who had been watching the back of the house. They had seen a lot of activity on the fire escapes. A *lot*. People with boxes going up, people with boxes going down again, but a hell of a lot faster; it looked like a cross-section of an anthill.

She walked round the three rooms of the flat, like a tracker looking for spoor. Just a few minutes past they had been here, the beer can still cold, the bed still rumpled, their movements still disturbing the air.

Forensics were setting up in the main room. Harriman had brought a video with him: a Clint Eastwood classic. He thumbed it in and the bootleg warning came up on the screen. "They were watching," he said.

Stella went into the bedroom, stepping carefully, though there was no real need for caution, their taint would be all over the place. She bent to the pillow: perfume with the scent of flowers.

The rain was coming in hard when the uniforms arrived. Donna and Sonny had crossed the road to the cemetery as the two ARVs and a police personnel carrier with twelve men aboard swept up toward the Strip, their bar-lights laying a slick on the tarmac. Two ambulances were coming down from Kensal Town, weaving through backed-up traffic. Pete Harriman and a couple of other officers had lifted the wounded man on to the pavement and given some basic first aid, but basic isn't much help when a femoral artery is hosing out blood. The other two lay still as stone, one hunched over as if still trying to protect himself, the other on his back, arms and legs flung wide.

The rain fell on his open eyes.

They had gone down the fire escape in the midst of chaos, no one looking, everyone shouting, and jumped out from the turn of the stair to the next backyard. From there they had climbed again, reached the landing, jumped again, and worked their way down the row like that, climbing and jumping. It had been a ten-foot drop each time, fifteen in all, and they had fallen, skinning their hands, rolling in the boxes and pallets and bottle crates the shopkeepers had thrown out.

Now Donna was looking for cover, somewhere off the streets. She didn't want to hail a cab or be part of the crowd on the Underground; Sonny was famous now, Sonny was a face. They went between the gravestones, heading for the far end of the necropolis, where the plague victims still lay in heaped confusion, leg bones and rib cages and sorry skulls and perhaps, for all anyone knew, the dark, viral root of their illness still in the soil. Donna stood still to look round, rain beating her head. She saw the mausoleum with its broken gate.

She thought it was someone sleeping rough, given the heat and movement between the stone coffins, but then two dogs ran out, followed by a third, and put a few yards between them and the intruders before stopping to look. Sonny kicked out at them and they shied off a little farther. Donna peered into the mausoleum and heard a low growl; saw a shadow move and the light reflected in the fourth dog's eyes.

Sonny picked up a handful of chippings from a grave and threw them at the other three. They turned and ran at once. "In there," Donna told him, and he threw a second handful deep into the mausoleum. The dog gave a barking yelp, circling and weaving, as if looking for a way out. Donna took the fish-gutting knife out of her bag and went a step or two into the mausoleum. Now she was sharing the darkness with the dog she could see it better: a mongrel that might have been part collie, part Labrador, its haunches down, the straw-colored fur on its back lifted in a narrow ridge.

She spoke soothingly, the knife held out like a gift.

There was nothing to say, but they said it anyway: more a need to talk away the nervous energy that stays with you after a street operation. They handed their guns back to the armorer; they started the paperwork. Blank sections on the attackers thanks to the ski masks. Blank sections on the Suzuki Jeep thanks to a lack of license plates. They thought back to the way Marcus and his six had moved in, cleaned up, moved out. Too fast for the AMIP officers to get close, though their pulse rates were still a little high and their fingers were tingling.

The team who'd been watching the backs of the houses told Stella more about the boxes that traveled up from the casino basement to the restaurant kitchen. She would let the locals know.

Maxine Hewitt wrote, a report concerning the probable tax and VAT evasion of Thomas MacIver and the connivance in that of his accountant Laurence Hall. Stella would pass that on to the fraud squad and to Customs and Excise.

"He's a shit," Maxine said, meaning Hall. "If they take their time, they could bring down half his client list."

Some stayed on to complete their reports, some went to the pub, some went home. Stella went to Bachelor Boy's loft, which was nothing like home, and opened the big kitchen drinks cabinet where her absent host kept a fine and comprehensive collection of liquor glasses, including twelve one-shot crystals.

She lined them up on the glass coffee table that stood in front of the black leather armchair and filled each with a shot of vodka, taking the liquid to the very top so that, if you got down on your knees to pour and sighted across the tops of the little glasses, you could see the way the meniscus rose above the brim, heavy and clear, like a sightless eye.

He loves me, he loves me not.

Working her way through them took an hour and was purest pleasure.

The dog was lying on its left flank, one leg protruding stiffly, its head thrown back; it was panting and its tongue lolled, as if it had come a long way and there was still a long way to go. The straw-colored coat was matted with blood.

Donna was working in a restricted space and she couldn't see as much as she would like of what was happening to the dog. She backed out of the mausoleum and stood to one side. It was a moment of stillness, the climber pausing to admire the view, the artist stepping back to admire his work.

The dog craned to lick its wounds, but they were too many, too deep and too wide. Sonny threw another handful of grave-chippings and the creature heaved to its feet, the muscles in its flanks and shoulders bunching and flexing as the feet scrabbled for a purchase, then it sniffed the air, fetid with its own blood and feces. Beyond the dark entrance to the mausoleum there were lights and the graveyard grass was wet and cool.

Three steps up to the broken gate. The dog worked hard and came out into the falling rain as Donna leaned in and struck—dancing round as the dog hopped and yelped—then struck again and again. Its hindquarters slumped and rose and slumped again: a cruel parody of the flat-out sprint that instinct ordered. Donna cut it across the backbone and it went down, turning belly up, legs raised, throat offered in submission.

It wouldn't be as easy as that.

Donna was working in a full drench, now, as the rain gathered force, but she could only feel heat.

They slept in the mausoleum for a few hours and woke before day-break. Sonny had a plan.

"We need somewhere to be, somewhere safe. Not to travel just yet. Not to be on the road."

Donna nodded. He tried to read her look, but her eyes were empty. He knew he'd done the wrong thing, but he'd said sorry. Now he said it again: "I'm sorry, Donna."

"Where?" she asked.

Sonny and Donna had met in Somerset, but she was the local girl, he the visitor. In London, he was on home turf. He told her about the Harefield Estate, where he'd lived for a while. Fortress Harefield. Empty units were the property of the local housing department to al-locate as it chose, but things never happened that way. Empty units were economic units, controlled by whoever ran that landing, that stairway. It wouldn't have been a good base for hunting: Sonny and Donna weren't gangsters, they were outlaws and different rules ap-plied. But it was a good place to become invisible for a few days.

The rain had stopped and the first break of light was in the sky, a false dawn setting clouds in dark relief. "We need to move now," Donna said.

They reached the gate and looked for police activity on the main road, but there was none: a few early trucks going through, the cars of shift-workers, a night bus. Donna set off down toward Ladbroke Grove, walking fast as if to put distance between herself and Sonny.

Dog Boy had seen them emerge from the mausoleum and walk to the gate. From his place by one of the cemetery's yews, close to the en-trance gate, he had watched everything, one hand on the neck-scruff of the big, brindled dog to keep it from breaking toward the action. The dog's big eyes had never moved from what was happening, nor had it blinked. Now and then a growl had rumbled in its throat, but too low to be heard over the thrash of rain.

On their way back to the road, Donna and Sonny had passed within six feet of the boy and the dog. There was light from the street lamps and the boy had noted the fierceness in the woman's face, the thin nostrils, the deep-set eyes. He could smell the blood on her.

The brindle nosed at the dead dog's wounds, then circled the mausoleum, marking each corner with a quick squirt of urine. The boy dragged the corpse to the back of the cemetery and left it between a plane tree and the bordering wall, half-hidden where it could be rendered down by the fox, the rat, and the crow.

68

While Stella had been observing her little communion of shot glasses and a lover's litany, John Delaney had eaten an indifferent hotel dinner and gone to bed to re-read the transcript of her interview with Thomas Allen, together with copies of Allen's trial and evidence reports. Now he woke to a fine spring day in the country town: clear sides and a warm sun, none of which matched his mood.

George's absence didn't appear to be playing in Delaney's favor. He believed Stella was assessing the blame involved, and doling it out between them. He'd waited for a call the previous night but it hadn't come. He could have made a call himself, of course, but by that time he was feeling resentful and—he realized—courting the self-righteousness of it all. He'd been there before and it had never turned out well.

He had several calls in to DCI Bill Stephens but he didn't really expect anything beyond a holding response and he didn't expect to be given the chance to meet officers Morgan, Harris, and Child. He'd placed the calls so he couldn't be accused of failing to check his facts with the people who mattered. He wanted to be able to say: . . . *were unavailable for comment.*

Despite having Stella's interview notes, Delaney had fixed a meeting with Allen and gone over the ground again, to hear it with his own ears, not Stella's. The only additional information Allen had been able to supply was that Stephens appeared to be suppressing Sonny's video-lift mug shot, because when Allen had tested him by pretending that Stella had mentioned such a picture but not given him one, a DS from Stephens's office said they were drawing a blank on that.

Delaney did what Stella would have done if she'd had more time and what Harriman would have done if DCI Stephens hadn't slammed the door: he took Sonny's face to the public.

There were seven pubs in the High Street and a lot more in the back-streets. There were a dozen or so clubs that didn't open until ten P.M. There were cyber cafés and Starbucks and Coffee Republics. There were Harvesters and Burger Kings. Delaney decided to concentrate on the pubs, hitting only one in three, since it was still morning—he could backtrack to the others later—but if he passed a coffee shop or a fast-food place he went in.

He showed Sonny's picture to barmen and drinkers, to waitresses and grill chefs, to the burger boys and girls, to the Internet surfers, to the kids drinking lattes and sending text messages. It was impossible to do this without attracting a little attention, and within half an hour a few phone calls had been made and Delaney had picked up a tail.

DS Child wasn't attempting a three-man switch-and-hitch sur-veillance or anything fancy of that sort. He found Delaney coming out of a cyber café in one of the hilly streets that led down to the town center, and simply tagged along in the car, careful to make sure that Delaney could see him. The man in the passenger seat was DC Harris. His square face with its neck-rolls, and the way he'd adjusted his seat so he could lean back and allow room for his gut, spoke of bad diet and a slow lifestyle. DC Harris was a known supporter of police being armed as a matter of course, mostly because if you could bring your man down from a distance, giving chase wouldn't be an issue.

Sometimes they overtook Delaney and eyeballed him from the

car, sometimes one of them got out and stood a few yards off the doorway of the pub or café where Delaney was doing his legwork. There was a kind of rhythm to this that both Delaney and the cops understood: there would be a moment when the distance narrowed and the cat-and-mouse convention broke down, though it wasn't easy to say what would make that happen.

Renata Fortune was sitting on her own in a designer bar with a stupid name, drinking her fourth BB of the day and looking forward to the next. Renata wouldn't have called herself a drunk, because there were days when she stayed sober, or only did drugs, or just slept, but her blight was boredom and her method was altered perception. The world looked better with booze. It looked better with coke or E.

She looked at the picture Delaney offered and said, "That's Sonny Martin."

If Child or Harris had been gifted with X-ray vision, and had been able to see through the wall of the bar to where Delaney and Renata sat deep in conversation, they would not have been happy men. Renata Fortune was one of their elimination witnesses. At the time of the investigation, they had wanted to concentrate on Albert Carrick: give him all their energy and attention, since he was their choice. To do this, they'd needed to eliminate everyone else who touched on the case. Not that they had other suspects, or even other thoughts, but there were ten or fifteen people who were connected to Marie Turnow in some way or another, and they had to be interviewed, alibied as a matter of formality, and ticked off.

Renata was one of the fifteen people able to vouch for the movements that night of Leo Martin—known to his friends as Sonny—and Donna Scott.

"We were in here," she told Delaney, "then we went back to Sonny's place."

"For more drinks?"

"More drinks, more anything."

"You have much of 'anything'?"

"Yeah, of course."

"Everyone was pretty stoned . . ."

"Yeah."

"And Sonny was there all the time?"

"All the time?"

"That's what you told the police, isn't it?"

"Yeah." Renata was staring at Sonny's picture. The fact that it was a video-lift meant that the color was dulled, the features fuzzy. A police artist had helped the blondness a little. "He's dyed his hair."

"But you're sure it's him?"

"Oh, yeah. That's Sonny." She looked from the picture to Delaney, then back again. "You're not a cop, so what are you?"

Delaney had wondered what would be best. He said, "Inquiry agent. I don't talk to anyone except the people who are paying me."

The notion of people being paid brought a light to Renata's eye. While Child and Harris sat in the car, thinking that their next move might be to find out what was keeping Delaney, a deal was going down in the pub and money was changing hands. Delaney had all he needed for Stella, but there were one or two things he needed for himself. A story of wrongful arrest needs to offer alternative theories.

"What else could we say?" Renata asked. "It was just a formality— was Donna with us that night? They only needed to know about her because she found the body. Everyone got asked; everyone that knew Marie. Al Carrick was the guy, the cops told us that."

"They just needed confirmation."

"That's it." She shrugged. "We weren't going to say they'd gone off to score some more stuff, were we?"

"How long were they gone?"

Renata laughed. "Who fucking knows? We were off our faces. Anyway, Donna would never have had any trouble with the cops, would she?"

"Why not?"

"She used to *be* a cop, didn't she?"

Delaney was making a call as he left the pub and DS Child joined him, walking alongside for a moment, before stepping sideways in a shoulder-to-shoulder nudge that put Delaney into the wall.

He said, "Get off the phone."

"Why?" Delaney asked, then turned slightly, fending off Child's hand as it came up to grab the phone.

"We can speak here, or we can speak at the nick," Child told him.

Delaney handed the phone over. "Well, first, maybe you'd like to speak to her."

Stella wasn't feeling as well as she had the night before. Twelve straight vodkas can bring a sort of joy, a sort of sharpness of the spirit that puts the world into perspective, but there's a price to be paid and the cola-ibuprofen cocktail Stella had downed earlier wasn't enough payback. However, Delaney's information was a big distraction and for that she was grateful.

When Child came on the line, she said: "Touch this man and you're in even bigger trouble than you think." She spoke on for a minute, maybe a touch longer. When Child handed the phone back to Delaney, he had a smile on his face.

"You think this is going to be easy?" Child asked. "No."

It was a sick smile, the smile of a man backing off in a street-fight.

Delaney said, "What do I think? I think you're fucked."

As he walked back to the hotel, weather was coming up from the west, cloud-cover and a rising wind. A long shadow rolled down toward the cop car, still parked outside the bar: the sun going in on DS Child's day.

69

Here's Janis Parker kissing Mark Ross goodbye, his smell still on her along with the faint but indelible scent of guilt.

Their lovemaking was intense and she wonders whether those orgasms that rocked the room might be the result of the no-ties, no-recriminations deal they had struck when things first started between them. The deal means they don't have to live with each other, they don't have to choose curtains together, they don't have to shop or look at holiday brochures or talk over breakfast. They don't have to make promises or say, "I love you." Especially not that. They can ask for anything they want in bed and get it. They can walk away any time.

Except walking away is fast becoming Janis's greatest fear, and "I love you" seems to be always on the tip of her tongue.

Here's another thing: she shares with Stephanie; she lives with Stephanie. She sits up at night splitting a bottle of wine with Stephanie while her flatmate—her *friend*—tells her about Mark, about their relationship, about the plans they have for the future, and about what a dynamite fuck he is.

Just lately, Stephanie has seemed less certain about the future, less secure in Mark's affections; they've been having bad rows, apparently, and Janis has found herself wanting to hear more of that, has found herself warning Stephanie not to ignore the signs, suggesting that maybe she and Mark should take some time apart. Janis wonders whether Mark's coolness toward Stephanie could be a result of his feelings for her, despite the no-ties-of-emotion deals and the no-recrimination deals. She hopes so. She feels guilt and hope to the same degree, which is what keeps her awake at night: that and the heartsickness that afflicts a lover when the loved one is absent.

The worst times are when they're all three together, of course. Those times are hell. And that's why Janis was so glad that Stephanie had decided to go away for a bit. She and Mark could be at her birthday party together, make an excuse to get away, spend some time. There's something she ought to tell him; something he ought to know.

I'm pregnant.

Each time she had started to say the words, she'd thought better of it, convincing herself that this wasn't the right time, that she shouldn't spoil the moment.

In truth, though, *I'm pregnant* sounded a lot like a deal-breaker.

So now Mark kisses her and slips a hand under her robe to cup her between the legs. She wants to bring him back to bed but that's another part of the deal—no overnights, no waking up in each other's arms, since one thing can lead to another. The fact is, Janis wants little else than to wake up in Mark's arms.

After he's gone, she tries to sleep, but can't. She puts the TV on but is instantly bored. It's not yet eleven and the streets in Notting Hill are full of people coming out of a late movie or fringe theater, people looking for a drink and something to eat, or just looking for some action. They might wind up at the Trattoria Romana, at Sadie's or the Pharmacy. They might wind up at the Ocean Diner, Janis's favorite. She's been there before on nights like this.

Janis gets dressed and goes out. Walking helps her to think and being surrounded by people helps her to feel less lonely. She walks two streets to the Ocean Diner and takes a table by the window, where she can look at the street. There are couples going by, arm in arm or hand in hand or, sometimes, lip to lip. That's not so good; that's not what she wants to see. She orders a white-wine spritzer and opens her copy of *American Vogue*.

Sonny sees her when he leans through the hatch to deliver a plate of potato skins with chive dip. He's seen her in here before and he knows where she lives. He calls her The Chosen.

Janis has almost finished her drink. One's enough: she's thinking of the baby. She has a tremendous urge to call Mark and tell him right now, but she closes up on the feeling. Better to tell him face to face, to watch his eyes, to be able to talk, to hold him, to take him to their no-deals bed.

She walks back through the busy midnight streets. She's only been home a moment or two when her doorbell goes. Like anyone, she has a fisheye viewer in the door. She asks who is it and a woman's voice says it's the police. Janis's heart leaps and she second-guesses a dozen bad-news stories. When she looks through the fish-eye she sees a woman in a dark skirt, a light blue shirt and a light cotton zipper jacket, her hair caught up in a bun. She is holding up a police warrant card. The fisheye doesn't reveal that it was issued in west Somerset.

Janis opens the door. She asks what's wrong.

And then it begins.

70

Now it was Sonny *and* Donna, two faces in the press and on TV. Now it was "team killers" and the tabloids were using full-page headlines. Now Mike Sorley was getting more help than he needed and more pressure than he could handle. The help and the pressure went all the way down to the civilian cataloguers, the switchboard, and the beat men. No one had yet leaked the fact that Operation Chop Suey had fucked up.

"Which can't last long," Stella told Delaney. It was late but he was working on his story, first because it was fresh in his mind and secondly because it was just too juicy to ignore. Stella had just got out of the shower and Delaney looked up to find her standing at the counter, naked, slicing a lime. It was a new kind of intimacy and he decided to take it as a sign, even though she was still going back to the loft each night.

The loft had become an issue, which is why she had been cleaning and hoovering over there, and making sure that everything was in its place. Bachelor Boy was due back soon to collect his things, and she didn't want to find herself shown the door. Staying with Delaney wasn't an option just now, but nor was going back to the flat she'd shared with George.

She put the lime into a drink and brought it to him, careless of the fact that she might be seen from the street. He put out a hand for the glass, deliberately missed, stroked her flank; she moved into the circle of his arm and bent to kiss the top of his head. It meant, *I missed you.* Somehow, the tiny separation had made their skin burn.

Stella fetched herself a drink and a T-shirt and started to make notes for the team meeting that she and Sorley would run next morning. As if to herself, she said, "Now we know how they got in."

"Being police," he said.

"She kept her warrant card."

"Can you do that?"

"Say you've lost it. You get issued with another. Gives you a spare."

"That easy?"

"More or less. Other nicks in the area will be faxed to let them know that a card's gone missing. So what?"

"So . . . are we saying that Donna Scott knew what she was going to do, even when she was still a police officer?"

"Maybe. Probably not. I expect she knew she wasn't going to be a cop for very long and thought a spare warrant card might come in handy: free travel and so on."

DCI Stephens had hesitated only for a second or two before releasing Donna's file. There she was in her uniform, hair up in a bun, hooky nose and thin lips, dark eyes staring straight into the lens. Two senior officers seconded to AMIP-5 were in Somerset, interviewing colleagues, going through records, looking at Donna's arrest pattern. Stella lifted the photo to the light and stared back at Donna. Then she held Sonny's picture alongside it.

Delaney glanced across and saw her with the two mugshots at arm's length, her own face, baffled by shadow, at the apex of the triangle.

. . .

Side by side by side. Sonny and Donna and Stella in the tabloids.
Ladycop and the Team Killers. Donna stared at Stella's face.

He talked to you, *bitch*. You want us, don't you, *bitch*. Maybe
you'll find us. The worse for you, *bitch*.

The press office had given them the goods: identities, backgrounds, even something of method, and had stressed the fact that
the man, Leo "Sonny" Martin, had been in touch with the police in
the person of DS Stella Mooney. They stated that Sonny Martin was
feeling remorse and might want to give himself up. They suggested
that it was a familiar pattern: making contact, taking ever greater
risks, asking to be caught. Despite that, women were warned to take
precautions, especially at night, if they had to travel alone.

To help eliminate false confessions and hoaxes, the press office
withheld the fact that Donna Scott had once been a police officer: at
least, that was the reason they gave themselves. Sorley did a second
spot on *Crimewatch*. It looked like progress, but in truth they had
gone backwards—a day ago they were almost close enough to touch;
now Donna and Sonny could be anywhere.

To make matters even more frustrating, Andy Greegan had found
four other possibles—killings with the Donna–Sonny MO, or something like it, at locations in southern England, East Anglia, and Es-
sex. Stella was pretty certain that they were genuine. She sent officers
to talk to the locals in case something came up that would give an in-
dication of where Donna and Sonny might have gone, but she wasn't
expecting to get lucky.

Side by side by side.

Donna read the papers as she sat on a plastic chair by the window
of the eighteenth-story flat on Harefield and discovered that she and
Sonny had pushed war and famine off the front pages. She and
Sonny and Ladycop.

She had perched on the same chair while Sonny cut her hair, not
just taking it off at the nape of her neck but, on her instruction, making it short all over. He first cut it for length, long hanks that had

once reached halfway down her back falling into his hands. Then he used his first two fingers to hold up layers, one by one, and cut just the ends, working down to the length she wanted. He'd watched this technique in the mirror whenever his own hair had been cut, and it wasn't a bad job. Then she had gone, after dark, to the nearest chemist and bought a treatment pack of Blondie. Sonny had stared as she'd emerged from the bathroom: now they were twins.

She had also bought some lipstick and blusher, eyeshadow and mascara. She had never been too skillful with the cosmetics, but more was better than none.

Not until she was blonde, short-haired, and made up like a geisha had she gone farther afield for the papers.

There were the front-page faces, hers and his. There was Lady-cop.

He said, "I'm sorry, Donna."

"You called her. You spoke to her."

"They don't know who we are," he said, then stopped. They knew everything now, he'd forgotten that. "Maybe I should change." He said it as if offering penance, but he was talking about his appearance. "I could dye it black, have a number-one cut. They say you look nothing like yourself if you're bald."

"You're okay," Donna told him. "We just have to sit tight."

"Shave the beard off," he offered. "Dye it black and lose the beard."

"Later, maybe. When we're ready to move."

Sonny had done the deal for the flat over the phone: he knew who to call and he knew what to say.

Just for a few days. Need somewhere to be. Moving soon.

That all added up to no questions asked. They had sat in the bull ring for ten minutes and a mule came with the key. The mule was a ten-year-old kid on a mountain bike, who also took their money: almost all they had. The kid liked *Terminator* videos but wasn't big on watching the news or reading the papers.

The new-look Donna went out for food and drugs while Sonny sat with the road map on his knee, planning routes to Scotland. The flat had three plastic chairs and an iron bed with a bare mattress.

Donna came back with kebabs, chocolate, wine, and a wrap of cocaine and they sat on the chairs, eating with their hands, then cut half the coke into lines on a hand mirror that had been propped up by the bathroom sink. They had to get down on the floor.

Sonny was greedy for it and Donna stood back, letting him root round like a pig, his arse lofted, his head lowered, traveling up the line on his elbows. She did one line herself, just to sharpen things up a little.

The flat had no TV or radio or phone. They sat in the plastic chairs and looked at one another. Sonny was smiling a sly out-of-focus smile. He said, "I'm sorry, Donna." He closed his eyes and dreamed for a minute or two that might have been an hour or two, then woke up and snorted the rest of the coke.

He said, "You want to do something? Let's do something." He crossed to where she sat and kissed her, which he had never done before; he put his hands into her clothing and she sat there for him.

"Donna?"

In the bedroom, she stripped and lay down on the bare ticking of the mattress. Her small, pointed breasts; her hips slender, like a boy's. It was broad day but there was no one to peer in: they were sky-high, coddled by clouds, keeping company with the birds of the air.

He lost himself in her, then slept. His dream was of the clouds and the birds, as if he were free-falling, arms and legs spread, the wind snaffling his breath. He floated through vapor, hearing the hiss of his own slipstream. Something big-winged swooped down to join him and he saw it had Donna's face.

Below him, a long way off, was the sea, bright blue creased with white. He wanted to bring his arms and legs in for the dive, wanted to arrow into the water without leaving a ripple, but the wind pressure was too great. He struggled, trying to force his elbows together, his knees, shouting to Donna for help, though the backwash of air gagged him.

He woke spreadeagled, as in the dream. His hands and feet were tied off to the uprights of the iron bed and his mouth was sealed with duct tape. Donna had piled the plastic chairs one atop the other, wedging the legs of one over the seat of the other, and taped the video camera to the back of the topmost chair, the lens looking straight down on to the bed.

She was standing to one side, as if not wanting to steal the show, though a film-maker would have wanted her in shot: naked, and masked to hide her new look. She had tied a T-shirt tightly at the neck and cut eye-holes, then dropped it over her head, an improvised hood. The T-shirt was from the Disney Store and Donna's eyes glittered darkly where Minnie's had once been. It took Sonny a second or two, then his back arched as he tested his bonds; he shook frantically from side to side, but he'd been tied for a while and his hands were already half-numb.

A bird coasted past the window, riding the tower-block thermals.

I'm sorry, Donna.

She couldn't make out the words, his voice was faint behind the gag and the syllables muddied into one another, but she smiled as if she had.

Don't hurt me was what she thought he'd said.

She slipped in with the knife, and cut, and moved back. He leaped like a landed fish. One stroke to the meat of his chest—there was a moment when it was nothing but a thin line, much like a graze, then it opened, the lips of the wound peeling back, the blood starting up.

Sonny's eyes were wide and running tears.

Don't hurt me, don't hurt me, don't hurt me.

Up there among clouds and birds there was no one to peek or pry.

71

John Delaney's car stood at the curb wearing its key-stripes, a London veteran. His second front door was in place and his answer-machine bore a series of silences joined one to the next by silence. He found himself going to his window more often than he had before. When he went out he checked the street, though he realized he had no idea what George looked like.

You think George did it? You're wrong.

He needed home-made pasta from the Italian deli: pasta, and a fresh block of Parmesan. Maybe tonight Stella would stay over; he hoped so, because he had decided that unless she found the heart to do that soon, things would start to slide. His story was written and filed and pretty soon the shit was going to hit. He wondered what she would really feel when DCI Stephens and DS Child and the others came under fire.

He closed his street door, looked left and right, and saw ordinary people doing ordinary things: a pair of joggers heading for the park, shoppers shopping, a traffic warden ticketing, a kid on a stunt-board. He'd seen the warden and the kid before.

Last night Stella had dressed, using the light from the hallway, and glanced at her watch like any adulterer. He'd pretended to be asleep, but then had got up and followed her to the door. She had heard him, but picked up her coat and left without a backward look.

The kid rode his board up and down the curb, jinking between parked cars, then came down the slight slope of the street, traveling fast. Delaney thought, *Good skills,* and stepped aside to leave a clear track on the pavement, but the kid was going to close-shave him and he changed his thought to *So fuck you.* The kids liked to do that: leave an inch or two, leave you gasping.

He was crouching like a surfer and Delaney felt a breeze as he passed. It was a moment before he registered the knock to his thigh and thought, *The bastard hit me,* then he looked down and saw blood gushing up through a rip in his jeans. He put his hand over the place and opened his mouth to cry out, but no sound came and he sat down, hard, the jolt loosening his grip on the stab wound.

Things were dim and seemed colorless: traffic in the street, a kaleidoscope of buildings and sky, people standing over him, their voices tangling.

The video had been addressed to Stella, so she had first viewing of it. After the first thirty seconds, she had got up and gone to Sorley's makeshift office, her face pale and showing a sticky sweat. Sorley had sat with her through the rest of it. It had taken half an hour and was like nothing they had ever seen before or would ever see again.

Sonny's suffering was full-on, Donna a figure on the sidelines who now and then came center-stage, breathing harder as things progressed. She was slim and toned; the long line of her torso and her extended arm as she bent over to him was athletic, like a Greek discus thrower's. The flexed ribcage, the taut flanks. Her small breasts bounced as she skipped back. She was wet; she glistened.

When it was over, the video ran to a blue screen.

Show a hill walker a rising patch of land and he'll tell you where it is; show a desert dweller some scrub and rocks and he'll take you right to the place. After the first shock, Stella had looked past Sonny's death to the room and the view; now, she told Pete Harriman to put together a task force of twenty officers and ask for weapons issue. She didn't expect to find Donna within a mile of the place, but if you're going in to Harefield mob-handed, you'd better go armed.

They were in the basement viewing room where Maxine had first found Sonny's face on the Kandy Kave security tape. Stella went up to the squad room and handed the video to Stuart Proctor, who would log it and take it to the exhibitions room. She should have handed in the note that came with it, but she hadn't shown that to anyone.

Ladycop—ask yourself, How does it feel?

Three personnel carriers, two ARVs, and an unmarked car carrying Stella and Pete Harriman rolled into Harefield and circled. The Estate's foot soldiers were out on the concrete walkways, just watchful for the moment, but careful to take the high ground.

There was a deal in the air, but no one was going to step forward to negotiate, no one wanted to be in the frame. Stella and Harriman walked in across the DMZ until they reached the bull ring, which was empty, the shutters up on the KFC and the off-license, a silence in the air that was the absence of sound systems and voices raised in anger or pleasure.

Stella looked up.

Faces at windows, foot soldiers leaning on the parapets, no one moving. A little way back, high on the eighteenth floor of the third block, a walkway where no one stood to watch, and a door half-open.

It was a forensics bonanza. They lifted fingerprints from the surfaces, several good palm-prints from the plastic chairs, DNA from everywhere. It didn't matter that much, of course, not now, but it made for a tidy file. They went through the motions, Andy Greegan taking charge of the operation, the stills and video men doing their jobs, the ME pronouncing Sonny dead at the scene of crime.

Stella thought she'd had enough of this stench, enough of these flying insects. When her phone went, she was glad and stepped out on to the walkway to answer it. The LCD display read "Office": the code for Delaney that she hadn't yet bothered to change.

The personnel carriers and the ARVs were still in position, but the unmarked car peeled away toward the North End Road, traveling at speed, Pete Harriman at the wheel. Stella was in the passenger seat, still talking on the phone. Her free hand came out of the window holding a magnetic roof light that was already rotating a blue beam.

Donna Scott stood among the crowd of watchers on the pavement, a presence that Stella hadn't second-guessed. The blonde crop-cut, make-up like a mask. As the car came out of the Harefield approach road, she saw Stella full-face.

"Ladycop." She said it under her breath. "I know you, but you don't know me."

Delaney was prepped for surgery and Stella only got in to see him by showing her warrant card to a young uniformed cop who was waiting to finish taking Delaney's statement. The charge nurse said Stella could have ten minutes. Delaney looked washed out and groggy from the pre-med. He lay almost flat, staring at the ceiling while she held his hand.

"They caught the kid," he told her. "It's called jooking, did you know that?"

"I did know that."

Jooking: leaving your mark. A blade or a broken bottle, it doesn't matter. Cut the guy and make sure he feels it: the thigh, the buttock, the belly; cut him to let him know what happens if you show disrespect.

"He was crossing the road on his stunt-board right in front of my car. I blew the horn—I dissed him. When I got out, he hopped the curb and shaved me. I called him a bastard—dissed him again."

"When was this?"

"Christ, I don't know. This is him talking. I don't even remember it."

"He tagged your door and trashed your car?"

Delaney nodded. " 'Good work' was what he called it, apparently. Check with the copper who took my statement. They think he was working up to this: first tags, then doing my car, then . . . jooking me."

"Being big for his friends."

"That's the idea." He smiled and said, "I'm sorry."

"You were entitled to think what you thought. You don't know George like I do."

There was a moment's silence while they both thought about that.

"They say I should be out tomorrow," Delaney said. "It's only a light anesthetic, but he cut through a few things." He sounded weary: the effects of shock and medication. She got up, then leaned over and kissed him. He said, "I love you," his voice ever more far away.

The young PC asked her when she thought he could go back in and she told him to wait until morning.

"The kid jooked him," he said.

"I know."

"That's London." The cop shook his head and laughed. "That's London life."

72

Deep blue of the moments before dark, clouds folding into the horizon, a solitary star holding steady in the clear skies to the east.

Another star appears behind it, shimmering as if seen through water, then growing, its radiants spreading into the ether. This is the convergence of the twin landing lights of an airbus, bellying down into the Heathrow corridor. When Stella Mooney was a girl, she used to sit in a high window on the Harefield Estate counting the lights of planes and waiting for her mother to come home from her night-time office-cleaning job. Stella would tell herself that one day

she would be aboard one of those planes, coming home from somewhere far away, somewhere beautiful, somewhere film stars go.

A second plane racked up behind the first, then another, then another. By the time the first passed overhead, she had been able to
count five. Anne Beaumont was reading Stella's notes for the case
update Sorley would pass on to the SIO in the morning. Stella had
included clippings from the press showing Donna's face. Anne said,
"Where's the video?"

"In the exhibitions room. You want to see it?"

"Jesus Christ, no. Do I look like a snuff fan?"

"What do you think she'll do?"

The note that Donna had left wasn't included in Stella's report,
but she'd told Anne about it.

"This one's pure sociopath," Anne said, "and very difficult to
predict. She's not operating out of homicidal rage—in fact, rage isn't
likely to be a part of her emotional set-up any more than remorse.
She likes what she does and, in some way, it connects with her life.
The patterns are too precise to be coincidental. She's involved in
some sort of complicated psychodrama and if I knew more about her
history, I might have a better idea of what's next."

"She doesn't seem to have a history," Stella said. "We know she
was a copper. We talked to colleagues, but couldn't find any really
close friends."

"It's a syndrome," Anne said.

"No friends?"

"Yes. But I really meant having been a police officer: liking positions of authority, positions of power, the ability to control. Sending
you the video was power-play." She handed the notes back to Stella.
"It's occurred to you that she probably won't look like that anymore?"

"We're compiling versions: short hair, wigs, coloring. Frankly,
the public isn't a lot of help when it comes to identification. Same
with anyone, really. Hear two cops telling exactly the same story to
a jury, you know they've got to be lying."

"She travels," Anne said. "Didn't you mention that?"

"When she had Sonny Martin with her. Who knows whether she'll travel alone."

"Wouldn't you?" Anne asked. "Wouldn't you look for new ground?"

Stella got up from her window seat and walked back to the armchair she sat in when they had their sessions: the client chair. She said, "Do I need you anymore?"

"Talking of new ground," Anne observed.

"When I was in Somerset I had a dream about the man I killed. I had the same dream when I was staying with Delaney: before George left."

"Are you surprised?"

"It wasn't the three A.M. dream," Stella said. "It wasn't dead babies hanging from the banister. It wasn't about the child I lost."

"When did you last have that dream?"

"I can't remember. It's gone." She paused a moment, then added, "George has gone."

Anne hadn't moved from behind the desk. They looked like interviewer and applicant: Stella applying for her freedom, perhaps. Anne asked, "What will you do?"

Stella laughed. "Are you supposed to ask me questions like that?"

"Not really, but I'm intensely curious."

"You think you know already, don't you?"

"If I thought that, I wouldn't have asked."

"My life seems to have sorted itself out. George has gone, Delaney says he loves me, he also makes me hot. I've got what I seemed to want without intending it to happen. Is that good? I'm not sure."

"What you *seemed* to want . . ."

"Exactly," Stella said.

She went back to Bachelor Boy's loft to find a note there saying he'd been and gone and thanks for keeping the place looking so good and stay as long as you like, which made her unaccountably irritable.

She cooked some food she didn't want and played some music she didn't like. She opened her laptop and wrote a report based on the notes Anne had been reading, then e-mailed it to Sue Chapman. She took a shower and got into bed with something from Bachelor Boy's scant collection of books, and read for ten minutes without registering a word. She tossed the book aside and closed her eyes for a moment. Sleep was a distant country.

She made a call and the charge nurse on Delaney's ward told her that he was out of surgery, had woken up briefly, was now sleeping, and she could collect him in the morning. He would need fresh clothes because his were pretty badly blood-marked and the doctors in A&E had been obliged to slit his trouser leg to get at the wound.

Stella got out of bed and dressed. At first she had thought she'd go to Delaney's flat and collect what he needed, but instead of getting into her car she started to walk through the Saints to Ladbroke Grove, then down toward Notting Hill. It wasn't late, not really; not for those streets. As she came into the Gate, she could see the plate-glass frontage of the Ocean Diner and inside, over the bar, neon script spelling out the name, and two cocktail glasses that filled and tipped and emptied.

She sat in a booth with a glass of wine in front of her and the dice on the table. It was a yes/no decision, like the flip of a coin. Under seven, one thing; seven or above, another. She would throw in a minute, or maybe after another drink, or maybe not here at all but somewhere else.

Chance isn't like luck: chance is what happens all the time everywhere; it's what casts the homeless out of doors; it's what puts the child in front of the runaway truck.

It's what brings people to the Ocean Diner at a certain time on a certain night.

Stella with her dice and her drink. Donna with her little bag of tricks.

73

Stella drank her wine and got up, leaving the dice on the table. She retraced her steps, heading toward the Saints where the streets were darker and less crowded, going home, except she no longer knew where that was. The night sky was clear, now, and a sudden wind was rattling trash in the basement areas.

George somewhere else; Delaney in the recovery ward. She had walked away from the dice because she thought it was time to leave chance to chance. But it was chance, after all, that she was passing the cemetery just then and, because of that, thought of Daz, stretched on a gravestone as the bullets took out his kneecaps and elbows; and, because of that, found herself walking along grassy paths toward the horizontal slab dedicated to the memory of Arthur Edward and Sarah May Stocker.

Donna walked behind her, light-footed in the shadows. She had transferred the fish-gutting knife from her bag to the patch pocket of her fashion combats, the pressure-molded leather scabbard hard against her leg; now she hung back a little to tease open the pocket-flap.

Stella didn't hear the soft rip of Velcro; she was too deep in her thoughts. She wondered where Daz was now and what his life was like; she wondered about Jackie Yates, missing presumed dead; she wondered whether anyone had mourned Nike Man and considered that, if there were such people, they must know her secret.

How to be free of such things? Anne Beaumont had once suggested to her that life was a system of choices and all you had to do was choose. Stella thought that most often choice was the problem. What about a world of no choice—a place run by the Emperor of

Emotions and enforced by his Feelings Police? She liked the sound of it. Tomorrow Delaney would be home and she knew that choices had to be made. You go through a door and it slams behind you.

She sat on the Stockers' slab with its patina of green and drew her knees up to her chin. She imagined a stirring in the stone as if its long-dead inhabitants were struggling to rise; or maybe it was an echo of Daz's agony as the bullets broke his joints and he lay in his own mire like a pinioned bird. That thought made her lie back, spread-eagling herself on the slab.

Like this. He lay like this.

Face up, arms and legs spread, ready to suffer the choice of no choice. That clear sky was the last view of the Chosen.

Ladycop laid out like a blood sacrifice, as if she knew what was required of her. Donna smiled in the darkness and saliva swamped her mouth as if she were anticipating the first bite from a peach. Except this would have to be quick: no opportunity to gag this one or tie her arms, no time to spend on her, and Donna felt a deep surge of regret, because it would have been keenest pleasure to see the fear in Ladycop's eyes, to watch as her suffering doubled with the second cut and tripled with the third, until the mathematics of pain could no longer calibrate the event and she moved to suffering that was beyond understanding.

This is for Sonny. He had to die because of you.

There was a sliver of moon, cold and white like the last of melting ice. Stella craned to see it, arching her throat, and Donna acknowledged the offer, moving forward, her lithe body suddenly in Stella's line of vision—a shadow, it seemed, a cloud across the moon. Then she was gone: swept aside.

The brindled dog had taken her in its stride, leaping like a deer and hitting hard. Donna cried out as she fell, her voice blurred by the dog's snarls. Its teeth closed on the boss of her arm, its neck and shoulder muscles bunching as it took hold. She kicked out, scrambling back and getting halfway to her feet, the dog still locked on, then lost her footing and fell, taking the granite corner of a tombstone on the jut of her cranium, just above the neck. The blow echoed in her skull and the world fell away. She couldn't see, but she could feel.

Don't hurt me.

The dog lunged at her throat and missed, getting instead the meat of her cheek, then bracing all four legs to pull back, jerking its head up and sideways. Stella had been watching, wide-eyed, shocked into stillness. Now she threw herself at the creature, her hands reaching for a collar, but there was nothing except the ruff of hackles over hard muscle. She stood above them both, hammering her fist on the dog's back until it turned, bloody muzzle lifted in a snarl, and Stella backed off, looking round for a weapon. There seemed a moment when everything was set at pause, then the dog trotted a few paces down the path before loping into the shadows.

Stella placed two fingers on Donna's neck and found the pulse; then she peeled back the eyelid and saw the pupil shrunk to a pinhead. Gone to a dark place. She put Donna into the recovery position and took out her phone.

Dog Boy watched the vehicles and lights from the far edge of the cemetery. An ambulance rolled slowly up the grassy path, followed by an ARV and two cars with their hazard-warning lights still flashing. The dog-killer was lifted on to a gurney and covered with a bright red blanket, then loaded in through double doors as the paramedics ran checks on her vital signs, put up drips, fixed an oxygen mask. There was little they could do about the great, ragged wounds in her face and shoulder apart from staunch the flow of blood and tape the torn edges.

The boy was sitting in the grass so as not to present a profile. The dog was beside him, lying straight-backed with its head up and ears pricked, like the hound silhouettes on an Egyptian tomb. The boy's hand lay across the knobby ridge of its spine, able to feel the excited spasms that ran under its skin. They would wait there until the dog's blood had cooled.

Four people got into the ambulance: the paramedics, a uniformed officer, and the woman who had lain down on the stone where, before, they had crippled the drunken man. The boy recognized her even in the dark, because she was the only other woman there. The ambulance moved slowly out through the graveyard gates, then hit the road and instantly gathered speed as the siren kicked in. The cars left in line, like a funeral procession, but two men remained, stringing police-line tape across the path by the Stockers' stone and across the entrance gates.

That was okay. There were many exits and entrances. In the far, dark reaches of the graveyard, where brambles grew over the old plague pits, the boy lay down to sleep, his head resting on the brindled dog's flank.

74

They had rounded Cape Horn and sailed out of the Beagle Channel into the fjords of Tierra del Fuego, the blue-green floating ice of the glaciers, the intense emerald of the mountain forests. Fighting the hundred-knot winds and fierce currents around the Cape, George had reflected on how drowning was supposed to be a gentle death; now he lay out on deck with others of the crew and watched a noisy flock of green parrots arrow up into the clear sky and drop in close formation toward the shoreline.

There was nowhere he wanted to be, so here was as good a place as any. Messages had been begun and abandoned but he had, at least, sent a fax to say that he was safe. He didn't feel safe; he felt at risk: a man adrift. He'd heard of an isthmus not far away where the Atlantic beat on one shore, the Pacific on the other, and only ten feet between them. I should go there, he thought. Bleak ground without a name, caught between two seas; Terra Nada.

Stella . . . We don't know anyone, really. We don't know ourselves.

.   .   .

His message was hanging from the FaxFone in his workroom, but Stella hadn't been there in days. She had spent a good deal of her time sitting by the hospital bed of Donna Scott, whose coma had been diagnosed as profound.

For a while, Donna had needed help with her breathing, but now that machine had been wheeled away. Other machines fed her and kept liquids flowing through her and collected her waste. A heart-rate monitor bipped like a time signal and showed a strong beat. Now and then, nurses came in and moved her, to prevent embolisms. This was the way Donna would live, her body working without her knowledge, her heartbeats telling the time, and for all the specialists could say it might never change. Stella was advised that sitting with Donna could be a lifetime's work.

The room was cool and white. Donna's face had been patched up and cobbled with sailmaker's stitches. If she came round, if she stood trial and was acquitted, if she came unexpectedly into money, then she could arrange to see a cosmetic surgeon. The cheek was lumpy and purple and her eye was lopsided where the dog's teeth had gone in high; the tear scar went all the way across her face and met a second rip just above the jawline. Stella had found it difficult to look at to begin with, but it didn't bother her now.

She drove back to the squad room and wrote a brief report on Donna's status, using the bleak prognosis given to her by the consultant. Almost all of the AMIP-5 personnel had been stood down: gone to the jobs they'd been doing before Mike Sorley had pulled them off to join the team. She e-mailed the document to Sorley, to find him at wherever he happened to be, then phoned John Delaney to let him know she would be home soon.

It was a dangerous word to use, but she could think of no other.

Some dreams console, some draw tears from stone. She woke at three A.M. with a vision still in her mind of the bald-eyed, marble angels in the cemetery, each of them weeping, and she herself weeping, though she couldn't remember why.

Delaney stirred and she realized she was lying in the crook of his arm, just as she had been when they'd fallen asleep. His breath fanned her face, sweet and warm. Most times, if she woke in the small hours, she would get up and take a drink and sit in silence; she thought about doing that, but before the impulse could become action, she had drifted back into sleep.

There's always noise on the night-time London streets: of traffic, of voices; a siren, perhaps, someone shouting in joy or despair. And there is always light: the suffused nimbus from street lamps and neon signs that gathers under the cloud-cover, glowing a dull orange and deceiving the city's songbirds.

Up on the Strip, the whores hustle and the deals go down.

Stella Mooney sleeps in the arms of a man who loves her; a man who, if her luck holds, might come to know her better, and love her still.

Donna Scott sleeps too, in a place deeper and darker than the blackest night. Who can say what her dreams might be?